War in the Valleys

War in the Valleys

Francesca Capaldi

hera

First published in the the United Kingdom in 2020 by Hera

This edition published in the United Kingdom in 2021 by

Hera Books
28b Cricketfield Road
London, E5 8NS
United Kingdom

A CIP catalogue record for this book is available from the British Library.

Print ISBN 978 1 80032 358 2
Ebook ISBN 978 1 91297 343 9

Look for more great books at www.herabooks.com

Printed and bound in Great Britain by Clays Ltd, Elcograf S.p.A.

To my great grandmother, Mary Jones, who struggled, through hardship and the premature loss of many loved ones, to care for her family. Gran, you'll always be a sunbeam for me.

Chapter One

21st July 1916

Violet Jones plonked her slight body onto the Windsor armchair, its creaking groan a reminder of its age. She surveyed the kitchen slowly. The stained oilcloth on the table was scrubbed, the dishes washed, the dresser organised. The range was blackened to gleaming. Although it was a warm July day, she moved a little closer to the fire in the stove. Its crackling flames and sulphurous aroma gave her the comfort of the familiar. The area was as neat as it was possible for a room with such shabby furniture to be. She knew 'shabby' was too kind a description for her belongings, as it was for the deep rose walls, now smoke-stained.

But none of this bothered her much today. It was the lack of another body on the matching chair, sitting on the other side of the range, that chipped away at her heart, like a pick hewing coal. Her children, four-year-old Clarice and twenty-three-month-old Benjamin, had been tucked up in bed ten minutes before for a nap, worn out by a morning running around the allotments as Violet had picked and planted. The house was unnaturally quiet.

Her husband, Charlie, had signed up with the Rhondda Pals in March 1915. She counted in her head… One year and four months ago. The 13th Battalion of the 114th Brigade of the 38th (Welsh) Division, as he'd been at pains to remind her several times when home on leave in November last year. Morose, he'd been, on that occasion. He'd spent more time out with his pals than in with his family. Her tears had welled up when Clarice had asked why he was out again. But she'd kept strong for the children. That was before his brigade had been sent to the Front. His short and infrequent letters did not reveal the exact location.

Oh Charlie, what changed, cariad? What happened to the happy, joking boy I married? He might have survived the carnage of the war so far, but his spirit had floundered. Was it lost forever, like so many of the limbs of their brave soldiers?

She rose to fetch the single photograph of him from the dresser in the front room. In this image he was upright and proud in his uniform, his hair combed back in a side parting. He'd grown a small moustache after he'd signed up. Standing in the doorway she looked down at his image, then towards the chair on the right-hand side of the range.

But it wasn't Charlie she pictured there.

The jolt in her chest came a heartbeat before she leant against the doorframe as she realised it was Hywel's form she imagined on the chair. Hywel was the uncle of Anwen Rhys, her best friend and had been Violet's lodger since last November. That was, until nine days ago, when he'd been shot defending his sister and niece against Madog Rhys, Anwen's father. After he'd come out of hospital, he'd moved in with Anwen's family. It was him she missed, his generous smile, his spark and vitality. But that was only because he'd been company for her recently, she told herself. Once the war was over, Charlie would return and be his old self again.

But which old self? She'd experienced three different Charlies over the seven years they'd been courting and married. The first one had been attentive and loving. The latest version, the one who'd been on leave the last time, had been sullen, not taking much interest in her. It was the original one she hankered after. As for the middle one…

The sudden clunk of the letterbox almost made her drop the photograph. 'What's that now?' she whispered.

She placed the picture back on the dresser, catching sight of the postwoman in her conspicuous blue serge skirt and coat, and blue straw hat, as she passed the front room window. Violet hurried out to the hall, via the kitchen. On the rag rug was a single letter. Perhaps it was from her mam. It was unlikely to be from Charlie, especially as she had read that the men were in the thick of it in the Somme. She reckoned that was where his brigade was now, in muddy, disease-ridden trenches, with guns firing overhead and bombs going off, if what she'd heard was true. The thought of him there, always close to death, turned her stomach.

She dipped down to pick up the missive. The handwriting was neat and precise, but she did not recognise it. She glanced up the stairs, afraid the noisy letterbox might have awoken Clarice and Benjamin. But no, there was no sound from there. She'd miss her daughter's lively chatter during the weekdays when she started school in September. Benjy was beginning to string enough words to make sentences, but only to ask for something or make an observation.

This letter wasn't going to open itself.

She ran her finger along the back, then slowly drew out the contents. A dread seized her gut, quickening her breathing. Slowly, she unfolded the paper.

Violet was confused at first by the address at the top of the letter. At the back of her mind she'd feared it would be news from the army to tell her Charlie had been killed. This was despite knowing that news like that arrived by telegram, and would have been dropped off not by the postwoman, but by the new telegram boy George Lewis, who'd recently taken on the job from the lad who'd been called up.

She looked next at the signature: *Pte Dylan Davies, 114th Brigade, 38th (Welsh) Infantry Division*. The same Pals' Brigade Charlie was in.

She sat on the stairs, frightened to turn it back to the beginning of the letter. Why would one of his fellow soldiers be writing to her? She took a deep breath for courage and began.

Devonport Hospital
Plymouth
Wednesday 19th July 1916

Dear Mrs Jones,

My name is Dylan Davies. I am sure you will not have heard of me, but I want to tell you what a great hero your husband, Charlie Jones, is—

Is. Not was. She read on, greatly relieved.

You may have read in the papers about the Battle of Mametz Wood. It's all over and done now, and we have captured an important German post, but if it were not for your husband, I would not be here to write this to you. We were in the thick of it, in the middle of the wood, Germans firing all around us, trees shot to pieces by our own shells because they were falling short of their marks. The trees still standing were on fire. Many of our men had already fallen.

I was hit in the leg by a bullet. I tried to pull myself through the mud, but my leg was burning and I could not bear the pain. More shells fell nearby and I knew my time would soon come. It was then that your husband, Charlie, ran back to help me. I told him to run to safety, but he would not hear of it.

For a long time, it seemed, we struggled, until finally we reached some kind of shelter. He stayed with me there a while. We talked as best we could, given the terrible din, and swapped addresses. He said I would be taken to a field hospital, then shipped back home. He asked me to write to him to tell him how I fared. Then he ran to help other men caught in the woods.

I was shipped out the next day. As far as I know he reached our target with the rest of the survivors. I know the men of the 114th are currently scattered, but are slowly being shipped home for leave. Perhaps he is already home with you, in which case may I request that you pass on to him the news that I am fine and in hospital in England, as you can see by the address. It is also an opportunity to let you know what a courageous man your husband is, for I am sure, from the little I got to know him while we were in the 114th together, that he is a modest man, who would not admit to such bravery.

I am from Bargoed, so who knows but I might bump into Charlie again one day as he told me his parents live there.

I hope you have not minded me writing to you.

Yours sincerely,
Pte Dylan Davies

She turned back to the beginning and stared at the address for some time. This man had taken the time to write to her when Charlie hadn't. Yes, this Dylan Davies was in hospital, with time on his hands to write letters, but... She sank onto one edge of the chaise longue. She was being unreasonable for she had no idea what her husband had been through. And what had become of Charlie since this battle? Skimming the letter once more she found the sentence about the men being shipped home on leave.

Maybe, if she showed him this letter, Charlie would open up a little more to her. He'd refused to speak of the training when he was last on leave, before Christmas, saying that he'd come home for a rest from it.

She was dying to show the letter to someone. Anwen. She'd be the most understanding, and anyway, their other friend, Gweneth Austin, would still be at the munitions factory in

Ebbw Vale at this time of day. Hywel would be at Anwen's house too, what with his injured leg. Maybe taking the letter and showing him the care and concern she had for her husband would put some distance between her and Hywel.

What a conceited little being she was. She scolded herself for thinking that her former lodger might be holding a torch for her. Yet she had wondered at one point whether this was the case, as he had shown her so much kindness. She'd even considered asking him to move out, especially after the fuss Charlie had made on his last leave about having a man in the house. He'd reckoned people would talk. Hywel being shot and consequently moving into his sister's house had taken the decision out of her hands.

So, to Anwen's she would go. But first she'd have to rouse Clarice and Benjamin.

–

Violet reached the top of Bryn Road and came to a standstill, turning to look out beyond the pit, nestled in the dip, to the valley beyond. The clouds' shadows skittered across the verdant hills, the grass shining where the sun's rays found it. The children stood either side of her. She was weary after a morning's scrubbing and cleaning of steps, doorways and windows. Her furniture might be past its best, but she was determined to keep the outside of the house as spotless as she could. She wasn't having her neighbours calling her a slattern, looking down on her like they did on some women in the village.

Clarice tugged on Violet's hand. 'Mam, when is the noisy dragon going to start up again?'

The pit had not yet reopened after the explosion three weeks back, at the beginning of July. The absence of the revolving wheels had brought a deathly silence over the village. Violet shivered, remembering the thirteen men who had tragically met their end in the underground tunnels. Bombs and bullets in

France, explosive pit gas: it seemed the men of Dorcalon could not escape danger in war or peace.

Clarice had referred to the pit wheel noise as a dragon since Idris, Anwen's fiancé, had told the children a story he'd made up about one who'd been trapped underground.

Benjy made a long, harsh noise at the back of his throat, trying to emulate the sound. 'Poor dwagon.'

'The sooner it starts up, the better,' said Violet. Though she loved the quiet that had resulted, the pit being still was no good for men's earnings. The money made from repair work didn't compare to that of filling trams. And the women who sorted the coal, like she used to with Anwen and Gwen, were getting nothing.

Nevertheless, she took a moment to close her eyes and enjoy the silence.

'Are you alright, dear?'

Violet's eyes popped open to see her next-door neighbour standing there, eyeing her with concern.

'Oh, yes, Mrs White, thank you. I was taking in the quiet, that's all.'

The older woman looked towards the pit. 'Aye, quiet as the grave it is. Monday they reckon it'll open back up.' Her body slumped as she walked away, dragging her feet like a much older woman. She'd aged overnight since losing her nephew in the accident. It was how so many of them seemed to walk around the village these days. Everybody knew somebody who'd been affected by the disaster.

She took the children's hands once more and led them onto Edward Street. As if to illustrate her thoughts, Gwilym Owen and his grandfather, Abraham, were shuffling along together in silence, staring at the ground. Gwilym's clothes were grubby: he must have been helping with the repairs at the mine. She followed on behind, since they lived two doors from her destination. Behind her she saw a few more men, adopting the same weary pose. Clarice chirped like a little bird, still relating the story of the dragon, blissfully unaware of the blanket of gloom that seemed to be laid across the village.

The three of them walked past Gwilym and Abraham, Violet intoning a subdued greeting, then took the path at the end to the back of the houses. On reaching Anwen's back door, Violet knocked gently on it. Clarice was running up and down the garden path singing, little Benjamin trying to emulate her, his shirt untucked from his baggy shorts.

'Clarice, hush your noise now. You're—'

The door opened and there stood Cadi, Anwen's grandmother, beaming broadly.

'Why Violet, *cariad*, how lovely to see you. And it's always a pleasure to see the little ones.'

'I hope I'm not disturbing you.'

'No, not at all. Come in.' The children hurried into the scullery, giggling. 'Elizabeth is already here in the kitchen. It's nice to have a natter.'

'Oh, I don't want to intrude on whatever she's here for.' She could have done without the mine manager's daughter today, but she'd become a firm friend of Anwen's since they'd started on the allotments together.

'Nonsense. Just dropped in, she has, to see how we all are. Come on now, in you come.'

Violet did as she was instructed, enjoying the inviting bready aroma of something as she stepped into the kitchen. Bakestones, if she wasn't mistaken.

Elizabeth and Anwen were sitting at the table. In the wooden armchairs either side of the stove sat Hywel and his sister Enid, Anwen's mother. Elizabeth was in her allotment attire of trousers, not elegantly dressed as normal. Cadi lifted Clarice and Benjamin onto the chaise longue, taking up one long end of the table, much to their delight, before going to the stove to make tea.

Hywel grinned broadly at her. 'How have you been, Violet?' He pushed his hand through his dark brown hair as his hazel eyes studied her.

'Very well, thank you, Hywel. How's your leg now?' She looked down at the bandaged limb, held aloft on a footstool.

'It's aching quite a lot. Still, the surgeon seems to have done a good job of removing the bullet without any danger to anything else.'

Enid tutted, tucking a piece of fine grey-brown hair behind her ear as she murmured. 'That Madog Rhys. Where'd he get a gun, that's what I'd like to know? Bringing trouble to my family and trying to' – she glanced at the children – "cause trouble."

An outsider wouldn't have guessed she was talking about her own husband, who'd become a dangerous tyrant in their midst, handy with his fists. Almost two years ago, not long after the war had started, he'd pushed Enid down the stairs in the hope of killing her, rendering her bedridden. That was, until Madog had shot Hywel and they had discovered she'd been able to walk for a while, but had been too frightened to let her violent husband know. There'd also been his involvement in criminal activity, what with the stealing and profiteering.

'And how are you feeling today, Mrs Rhys?' said Violet.

'Me? I'm fit as I was before… the incident. Walking out on the hills, every day I've been, and I'll keep on doing it regular like. It was a bit of a struggle at first, but it's done me the power of good. See.' She jumped out of the chair and started running on the spot. 'I'm not going to let that madman's actions keep me a prisoner anymore.'

'At least he's safely locked away now,' said Violet.

'Aye, but we've the court case to get through yet. October, they reckon.'

'Enough of that for now,' said Anwen. 'I'm glad you've called round, Violet, for I was planning on popping down as I have something to tell you. And since Elizabeth is here too, this might be the time…'

'Oh, what is it?' Violet always worried when people told her they had something to tell her, instead of just saying it.

'Don't look like that, it's nothing bad. Idris had a letter from the hospital in London yesterday. The operation's at the end of August. Monday 28th.'

Was that good? Operations were not without their dangers. She'd heard of a couple of people who'd died on the operating table. Not that she knew what was involved in operating on an overactive thyroid. 'I suppose it's best to get it over and done with.'

'Yes. But that's not all.' Anwen looked a little sheepish. 'Since he'll be in London a few days, we thought we might go a couple of days before. Make it a bit of a, um… honeymoon, like.'

Violet's hands flew to her mouth in joy. 'You're getting married!'

'Monday August 21st. We've already arranged it with the minister. I really want to be there for Idris while he's in hospital, but it wouldn't be seemly for me to go with him if we weren't married.'

She was about to get up to hug Anwen where she sat, but Elizabeth beat her to it. 'That's wonderful! If there's anything we can do…'

Anwen's expression became serious. 'Oh dear, Elizabeth, I'm afraid it's not all good news. I'm going to have to give up my job at McKenzie House for now, not just the three weeks I've had so far to look after the family. I know it won't be easy to get another maid.'

Elizabeth took Anwen's hands. 'Don't you worry about that. But are you sure you want to? We're not about to sack you just because you're getting married. It's not like you're a teacher or a nurse. Not that *that's* fair either.'

There she went again, on her soap box, thought Violet, resisting the urge to tut. As if it was any of her business what Anwen decided. She really had no idea how life was for them, being the manager's daughter.

'I told her that,' said Enid. 'And since Idris will be out of action for a while…'

Anwen huffed out an impatient sigh. 'Exactly, Mam. And I want to look after him while he recovers. I've already explained this to you.'

Violet got up and headed towards her friend as Elizabeth stepped away. She hugged Anwen. 'The wedding is wonderful news, especially with all the trouble and sadness we've had lately.'

'Don't worry about the job,' said Elizabeth. 'I'll talk to my mother. She'll be disappointed, especially after having to dismiss Rose Pritchard, but you have more important things to deal with now. Did you hear that her father's taking over the butcher's shop?'

'Yes. I hope he isn't as unpleasant as Rose.'

'No, he seems quite reasonable.'

Violet put her hand in her pocket and felt the letter. Was now a good time to tell them about it? No; nobody would be interested in her bit of news.

Cadi passed her a cup of tea, then offered the plate with the bakestones. Violet hesitated.

'Go on, *cariad*,' said Cadi. 'I put some flour, margarine and an egg by especially for these. It's a celebration.'

'Thank you.' Violet's mouth watered as she picked one up. She hadn't had a bakestone in a while.

Cadi offered them to the children next, who eagerly pounced on the plate to take one each. Poor little loves, thought Violet. They didn't get many treats these days.

'So, Violet,' said Enid, 'has there been any news from Charlie?'

'Well... Since Mrs Rhys had mentioned him, she might as well tell them about the letter. I got this today.' She pulled it from her skirt pocket. 'From a Private Dylan Davies, who's in the Rhondda Pals. It says—'

'Well read it to us then,' Cadi interrupted.

'Mamgu, it might be private,' Anwen admonished her grandmother.

'No, it's all right,' said Violet. She unfolded the letter and started to read. By the time she'd finished, her eyes were glassy with tears. It had not affected her like that the first time she'd read it.

'That's wonderful,' said Hywel. 'Charlie is a hero indeed. And it sounds like they might all be home on leave soon.'

Violet realised once more how foolish she'd been to think Hywel was interested in her. Perhaps she just liked the idea of being attractive to someone.

'D'you hear that, *cariadon*?' Cadi said to the children. 'Your da's a hero, saving people's lives.'

The children cheered, though Violet doubted they really understood what that meant.

'I suppose I should pass on the news about the leave to others with men in the Rhondda Pals,' said Violet. 'There are a few in the village.'

'Twenty-nine enlisted altogether, including Gwen's brother Henry and Idris,' said Anwen. 'But of course, two have already died, and Daniel Williams has joined the Pals since then, so that leaves twenty-seven still over there. Tell you what: Rhonwen Evans's son-in-law, Maurice Coombes, is in the Pals. If you tell her it will soon get round to the others.'

Enid clattered her teacup onto the saucer. 'Never a truer word.'

Elizabeth rose from her seat, fiddling with the belt holding up the trousers. 'I must be getting over to the allotment. It's such good news about you and Idris getting married.'

'It's only going to be a small affair at the chapel. You're all invited, of course. There'll be a bit of tea afterwards back here.'

'I'm sure it will be lovely. Small and intimate can be good.' Elizabeth kissed her cheek. 'Cheerio for now.'

She exited into the hall to leave by the front door. Violet experienced a stab of jealousy at her easy friendship with Anwen. She didn't even understand it: Elizabeth was a different class to Anwen, and lived in the Big House on the other side of the village. She knew she was being petty, but she'd been friends with Anwen and Gwen for such a long time. She recalled Anwen moving into the village as a six-year-old, not long before Gwen. They'd got to know each other at school. After, they'd started work sorting coal together. She'd always thought of them as a trio.

She stood. 'I'd better get going too. If you'd like help with a dress, or anything like that…'

'I'll pop over in a day or two, when Gwen's back from work, and we'll talk about it.'

There was a twinge of excitement in Violet's belly such as she hadn't felt in a long time. This could be fun. There'd been little enough of that in her life. *Since Charlie changed*, a small voice at the back of her mind said. For now, she'd better call on Rhonwen Evans to impart her news.

–

Clarice and Benjamin were pottering in the back garden the next day as Violet worked in the scullery, scrubbing the stone floor. She'd left the door open to keep an eye on them. If only she could have been out there too, or working on the allotment, on this mild day, cool for July but just right for her, with the sky an intense cobalt blue. It was the kind of day that made her heart sing, just as the birds were singing in the bushes on the hill, unseen. Still, the work in the house came first.

Since the letter had come from Private Davies yesterday, she'd been expecting Charlie to walk through the door any moment, knapsack over his arm. It wouldn't do for him to come back to a mucky house. Perhaps coming home in the summer, the sun shining and the valley decorated with wild flowers, would put him in a sweeter mood than when he'd returned in November, with the slate clouds and rain creating a gloom around the village. In her imagination she had him framed by the open back door, a smile on his face on seeing her. Next, he dropped the knapsack, ran to her and flung his arms around her small body.

She'd missed that when he'd come home last time, the warmth and security of his embrace. He hadn't even held her at night. There certainly wouldn't be new babbies anytime soon, which was a blessing at least.

She pulled herself up from the floor, stretching her arms high. A painful twinge ran down from her hip to her foot and she gritted her teeth as she held her leg out to relieve it. Time to get some clean hot water from the pan she'd placed on the stove in the kitchen.

Since the water hadn't yet come to the boil, she took a brief rest in the garden, watching the children as they sat inspecting the weeds. She'd had no time to attend to flowers. Strands of her long, black hair were straying over her face, so she took the opportunity to pin them back up.

It was then she heard it, the air-rending shriek, like someone in agony. It was coming from the direction of James Street or the adjacent Jubilee Gardens, the back yards of which faced hers.

The children stopped what they were doing and ran to her.

'Mam, someone hurt?' Clarice's little voice piped up. She lifted the hem of the white pinafore that covered her shabby blue dress, to fiddle with it.

Violet bobbed down to wrap her arms around the two tots, holding them close. 'Maybe someone's fallen over and hurt their knee. Let's go inside for now.'

She ushered them in, lifting them over the wet floor to the kitchen. She wasn't convinced by her excuse for the scream. It was more like that of a wife or mother when a miner was killed in the pit. It wasn't re-opening until Monday, but who knew if some other death had occurred? She sent up a silent prayer for whoever it was. Hopefully not another child with the consumption, pneumonia or the diarrhoea.

'Let's get your paint box out, Clarice, and you can do me a nice picture. Will you let Benjy use them too?'

The little girl nodded. 'I kind to Benjy 'cos he like painting, don't you, Benjy?'

He copied her nod, more strident in his head movements. 'Benjy like paitin.'

Violet kissed his head. It was hard to believe he'd be two next month.

She was just fetching the paint box that Anwen had been kind enough to buy for Clarice's fourth birthday, when there was a knock at the door.

'Oh, who's that now when I need to get on,' she muttered. 'I won't be a moment, *cariadon*.' As she approached the door into the hall she wondered if it could be Charlie. No, he'd come the back way and certainly wouldn't knock.

Opening the door cautiously she peered round.

There on the doorstep was young George Lewis, smart in his new telegram boy uniform, the cap and trousers, the long jacket with a belt and brass buttons and a 'T' on the collar. Her breath caught in her throat as the bolt of dread shot through her.

Telegram boy.

Chapter Two

The temperature was pleasantly warm as Elizabeth Meredith marched down the road from McKenzie House, on her way to the village of Dorcalon, on the other side of the colliery. The Edward Street allotment, at the top and on the eastern side of the village, was her destination. She could spy the edge of it as she wound her way round the bend and over the tiny bridge of Nantygalon stream. Several people could be spotted at the edge of the field, working on the rows of vegetables for the community allotments.

Bypassing the village centre, she took a short cut up the ends of the terraces instead, arriving at the plot slightly breathless from her haste. She surveyed the field, breathing in the earthy aroma of the soil from where it was being dug nearby. Yes, there was Gwilym Owen, in the middle. She made her way across the crumbly mud, dry in the July sunshine. The mood was sombre among the men, no doubt still remembering their ill-fated colleagues. She greeted them, aware of their slight frowns at the apparel of their manager's daughter. She'd pinched yet another pair of her brother Tom's old trousers, keeping them up with a belt around her waist. Over that she wore a shirt he'd grown out of some years back.

'Gwilym,' she called, when a few yards away from him.

Until the pit accident he'd been a cheerful soul. Now his face always wore the same neutral expression. Hardly surprising since his father, Earnest, was one of those killed in the tragedy. Anwen, her fellow allotment organiser as well as her family's maid, had told her he was having to support his mother and

16

grandfather in their sorrow, along with his fifteen-year-old brother, Evan. Despite that, he was working all the harder on the allotment. She'd done much the same since Tom had enlisted after his recovery from the lingering after-effects of a nasty bout of influenza.

Gwilym straightened up from his efforts to pull the mature carrots from the earth. 'Miss Elizabeth. Is something wrong?'

'No, not at all. There seem to be a lot more men helping than there were previously.'

'Aye, they're looking for ways of filling their time until the pit reopens. The repairs don't produce enough shifts, see. But looks like we'll be back in a couple of days, so I dare say they'll drift off again.'

'As long as they're back at work, that's the main thing. I notice you've been doing sterling work while Idris has been unwell. I'm aware that you've taken charge, Gwilym.'

'I wouldn't go that far, Miss Elizabeth. I'm aware of what needs doing, that's all.'

'The thing is, since Anwen and Idris are standing down for the time being, I'd like you to step in to be one of the organisers, alongside me and Mary Jones.'

Gwilym frowned, hunkering back down, lifting his face to her. 'Not sure I'm capable.'

'I understand that the last weeks have been trying and you may not feel up to it. Hopefully Idris's operation will be a success and both he and Anwen will be available once more. But if you'd rather not, I quite understand.' She didn't want to push anyone past their endurance.

He blew out a long breath. 'Let me think about it, Miss Elizabeth, if that's all right.'

'Of course. And it's just Elizabeth. The *Miss* isn't necessary.'

'As you wish, Elizabeth.' He touched the peak of his cap and nodded his head very subtly, contradicting the more casual use of her name.

At that point, two youths ran down the road, calling and waving. One was Idris's brother, Jenkin, the other Gwilym's brother, Evan. She recalled the heartache they and a few other underage boys had caused their families by running off to join the war a couple of months back. They'd returned a few days later, hungry and ashamed.

'Gwilym,' Evan called, as he and Jenkin ran towards them. Coming to a breathless halt he added, 'At last, we've finished school.'

'For the summer at least,' said Gwilym.

'No, for – for good,' Evan stuttered.

'What?'

'Don't argue now, for you did the same. Will you be at home this evening?'

'I'll be in for supper,' said Gwilym. 'Why? Oh. Of course. You want me there when you tell our parents. Look, I know I left school, but—'

'I won't change my mind.' Evan was defiant. 'And at least it'll save our parents the bit of money they have to pay for school.'

'If we can't sign up, we want to be some use to our country,' said Jenkin. 'Please don't be telling Idris till I see him.'

'Well – all right.' Gwilym looked resigned to the situation.

Elizabeth thought it a shame that they should give up their education, but it wasn't her place to say anything.

Evan became serious. 'We're going to visit Mr Beadle in hospital now.' He turned his attention to Elizabeth. 'The scout master woke up yesterday.'

'So I heard,' she said. 'That's good news at least.' But will he ever be the same again, she wondered, after being attacked so viciously by Anwen's vile father, Madog. The brute was now in police custody, and long may he stay there after what he'd put his family through.

'*Hwyl fawr!*' the boys called in turn as they ran off towards Evan's house at the other end of the village.

'Oh to be fifteen again,' Elizabeth said with a sigh. 'Life seemed so much simpler.'

'Unless you've just lost your da,' said Gwilym.

She could have kicked herself for her crass words. Life had long been simpler for her; her family had not had to think about working all hours for a basic existence for a good number of years. Yet, she had lost precious moments along with that life too, the simpler, more loving times.

'I'm sorry Gwilym, it was a silly thing to say.'

He shrugged. 'I'm sure you meant no harm. I must get on with pulling these carrots.'

'Do please think about what I said, about being in charge.'

He nodded, before hunkering down once more.

Now to cross the road and pay a quick visit to dear Anwen. She had a question to ask her about the Alexandra Street allotment to the west of the village, before she went over to work on it.

–

Violet stared at young George Lewis, standing on the pavement in front of her. As if to confirm her fear, his face was puckered with concern, his lips slightly apart as his arm crept out. In his hand was a cream envelope, the address obscured by his fingers. He said nothing at first.

If she didn't take it, whatever was in it wouldn't be real. She remembered the primal scream she'd heard in the back garden.

'Are you sure that's for me?' she said, her voice unsure and husky.

George pulled the envelope back, doubt in his expression. He read out the address. 'Mrs V Jones, 5 Bryn Road, Dorcalon.' He looked at the door number. 'Aye, missus, I'm sure.' His hand shot out, his eyes widening in appeal for her to take it.

When she didn't move, George gently placed it between her thumb and fingers. No sooner had he done so than he turned on his heel and ran up the road, towards Edward Street.

The scream. It was a telegram that had caused it. How many had he delivered? How many were there?

As these thoughts passed through her head, delaying the inevitable, a wave of nausea overtook her. She clutched her stomach and before she could stop herself, she was sick on the pavement.

A woman coming down the hill crossed over, murmuring something Violet couldn't hear. Normally she'd have been mortified at losing control like that, but at this moment she couldn't care less.

What if it wasn't what she thought? What if it was news of Charlie's return?

But the scream, the scream.

She shoved the telegram in her pocket as she ran back to the kitchen, leaving the doors open in her wake.

'You get paint box, Mam?' said Clarice.

'Not now, *fach*. We've got to go out. I'm going to clean the step first.' She went to the stove, fetching a teacloth off the hook nearby to pick up the saucepan. Through the hall she went with it, tipping its contents onto the step when she reached it. The water and debris flooded into the gutter though some continued down the street. That would have to do for now.

After the initial shock, she felt immensely calm. The telegram wouldn't be what she'd thought. She'd take the children to the Rhys's house to open it there anyway.

'Come along now, we're going to Aunty Anwen's.' She placed the saucepan back on the stove.

Clarice jumped down, then helped Benjamin. Violet experienced a swell of emotion building in her chest.

'Come on, quickly, we're in a hurry.' She needed to move.

'Why, Mam?'

'We just are.'

She took several gulps of the weak tea she'd put on the table for Clarice, to get rid of the sour taste that burnt her throat. Next, she shuffled the children along the hall, taking their hands once they were outside.

'What that water there for, Mam?' Clarice pointed to the pavement.

'Nothing.'

She rushed to Anwen's as quickly as she could with them, a constant prayer looped in her mind. *Please let her be in, Lord, please.*

As she approached Anwen's house on Edward Street, the front door opened. Cadi stood on the step and shook out a mat. When she spotted Violet she waved. 'Come to see us have you, *cariad*?' Her smile slipped as she peered behind Violet. 'Oh Lord, what does she want now?'

Violet turned to see Esther Williams, the busybody of the village. Her husband, Edgar, was also in gaol for various crimes. They included stealing and profiteering, but worse than that, he'd beaten the scout master, Cadoc Beadle, unconscious, because he blamed him for their son, Christopher, trying to enlist underage. Edgar had been the under manager at the mine, efficient but with a malicious streak that he'd particularly taken out on poor Idris. Violet hoped the judge at the impending court case would have him locked away for a very long time.

'I'm not after talking to you,' said Esther, 'so you can put that face away. It's the Owens I'm after giving a piece of my tongue. Decided to leave school a year early did Evan and persuaded my Christopher to do the same. Won't budge on the matter he won't. If their parents—'

'As usual, you blame everybody else but your own family,' said Cadi. 'You'll get no sympathy from me and I'm sure you'll get even less from the Owens. And have you forgotten that they're still mourning Earnest's passing?'

Esther clomped on, regardless, her face set hard.

Cadi turned to Violet. 'Come on, *cariad*, ignore her.'

'Why that lady so angry?' Clarice asked.

'That's no lady,' said Cadi. 'And she's always angry.'

Violet took a deep breath and stepped over the threshold with the children.

'What's wrong? You've got a face on—' Cadi started.

Violet pulled the telegram from her skirt pocket briefly, before pushing it back.

'Oh, *cariad*. Come in here. Anwen's in the garden. We'll fetch her, won't we, children? Then we'll have a look at the flowers there.'

'I love flowers,' said Clarice.

'Me too,' said Benjamin.

Talk of flowers and gardens made Violet wonder if she'd imagined the telegram. It was an ordinary day after all. She slipped her hand into her pocket once more. No, the offending piece of paper was still there.

In the kitchen, Hywel looked up from the newspaper in his place by the stove. 'Can't keep you away, can we?' he said to Violet, smiling. It soon melted when he saw her expression.

Hywel removed his injured leg from the stool, placing it on the floor before leaning forward. 'What's happened?'

'Mind your leg.'

'What's wrong?'

She held up the telegram as Anwen entered the room.

'Oh sweet Lord!' Her friend ran to her side.

Behind her came Elizabeth, clasping her hand to her mouth when she realised what was happening. *Not her here, not now.*

'It might be good news, Charlie coming home.' Violet's voice quivered and she tried to pull herself together. 'Could you read it please? I'm too scared.'

'Shall I leave?' Hywel went to pull himself up.

'No, please stay.'

It was Elizabeth she wanted to leave, but Violet wasn't brave enough at that moment to express her wishes.

Anwen took the telegram and lifted a knife from the table to slit it open. She unfolded it. 'You want me to read it out loud?'

'Please.'

'All right. So... *Deeply regret to inform you... 33088 Private C Jones died – died of wounds on July 11th*'. Her chin wobbled before she continued. '*The Army Council express their sympathy.*' Anwen placed the telegram on the table and put her fingers to her forehead.

Hywel stood, limping over to the table to look down at the telegram. 'I'm so sorry, Violet.'

It was true. Charlie was dead.

Elizabeth took one step forward. 'Oh Violet, how awful. You have my deepest sympathies.'

It was unbearable enough to suffer this with people she knew well. Violet took a deep breath, as if sucking in courage. 'Please leave, Elizabeth.'

'Oh, of course. I'm sorry.' She scuttled out through the door to the scullery, unusually awkward.

Charlie, Charlie. It was unreal, something she was surely dreaming, or seeing on the screen at the picture house. She'd have to send a letter to his parents, or travel to Bargoed to tell them. What would she do for money? She'd heard there was a widow's pension. How would she tell the children? She felt the acidic burning in her windpipe and knew she was in danger of being sick again. No. She had to be strong.

Anwen touched her arm. 'Violet?'

At that moment, the front door slammed and rushing feet were heard in the hall. Enid flew into the room, catching her breath.

'Oh dear Lord, I've just heard Farmer Lloyd's Bryn has been killed – then, as I was coming back, Winnie Price told me Walter Burris from number nineteen's gone too. And she said George Lewis has been leaving telegrams at lots of doors. *O Duw!'*

It was only then that she noticed the telegram on the table. She turned to Violet who felt she was hearing the news from a long way away.

'Oh Violet, not Charlie too?'

'Yes,' said Violet. 'Char – Charlie – t-too.'

It was only then that she started to sob.

–

23

Elizabeth surveyed McKenzie House as she approached it, perched on the side of the hill as it was. They'd lived there six years, ever since her father had become the manager of the McKenzie colliery in Dorcalon. She'd quickly got used to its larger size and elegance. Maybe a little too quickly.

She halted at the gate, grabbing the top of it and leaning over slightly. Poor, poor Violet. The thought of another loss in the village, maybe many more, was tragic. But lurking beneath the sorrow was a disappointment at being sent away by Violet in that manner. She knew she was being selfish – after all, the woman had just lost her husband, but it gave Elizabeth the feeling, once more, that she was impinging on the lives of people who didn't want her around. The nosy manager's daughter who should keep to her own class.

'You are a self-centred body, Elizabeth Meredith,' she told herself. 'It's Violet's loss, not yours.'

That's what Mamgu Powell would have said to her. No doubt she'd have wagged a finger too, as her lips disappeared into a thin line, always a sign of her disapproval. How she missed her maternal grandmother, and her warm kitchen full of cuddles as well as the odd scolding.

Pulling herself together, she walked round to the back of the house and entered via the scullery, looking around with a sigh of relief. The washing up from breakfast and lunch had been done. She'd been braced to do it herself but was weary after her stint at the allotments and the bad news. Onner, their washer woman, must have completed the task. Her mother had recently offered her a further four hours a day to help with cleaning, giving Anwen time to help with meals after they'd dismissed their cook, Rose, for stealing food.

Elizabeth removed her muddy boots, leaving them near the back door to clean later. Mother wouldn't appreciate soil being trampled all through the house.

She carried on to the hall, via the kitchen, wondering where Mama would be. Most likely the drawing room. She'd not had the opportunity to impart Anwen's news yesterday. Heading down the hall and around the corner, she peered at the floor. The usually attractive green and terracotta floor tiles were grubby. After she'd spoken to her mother she'd find the mop and bucket in the scullery and boil some water. She was dying to get back to a book on horticulture, but it would have to wait until later. Then there was the dinner to think about.

In the drawing room, Margaret Meredith was sitting on one of the cream velvet Chesterfields, a pot of tea on the table in front of her and a cup and saucer in her hands. She had kept this room clean and tidy herself; the wooden floors waxed, the furnishings polished, the mats shaken out and the yellow damask curtains dusted. Elizabeth hadn't seen her do this much housework since they'd lived in a terrace in Georgetown, where her father had been a lowly examiner.

'There you are, Elizabeth. Good heavens! Look at the state of you. I don't know why you can't tend the allotments in a skirt like the women of the village do.'

'Because it's much easier in trousers, and without corsets.'

Margaret's eyes popped open. 'Without corsets? Are you mad?' Her usual genteel accent, with only a hint of her Welsh heritage, returned for a moment to its Valleys origins. 'Goodness, how will you ever get a husband looking like that?'

Elizabeth decided it was better not to reply. About to take a seat, she was halted by her mother. 'Do not dirty my beautiful settees with those *clothes*. Go and change immediately. And look at your hair. What a mess!'

Elizabeth pulled at a wandering honey-coloured strand self-consciously. 'I only came in to tell you some news.'

'I hope it's about Anwen's return. I understand all the upheaval they've been through but surely they'll need the money.' It came out all in a rush, as her words always did when she was stressed.

'First of all, there's been a war death in the village. Violet Jones's husband, Charlie.'

'That is unfortunate.' Her brow creased to convey sympathy, though Elizabeth wasn't sure how genuine it was.

'It may not be the only one. I spotted the telegram boy in the distance as I was heading back over.'

'Oh dear.' Margaret tutted and shook her head. 'Hopefully not too many.'

'Also, Anwen told me yesterday that she won't be returning. Not in the foreseeable future. She and Idris are getting married and she wants to look after him until he's well again.'

Margaret's eyes and mouth drooped, along with her posture. 'How will they manage for money with her father gone?'

'They'll be able to manage for now as Cadi, Anwen's mamgu, earns a bit from sewing, and Enid is looking for a job.' She didn't add that they'd found thirty pounds under Madog's mattress. It was likely garnered from the profiteering he'd been indulging in. Anwen had been keen to give it to the police, but Elizabeth had persuaded her otherwise. After all, who exactly would they return it to? And they deserved it after all they'd been through.

'I don't suppose...' Margaret started.

'That Enid would come here to work?'

'Though she has been bedridden until recently, so would she be up to it?'

'She hasn't been actually bedridden for a while and seems quite healthy now. It's certainly worth asking.'

Margaret stood, placing her teacup down. 'I'll take this tray to the scullery and wash up the things.' She bent to pick up the tray. It wobbled initially, until she straightened herself. 'Then I suppose I'd better start the dinner. Your father will be in soon and will be ready for a meal. That's if he hasn't found something else to do in the meantime.'

'I'll come and help you when I've got changed.' The mopping of the hall floor would have to wait.

'Perhaps instead you could take the car and call on Enid Rhys, to ask her about the job. The sooner I get a new maid, or cook, or someone who'll do a bit of both, the better.'

'Not just at the moment, as Violet is there.'

'Violet?'

Did her mother ever listen properly when it didn't concern her? 'Violet, who's just lost her husband?'

'Oh, her. Of course.'

'And if Enid doesn't want the job?'

'We'll cross that bridge when we come to it.' Margaret flicked her hand to signify that was the end of the conversation for now.

Chapter Three

Elizabeth stood upright, glad to give her knees a rest after weeding on the corner of the Edward Street allotment. Men were starting to drift up Bryn Road after the early shift. Five days they'd been back now, since the mine reopened. There was a pervading odour of carbon dust, the absence of which she hadn't noticed until it returned once more.

It must have gone two o'clock already and she hadn't been home for lunch. The weather was mild today, if a little over-cast, making it easier to work on longer than normal. On the allotment with her were six other women, some with children who were now on their summer holidays. The older children were helping out. She'd had no luck persuading any of the other women to don their husband's or son's clothes to do the work. Instead they trailed their long skirts, outdated with the new shorter fashions, through the earth, or the mud when it had been raining.

The last few days she'd seen the men walking home after a shift there hadn't been any of the usual smiles of relief that they'd displayed before the accident. The relieved expression was something she'd noticed since she was a little girl, living in Georgetown, when her father returned with them, black with soot. News of the deaths of their former colliery pals in the trenches had added to their sorrow. Now they all dragged themselves up from the valley floor, backs bent and faces long. The circles of white skin round their eyes were in sharp contrast to the rest of their skin. They were like walking corpses.

The pit wheels grinding, as they had done for the last five days, seemed to accompany their weary progress, replacing the lively chatter. It seemed louder now than before, though she knew this was only in contrast to the recent silence.

Among the men she spotted Gwilym, lumbering up the incline. He lived at the very last house of Edward Street, at the end of the village, so he'd have to pass her to get home. She walked to the pavement to await his arrival.

'Gwilym, how are you?' she called softly when he was a few yards away.

He looked up, surprised. After rubbing his hands forcefully on his trousers, he lifted his cap to rearrange it, revealing the reddish-brown curls that constant haircuts never seemed to tame.

He waited until he reached her before answering. 'I'm fine, Miss Elizabeth.'

'Really, I wish you'd stop this "Miss" business, especially when I'm working the allotments.'

'You're the manager's daughter, it's only proper, like.' He seemed uncomfortable, shifting his feet several times as if he wanted to be on his way. It was a different reply to the one he'd given last time she'd corrected him, when he'd seemed to accept her request.

'It was terrible news about Violet's husband. How is she, do you know?'

'As you'd expect.'

'Yes, yes, of course.'

She looked up, alerted by a sudden sensation of cold. The sky was now obscured by dark clouds. Her time outside might soon be curtailed by a shower.

'I'm so glad, by the way, that you decided to become one of the allotment leaders.'

Instead of replying, he looked down Bryn Street. She followed his eye line to see four soldiers walking up, in two rows of two. Their posture emulated that of the miners ahead of them, dragging footsteps, faces covered by their caps as they examined the road. On their backs were knapsacks. Their khaki uniforms were grubby, brass buttons and cap badges dull. One of them had a bandage round his eye. As another of them lifted his head, Elizabeth recognised Maurice Coombes, the brother of Polly Coombes whom her family had paid off earlier in the year when she had become pregnant. She'd apparently gone to Surrey to stay with an aunt. Maurice was limping quite noticeably.

A murmur went around the women on the allotment and one by one they switched their attention to the straggling band.

'So they've returned.' Elizabeth knew her words were inadequate to the event.

'A few. Too few.' Gwilym's muttered reply was barely audible. 'Thirteen of them were killed at Mametz Wood. With Percy and Robert killed earlier, that leaves only fourteen men of the thirty who enlisted. Plus Idris, of course. So, only half of them left.'

Elizabeth considered this appalling statistic with tears in her eyes. And who knew if more would be gone before this unbearable war was over?

Four of the men, including Maurice and Henry Austin, turned onto Lloyd Street.

'I'm glad to see Gwen's brother is among those on leave. She'll be glad to have him return.'

'Aye, until they send them back again.' Gwilym stared ahead as he said this.

As the two remaining soldiers got closer, one of the women on the field ran across it, skirt lifted to her calves, shouting, 'Teilo, oh Teilo!' Elizabeth saw the tears on her cheeks as she hurtled by, jumping over rows. She met her man three-quarters of the way up the road and they embraced before moving on.

Gwilym stepped into the road, waylaying the remaining soldier, Douglas Ramsay. He had a bandage wound around his head and a patch on his eye.

'Douglas, are you all home on leave?'

'Almost all, those of us who survived. Damned blood bath, it was.' Douglas turned towards Elizabeth and lifted his cap off briefly. 'Begging your pardon, Miss Meredith.'

'No need for apology. These are desperate times.'

'Aye, they are that, Miss. Wiped out we were, near enough. They reckon around four thousand of our brigade were killed or wounded.' Douglas's chin jutted out. 'Given us two weeks leave, they have. Elfin Gillam and William Griffin are in hospital still at Devonport. William lost his leg, he did.'

Gwilym shook his head. 'I'll stand by what I said when you all signed up, that it's a fool's war, but I'm sorry for you all. Sorry to the heart of me.'

'And you were right, Gwilym *bach*,' Douglas said. 'We should have listened to you. But I've heard there's been tragedy here too, and a dozen killed.'

'Aye, we've not long gone back to work.'

'Seems to me you can't escape death if it has its sights on you.'

Elizabeth wished she could contribute some words of hope, but what was there to say in such times? To talk of a better future did not help when people felt so desperate today.

'You sustained an injury yourself, I see,' she said.

'Aye, only minor though. Still got my sight.'

'I'm glad to hear it.'

Gwilym lifted his head to the sky as the first drops of rain descended. 'Better get in for my bath. And your mam and da'll be glad to see you.'

Douglas nodded and started off again, lifting his arm and calling, 'Maybe see you in the McKenzie Arms.'

'I'll let you get on then,' Elizabeth said to Gwilym.

He simply nodded and carried on to his house.

—

The small clock on Violet's dresser indicated it was ten minutes to three. She put the kettle on the stove. Gwen and her brother Henry would be arriving soon, as they'd promised when they'd called by after chapel this morning. Violet had stayed home this Sunday, not able to cope with the mournful declarations of sadness at her loss. She didn't think they'd be insincere, but they could not guess at the depth of her regret.

Regret. She mulled over her choice of word. She surely meant grief. Weren't they different sides of the same coin? There'd be no more chances of a good life with Charlie; that was what she regretted.

The children were playing on the table with a toy train and carriage and several wooden people. It was like any other day for them, as they had no idea yet that their lives had been turned upside down. They were taking turns to load the passengers, set them on a round trip, then unload them, making chuffing sounds and their attempt at a whistle. She'd taken them several times to Dorcalon station, down near the pit, when a train was due. They'd never travelled on one, though. She hadn't been on one herself since the time she'd visited Cardiff with Anwen, Sara and Gwen, six years back.

There was a knock at the front door. She looked down at her old blouse and skirt, only fit for cleaning, with its faded fabric and patches. Too late to change now.

Clarice's trip came to a halt. 'Is that Aunty Gwenny and Henry?' Clarice asked.

'Yes *fach*, I believe it might be.'

Violet went to the front door, gesturing them in without a word. In the kitchen, Henry removed his cap and sat down in the old wooden armchair. He wasn't in uniform this time, as he had been when he'd called this morning, but in what she guessed was his best suit, his hair neat and parted to one side. Like Gwen, he was blond, though his hair was a little darker than hers and not curly. He had the same large blue eyes. Gwen was still in her Sunday best, an outfit more modern than anything Violet owned, with its chiffon overskirt and wool embroidery in a lovely forest green. Violet knew she'd bought it from Mrs Bowen, who stocked second-hand clothes as well as making new ones. Even second-hand, Violet could never have afforded it, not like her friend on her munitions wage.

Gwen took a seat next to the children, chatting to them about their game.

Violet lifted the warming teapot from the stove. 'The kettle's just boiled so I'll do some tea.'

'That would be very welcome,' Henry said, stiffer than he normally was with her.

Dread crawled around Violet's stomach like the slow worms she'd seen among the heather on the hills. Henry had come to tell her of Charlie's last hours. Part of her wanted to know, but most of her wanted to run away.

'I know a new hymn from Sunday School,' Clarice trilled, before embarking on '*I'll Be a Sunbeam*'.

Benjamin tried to join in, much to Clarice's irritation as he didn't know the song, causing her to shush him before she continued.

When the tea was made, Violet set the three cups on the table. 'Shall we take our drinks to the front room to talk?'

'Can we come to front room too?' pleaded Clarice, her cherubic face tipped to one side.

'Not today, *cariad*. We're going to talk about boring things and you're better off playing with your train.' Violet was relieved when Clarice didn't argue, instead taking her turn at the game without a word.

Henry arose and coughed, causing him to lean over and clutch his chest. The sharp sound sent a shudder through her.

'Chlorine gas,' Gwen mouthed, turning her worried frown on her brother.

Violet led the way to the front room. It was lighter than the kitchen but no more cheerful, its long-term neglect only too apparent. It had the musty whiff that accompanied unused rooms. It was just as well Charlie had not been brought home to be laid out in here, what with her selling some of the furniture last year to make ends meet. With no table, the coffin would had to have sat on the floor. But then, it was Charlie's stinginess when passing on money to her that had caused the situation. She lamented the thought immediately. How wicked she was, thinking of her late husband in this way.

They placed their cups on the small occasional table, one of the few pieces still left in the room.

'I'm sorry there are no chairs. Would you like to bring some from the kitchen table?'

'No, that's fine,' said Henry. 'We were sitting down at church and then at dinner.' He took out his handkerchief and coughed once more. 'I'm sorry, I might do that quite a lot.'

'No need to apologise.'

He took a sip of the tea, putting the cup on the mantelpiece when he'd finished. 'It won't be easy to relate what happened, but I think you should know. Especially as Charlie's body won't be returned.'

Violet pressed her eyelids together, willing herself not to cry. She couldn't bear the thought of him so far from home, from family, for evermore.

'I'm sorry Violet, would you rather I didn't speak of it?'

She opened her eyes. 'No, I need to hear what happened.'

Henry pushed both hands against the mantelpiece and stared down into the empty fire grate. 'I hear you had a letter from Dylan Davies.'

'That's right, telling me Charlie saved his life.' She was regretting not bringing the chairs in, feeling a little weak in the stomach.

Gwen leant against the dresser, hands behind her back, gazing at the floor.

'Well, that's right enough, he did,' Henry said. 'And Dylan wasn't the first one. He was brave like that, was Charlie. Or foolhardy, always looking out for everybody, and going back for people.' He looked up. 'Not that I'm saying I'm a coward, look you, or didn't keep an eye out for my pals, but there are times when you just have to keep running or you'll be cannon fodder.'

'You're right of course, Henry,' said Violet, not wanting the ailing man thinking she considered him a coward.

'Anyway, Charlie wouldn't be told, even when the lieutenant ordered us on, he wouldn't leave. He brought in two more soldiers.'

Gwen stepped towards Violet at this point, placing an arm around her.

'As he was bringing in a third, I was watching from behind a tree. That's when it happened. Him and the poor sap he was carrying. In the back, quick, it was. He probably didn't even know what had hit him.'

Violet put her hand to her mouth, afraid she might be sick. Shot in the back. However quick, it must have been agony. She couldn't bear to think of him suffering, her Charlie. The pressure built up behind her nose and eyes. She breathed in several times, suppressing the emotion, like a dam holding back a river. What a true hero her husband had been. Never in all the time she'd known him had she felt prouder of him. But why had he been so eager to put his life in danger when he had her and the children waiting at home? It was like he'd forgotten their existence.

It was Gwen rubbing her arm and consoling her with, 'Oh Violet, I'm so sorry,' that finally made her lose control. The tears gushed forth and she let out a long, low howl of lament, clutching Gwen as she jammed her head against her friend's shoulder. She tried to keep the volume down for the children's sake, though she'd have liked to shriek.

Despite her effort, the door swung open and there stood Clarice, Benjamin just behind her.

'What that noise, Mam? Benjy and me don't like it.'

Violet stood away from Gwen, composing herself. She took a handkerchief from her skirt pocket and dabbed her eyes.

'I'm not feeling too well, *cariad*, that's all.'

'Now might be the right time,' said Gwen. 'You can't leave it forever.'

Violet considered her two little babbies. It wasn't fair, burdening them with this tragedy. Would Benjy even understand? But Gwen was right. And there'd never be a good time to tell them their da was never coming home.

'Would you stay while I tell them?' She looked from Gwen to Henry.

'Of course,' said Gwen.

Henry nodded.

She smiled sadly at the children. 'Let's all go back to the kitchen and sit down. I've got something to tell you.'

Chapter Four

Violet came to a sudden stop just before reaching the doors of the Ainon Baptist Chapel. She looked up at its pointed roof and five first-floor windows, aware of the wave of panic that had stolen her breath.

'What's wrong, *fach*?' said her mother, Doris Wynne, clutching her arm.

'I – I—' she looked behind at Anwen and Gwen's families, at the queue of people politely waiting to get inside the building, being patient because they knew she was one of the bereaved. No, this faintheartedness wouldn't do. 'It's all right, I'm all right. I'm sorry,' she said to those behind, before moving swiftly through the double wooden doors.

'No need to apologise, *fach*,' said her father, Ioan.

Charlie's parents, Olwen and Brynmore Jones, had already found a row of five seats for the family. Olwen beckoned them over.

'I'd like Anwen's family to sit with us too,' said Violet. 'And Gwen's. There are more rows together in the middle.'

Olwen frowned. 'But these are at the front.'

'If it's all the same to you, I'd rather sit further back.'

Violet led the way to three rows about halfway down. 'This will do.'

Olwen insisted on sitting on the outside with Brynmore, so Violet sat at the opposite end of the pew with her parents. Anwen, Idris, Enid and Hywel sat behind. In front of Violet sat Gwen, her parents and her brother. Henry was wearing his uniform today, as were the rest of those home on leave. Soon the chapel was filled both on the ground floor and the gallery above, with many standing at the back. Violet spotted Elizabeth sitting on the other side of the aisle, near the front, with her mother.

Now she was here, waiting for the memorial service to begin, she felt the opposite of the panic she'd experienced in the doorway. Life had been like this since telling the children, her emotions swinging from feeling it was all too unbearable to – nothing. A numbness.

Clarice had sobbed for an hour after she'd been told about Charlie. Benjy had too, but only because his sister had. He'd asked yesterday when his da was going to come back from the dead place. The sad thing was, he'd probably not remember him at all in the next year or so. Even Clarice would have difficulty hanging on to memories of him as she got older. The realisation of this inevitability made Violet grip her hands. How desperately sad that was for them. Anwen must have noticed her reaction, for she placed her hand on her shoulder reassuringly.

'I'm grateful to Cadi for looking after the children,' Violet said.

'She says she's been to enough funerals and memorials for a lifetime.'

'We all will have by the time this war ends.'

The congregation hushed as the new minister, Pastor Lewis Thomas, took to the pulpit. Only in his late twenties, he'd arrived recently from Carmarthenshire. He was reasonably tall and slim, with an already balding head. His kind face matched his softly spoken voice. His young wife, Anabel, was pretty and delicate, with fine, mousy hair. They had no children as yet. He introduced himself for the benefit of those who'd not met him before and started with a verse from the gospel of St John.

'*Greater love hath no man than this, that a man lay down his life for his friends.*' He paused a little, as if to let the quote sink in. 'A great sacrifice has been made by a good deal of men in this village, and in many villages and towns in this country. And I fear a lot more names will be added to the Roll of Honour before this war is over.'

A series of sobs came from the end of Violet's row. Without looking, she knew it was her mother-in-law. Would people think her cold for not doing the same? But she couldn't show her feelings, not to the outside world.

Her attention was drawn back to the service, in time to hear Pastor Thomas say, 'We must remember the ravages death is making on *all* sides.'

There was a brief grumble among the congregation; suggesting having any sympathy with the enemy was not a popular opinion with many. The pastor hesitated for some moments before ploughing on.

'Charlie Jones, Bryn Lloyd, and the brothers, Aneirin and Ianto Pendry, were all old members of Sunday School here, while Harold Prothero and Meirion Peirce had been loyal members of the chapel since they moved to the village.' He continued to tell a little of their connection with the chapel, his knowledge gleaned, Violet knew, from the families of the lost. He'd been to visit her just a few days ago to offer comfort and find out a little about Charlie. She didn't yet know what to make of this new, inexperienced minister. He'd said nothing yet of Charlie's bravery in helping several men to safety. She thought he might, since he'd borrowed the letter she'd received from Dylan Davies.

'It's particularly tragic that they should have been taken in this way, considering the thirteen men who died little more than a month ago, and the loss of Percy Vaughan and Robert Harris in the war barely three months past.'

After enlarging on this, he listed the names of the remaining men lost, who were not attendees of the chapel. After he had finished speaking, there was a rendition on the organ of Handel's 'Dead March' from *Saul*, a piece she'd heard at so many funerals. Violet felt once again that this could be a memorial for anyone. There were no bodies, a fact that pierced her heart.

There'd be nowhere for her children to visit their father, to offer flowers. It would be like he'd never existed.

The prayers came next. She recited them by heart, the individual words meaning nothing today. How she longed to get back to her little house and cuddle her babbies.

Pastor Thomas was back in the pulpit after that. 'And now, I'd like to emphasise the bravery of these young men, who, you may recall, signed up to fight before conscription, therefore did so of their own volition. And here, I have further proof of the courage and heroism of the ordinary sons of God.' He held up a piece of paper, before reading what Violet soon realised was the letter Private Davies had sent her.

She lowered her head, burying her face in her hands. She couldn't stand to hear it again. Why had Charlie done it? Yes, he'd been valiant, he was a hero.

But he was dead.

She felt the hand stroke her back, wanted to brush it away, but she knew it came from the care and love Anwen felt for her.

There was a rustle that made Violet uncover her eyes. Everyone was standing. When she heard the pastor say, '…which was the favourite hymn of the late Lord Kitchener,' she realised she must have missed some instruction. The organ struck up, the introduction to *Abide With Me* ringing out. Determined to see this thing through to the end, she stood with everyone else. After this, she could be on her own with the children.

But she wouldn't be on her own. First, she had to attend the tea. Then Charlie's parents were staying overnight. So be it. She'd soldier on, as she always had done.

–

Violet hadn't wanted to attend the tea after the memorial, organised by the pastor's wife, held in the chapel hall. Olwen had insisted it was only right and proper, overriding Violet's wishes. So here she was, not knowing what to say to people, dreading what people might have to say to her. It was all so – predictable. Did they really mean any of it?

Her parents were standing either side of her, as if to protect her. Her mother was still much thinner than she had been, the result of a bad bout of influenza she'd suffered at the beginning of the war. Violet's older sister, Ivy, had lived near them in Bargoed then and had taken care of her, but she'd recently moved to Hereford with her own family. She'd sent her apologies for her absence from the funeral, something about her two youngest having a cold, though Violet suspected she simply didn't want to come.

Facing her and her parents were Anwen and Gwen, talking solemnly of the service, and of the others who'd been lost. Their family members were spread around the room, speaking to the relatives of the other lost men.

Violet felt detached from it all, remote, as though she were on the ceiling, looking down. Was that what Charlie was doing right now? Could his soul travel here, if he were buried so far away in France? The panic began to expand in her chest, making her breathe too fast.

'Violet?'

She came to, faced by Hywel who was holding out a cup and saucer.

'Sorry?'

'I said, would you like a cup of tea?'

About to refuse, she realised she was parched. She'd had nothing to eat or drink today, her stomach threatening to eject anything that might be placed there.

'Yes, thank you, Hywel. That is most kind.' She took the beverage and had a sip.

'So, you've moved back in with your sister now,' her father, Ioan Wynne, said to Hywel.

'I have, regrettably, for Violet was a grand landlady indeed and made me feel very welcome. But with my accident, I've needed looking after and have no work at present.'

'Aye, Violet wrote to us what happened. Terrible business indeed. Never did take to Madog Rhys when we lived here. Begging your pardon, Anwen, since he is your father.'

'You've no need to apologise to me, Mr Wynne. We are certainly better off without him.'

Violet was content to sip the tea and contribute nothing. She wished she could fade and disappear, without anyone noticing, like a snowflake on skin. She recalled a time as a child, standing in the garden of Edward Street, where she'd lived with her parents and sister, her tiny hand held out as the cold, white flakes drifted down. They'd had a dog, Bledig, who'd barked at the snowy intruders. It was an insignificant memory yet filled her with nostalgia. How she wished sometimes she could return there.

'Isn't that right?' she heard her mother say. It was some moments before she realised she was talking to her.

'What's that, Mam?'

'You said what a good lodger Hywel here was. Always produced the rent on time and helped out a lot.'

A voice in her head carried on with, *unlike Charlie*, though she was certain her mother hadn't meant that.

'Yes, that he was.' She gave Hywel a brief smile, then looked away. He had been most helpful and thoughtful.

Charlie had been like that in their early life together. She'd adored his ready laugh and easy-going manner, the little gifts he'd brought her when they were courting, sometimes only wildflowers from the hillside, but picked with love.

'And I dare say our Violet could do with a lodger again now that she'll only have the widow's pension.'

'Mam!' she warned. 'Hywel doesn't need lodgings. He has his family, who he'll need to look after when he's properly well again.'

'I'm sure I meant no offence, *cariad*.'

'And I haven't taken any, Mrs Wynne,' said Hywel. 'If circumstances were different, I would be more than glad to lodge with Violet once again.'

'I'm sure that won't be necessary,' came a new voice. It was Olwen's. She looked Hywel up and down with disdain. 'It's not seemly, a young widow having a single man as a lodger, especially a young one like you.'

It was true that he was only thirty-seven, being Enid's youngest sibling, yet still fifteen years older than her. Violet had never really thought of him as being that much older though.

'It didn't seem right even when my dear Charlie—' Olwen stopped to dab her eyes. 'When Charlie was still with us. If Violet needs financial help, I'm sure she could get work, especially with the war on and the lack of men.'

'Not with two small babbies,' countered Doris Wynne, her voice betraying a hint of irritation. The two mothers had never got on together, unlike the two fathers.

'It's not going to be an issue,' said Hywel, his voice light, clearly trying to defuse the atmosphere. 'For I'm staying at Enid's for now.'

'Excuse me,' said Violet, desperate to leave the strained mood of the group. 'I want to speak to Ianto Pendry's wife.'

Violet had spied the woman in question alone by the table, stirring a cup of tea for longer than was necessary.

'Alison, I've not had a chance to say how very sorry I am about Ianto.'

Alison put down the spoon. 'And I for Charlie's loss. What made them do it, eh, sign up like that? They'd no need. Even when the conscription came in, they would have been exempt.'

Violet lowered her head. She didn't want to admit that Charlie had been one of the ringleaders, keen as mustard, encouraging several pals and colleagues to march off to the recruiting office.

'I blame Lloyd George, with his fancy speeches about defending Belgium,' she said instead. 'It's what Charlie quoted to me the day he enlisted.' After he'd already done it, giving her no clue beforehand of his intention, let alone any say in the matter.

'And look now,' said Alison, 'Lloyd George is Secretary of State for War. It's a Secretary for Peace we could do with. Look at them, the poor lost souls.' She nodded towards a group of eight of the soldiers home on leave, the others being distributed among the congregation.

All fourteen of them had turned up to the memorial, even though some were from different denominations. Tomorrow there'd be another service at the parish church. No doubt they'd all turn up there too. Not Violet though.

The eight men stood silent, all apparently wrapped up in their own thoughts, until Pastor Thomas approached them. He was followed by Gwen, whose brother was among the soldiers. Violet had a longing to join those who'd been with Charlie at the end. Somehow the thought brought her closer to him.

Florrie Harris, mother of Robert, who'd been killed earlier in the year at the Nord-Pas-de-Calais, approached Alison to speak with her, giving Violet the opportunity to escape.

She joined Henry and Gwen as Alun Lloyd, the farmer's surviving son, said, 'Reckon you got it right, Pastor, about ravages on both sides. Don't reckon those poor young Huns want to be there any more than we do.'

Violet hadn't noticed her mother-in-law coming towards them until Olwen said, 'How can you say that? Evil they are, led by that mad Kaiser Wilhelm. Hungry for blood and a bigger empire, the lot of them. And him a cousin of our dear King George.'

'Of course, it's not quite as simple as that,' said Pastor Thomas. 'These things never are. Leaders get embroiled in their own vainglorious conflicts, then drag their subjects into them.'

Olwen pinched her lips in. 'Don't you bandy fancy words at me. It's a conscientious objector you are, is it? My Charlie was a hero. You're still young, why aren't you out there, on the front, fighting?'

Olwen's raised voice had attracted the gaze of many in the room. A knot formed in Violet's abdomen at the thought of the unwanted attention. She was considering how to silence her mother-in-law when Henry stepped forward.

'Ministers of the church are exempt, Mrs Jones,' he said, flatly.

'But many are out there as army chaplains,' she countered.

'And what would we do at home for spiritual guidance if all our ministers went to war?' Gwen asked. 'We need them as well, to keep up *our* spirits, more than ever now. We all have our part to play.'

Olwen's eyes blinked rapidly as her lips trembled. All at once she let out a howling wail. Tears cascaded down her cheeks. The rest of the soldiers in the group looked in other directions, some taking a step or two back.

Deep inside, Violet was furious with Olwen for making herself the centre of attention, as if no one else's grief was worth as much as hers. She'd always been inclined to such self-indulgence. But now was not the time to show annoyance at Charlie's mother. The woman had lost her only son. What would she feel like if Benjy was older and killed at the Front? She didn't even want to consider such a situation.

Violet went to her mother-in-law, enfolding her in her arms as Olwen sobbed. She tried to shed a few tears in solidarity with her, but they wouldn't come. The rest of the group fled. It wasn't long before her father-in-law arrived, taking his wife from Violet's embrace.

'I think it's time we made our way back to your house,' he said. 'You don't need to come yet, if you don't want to.'

Violet nodded as if with regret, but she was greatly relieved to be rid of Olwen for a while. 'I will stay a little longer, to speak with the other widows.'

After several muted farewells, Olwen was led away out of the hall.

Elizabeth was first by Violet's side. 'Are you alright, *cariad*?'

Violet put to one side her wariness of Miss Meredith, as she'd still rather call her. What business had she here, intruding on her grief as if she'd known her for years? She swallowed to calm herself.

'I'm as alright as I can be, under the circumstances.' She suspected her tone was a little spiky, despite her resolve.

Hywel appeared next.

'I am fine, Hywel, before you also ask.' That had definitely come out harsher than she'd intended. 'I'm sorry, I am tired.' Her yawn came at the right time.

Hywel, about to speak, was pre-empted by Elizabeth. 'Of course. You should sit down and have a rest. There are some seats by the wall here. Shall I sit with you?'

She could do with sitting down, so weak did her legs feel. 'I'd rather you fetched Anwen or Gwen.' She admonished herself as soon as the words were finished, for she knew they were intended to exclude Elizabeth.

'Very well.' She showed no signs of being hurt by the snub, displaying only concern as she fulfilled Violet's request.

Hywel took her arm. She resisted shaking it off as was her first inclination. He led her to a seat.

'Can you cope, having Charlie's parents staying? Do say if you need any help. I might be limping, but I could be of some use.'

Violet had more of an urge to cry at Hywel's kindness than at Olwen's grief. What sort of person did that make her? 'You are a good man indeed, Hywel Llewellyn. You should find a deserving woman to be a good man to.'

He widened his eyes and started to open his mouth to speak. Whatever he was going to say was halted by the appearance of both Anwen and Gwen.

'I'll leave you three alone,' he said instead, and headed off into the throng.

Chapter Five

'I hope they haven't got held up anywhere,' said Elizabeth, taking her grandfather's fob watch from the pocket of her velvet jacket. She'd decided it would be best to wear something more presentable than her usual work garb today, given that she was meeting a group of representatives from other villages, along with a local councillor.

'At least it's not raining,' said Anwen, standing beside her. 'It will be a better tour in the sunshine.'

Behind them, Gwilym, Idris and Abraham chatted in a group, the older man pointing at several places on the Alexandra Street allotment in turn. To one side, Mary Jones kept hoeing.

'Only ten days until your wedding,' Elizabeth said to Anwen. 'Are you excited?"

'I'm not sure, to be honest. It's such short notice with so much to do, even if it is a small affair.'

Elizabeth put her arm through Anwen's. 'I'm sure it will be lovely, despite that.'

'Thank you so much for finding that wedding dress at Mrs Bowen's. With a little alteration here and there, I'm sure Mamgu will have it looking just right. And it'll be cheaper than Mrs Bowen doing it.'

'She's certainly a whiz with the needle, is Cadi. The dress was a good find.' Though she hoped Anwen had more luck with her marriage than poor Sophia Quinn who'd sold it to the local seamstress. Her husband had run off after only eighteen months of marriage. She suspected the dress had been around a number of brides, as the style was a few years out of date, but it was still pretty.

'I did think of postponing the wedding, what with Charlie's passing and all. I didn't think Violet would feel up to being my matron of honour, but she said she was looking forward to a happy occasion for a change.'

Elizabeth patted her hand. 'She's right. There's been too much sadness.'

'This looks like them now,' Anwen called, waving towards a group of people. Men and women of mixed ages were heading up the main road towards them.

'Nice to know that other villages are catching on to growing their own veggies,' said Abraham, joining them with the other two men. He lifted his cap and scratched his head. 'Bit behind the times, they are.'

'Their allotments will be different to ours, Mr Owen,' said Elizabeth, 'as individual families will be renting a small piece of land and growing for themselves.'

'That doesn't sound as efficient and fair as our set-up,' said Mary, coming to a stop beside Anwen, her lips pressed together in disapproval.

'You're right,' said Elizabeth. 'And there's been a lot of wrangling about where to put their allotments and whether land should be compulsorily purchased from farmers and the like. We were very lucky that the coal company owned this spare land and saw the merit of us growing food to feed their workers.'

'That was down to you,' said Anwen.

'And my mother, who can be quite persuasive when the mood takes her. Let's walk over to meet them. You too, Mary.'

The others followed behind, each picked by Elizabeth to represent their little co-operative.

'Councillor Tallis.' Elizabeth held out her hand in welcome, presenting a wide smile that she was barely in the mood for.

The soldiers from the Rhondda Pals had returned to the war this morning. She'd been at the station, watching the crying families wave their beloved sons, husbands and fathers goodbye. Who knew if they'd see them again? It had made her think of her brother Tom, who was still training but would be off to war in the next few months. She composed herself. This was not the time for melancholy.

'Miss Meredith, I presume.' The councillor took her hand and shook it. 'These good people are representatives from Rhymney and Bargoed. They are hoping to set up their own allotments, as you know. I must say, it certainly looks quite impressive and industrious from here.' He swept his hand to take in the scene of the dozen workers.

'And we have two other areas, over there—' She pointed past the Workmen's Institute towards the Edward Street allotments, opposite the houses. 'And on the other side of the village, behind the cottages and my home, McKenzie House.' She indicated the other side of the valley, past the colliery that sat in the dip.

The group with the councillor murmured their approval, pointing and nodding as they did so.

'And these are some more of your workers?' He nodded towards the people with her.

'Let me introduce you. This is Anwen, who created the allotment project with me and has been instrumental in attracting so many helpers.' She pulled her reluctant friend forward, knowing she'd be embarrassed to be lauded so, but convinced she deserved the praise.

Anwen took over, saying sheepishly, 'This is Idris, who led the men on the far allotment with Mr Owen here. Mary is in charge of the field here and this is Gwilym, who's set to take over while Idris and I – um – take some time off.'

'I see,' said Councillor Tallis. 'Of course, everyone on our projects will be responsible for their own pieces of land, but I dare say we can learn much from you about planting and cultivation. Perhaps we could split into six groups, with one of you in charge of each, and undertake a little tour?'

'Just what I had in mind,' said Elizabeth. 'Please feel free to ask questions as we go along.'

They divided into groups, Councillor Tallis joining Elizabeth's, and set off in different directions to begin their excursions. She had absolute confidence that the other five could conduct an informative talk. They had learned so much on their agricultural journey together.

Elizabeth's group took the longest and so was the last back to the starting point. She'd had to field numerous questions from the councillor, who'd taken up much of her time, allowing few questions from the rest of the group. Despite this, he'd been charming throughout, and what was more, amusing. She wondered briefly if he were married, berating herself for such an uncharacteristic thought.

'That was most enlightening,' said Councillor Tallis. 'Perhaps now we could walk over to the far allotment, as I understand it has its own problems, being on steeper land and more exposed. Some of our land may well have the same issues.'

'Of course. Gwilym, Idris and Mr Owen will have much to say about that, I'm sure.'

'How lucky we are that you have all this experience between you.' He extended his hand. 'Please, do lead the way.'

Elizabeth treated him to a smile, from the heart this time. Yes, he was a pleasant and thoroughly gallant man indeed.

—

Anwen's heartbeat hadn't calmed down since she'd woken this morning, convinced that some catastrophe would occur to prevent her marrying her beloved Idris.

'Come on now, don't think like that,' said Gwen, placing a little mattifying powder at the roots of her hair. 'With all that's occurred, I think we've all got into our minds that only bad things can happen.'

Anwen wriggled on the seat of her mother's dressing table. 'You're probably right. It's been such a struggle getting to this point, what with Idris making me think for so long that he didn't love me anymore.'

'Keep still while I do this next bit.' Gwen started to roll the mass of Anwen's umber hair at the back. 'You know he did it to protect you, because of his illness. He thought he was going to die on you and leave you with a family to bring up. But now he knows what's wrong, and he can have the operation on his... whatever it's called... and be well again.'

'Thyroid, it's called.' She'd found a medical book in the library to read as much as she could find on the thyroid lobectomy, how they removed some of the thyroid so the person didn't produce so much thyroxin. It was making Idris terribly ill, what with the shakes and sweating and being increasingly tired. And his heartbeat was still at around one hundred and twenty beats per minute, as it had been when recorded by the army doctor last November. It was what had got him discharged at the end of his training, before he'd seen any action at the Front. That had been a mercy, at least.

The bedroom door creaked open, revealing Violet and Elizabeth.

'Your mam's made us some tea,' said Violet, as she placed an old wooden tray on the bed. 'How are you getting on?'

'I've done the roll at the back.' Gwen held up the comb. 'I think Elizabeth can take over with the plait now. It's already nearly quarter to ten. You need to get dressed soon. And do your make-up.'

Anwen screwed up her face. 'Do I have to?'

'Just a smidgen of powder, a little rouge for your cheeks and some geranium stain to redden your lips.'

Anwen considered her image in the speckled mirror. Idris had said she was beautiful, so did she have to paint herself? Then again, you only got married once – she hoped – so why not make the best of it?

'Your eyebrows are dark enough without adding pencil.'

Just as well, as she'd have drawn the line at that. 'Go on then, but we'd better finish my hair first.'

Gwen clapped her hands, springing up and down on the spot. 'You're going to look so lovely. I'll go to your room and change while Elizabeth's doing your hair.'

Anwen watched Elizabeth in the mirror as she expertly brushed, smoothed, twisted and pinned her hair in place. Violet stared, either mesmerised or miles away. It wasn't long before she got up and went to the open window, leaning down to stick her head out.

'Why are you smiling like that?' Elizabeth asked Anwen, her forehead crinkling a little.

'I was just remembering when I first turned up at the Big House, that is, McKenzie House.'

Elizabeth laughed. 'You were like a scared little mouse.'

'I didn't know what to expect. And your mother was quite – intimidating.' Anwen hoped she hadn't offended her friend.

'She certainly likes to give that impression.'

'If it hadn't been for your friendliness, I'm not sure I'd have lasted long. Especially with bossy Rose in the kitchen.'

'Well I'm glad you did,' said Elizabeth.

'I was quite surprised that you wanted to be friends. I did wonder if you had, well, some ulterior motive.'

Elizabeth stopped for a moment and considered Anwen's reflection. 'Like what?'

'I don't know. I suppose I expected you to be snooty, like all the other young women of your class.'

'Of my class. I sometimes wonder what exactly my class is.'

Anwen turned her head. 'What do you mean?'

'Ah, don't move, otherwise I'll have to start again.'

Gwen came back into the room at this point, in another new dress. Or new to her. Anwen certainly hadn't seen it before. Violet took the opportunity to slip out and change.

With the hairstyle complete, Gwen took over, dabbing and rubbing Anwen's face with the cosmetics.

'Time for your gown now,' said Elizabeth.

Anwen stepped out of her working dress. She was already attired in her corset, over which she wore a camisole and knee-length drawers. Over that she had a petticoat.

Gwen undid the buttons on the back of the cream dress, where it hung on the picture rail. It was plain apart from the lacy high neck and yoke and the lace around the bottom of the half-length sleeves and waist. She removed it carefully from the coat hanger, then helped Anwen place it over her head. Gwen did up the buttons for her, humming the 'Bridal Chorus' quietly. Elizabeth unfolded and straightened the hem before placing a band of flowers across her head.

It was at this point that Violet re-entered the room, fiddling with the skirt of the outfit she'd worn to her own wedding: a plain mid-blue dress with a lace yoke. The satin sash she'd worn that day was missing. Violet's mother had made the frock, which Anwen had not seen her friend wear since she married Charlie. She wondered at the timing, with him gone. But maybe that was the point; Violet perhaps wanted to remember a happy day with her husband.

A melancholy descended over Anwen which she did her best to hide. So many people had gone from the world since Violet had got married.

When Violet finally looked up and noticed Anwen in the dress, she looked shocked.

'Oh, what's wrong?' said Anwen.

'N – nothing,' said Violet. 'You look beautiful. But I thought you'd wait for me to come to help you, like you and Gwen did for me.' She glanced at Elizabeth.

Had that been an accusing look, or was Anwen imagining it?

'Never mind,' Violet added quickly. 'You look lovely, *cariad*.' She stepped forward to hug her friend but halted before she reached her. 'Better not. Don't want to smudge or crease anything before you get to the chapel.'

'She's right, you look *so* beautiful,' said Gwen.

Elizabeth agreed with great enthusiasm, causing Anwen to well up.

'Oh, don't cry,' said Gwen, reaching for a clean handkerchief from the dressing table and handing it to her friend. 'This is your special day.'

'And just two months ago I thought it would never happen.' She dabbed at her eyes wondering if she was having one of the happy dreams she'd had in those dark days after Idris had rejected her. In the morning she used to wake up content for all of two seconds, until she remembered the true situation.

'But it has, and in little over an hour you will be Mrs Hughes.'

'My only regret is that Sara can't be here,' Anwen said, remembering her sister who had died last Christmas morning of the consumption. She'd only been fifteen.

The memory of it was too much. She wept into the handkerchief, aware of Gwen's arm around her on one side and Violet holding her hand on the other. When they led her to the bed she sat on the edge with them.

'Sara and I often talked about how we'd like our weddings to be. Usually it was pure make-believe, with carriages, long veils and tiered cakes, like the weddings we saw in the magazines. Of course, I'd long decided that I would marry Idris. Sara had a crush on Jenkin when she was younger. I used to tease her that we'd have a double wedding, two brothers marrying two sisters. That would have been something, wouldn't it?'

When she was finished, she opened her eyes to see Elizabeth regarding her, her face sad. Anwen dabbed her eyes once more and blew her nose. 'Right, we have a wedding to get ready for. Elizabeth, you're not changed yet.'

'Let me put a little more powder on you, then I'll change my dress.'

'I'll do that,' said Violet, jumping up. 'You go and get yourself ready.'

When Elizabeth returned, she was, of course, wearing the most fashionable dress, with a shorter, wider skirt, in a dark green silk with a V-neck collar. Anwen knew she owned fancier outfits so was thankful to her for not outshining the bride.

The four women stood together in front of the mirror, peering down to see what they all looked like. The door opened.

'Come on girls,' said Enid. 'Cadi and I have been ready ages, and it will be time to walk to the chapel soon.' She stepped in properly. 'Oh Anwen, don't you look a picture?' She ran to her daughter and placed her arms around her, being careful of her hair and dress. 'I just wish our Sara was here.'

'I was saying the same, Mam.' She held Enid's hands tightly as they both fought off the tears.

Anwen was aware that nobody had commented on Madog's absence. She felt no regret at that at all. Uncle Hywel was going to walk her down the aisle, or rather, limp her down there, and he was a far better person in all respects to give her away.

–

'Those whom God has joined together, let no man put asunder. In so much as Idris and Anwen have consented together in holy wedlock, and have witnessed the same before God and this company, having given and pledged their faith, each to the other, and having declared the same by the giving and receiving of a ring, I pronounce that you are husband and wife. I ask you now to seal the promises you have made with each other this day with a kiss.'

Anwen tipped her head up at these last words, blushing at the thought of Idris kissing her in front of the congregation. He closed his eyes and bent to conform to tradition, making contact with her for a second. The organ struck up, being their cue to walk back up the aisle. They were treated to numerous smiles from guests and village residents who had arrived at the chapel to wish them well.

'I didn't expect a turn-out like this,' Idris bent down to whisper. He was certainly handsome today, with the three-piece suit, his black hair cut neatly and slicked down into a side parting. The moustache he'd been growing the last couple of months had also been trimmed and tidied up. She was sure she must be the envy of many a young female attendee.

Outside, at the top of the chapel steps, the couple waited for Elizabeth, who soon appeared behind them with her Box Brownie camera.

'You're so lucky to have such a sunny day,' she said. 'It will give us better photographs.'

'Thank you so much for doing this,' said Anwen. 'It will be lovely to have a record of the day.' A little voice inside her head said, *in case something goes wrong with the operation*. She batted the errant thought away. This was going to be a joyful day, one to look back on with happiness in years to come.

The rest of Anwen's family and friends appeared through the doors, but it wasn't long before their well-wishers were also eager to leave and go home, now the ceremony was over.

'Oh dear,' said Elizabeth. 'We'd better wait till everyone's gone, otherwise we'll have other people popping up in the photographs.'

The couple stood to one side, thanking those who called their congratulations. Some lingered on the pavement nearby to watch the photographs being taken.

After Elizabeth had taken a few with just the couple, and then family and friends, Idris called to the small gathering, 'Could one of you come and take a photo so we can include Miss Meredith?'

Mr Schenck, the Dutch bookseller, came up the steps. 'I have such a camera, so know how they work and would be glad to oblige.'

Elizabeth stood at the end next to Gwilym, who had acted as the best man.

When it was all finally over, Anwen breathed a sigh of relief. She longed to be back at the house where she knew her mam and mamgu, along with Meg and Rachael, had already laid out a good spread, or as good a one as could be gathered in these days of shortages. Farmer Lloyd had provided a couple of rabbits and a brace of partridges as a wedding gift, in appreciation of her work on the allotment scheme and providing him with a rota of workers. She'd had nothing to eat that morning, what with her nerves robbing her of her appetite, so she was looking forward to his contribution, along with the other treats. She realised how lucky she was: Violet's wedding breakfast had consisted only of tea and cake, as did many of the weddings in the village.

Back at her house, the front room had been polished to gleaming. The last time she'd spent any time in here had been for Sara's funeral. She took a moment to consider this.

'What's wrong, *cariad*?' said Idris, approaching her with a cup of tea.

'Just remembering my sister.' She looked towards the framed photograph of Sara on the pianoforte.

'Dear Sara,' he said, handing her the cup.

Anwen drank it in one. 'Come, I'm starving. I've been looking forward to this.'

Idris laughed. 'Is that all you married me for? The wedding breakfast?'

She chuckled. 'Farmer Lloyd wouldn't have given up his partridges for anything less.'

'I'm glad to see you both so happy,' said Idris's mother, Meg, beaming. 'Such a glorious day. And what did you think of the new pastor? Takes a better wedding than a memorial, I reckon.'

'Yes, he did well,' said Anwen. 'Still, it would have been nice to have been married by Pastor Richards, since we've known him such a long time.'

'Strange, the Richards family leaving the village with so little notice,' said Idris. 'Though maybe with losing Joseph in the mine accident, they just wanted to escape the memory. Where is it they moved to again?'

'Porthcawl, to a chapel there,' said his mother. 'Maybe they fancied a spot by the sea. Strange though, that Joseph's wife,

Jenny, has been left behind with the new babby, since she was living with them. Gone to live with an aunt now, she has, on Gabriel Street.'

'Perhaps she didn't want to leave Dorcalon,' said Anwen.

Meg humphed. 'Seaside or coal dust, I know what I'd choose. Maybe Miss Meredith knows something about it, as Jenny was their maid before she married Joseph.'

This comment was prompted by Elizabeth passing by. 'Know what about Jenny?' she asked.

'We were wondering why she hadn't gone with the Richards family.'

Elizabeth opened her mouth but hesitated. 'I really don't know, Mrs Hughes.'

But Anwen had a feeling she did know something.

'Well, I dare say it's none of our business,' Meg concluded. 'Now Miss Meredith, I must thank you for taking the photographs. How lovely that it's possible these days with your little camera. Not like when Isaiah and I were married.'

And so continued the conversation between the two women, with Idris chipping in now and again. Anwen looked around the front room at the happy faces, chatting about this and that. Gwen and her mother giggled as Jenkin told them a silly joke. It was a joy to see and lifted her heart. Cadi came into the room with a tray full of cups of tea, the tray lent to them by Elizabeth and the cups borrowed from various neighbours. Her mamgu was in her element, her cheeks plumped up like ripe apples as she grinned fit to burst. Anwen smiled in response, welling up as she did so with the sheer elation of it all. And best of all, there was her handsome Idris, her husband at last.

As she turned to take it all in, she spied, through the open door, Violet, standing dead still. She seemed to be looking at the floor. Poor Violet. Anwen lifted her dress and went through to the kitchen to join her. Enid had already placed the children at the kitchen table so they could tuck in straight away.

'Violet, are you all right?'

Her friend turned with a start. 'Oh, yes, of course.' A smile appeared in place of the frown.

'I don't know about you, but I really *must* get something to eat. Come on, there's food in the front room.'

Violet followed her in. As they passed Idris, Anwen turned and grinned at him, and he returned a look of pleasure and love. Her stomach melted. The niggle of fear she had about his upcoming operation she put to the back of her mind. Today was a celebration, of her love for Idris, and for her wonderful family and friends.

Chapter Six

'Here's the train now,' said Cadi, leaning out from the platform on Dorcalon station.

'Careful Mamgu,' said Anwen, pulling her grandmother back as she spotted the smoke and heard the distant chuff of the locomotive.

'I do hope there won't be any air raids while you're in London,' Enid's voice croaked. 'What a time to be going, when the Zeppelins have started upping their campaign in southeast England.'

'Aye, I agree,' said Meg.

'Now don't fuss, you two,' said Idris, encircling his mother with one arm.

As the train got nearer, Anwen hugged her well-wishers in turn; their mothers and Cadi, Violet with the little ones and even Elizabeth had walked down to see them off. Anwen had the feeling that it was the beginning of an *awfully big adventure*, as Peter Pan would have said. She had a brief pang, thinking of her sister Sara, whose favourite book that had been. A copy, intended as a Christmas present last year, still sat on the chest of drawers in her bedroom.

'What's the matter, *fach*?' said Idris. 'Not having second thoughts, are you?'

'No. No, of course not.' She brightened, not wanting to upset anyone, least of all her mother.

'Come on now,' said Elizabeth, as the train pulled in with a *shushhh* of brakes and hiss of steam.

Idris picked up the small case he and Anwen shared and looked round at the group. He must be feeling a lot more nervous than she was, Anwen realised, with an operation to face. She shuddered inside, sending up a small prayer of petition to the Almighty.

'Take care, *cariad*,' said Enid, as she hugged her daughter once more.

Idris had already unclicked the heavy door and stepped inside by the time Enid let her go. Anwen took his hand so he could help her up, then clunked the door shut. As the train chugged off, they waved out of the window. The group followed the train to the end of the platform, waving back until they were finally out of sight.

—

The train pulled in at Paddington station with decreasing chugs and a loud hiss. Idris, already rising from the seat, was pulled back down by the deceleration.

'Oof,' he said, as his head thumped against the headrest.

'Are you alright, *cariad*?' said Anwen, turning swiftly with concern.

'Aye. Soft landing, luckily.'

'You should sit until we come to a standstill.' She rubbed the sleeve of his jacket.

'I realise that now.'

When the train came properly to a stop, Idris rose to lift down their suitcase, then took down another for the lady sitting opposite when she seemed to be struggling.

Out in the corridor, Anwen went ahead to open the outside door, climbed down to the platform and took the case from Idris before he too came down the steep steps.

She looked up at the immensely tall, grubby glass ceiling and the huge arched girders. The platform was wide. A large clock hung over them. Arched doorways to one side displayed signs above, telegram office, lavatories and cloakroom among them.

Anwen wrinkled her nose at the stench of smoke. People were rushing off the train, down the platform to the exit, adding to the din of a shrill whistle and another train chugging onto the platform opposite theirs.

'I'll carry this,' she said, when he tried to take the case off her.

'Pardon? Can't hear you above the noise.'

'I said, *I'll* carry the case. You keep up your strength for the operation.'

'That's not right—' he started to protest.

'Excuse me,' came the impatient voice of a man with a bowler hat and briefcase, trying to get off the train behind them. He didn't wait for them to move fully out of the way before barging past.

'How rude!' said Anwen. 'I hope not all Londoners are like that.' She watched as several other people darted past, avoiding them both by inches, before turning her attention back to the suitcase.

'Now don't you start with your *it's not right for a lady* rubbish. After you've recovered from the operation you can carry all the heavy bits and pieces you like. I'm sure I'll find plenty for you in the home,' she said, wagging her finger.

'Alright, alright,' he said. 'Carry it if you must.'

Oh Lord, she thought, *I'm sounding like my mother.* 'Sorry, but I want you to be as fit as you can. Let's get off this platform before we're knocked over by the mob, and find this Baker Street and Waterloo Railway underground train we've got to travel on next.'

'Move along there!' the guard called as he passed them.

'Goodness, why is everyone in such a hurry?' said Anwen as they started following the other passengers out. 'Was it like this in Winchester when you were there?'

'Yes, because all the soldiers were getting on and off trains. Dunno what it would have been like normally.'

Dominating the crowded station were men in uniforms hanging around in groups, most with caps, a few with Tam o' Shanters. They had bags hanging off their backs and slung across their bodies. Their clothes were caked in mud. They passed around cigarettes and chatted good-naturedly. A few eyed Idris up as he went past. He looked straight ahead, but Anwen could tell by his expression he felt awkward. And here she was carrying the case and probably making it worse.

They stopped to ask a guard the way to the underground. When he'd explained and walked away, a voice called over, 'Oi, mate. You one of them conshies? Out gallivanting with a girl while we fight the war for you?'

Anwen put down the case and sucked her lips in.

'Ignore it,' said Idris. 'It's none of his business.'

But she was livid with the assumption that her husband was some idler. She wasn't allowing the soldier to get away with it.

Taking three steps towards the offending soldier she said, 'Actually, my husband is a coal miner, which is a reserved occupation, see. But he did sign up for the army and did his training nevertheless, and then was discharged because he has Graves' disease.' She didn't expect they'd know what that was, but it sounded serious enough. 'But still mining the coal, he was. And now we're here for him to have an operation so he can get on with digging out more good steam coal for our navy. So there.' She let out a, 'Hm,' as a full stop.

The soldier and his friends were wide-eyed with surprise at first. She wondered briefly if they'd understood her accent. She only normally spoke English to those who didn't speak Welsh, like Mr Schenck, and some of the English and Scottish families who'd moved to Dorcalon. Or the posher families who wouldn't speak it even though they could. Then she noticed the soldiers all looking embarrassed.

'Sorry missus,' said the man, who had a scar down one cheek. 'Didn't know, did I? You get a lot of shirkers round 'ere.' He looked past Anwen to Idris. 'Sorry mate, no 'arm done.'

'Easy mistake to make,' said Idris.

'Good luck to ya in the op.'

Idris lifted his cap in thanks as Anwen took his arm and, with her head held high, led him away.

'See, people need to know it's not only the soldiers doing their bit,' she said, feeling that he was still embarrassed by the scene.

'Aye, I suppose so.'

They found the entrance to the underground trains, following the signs carefully and asking directions to make sure they didn't go the wrong way.

Anwen stopped suddenly when they reached the escalator. 'Oh my goodness, a moving staircase.'

A woman in a large hat, carrying a parasol, tutted as she almost bumped into them.

'It's all right,' said Idris. 'It looks like you just step on and it takes you down. Come on.'

Anwen's heart thumped as he took the case off her and then took her hand to lead her towards the escalator.

For the first time, the confidence with which Anwen had decided she was going to face this trip started to slip. She wanted to stop, to take a moment, but there were people behind them. She jumped on a moment after Idris stepped on, wobbling as it went forwards. When the escalator went over the precipice and started on its downward journey, she almost toppled, realising suddenly she was standing on two steps. Idris caught hold of her.

'Oh heavens,' she said on a hefty breath out.

'You all right, love?' said an older woman behind them.

Anwen looked up. 'Yes, thank you. Not used to these things.'

'Had a bit of a wobble myself when I first went on it. Where're you goin' to?'

'Waterloo.'

'Ah, you'll be all right there. It has a lift.'

Anwen sighed with relief once they got off the escalator and onto the platform, for a short while at least. She looked up at the curved, tiled walls and ceiling and the overhead lighting.

The wall on the other side of the rail was plastered with adverts. The air was stuffy down here; she soon felt overly warm.

'How do you bear it, being underground for so many hours?' she said to Idris. 'It's bad enough here.'

Idris laughed. 'This is luxury in comparison: properly constructed tunnels, areas to sit in with lights. Not much chance of these roofs falling in on you.'

They heard a sound like a wind rushing through the tunnel, before a long, low set of carriages whirred into the station.

'This is a novelty,' Idris said, when they were finally settled in the long carriage.

'When you work underground all the time?' she asked.

'I mean travelling so fast underground. Bit different to the ponies pulling the trams.'

'Just as well, for what a racket it makes. It'd soon have those coal tunnels down.'

They sat in silence the rest of the journey, holding hands, watching people get on and off at the various stops in between. Anwen's mind wandered. What if the train came to a halt and they were stuck in the middle of this tunnel? She broke out in a prickly sweat. It was the first time she'd been so far underground and it gave her a vague idea what it must be like for the miners in the village.

Idris rubbed his neck, his face creased.

'Is it the goitre irritating you?' she asked, referring to the protrusion in his neck that stuck out a little more than an Adam's apple.

'No,' he chuckled. 'It's this collar your mother starched and insisted I wear. It'll be the first thing to come off when we get to our guest house.'

'She was only trying to smarten you up for London.'

When she noticed *Waterloo* written on the signs of the next station, she was relieved. 'Here we are.' She picked up the case and led the way.

Following the other passengers up and out, they found themselves on the street in front of the station.

'Everything seems so much *larger* here,' said Anwen, peering up at the classical-looking building with 'South Western Railway' emblazoned across the triangular pediment. The buildings generally were very much taller even than the Workmen's Institute and the McKenzie Arms. There was no greenery, no hills to be seen. There were more cars here than even in the larger towns near them at home, interspersed with horses and carts, some piled high with goods. The noise of the engines, with the odd hooting of a horn, was even more deafening than being on the station platform.

'People are so impatient here,' she added. 'And I thought the pit wheels were noisy. Where do people go for a peaceful walk?'

'I read there were some big parks in London. Not around here though, by the looks of it. We'd better find Roupell Street, and our lodgings.' He pulled an envelope out of his pocket, containing a letter from the landlady with a basic map and some instructions.

'Watch out!' she said, pulling Idris from the edge of the road as a car came speeding by. 'We're not walking the streets of Dorcalon now.'

'Yes, have to have your wits about you here.' He pointed across the road. 'Looks like we can go down that side street by the public house. Then turn left and it should be second on the right.'

'I hope it is that simple.' Anwen patted her tummy. 'I'm starving already. I shall be ready for the dinner. I hope the landlady's a good cook.'

'I'm so hungry I'd be happy with anything,' he said.

'Tomorrow we'll do our bit of sightseeing. It's a play in the West End I'm particularly looking forward to, though we need to find out how to get there. I just hope there are tickets available for something worth seeing.'

She thought back to April, when she was still working at the Big House and Tom Meredith was still at home recovering. He'd asked her to sit with him in the garden for lunch and had told her that one day she must visit the West End. She hadn't even known what it was till he'd told her. She had certainly never expected to see it.

'Don't know why it'd be any better than a performance in our Workmen's Institute, but we'll see.'

'Oh Idris, of course it will be. It'll have proper actors and actresses.' She hooked her free arm around his. 'Now let's look at these directions and get to where we're going.'

–

Elizabeth and Gwen joined the queue outside the Imperial, falling in behind two older women. Determined to watch *The Battle of the Somme*, Elizabeth had been keen to come with someone, but now she was having second thoughts about having asked Gwen. She'd seemed quite surprised when Elizabeth had suggested it to her. Whether this was a delighted shock, or the opposite, she wasn't sure. She only hoped Gwen hadn't come simply to be polite. She'd been quiet in the motorcar driving here when she was normally so chatty with Anwen and Violet. Perhaps that was the problem: Elizabeth wasn't an old pal like the other two. It could be she'd got the wrong end of the stick about their friendship.

'I hope it's not too gory,' said Gwen, looking worried.

Elizabeth was about to reply when a man's voice said, 'Well, Miss Meredith, good evening.'

Gwen looked round Elizabeth, giving the man a quizzical stare as he lifted his bowler hat to them in greeting.

'Mr Tallis! Have you come to watch *The Battle of the Somme* too?'

'Indeed I have.' He turned his attention to Gwen, giving her a smile. 'Good evening, Miss.'

'Oh, where are my manners? This is Mr Tallis, the councillor who came to see the allotments. This is my friend, Miss Austin.' She hoped 'friend' wasn't too much of a presumption.

'How very nice to meet you,' said Tallis, shaking Gwen's hand. He had a twinkle in his eye as he smiled.

'Likewise, I'm sure.' Gwen beamed at him.

Elizabeth felt a twinge of disappointment. She couldn't really blame him for taking a shine to Gwen. She was pretty, with her large blue eyes and blonde curls, and the most fashionable young woman in the village, apart from herself. Even the yellow tinge to her complexion, caused by her job in the munitions factory, was not so obvious in the evening light, especially with her make-up and the smart hat.

'Would you mind if I joined you, ladies? The friend I was supposed to be coming with has been unavoidably detained.'

'No, of course not,' said Elizabeth. That did at least suggest there wasn't a Mrs Tallis, otherwise surely he'd be coming with her? 'I have no idea what to expect, and whether I will regret finding out what it's like over in France,' she said. 'Miss Austin has a brother over there, and mine will be going shortly, you see.'

'Whereabouts is your brother?' he asked Gwen.

'In France somewhere, that's all I know. He was at the Battle of Mametz Wood recently.'

'A fierce battle, I'm given to understand.'

Something occurred to Elizabeth that had not at their first meeting. 'Do you mind me asking why it is you're not in the army?'

'Not at all. I have a condition called gout. Not a disease that is likely to kill me, but one which precludes me serving my country in that way, sadly.'

She felt dreadful for asking now. 'I'm sorry to hear that.'

'It's fine. There are other ways I can serve,' he said, his smile stretching the neat moustache. 'I do want to find out what is going on over there, though. I was going to sit in the front circle. Would you ladies allow me to treat you to that?'

Elizabeth was about to decline, but was pre-empted by Gwen saying, 'That would be most kind, thank you.'

So be it. It wasn't as if one of them was with him on their own and he was likely to take advantage. No, he was simply a nice man.

In the theatre they quickly found seats in the second row of the circle. Mr Tallis managed to position himself between them. Elizabeth would rather have been in the middle herself, and able to converse easily with both. The other customers sat chattering as they waited for the first film to start, some clearly wondering what they were letting themselves in for.

'Can't say I'm too bothered about the other film, what was it called?' Tallis clutched his chin as he tried to remember.

'*His Majesty the Baby*,' said Elizabeth. 'A piece of light entertainment, though odd to match it with a serious battle film. It could be worse I suppose, Charlie Chaplin or a Keystone Comedy.'

'Don't you like those?' said Gwen, leaning forward.

'I like them well enough normally, and Mr Chaplin is very amusing, but not along with *The Battle of the Somme* I think.'

'No, you're quite right,' said Tallis.

Soon the lights dimmed and people's chatter ceased for a while. The newsreel started, showing first a hurricane in Texas. The audience gasped at the brief footage of the damage caused. Next, the white writing on a black background told of two British submarines colliding in the North Sea, eliciting several cries of shock. Whispers of conversation began. A battle between Italy and the enemy on the Austro-Hungarian border was outlined, with several comments and tuts accompanying the news.

The chatter grew in volume once more as they changed the reel. 'I wonder how the Italians will fare in the end,' Elizabeth commented, for something to say.

'A few of our allies must be regretting by now they ever joined this mess,' said Tallis. 'I wonder how long it will be before every country in the world's involved.'

She was about to reply when the pianoforte struck up at the front and the first film came on. Elizabeth found herself only half concentrating on *His Majesty the Baby*, as charming a story as it was. The audience cheered the protagonists on while Elizabeth's mind wandered.

The film they'd come here to see started at last, the piano pieces accompanying it less chirpy than they'd been for the previous film. Elizabeth adjusted her position and her skirt to make herself comfortable, then placed her blue leather handbag in her lap.

Mametz was mentioned on the first shot of writing. There were comments from the audience. She guessed there would be others in attendance with men who had fought there, maybe even some who'd lost family and friends.

A mountain of ammunition was displayed, with a comment of thanks to the munition workers.

'That'll be me,' Gwen told Tallis, smiling.

'Well done,' he replied.

When the huge Howitzer guns came on screen, being loaded and bouncing as they fired their shells, people yelled with disbelief. 'It's as big as a steam engine,' exclaimed a woman behind. The gasps and 'oohs' came ever swifter. The pianoforte, in response, mimicked the unheard explosions, making several people jump. The images of the artillery were interspersed with those of the various battalions, some of them in shorts or kilts. Many smiled for the camera, some clambering to get in shot.

Between the reels, five in all, the multiple conversations became louder, concerned, full of tuts and huffs. Two young women left after reel two, shaking their heads.

Elizabeth noted the living conditions – the trenches, barely habitable, or, in some cases, fields of tents. This had been filmed at the end of June and beginning of July, this summer. What would it be like in winter, with cold frost, freezing rain, mud and snow? She shivered, thinking of it.

'Are you all right?' Tallis asked, turning a concerned expression towards her.

'Yes, it's an eye-opener, even when you think you know something of what's happening.'

'It is indeed.'

When two men were seen to rescue a comrade, Elizabeth thought of brave Charlie, the tears stinging her eyes even though she'd never known him. She was touched once again when British soldiers were seen bringing in the wounded from both sides. They carried the Germans as carefully as their own. That they could still display some human kindness in the midst of that lot was wonderful indeed. This time she couldn't prevent one tear spilling onto her cheek. She gently pulled her hand-kerchief from her bag and dabbed her eye, trying not to make it obvious. Luckily, Tallis seemed oblivious, mesmerised by the screen. The tears came again when scenes of the dead from both sides were displayed.

The film ended with smiling troops and a caption that informed the audience they were getting ready for the next surge. A Worcester battalion waved their tin hats in greeting, as if the whole thing had been a jolly jape. Elizabeth guessed it was all part of keeping up the hopes of those on the home front. Much of the audience waved back and cheered.

The lights went up and people started to stand, chatting about all they'd seen.

'To be continued, as they often say on these series,' said Tallis. 'You look a bit pale, Miss Meredith.'

'All the loss of life.' She shook her head.

'I don't think it's right to be showing the dead,' said Gwen, 'though at least they're not pretending everything's wonderful and we're winning. And I dare say it's worse than they're making out.'

The three of them stood and shuffled out of the row. As they left, Tallis talked of the allotments and how much he'd enjoyed the tour. Gwen was silent.

Outside the picture house it was now dark. Tallis nodded his head towards each of them in turn. 'It's been a pleasure to spend the evening with you, Miss Meredith, and you, Miss Austin.' His eyes lingered on Gwen. 'Can I give you a lift anywhere?'

'That won't be necessary,' said Elizabeth, 'as I have my motorcar here.'

'Hopefully I'll see you ladies again. Good night.'

When he was out of earshot, Gwen giggled and said, 'Oh I do hope so. When Anwen talked about his visit she didn't say how handsome he was.'

'Probably because she's smitten with Idris. I wonder how they're getting on?'

'Having great fun by now, I should think. I would so love to visit London.' Gwen looked wistful.

'They're more likely exhausted, poor things.'

They walked to the car in silence, all the while Elizabeth wondering how the evening might have been without Gwen there.

—

Anwen woke with a start, confused at first as to where she was. It was pitch black, yet the bed didn't feel right. There was too much room. She and Idris were still squeezed into her single bed at home. Here, Idris seemed further away.

The guest house. But there was something else. A booming sound. What on earth was it? Her heart raced. She sat up and dangled her feet over the bed, feeling around on the bedside table for the candle and matches. No electric lights in this house, not like at home. She fumbled in the dark, eventually managing to light the candle. Carrying it over to the clock on the mantelpiece she saw that it was just after half past one. Perhaps a motorcar had gone past, or someone had dropped something in another room?

She crept back to bed but had only just sat on the edge and put the candle down when there was another thud. This time she felt the house move. She clutched the front of her nightdress. It was a sound that was only too familiar from the pit disaster back in July.

There was a moan from Idris. 'What's going on? Thought I heard something.'

Anwen pulled her feet into the bed and shuffled up closer to Idris, throwing her arm around his waist. A small sob escaped her mouth. 'It was an explosion.'

'It's alright, *cariad*, I'm here,' he almost sang, stroking her hair.

'It… it must be the Zeppelins, bombing.' She felt the shaking begin in her hands and slowly travel across her body.

Idris placed his arm round her shoulder, pulling her in. 'That seems the most likely explanation. That would be good, wouldn't it, blown up before I even got to the operating table.'

'Oh don't say that, *bach*, not even in jest.'

'Don't worry. We'll sit tight here, and it'll stop eventually,' he said.

He'd barely got to the end of his sentence when there was a hammering on their door and the landlady's voice called, 'Come down to the cellar with you, before the next explosion. The Zepps could be coming our way.'

The pair of them sprang out of bed, Anwen calling, 'But we're in our nightclothes.'

'Better that than being blown to kingdom come,' came the landlady's reply.

Please, if a bomb falls here, let us both be properly alive or both be gone, she prayed, hardly able to breathe, a second before there was yet another explosion.

Chapter Seven

Elizabeth had been out hoeing, digging, planting and harvesting for the best part of three hours now, on the Edward Street allotment.

Needing a rest from bending, she was walking around the field, rubbing her back. It was when she came to a halt near the end houses that she spotted him, coming along the road. Councillor Tallis. She looked down at her brother's shabby cast-offs. Dash it, she didn't want him seeing her like this. Still, what choice did she have? Too late now anyway: he'd spotted her.

She tidied her hair, realising too late she'd probably only put more soil into it. Did it matter? He'd be here to see the allotments, not her. *More's the pity*, she thought. She was glad Gwen was at work and not helping out, as she'd have looked far more elegant, even working on the soil.

'Miss Meredith,' he said, looking as dapper as he had the last time she'd seen him, though a little more serious.

'Mr Tallis. How nice of you to grace us with your presence. Do excuse my work outfit, but I didn't expect any outside visitors today.'

'Don't worry about that.' He waved the matter away. 'What does concern me is whether you actually have permission to dig these fields up. We didn't discuss it last time, as I assumed you'd been given permission by the council before I was appointed. But what I've heard suggests not.'

'The reason—' Elizabeth attempted to enlighten him when he ploughed on, interrupting her.

'I'm afraid that just because you are the mine manager's daughter here, it doesn't mean you can dig up the ground willy-nilly.' He looked at her as if she were a naughty child and he was disappointed in her, much like her father used to when she was little. That annoyed her more than his words.

'No, but the thing—'

'We take a dim view, on the council, of people who take matters into their own hands. If you want to use council land you must seek permission to rent it, and then there's a due—'

'*If* you would let me finish, Mr Tallis.' When he looked abashed, she carried on. 'The reason we did not seek permission from the council is because the land is not council property. It belongs to the Tredegar Iron and Coal Company, who own McKenzie colliery, and it was from them we obtained permission.'

Mr Tallis raised his eyebrows and pressed his lips together. 'And they'd allow you to do that for nothing?'

'Yes, because they could see the good sense of growing food to keep their workers fit and healthy, which in turn would mean more coal excavated.'

'And who exactly persuaded them of this?' This question was asked with interest, rather than irritation.

'My mother and myself. My mother is acquainted with Lady McKenzie, whose husband is on the board of directors.'

'Ah Lady McKenzie, is it?' He seemed impressed by her connection. 'A couple of people at the council seemed to think the ground was common when I mentioned your project to them. I was sent to sort it out, since I'd met you.'

'You can check it with my father, if you like. He was present when it was agreed.'

He held up both his hands in protest, shaking his head at the same time. 'No, no, there's no need for that.'

'I can assure you Miss Meredith is telling the truth.'

Gwilym had come up behind them, freshly washed, his hair still wet where it was slicked back.

'No need to stick up for her, old chap. I'm not doubting her word. My colleagues at the council should clearly have checked their facts. I shall be having stern words with them.'

'Aye, you should,' said Gwilym, before fetching a spade and starting to dig out of earshot.

'My, he was quick to defend you,' said Tallis. 'Is he... I mean, are you and he—'

'Courting?' Elizabeth said with surprise. 'Goodness, no.'

'Of course. You are clearly out of his class.'

She looked towards the handsome but cross face of Gwilym, taking some irritation out on the earth. Would she have courted him if the two of them had been attracted to each other? Her mother would certainly have had much to say. She wanted to laugh at this thought but instead said, 'Maybe so, but he's an intelligent man and one of the team leaders, so I consider him an equal. I am not spoken for.' She wasn't sure why she'd added the last sentence.

'I can't imagine why not.'

Her face reddened and she felt a fool. It was more than likely an empty compliment. Well, she wasn't a silly schoolgirl about to fall for that again. Unbidden, an image of Max, the brother of an old school friend, came to mind. He'd been the son of the owner of a shipbuilding company. She'd adored his auburn curls and intelligent green eyes, not to mention his enquiring mind. He'd been good at everything, schoolwork, sports, the piano. He'd gone on to Cambridge. When she'd visited her friend, she'd often found an opportunity to speak to him, enjoying their conversations. She'd been twenty, and he'd been home on holiday, when she'd overheard him telling his friends that his sister's 'passably pretty but irritatingly dull' friend had come around, and how he was sure she had a soft spot for him. 'It's fun to lead her on a little,' Max had said, 'but what is she but a jumped-up miner's daughter? Thinks she's something because he's a manager now.' They'd all laughed, adding to her humiliation. Not long after, her friend had become engaged.

She'd seen little of her since then. The memory never ceased to shame her anew. No, she wasn't falling for shallow compliments again.

'Anyway,' Tallis continued. 'I had better be getting back to sort out this misinformation at the council.'

'That would be appreciated,' said Elizabeth.

'I'll bid you good day then, Miss Meredith.'

'And to you.'

He had turned to head off but whirled round once more to face her. 'I've just remembered that there's a talk on allotments next month at Bargoed Parish Hall. I wonder, with your interest here, whether you'd like to accompany me.'

She experienced a small glow of pleasure. 'Well it so happens that I'd heard of the talk and was thinking of going.'

'Then I dare say you have others to go with.' He looked disappointed.

'As a matter of fact, I haven't arranged anything yet.'

'In that case, let us keep each other company. I would offer to give you a lift, but I will have meetings beforehand, so could we meet there?'

'Of course. It starts at seven thirty, doesn't it?'

'Indeed. I shall meet you outside the hall.'

'Yes, that would be fine.' And would stop any tongues in the village wagging and making up their own stories, she thought.

'Oh, but there is one thing I'd ask you.' He looked serious enough for her to worry about what was coming.

'What is that?'

He looked embarrassed. 'I feel awkward saying this, as it makes me sound rather arrogant, but… the young lady who accompanied you to the picture house, Miss Austin, wasn't it?'

'That's right.'

'As we were sitting together the other evening, she, well, she took my hand for a while and whispered to me, giving me to understand that she was interested in me. Oh dear, this does sound bad, and her your friend.'

'My goodness, that doesn't sound like Gwen.' Then again, how well did she really know her?

'Well, it's just that I'd rather you didn't say anything to her, or to anyone who might tell her. I wouldn't want her to be upset with you.'

'All right, I'll keep it to myself. And we're only attending a talk, after all. It's not like we're walking out.'

'Thank you, Miss Meredith, for being so understanding. May I, um, call you Elizabeth?'

'Of course. And your name is…? Apart from Mr Tallis?' She leant her head to one side and smiled, realising she hadn't a clue about his first name.

He pointed to himself. 'Me? Of course! I'm Ralph.'

'Then I shall look forward to our evening at the talk, Ralph.'

When he'd walked away a fair distance, Gwilym came back over to her.

'I was wondering if you'd heard about the Zeppelin raid in London early Friday morning.'

She gave a small yelp. 'Zeppelin raid? No. Where did you hear that?'

'Someone at the pit mentioned it as we were leaving our shift, then gave me the newspaper.' He pulled it out of his jacket pocket.

She looked at the headline. 'Do the Rhyses know about it?'

'I dunno. Should we worry them? London's a big place. And they'll be told soon enough if something's happened.' Despite his words, his frown gave away his concern.

'Not—' she was about to say *not if nobody knows who they are*, but couldn't bear the image that came to mind, of Anwen and Idris among the rubble, like those poor soldiers lying in the mud in the Somme. 'It's not something we can assume.'

She'd seen Florrie Harris knocking on the Rhyses' door, not five minutes ago, no doubt arriving for a gossip. As she was considering this, the door opened and out flew Enid, looking around blindly. She spotted the two of them, lifting her skirt to run towards them, her shawl flying behind her.

'Miss Elizabeth, Gwilym, have you heard?' Tears were running down her panicked face. 'Florrie says there have been Zeppelins in London, dropping bombs.'

'Calm down now, Mrs Rhys,' said Elizabeth. 'Gwilym was showing me the newspaper. Let's see what it says.'

Gwilym unfolded it. 'There were twelve Zeppelins but only one got through—'

Enid grabbed the paper from Gwilym. 'I'll read it for myself, rather than have you tell me only good news.' She scanned the paper closely. 'My reading may not be as good as yours, but I can read well enough. Here we are. Eight killed and eighteen injured. *O Duw*. The Zeppelin… came in from the southeast coast to the… outskirts of London.' Enid dropped the newspaper. 'But that was on the address: London SE. SE for southeast London.' She lowered her head and sobbed.

Elizabeth felt sick. Only eight killed, she told herself. Eight too many, but it made the chances of two of them being Anwen and Idris small. The thought did little to comfort her. She picked up the discarded paper, noticing the bottom line of the report. One hundred bombs were thought to have been dropped in all, maybe only forty hitting anywhere. Forty. She shook her head.

Cadi appeared from across the road, taking hold of Enid. 'What's happened, *cariad*? I've been gone no more than half an hour.'

'Florrie did call by to say—' but she was unable to finish.

'There was a Zeppelin raid early yesterday morning,' said Gwilym. 'It went over southeast London, where Anwen and Idris are.'

'*O Duw*,' said Cadi, cradling her thin daughter-in-law in her well-rounded embrace.

'Here's the report,' said Elizabeth, showing her the paper.

'No good showing me, for I can't read it.'

Elizabeth read the whole report carefully, so they'd get a proper idea of what had happened. Slowly a crowd of allotment workers gathered around, the closer ones alerting those further away.

'Someone should take that to the Hughes family,' said Mary Jones, the closest to them.

'I will,' said Gwilym.

'Let's get back to the house, *cariad*,' said Cadi. 'For we'll need to tell Hywel when he returns from his walk.'

Enid nodded and let her mother-in-law lead her home. The allotment workers drifted back to their jobs, whispering among themselves and shaking their heads.

'I would imagine there's little chance of them having been involved,' Elizabeth said to Gwilym.

'We can only hope,' he said, before he sauntered off across the field, towards Alexandra Street.

—

Violet looked for a while at the empty school playground, after Clarice and the other children had gone inside. Taking hold of Benjamin's hand, she moved off at last. She'd miss the little girl's chattery presence in the house all day.

'Mam, when Clarry come home?' said Benjy. 'I want play wiv her.'

'She's only been gone two minutes. We'll fetch her back in the afternoon, after dinner.'

'That's long time away.' He started to grizzle, the tears flowing readily.

'I know Benjy, love.' She bent down to pick him up. 'Would you like to help me on the allotment? There might be other children to play with.'

He nodded his head. She hadn't been for a while but wanted to get back to some kind of normal routine. The tot put his head on her shoulder; she realised she'd have to carry him up hill to the Edward Street allotment. He was getting a little big to carry now, at least by her. Hywel had managed it all right at Anwen and Idris's wedding, despite his limp.

Anwen and Idris. Her stomach lurched. They still didn't know if they'd been involved in the bombing raid.

As she reached the allotment, she saw Enid from afar, talking with Elizabeth and Hywel, a piece of paper held aloft. She ran down the road towards her. Violet marvelled at the change in her since Madog had been arrested.

'Violet! I'm so glad you're here. We've received a letter from Anwen. The two of them are fine.' She came to a breathless halt. 'Idris has had the operation and is making a good recovery. The pair of them heard the raids to the southeast of London, but they were over places called…' she checked the letter, 'Dept – ford, Green – wich, Blackheath, El – tham and Plumstead. Anwen was in… Lambeth, which was, she was told, about five miles from where the nearest bomb dropped, thank the Lord.'

Violet placed Benjamin down, uplifted by the good news. 'None of those places mean a thing to me, but I'm so relieved to hear they're safe. Five miles. It's not that far, is it? Are they still due back on the 6th September?'

'That they are. It'll be a long stretch of bedrest for Idris after that, though.'

'Talking of which, what is Hywel doing on the allotments?'

'Said he was going crazy not being useful. I thought he could do a bit of easy work here. He did seem to be getting a little melancholic.'

'Poor Hywel.' He hadn't seemed quite his jolly self when Violet had visited the house. 'It will do him good to be out here.'

'Have you come to work on the allotments?'

'I have.'

'Come on then.' Enid held her hand out to Benjy. 'Mary Jones has her little Charlotte out. A bit younger than you, she is, but a little friend to play with nonetheless.'

'I like Charlon,' said Benjamin.

Enid led him across the road to the grass verge where Charlotte was playing. They were soon running around and laughing.

Elizabeth came over to speak to Violet. 'I'm glad you've come to help again. Perhaps you could sow the seeds for the broad beans and peas where Hywel is preparing the ground. He can push a tiller as he doesn't have to bend his leg for that.'

'If that's where I'd be most useful.' They moved in that direction together. 'I wonder what he'll do for work when he's better. I doubt he'll be able to dig coal again with that leg.'

'There are always plenty of other jobs in the mine need doing. I will speak to my father. But please, don't tell him I've got involved. I know about men and their pride. I believe Idris got cross with Anwen when I suggested him for the job of examiner to Papa.'

Papa. Elizabeth couldn't even use ordinary words like the rest of them. She put the thought to one side to say, 'Charlie would have been the same.' She came to an abrupt stop as her chin wobbled. The last thing she wanted to do was cry in front of Elizabeth, and risk her putting an arm around her. However, the other woman waited patiently as Violet composed herself. 'I'm sorry.'

'It's perfectly understandable. I know it's not the *done thing* to show your emotions in public, but in my experience it doesn't do any good hiding them. Don't apologise for caring.'

'I had better get on with some work,' said Violet.

'Of course.'

Violet moved off, not waiting to see if Elizabeth had any more to say.

–

'All I'm saying, Mam, is that it's going to be a tough few months, what with the men of the family unable to work and little money coming in.' Anwen had taken the opportunity while Hywel and Idris had gone to sit in Jubilee Gardens to share her concern with her mother. She'd only returned from London yesterday evening, but there was no time like the present to talk of the future.

'Hywel is well on the mend and I'm sure he'll be doing some work or other soon.'

'He was a hewer, Mam. He won't be able to bend his leg well enough to do that anymore. We've got to face facts. That thirty pounds I found under Da's mattress isn't going to last forever, neither will Idris's savings, a large part of which went on going to London and some of the hospital bill that the workers' health fund subs didn't pay. And Cadi's bits of sewing work aren't enough. Perhaps I should go back to the Big House as maid again after all. I know that means you and Cadi looking after Idris and Hywel, but, well…'

Enid bit her bottom lip and looked away. She crossed her arms before saying, 'I wasn't going to tell you yet, mainly 'cos I hadn't made up my mind, but Miss Elizabeth has asked me if I'd like to take up the position. It makes more sense that you stay home to look after your recovering husband, which is what you wanted to do.'

Anwen was miffed at being so easily replaced by the Merediths. But then, wasn't it she who'd given up the job? They couldn't be blamed for seeking another maid. And why not her mother? She'd done a similar job before she'd married her father.

They heard the back door open and the chatter of the two men.

'Are you sure you're fit enough to do that?' Anwen asked.

'You know I am. Haven't I done my bit with the housework, shopping and the garden here?'

She certainly had, as if she was making up for the lost time. It was such a shame that Sara hadn't lived long enough to see their mother so active again. 'I suppose it makes sense. When will you start?'

'I'll walk over to the house today, unless Miss Elizabeth's on the allotment here.'

'She is that,' said Hywel, hobbling through the door. 'Are you wanting to talk to her?'

'Aye, later. How was your walk? I 'ope you're not too tired, Idris *bach*,' she said as he followed Hywel in.

'I do need a rest now, but it was good for the soul to sit in the gardens on a sunny day for a while, instead of being mollycoddled sat on the chaise with a blanket.' He plonked onto a dining chair, as if in protest.

'You want to enjoy it while you can, *bach*,' said Hywel, winking. 'Though I must say, I'm keen as mustard to get back to some kind of work, to pay my way.'

'We'll talk about that later,' said Enid. 'Sit down and I'll put the kettle on.'

Hywel did as his big sister told him, pulling out a newspaper from his jacket. 'Wonder if any more countries have joined the war. What with Rumania, Turkey and Bulgaria joining recently, I do wonder how long it'll be before every bleeding country in the world's involved. Then how long will this whole thing last?'

Enid tutted. 'Enough of your swearing. We've got enough to worry about here. I've just been telling Anwen, so I might as well tell you two. I've finally decided I'm going to take the job at the Big House. I wasn't going to, but they still haven't found anybody, and it will help out with money.'

'What, the one Anwen had?' said Idris.

'That's right. Though I don't want to do as many hours as she did, so Mrs Meredith will have to like it or lump it.' Enid picked up the kettle's handle with a teacloth. 'Let's have some tea and you two can tell us more about that London.'

Chapter Eight

Violet had spent the time since dropping Clarice off at school getting through the housework at a feverish pace. Benjy had devoted some of the time to playing with the train, and some of it to the garden, running around the weeds, pretending *he* was a train. By midday he'd been bored and grizzly. Because Violet had done all the tasks she'd allotted herself, she had set dinner early to cheer him up.

'When Clarry come home?' Benjamin asked forlornly, in between bites of bread and dripping.

'Same time as usual.'

So sad did he look, it struck her to the heart. Poor lonely little boy without a da. She scraped her chair out and went to the kitchen window, peering out into the yard, trying to catch a glimpse of the sky. 'Shall we go for a walk after dinner, to the gardens? Then maybe call in on Anwen?'

Benjamin lifted his head and smiled. 'I like do that.'

The Rhyses always made a big fuss of the children, so it wasn't surprising he was keen to go. She wondered when Anwen and Idris would have their first child. Probably a burden they didn't need at the moment, with him recovering from the operation. But babbies came along when they wanted to, without regard for your own wishes.

They left soon after dinner and were heading along James Street, towards the park, when they were overtaken by Esther Williams. She was on her own, as she had been increasingly recently, her group of cackling harpies having deserted her when her husband, Edgar, had been arrested. Reaching

Schenck's bookshop, opposite the gardens, Violet met Elizabeth coming up Station Road. Violet supposed she should be civil to her, but she was fed up with her popping up in their lives.

After greeting each other, Elizabeth said, 'Where's Esther off to in such a hurry?'

'Home, I should think,' said Violet, 'since she lives on Jubilee Green.'

'I wonder how she'll afford the rent on the house, with Edgar in gaol. Her younger son, Christopher, has started working at the mine, but he won't be earning much yet.'

The houses on Jubilee Green were certainly among the fancier ones in the village, with their stonework and tiny bit of front yard. Violet would never be able to afford to live there. Keeping up with the rent on her current house was starting to get difficult. She pushed the thought away. 'He's not been convicted yet.'

'But he will be,' said Elizabeth. 'He confessed to the crimes. I should imagine he'll be put away for quite a while.'

Violet wished her unwanted companion would go about her business. She'd been too friendly in their last chat and this had only served to encourage her. But instead, Elizabeth bent down to her son's level.

'Why, hello Benjy. And where are you off to? Anywhere nice?'

'We go gardens, then see Aunty Anwen.'

'That sounds lovely. I hope you have a good time.' Elizabeth straightened herself. 'Are you working on the allotments later today?'

She could have been, instead of indulging her son, but they were only little once and she'd been there the last three days in a row, with Elizabeth working close by much of the time. She needed a rest from her.

'Not today,' Violet said, maybe a little too sharply. She softened her voice to say, 'Can't be bringing the children every day.'

'I suppose not. I must be getting on. Cheerio, Violet. Take care.'

'Goodbye Miss Elizabeth.'

Violet was aware of Miss Meredith opening her mouth to correct her, but she hurried across the road before she was able to. She should keep to her flower shows and afternoon teas with the ladies of the district, not try to pretend she was part of their community.

Violet opened the bottom gate to the gardens and Benjy surged ahead, stopping at all the plants still in flower to sniff at them. She sat herself down on the bench and watched as he skipped up and down the path. Perhaps she should forgo the visit to Anwen's and take him on a longer walk on Twyn Gobaith, the hill behind her friend's house. Or to the other side of the village, to the evergreen woods. She hadn't been there since her walk with Anwen and Gwen in February. Thinking about it, Elizabeth had disturbed that too, fetching Anwen to speak to Mrs Meredith.

Benjy ran up to her, leaning on her knees. 'We go Aunty Anwen's now?'

'I was wondering...' she began, when the top gate creaked open and two figures entered: Hywel and Idris.

Hywel's limp was still pronounced and Idris was bent over slightly, so they were both taking each step slowly.

'Nice to see you out and about,' said Hywel. His smile formed dimples in his cheeks. His dark brown hair, parted in the middle, looked like it had been cut.

Violet wondered if smiling was fitting for a still-new widow, so tried a half smile in compromise. 'I could say the same.'

'We do try to do a walk every day.'

'Aye,' said Idris, sitting at the other end of the seat.

This left Hywel no choice but to sit next to Violet. Searching her brain for something to say, she came up with, 'I was thinking of taking Benjy for a walk in the woods beyond McKenzie House. It's not a bad day, and mild.' She looked up at the sky, half covered in cloud.

'Wish we could do that,' said Idris. 'Love walking, I do.'

'We go see Aunty Anwen,' said the boy, a frown marring his chubby face.

'I'm afraid she and Cadi have gone out,' said Idris, 'to visit Cadoc Beadle. He's at home now, so people are dropping in all the time to do his shopping and the like. He seems a little better, though terribly melancholic.'

'What mellycolly?' Benjamin asked.

'It's being sad,' said Violet, wondering if she could be described as such.

Hywel slipped off the bench and hunkered down awkwardly next to the boy, one leg sticking out. He leaned forward, placing his hand by his mouth as if to whisper a secret. 'I'd go for that walk if I were you,' said Hywel. 'And on the way, I'd get your mam to stop off at Mrs Davies's for some chocolate. I hear she's just had in some bars of that Cadbury's Mexican.'

His face lit up. 'I like choclit.'

'Who doesn't *bach*?' He pulled himself up awkwardly, a grimace on his face, prompting Violet to stand and help him.

'Thank you. I still haven't got used to the fact I can't bend in the way I could.'

'It's getting better though, it seems,' she said.

'Yes, but I doubt my leg will ever be quite the same.'

Violet took Benjy's hand. 'We'd better get going if we're to get that chocolate and take that walk before Clarice finishes school.' She was grateful to Hywel for cheering her son up, but she knew the chocolate would stretch the coins in her purse. 'You'll have to share the chocolate with Clarice though,' she added.

The boy pulled his mother along, eager now to get going.

'Do call by after school, if you want to see Anwen,' Hywel called. 'She should be in then.'

Violet turned her head back to wave at the two men. 'I'll see how things go.'

She chased Benjy to the gate, not looking back again.

Despite the sun having long since disappeared over the horizon, there was still a slight pinkish light in the sky when Elizabeth arrived at the parish hall in Bargoed at quarter to seven. Several people were going in, but there was no sign yet of Ralph Tallis. She felt a pang of nerves, wondering what to do if he didn't turn up. Go in by herself? She might as well, rather than waste the trip. She patted down her clothes to consider once more what she'd worn. The green velvet skirt and matching jacket were favourites of hers. The skirt was the shortest she owned, between her ankles and mid-calf. Her hat was an elegant one, with the brim rolled up at the back and trimmed with dusky pink fabric roses and green foliage. She still couldn't decide if she'd made the right choice or whether it was a little too bold. Too late now.

When she saw Ralph across the road, lifting his arm in greeting, she was filled with relief. He was wearing a smart dark brown suit this evening. On his head was a felt Homburg. A couple of women looked round as he reached her, giving him admiring glances.

'Are you early or am I late?' he quipped.

'Neither. I've only been here a couple of minutes. We have plenty of time to find a good seat.'

He offered his arm, which she took with a smile.

The hall was so far only half full when they sat six rows back from the front.

'What a shame there aren't more people,' she said. 'For I'm sure Mr Lawley will be a mine of information.'

'You'd hope so, with him being a Board of Agriculture inspector.'

Only a few more people turned up before the doors were closed and a small, balding man stepped onto the podium. He gave a brief introduction before Mr Lawley himself appeared through a door, taking the man's place on the podium to greet them. Elizabeth removed her notebook from her bag, along with a fountain pen. She was determined to glean all that she could from the knowledgeable Board of Agriculture inspector.

Ralph leaned over to whisper, 'That's very efficient.'

'I want to be able to go through it with my allotment team.'

He nodded and looked impressed, which pleased her no end.

Mr Lawley spoke of acquiring seed immune of disease, of the best varieties for the land, the use of manure and of recommended literature on the subject. She scribbled frantically, afraid she'd miss a valuable nugget of information, yet despairing at her deteriorating handwriting.

After Mr Lawley had finished his speech there were numerous questions, particularly pertaining to local land, that the man answered admirably. Elizabeth asked a couple of them herself, pleased with the replies she received.

At the end of the meeting, as everyone rose to leave, Ralph said, 'You seem to have written a lot.'

'I'm afraid I was the same at school,' she laughed, 'which didn't always make me popular with my fellow pupils. But I have always loved learning.'

'That is an admirable trait indeed. Many privileged young women like yourself are more than happy simply to spend money on clothes and sit at functions all day long.'

She wondered just how 'privileged' he imagined her to be.

They made their way towards the doors. 'My goodness,' he said, 'I almost forgot to tell you. I met your mother at a Dorcalon school committee meeting. Most friendly she was too, especially when I mentioned I'd met you at the allotments.'

'Oh, really?' said Elizabeth, thinking instead, *I bet she was.* That may well be why he considered her privileged, what with Mama's airs and graces.

'She is clearly not enamoured of you wearing men's clothes for the allotment though, for she was at pains to point out how well you normally dress. I told her you were well turned out the first time I met you, which seemed to be a relief to her.'

'How embarrassing!' said Elizabeth.

They were outside now, the mild air of earlier having turned a little chilly. She wondered if he'd suggest a cup of tea or coffee somewhere, as there were a couple of cafés open this time of the evening. They stood by the hall for a few moments, saying nothing.

'I can't wait for next spring,' said Elizabeth, hoping to prolong their evening. 'When we can put some of these suggestions into practice, and maybe get an even better crop of vegetables than this year. I'm afraid we had some unfortunate incidences with some less salubrious members of the village.' She recalled how Edgar Williams, Madog and Prosser the Meat had organised the destruction of the vegetables on the Cottages allotment.

'What a shame. Well, it's a little cold now, so I won't hold you up getting to your motorcar, especially as you, like I, have not brought a coat.'

She was disappointed, she couldn't deny it. Perhaps this had, after all, been only about having company at the talk. Or she'd frightened him away because she had some intelligence. It didn't suit all men for women to have thoughts and opinions.

'However, I would like it if we could do something else together at some point in the future.'

Her spirits were lifted no end. Maybe she wasn't as boring as she feared.

'That would be very agreeable, thank you.'

'Let me walk you to your motorcar.'

'It's only around the corner, but all right.'

When they reached the Morris Oxford he said, 'Do you have a telephone at your house? I imagine you do.'

'Yes. My mother had it installed a couple of years ago.'

'Splendid. Maybe you could write your telephone number on a piece of paper from your notebook.'

'It's very easy to remember. It's Rhymney 13.'

He laughed. 'I hope that will be lucky for me. Now, I don't know about you, but I'm getting a little cold. And I have a full day tomorrow, what with my own business and the council business too.'

'What is your business, you haven't said?'

'I own a surveying and estate agency business for the upper end of the housing market with my cousin. Tallis and Fair-weather.'

It was said in a way to impress her, though she worried little about his profession. It would at least impress her mother if she ended up introducing him as... but she was running away with herself.

'I'm sure it must keep you busy. Good night, Ralph.'

He took her hand long enough to say, 'Good night, Eliza-beth.'

She gave a sigh as she watched him disappear into the dark.

—

Three days later, Elizabeth arrived home from the allotments just before seven. Due to the gloomy day, the sky had already darkened. There was a distant noise she couldn't make out. She removed her muddy boots in the scullery, to clean later, then headed into the kitchen on her way to get washed and changed. It was then that she realised the sound was her mother shouting. A deeper voice interrupted, though the words were indistinct.

She held back, sitting on a chair, dog-tired and not wanting to get involved with whatever it was between her parents.

The shouting stopped. She was about to rise when the door was flung open and Margaret stormed in. Seeing her daughter, she came to a sudden halt.

'Oh, you're back.'

'It is seven o'clock already. It's dark outside.' As if to back her up, the hall clock chimed the required number of times.

'Aren't you going to get changed? I could do with a hand finishing the meal.'

'I've been working on the allotments all afternoon. I need a bath.'

'Your father's eating out this evening, with the gentlemen's club lot. I trust you're not attending another talk with the *hoi polloi*.'

She hadn't been going to tell her mother who she'd gone to the talk with, but she was annoyed now. 'I didn't realise you considered Councillor Tallis the *hoi polloi*.'

The broad smile was instant. Margaret fluttered her eyelashes and gave a little shiver like a smitten girl. 'Councillor Tallis, is it? He's a fine catch. I hear his estate agency is doing very well. Descended from landed gentry, I believe, and has a lovely house, just outside Rhymney.'

Elizabeth already regretted telling her. 'Don't get carried away, Mama; we were only keeping each other company. And please, you must keep it to yourself for now. I don't want people to know.' Or rather, Gwen in particular.

Margaret wasn't to be discouraged. 'Will you be walking out again?'

'Did you not hear what I said?' Yet she'd been waiting eagerly for his phone call.

'There's no need to speak to me like that. I'm only asking.'

'I'm sorry.'

Perhaps now wasn't the time to get cross with her. The argument with her father must have been about him going out again. She couldn't blame him in some ways, yet no wonder her mother was constantly upset. It was a vicious circle. Her mother had been far more sensitive about such things since Tom had enlisted, yet her father had failed to notice this. Or was he burying his dismay in jaunts out with his friends? She was thinking too deeply about it again. It was her parents' affair and they had to sort it out.

'Why are you shaking your head?' said Margaret.

'Am I? I, um, guess I was thinking about all the work that needs doing on the allotments, ready for autumn.'

'Autumn.' Her mother walked to the window to peer out at the night. 'October tomorrow already, and it will get dark an hour earlier with us losing the daylight-saving hour. What happened to the summer?' She let out a long, dispirited sigh.

This was a different point of view from her mother, who'd declared the new summertime hours, back in May, to be ridiculous.

'Mam, are you all right? You're not coming down with a cold or something?'

Margaret regarded her crossly. 'Mama, it's *Mama*! Mam is for babies and, and…'

She was sure her mother was going to resort once more to *hoi polloi*, but she didn't finish the sentence.

'It was good enough when we were children, not just babies. It was only when Papa, or *Da* as I used to call him, became under manager at the Whitworth pit that you made us change what we called you. We were *hoi polloi* once too. Still are, at heart.'

Margaret stomped from the window to stand in front of Elizabeth. 'We most certainly are *not*. And let me remind you that my father was a bank clerk. Now, get yourself washed and changed, and we shall have dinner together in the dining room.'

'Why don't we have it here, in the kitchen, with it being just the two of us? It's much cosier. Like we used to at your mother's house.'

Margaret didn't reply, instead walking towards the pantry. 'The quicker this war is over and we can get a proper cook again, the better.'

She opened the pantry door and stepped inside, grumbling. Elizabeth took it as her cue to leave.

–

'Thank you for coming with us, Hywel,' said Evan, as they entered Cadoc Beadle's back garden, at the house right at the end of Islwyn Street on the edge of the village. They were all damp from yet another passing shower that day.

'Aye,' agreed Jenkin. 'It's hard to know what to talk about sometimes. We tells him what's going on at scouts, and how Mr Breckon has taken over, but he doesn't seem as interested as he was.'

'It's good of you boys to keep coming,' said Hywel. 'It's a shame Cadoc hasn't returned to chapel. Thought we might have seen him there this morning, after Pastor Thomas's visit last week. It seemed promising.' He knocked on the scullery door and entered. 'Just us,' he called.

They found Cadoc sitting on a wooden armchair by the range, as always. A book was open on his lap, face down.

'Cadoc, mun, how are you?' said Hywel.

'Bit cold today, if truth be told.' He took off his round spectacles and rubbed the bridge of his nose. 'Looks a bit damp out there.'

'Aye, it is.'

He went to get up, saying, 'I'll get us some tea.'

Hywel put out his hand, 'No mun, you stay put. We can do that now we're here.' He lifted the kettle from the range. 'Fill this up would you boys? And fetch in the tea things.'

Evan took the large copper kettle and ran off to the scullery, Jenkin in tow.

'How are you coping, mun? Has Dr Roberts said when you can go back to work?'

Cadoc looked at his hands, knotted together on the book. 'He's not said much. Heard him say to Jozef though that he doesn't think I'm the full ticket. Whatever that means.'

'Jozef?' Hywel queried.

'Mr Schenck. Friends we've been, for years. Been visiting me every other evening after the shop closes.'

'That's good of him,' said Hywel. 'You know, you took a battering and were unconscious for a good long time. Bound to take a while.'

'I dunno about that. Can't concentrate on anything. Used to love reading, I did, now I can't remember the story from one sentence to the next. What day is it?'

95

'Sunday October 1st.'

The boys came back with the full kettle and the teapot between them.

'Oh, hello boys,' said Cadoc. 'It's nice of you to come and visit.'

Hywel looked sidelong at the boys. Did he not remember them being here only two minutes ago? Or maybe it was because he didn't greet them the first time. He took the kettle and lit the stove.

'Are you boys still going to scouts then?' Cadoc asked.

'You know we are, mun,' said Jenkin. 'We help Mr Breckon, and he's doing a good job, but not as good as you did. When are you coming back?'

'I couldn't say. How's school then?'

'Oh Mr Beadle, we already told you we'd left. I'm a trapper and Evan's a putter in the mine.'

'Of course, I remember now,' he replied.

Sitting himself opposite Cadoc, Hywel asked, 'Has your sister said when she's coming up from Porthcawl to visit yet?'

'I think I 'ad a letter. Yes.' He rose and fetched it from the end of the table. 'Here we go.' He opened it. 'Said she's busy in school now, so will come one weekend. Doesn't say when though.'

She wasn't busy in the summer holidays when she wasn't teaching, Hywel thought. She didn't come then either. He kept this to himself, not wanting to give Cadoc any more reason to be down.

Waiting for the kettle to boil, the boys chatted on about what they'd been doing at scouts, along with who'd left and who'd joined. Cadoc nodded his head slightly at each bit of news, though Gwilym wondered if he were really taking it in. He asked no questions and his expression was a little glazed.

'There we go,' said Hywel, when steam flew out of the spout of the kettle.

Jenkin made the tea while Evan fetched four cups from the scullery.

'There was something I was going to ask,' said Cadoc, his brow furrowed as he struggled to remember. 'Christopher Williams. What was it now?' He bent down to pick up a newspaper next to his chair. 'Here it is, I wrote it down. What happened to the boy? There was some story, I can't remember what I was told.'

'Edgar Williams tied him up in his bedroom, when he tried to run away to enlist,' said Hywel. 'We discovered him upstairs, when we went to the house. Edgar was loaded and admitted to attacking you. Do you remember it yet?'

'No,' he said on a long sigh. 'Don't remember a thing.'

'Only a couple of days now till the court case,' Evan piped up, handing Cadoc a cup of tea.

'Shh now,' Hywel warned.

'It's all right,' said Cadoc. 'Several people have told me. I know, 'cos I wrote it down here.' He picked up the newspaper once more to reveal he'd written things in several spaces on the front page.

'Looks like you could do with a notebook, mun,' said Hywel. 'I'll see if I can get you one.'

'That would be kind.' He took a long slurp of the tea.

The boys gabbled on about an overnight trip that Twm Bach, or Mr Breckon as they called him, had taken them on, camping in the evergreen wood near McKenzie cottages. They didn't notice Cadoc was miles away, staring at the fire in the range.

'Why don't you lads do the washing up now,' Hywel said when they'd finished their tea.

They gathered the crockery up. Hywel waited until the boys had gone into the scullery before saying, 'Are you going to be called to court at all?' There was no reply. 'Cadoc?'

He looked up in surprise. 'Mm?'

'Court. Are you being called to Edgar Williams's hearing?'

'No point. I don't remember nothing.'

'That wouldn't stop his lawyer. Could be to his advantage. But I'm glad they've decided not to call you. Now, if you want anything doing mun, let me know.'

'The women do come in to help, so I'll be all right.'

'I'll pop in again another day.' Hywel stood and stretched.

'As you wish.'

When the boys had finished and said their goodbyes, they left via the back door and headed down the path behind the houses.

'Is he off his nut, do you think?' said Evan, with no preamble.

Hywel considered how best to answer this. 'I think he's still recovering. Time will tell how much damage was done.'

'I 'ope he recovers,' said Jenkin, slinking along with his hands jammed in his pockets. 'For I do miss him from scouts. Mr Breckon's fine, but, he don't quite have Mr Beadle's enthusiasm.'

Hywel patted him on the shoulder. 'He's rather down at the moment, so let's all do our best to cheer him up, eh?' He looked up at the sky. 'Here it comes, another shower. Let's get home before we get soaked.'

–

Anwen held her mother's hands in her lap, looking down at the proceedings in the courtroom at the Monmouth Assizes, from the seats on the balcony. At last the day of the court case had come, and soon, hopefully, Madog, Edgar Williams and the others involved in the thefts from carts and motorvans, and the subsequent profiteering, would get their comeuppance. The judge sat in a high-backed seat, akin to a throne, raised above the other attendees in the court, a wooden, triangular pediment above him, as if he were sitting in a Roman temple. All the benches in the room were made from a dark brown wood, lending a gloominess to the already glum proceedings. She glanced towards Gwen, Violet and Elizabeth, on the other side of her, who'd come along to support her and Mam today. Cadi had agreed to look after Clarice and Benjy as she had no intention of coming to the courthouse.

At the other end of the balcony sat Esther Williams, with whom they had not exchanged a single word, though she had treated them to several pinch-faced glares. On a bench at ground level was a group of reporters from the press. Anwen dreaded to think what might be written about her family in the newspapers.

At least all the prisoners had pleaded guilty, including her father. She'd been surprised about this, with him and Edgar, along with Iolo Prosser the erstwhile butcher and Reginald Moss, the former landlord of the McKenzie Arms, being the sort to fight everything. It meant none of them would be called as witnesses and precluded the sorry incident lasting longer than a day. This had been a relief to Idris who hadn't yet felt up to travelling to Monmouth.

The prisoners, lined up in the dock, were awaiting sentence. The three men who had been accessories to the thefts and the profiteering were given nine months imprisonment. Enid clutched Anwen's hands tighter.

'It doesn't seem like much,' Gwen whispered behind her hand.

'I'm sure the others will get longer,' Anwen murmured back.

Next, Iolo Prosser and Reginald Moss were given three years' penal servitude. They had been among the organisers of the scheme and more involved, so were more severely punished. The look on their faces was of immense shock. Their wives were notable by their absence.

'Don't look so smug now, do they?' said Gwen. 'What is penal servitude?'

'Hard labour,' Anwen mouthed.

'Good job too.'

'Edgar Iago Williams, you are sentenced to five years' penal servitude.'

Even from where they were sitting, they heard Esther gasp. Everyone in the balcony looked at her. He'd got two years more than Prosser and Moss, no doubt because of beating up Cadoc Beadle and imprisoning his own son, in addition to his deep involvement in the profiteering scheme. Williams showed no emotion whatever.

There was only Madog left now. The spectators leaned forward as one. Enid's eyes were wide with anxiety. She surely didn't think he'd be let off. Or maybe, like Anwen, she was worried he wouldn't get long enough.

'Madog Rhys, you are sentenced to three years' penal servitude…'

The courtroom erupted in surprised exclamations, with Enid yelling, 'That can't be right! He tried to kill me and my brother.'

The judge hammered his gavel against the block several times, shouting, 'Order in court!' When the crowd was silent once more, he said, 'If there are any more disturbances, those causing them will be ejected from this court.' He narrowed his eyes and peered round, taking each layer of seats in turn. 'Now, if you'd let me finish… You are sentenced to three years' penal servitude for your part in the thefts and the profiteering and a further nine years' penal servitude for two attempted manslaughters, making twelve years in—'

He hadn't finished before Madog started bellowing and swearing. The judge banged his gavel repeatedly, but Madog simply pushed past his fellow felons and attempted to get out of the dock. Two constables rapidly grabbed hold of him. By this time there was uproar in the court with people chattering and the judge hammering with his gavel.

The scene was so farcical that Anwen had the urge to laugh. This urge was brought to an abrupt end when Enid turned to her with a face like thunder.

'I'd have put him in there for life and thrown away the key. Or sent him to the hangman's noose.'

Anwen offered no reply. The reality of capital punishment had long concerned her. Where did forgiveness and compassion sit with such a verdict? Yet could she blame her mother for feeling this way, after what he'd done to her?

'Si – lence,' the judge finally yelled. The courtroom fell silent. He straightened his wig, which had slipped slightly over his forehead in his frantic attempt to quell the noise.

The prisoners were hauled away, Madog struggling all the while. She knew they'd be taken to the Monmouthshire County Gaol in Usk. Enid stood, pulling herself up tall as she removed the gloves from her old, battered handbag and placed them on. She headed for the door without a word, followed by Anwen and the other three.

They lost her in the crowd, looking round for her as they made for the exit. Anwen scrutinised the six large arches of the stone building, trying to find her.

'There she is,' said Violet.

Enid was looking up at the statue of Charles Rolls, who held a small aeroplane aloft.

'You took your time,' she said, spotting them.

Since working at McKenzie House, Anwen realised, her mother had never really kept still for any length of time, always finding something to do. It was as if the job, along with Madog's arrest, had given her a new lease of life. Mrs Meredith had certainly been pleased with her efforts.

'Would you like to get a cup of tea before I drive you all back to Dorcalon?' Elizabeth asked Enid. 'I should think you need one.'

'I would indeed. And a piece of cake too. That was an experience I do not intend to repeat. I noticed a nice tearoom on our way here. So let *that* be the end of *that*. That's the last time we need to worry about Madog Rhys.' Enid turned right and headed off down the street.

Anwen suspected that it would not be as simple as that.

Chapter Nine

Hywel had endured enough now of his sister's hectoring tone. He was ready to go out, down to the colliery, his cap placed firmly on his head, but still her voice was like a chain, shackling him there in the kitchen, on a seat by the door to the hall.

'But it's too soon, *bach*! You're still limping.'

'And may be doing so for the rest of my life. But I can walk fine now. I feel well in every other way. I can't sit here for evermore, pondering the stove or pottering in the allotments. Madog's convicted and won't be contributing to this household anymore. There's not enough to keep us all in food and clothes in the long run and the doctor reckons Idris needs another month's rest.'

'You can't kneel down all day with that leg.'

'No I can't. But there are plenty of other jobs in the mine that don't require that.'

'No, but—'

'You're my sister, and a good one at that, and I appreciate you looking after me, but I've got to go and do something for myself. You still see me as your baby brother, but I'm all grown up now.'

Enid let out a tired moan and plonked herself on the edge of one of the wooden armchairs. 'I know that, Hywel. It's nearly thirty-seven you are now, and still no wife or family.'

This was an old theme he thought she'd given up on. One of the reasons he'd left his and Enid's home county of Cardiganshire, apart from talk of the money to be made in the mines, was because of Catrin. Even now the name summoned up a vague wave of pleasure and pain. She was the daughter of the farm owner next door and they'd been sweet on each other – at least, he'd thought it mutual. But her father had considered him, a farm hand, not good enough for his daughter. In the end, she'd clearly thought herself a cut above him too. Catrin had married the dairy owner, a good seventeen years older and a widower, without any visible sign of regret, strutting around the town like the lady of the manor. It had cut Hywel to the core each time he'd encountered her, especially as she'd ignored him like they'd never been acquainted. Three years later, at twenty-two, came Hywel's opportunity to escape to the other side of the country, when Enid suggested he try hewing for a living. She and Madog had seemed to be doing all right, renting a nice little house in a newly built village. He'd already sworn off women by then, not expecting to ever meet one as fine as he'd first thought Catrin. And he never had. Or not until recently.

'Hywel? Have you gone off to your dream world again?'

'Sorry? Oh, no, just thinking.' He hated arguing with Enid, and they seldom did. He should just get up and go, and that would be an end to it. 'I'll see you later.' He escaped through the door into the hall, then ran awkwardly to the front door before she had time to pursue him.

Out on the street, he increased his speed, disappearing down Bryn Street. He must look a right sight, joggling along like he was.

Making his way to the village centre, he turned onto Station Road at the corner of Jubilee Green, which would take him straight down to the pit. Here he slowed to a walk. He wasn't sure what he expected. His gift was churning out the most trams of coal. There weren't many who could beat his output. But those days were gone.

The colliery loomed up as he reached the bottom of the hill, its church-like edifices built only for the worship of steam and electricity. The pit wheels were ominous, overbearing gods, their raspy moaning an instruction to work harder.

'Morning, Hywel,' said one of the old timers as he entered the colliery. He was leaning against a wall, smoking a roll-up. The man worked at sorting the coal with the women these days.

'Morning Dewi. Mr Meredith about, is he? Or Mr Bowen?'

'Saw Meredith go underground ten minutes since. Think Bowen's in his office though.'

'Thanks Dewi.' The under manager would have to do. At least it wasn't that nasty piece of work Edgar Williams anymore. Though, from what he'd heard, Bowen wasn't any great shakes in the job. At least Edgar had been able to manage them.

He knocked on the office door, entering when a sing-song voice invited him to.

'Ah, Hywel Llewellyn. I wondered when we might see you again. Missing your output, we are. How are you then?'

'Fit as a fiddle I am, John. But to be honest, my hewing days are over. Can't bend the old pin without it stinging, see.' He demonstrated, grimacing for effect.

'Sorry to hear that, I am. What can I do for you then?'

'I'm reckoning there must be other jobs going like, something which don't require me kneeling or stretching my thigh. I can walk perfectly fine. I can bend my back to walk through low places.'

Bowen tapped his chin. 'Mm. Well, we can always do with firemen of course, having lost two or three to the war, and Philip Hubbard to the explosion. But it takes training see, and some exams.' He considered Hywel carefully.

'I can do that. But does it mean I can't earn anything until I've done the training?'

'Have you seen the adverts for lessons by post in the *Monmouth Guardian*, mining exams and what not?'

'I've noticed them, yes.'

'If you could get on one of those courses, I could put you in as assistant fireman here, to Johnny Jones, which would get you trained up a bit quicker. He'd still set the shots for the blasts until you were qualified, but you'd do things like erect the brattice cloths for ventilation, examine the fire stoppings and so on. You're lucky: the previous candidate didn't last five minutes, and we've recently had a vacancy.'

Hywel considered the offer. Fireman. He'd never had any inclination to that, not like some, who wanted to get away from the heavy manual labour. But if it meant earning some money, why not?

'Go on then, I'll give it a go.'

'You'll have to give it more than a go, mun. If you want me to give you the job, I'll want to be sure you'll see the training through and be here a while.'

'Aye, I'll do that, don't you worry. Good worker I've always been.'

'I know that, Hywel. It's why I've offered it to you. You apply for that course and come back when you've heard.'

'Righty ho. And thank you, John.'

Bowen stood and reached his hand across the desk. Hywel took it and they shook. 'Mr Bowen it'll be from now on,' he laughed. 'Only at work like, though. Right, I've got a round to go on.'

Out on Station Road again Hywel felt his spirits lift. He passed the McKenzie Arms at the crossroads, half considering a celebratory pint. He'd already dismissed the idea a moment before he remembered they weren't even open this time of day anymore.

About to cross to the pavement on the gardens side, he saw Violet crossing with Benjamin from outside Schenck's book-shop. She'd reached the other side before she noticed him, jumping with surprise as he reached the pavement the same time as her. He was keen to tell her his news.

'Why hello, Violet. Nice to see you. Off to the gardens with Benjy, are you?'

'No, collecting Clarice from school.' Her words were rapid and she'd passed on before he could suggest he walk there with her, enjoying the idea of her company.

He watched her departing back, poor old Benjy being pulled along a little faster than he'd have liked as he tried to stop to smell a flower poking through the railings of the gardens. She seemed a little put out. Probably nothing he'd done. He'd find Idris on the allotments instead, maybe give him a hand and tell him his news.

He was sure Enid wasn't ready to hear it yet.

–

'Draw the curtain would you, Hywel *bach*?'

Hywel did as his sister asked, getting up from the kitchen table, where he was reading a booklet for the fireman's course, and limping over to the window.

At the table, Idris sat reading a newspaper whilst Anwen laid the cutlery. Cadi was in the scullery, chopping some vegetables that had been grown on the allotment. Enid, at the stove getting a pot of boiling water ready, stepped over to the light switch to put on the electric lights.

'Now here's one reason I'd never want to leave a pit village,' she said. 'Still using gas lamps on the farm back in Cardiganshire, are our family.'

'So you always say, Mam.' Anwen gave her an indulgent smile.

Hywel surveyed his family as he turned back from the curtain. In the last couple of weeks a peace had settled on them. Enid had accepted his new job when she'd heard he'd be training as a fireman. It was something to have a little boast about in the knitting group. And to Mrs Meredith at the Big House on the few occasions she asked how she was. Idris would get back to work soon and then they could all get on with their lives. He didn't think too deeply about what that meant for him. Or didn't mean. A brief image flashed before him, of a smiling Violet – rare as that was – her deep brown eyes crinkling with delight, her ebony hair down and nearly reaching her waist. Odd to think of her wearing her hair loose: he'd only spied it a couple of times when lodging there. Mostly it was pinned up simply and neatly.

'Aye, well, I also say—' But whatever that was going to be, Enid was interrupted by a loud rapping at the front door. 'Now who on earth would that be?'

'I'll get it,' said Hywel, tramping past his sister to the hall.

When he opened the door, the first thing that struck him was how light it still was, with the golden sky of sunset. It hadn't been obvious through the small kitchen window that overlooked the yard and faced the mountain.

Adjusting his eyes, he noticed a large woman on the pavement, almost standing in the road. She was tall with pitch-black hair, half hanging down, pale skin and piercing jet eyes. He quickly realised she wasn't so much large as heavily pregnant, with a loose, high-necked blouse stretched over an extended stomach. She wore a blue shawl, but it was open, as if to emphasise her condition.

'Can I help you?'

'I bet you're Hywel, aren't you?' she said, as if being 'Hywel' was a disgrace.

'You have the advantage over me. You are?'

'You won't have 'eard of me yet, but you will from now on. Where's Enid?'

He stepped forward to fill the doorway. 'Who wants to know?'

'Just get her.'

'Who is it?' came Anwen's voice as she entered the hall.

The woman shifted back and forth in an attempt to see behind Hywel.

'It's no one,' he called back.

'Is that you, Enid?' the woman shouted, her voice rising up the scale.

Anwen nudged her uncle to the side. 'No, it's not. Who are you?'

Good luck with that, thought Hywel.

'Someone who do want to see Enid!' she yelled, her arms folded across the top of her belly. 'Now be a good girl and fetch her. Anwen, is it?'

Hywel noticed his niece's shoulders stiffen. The woman couldn't have been many years older than her.

'I might if you tell me who you are and what your business is.'

'What's all this shouting?' said Enid, rushing into the hall. 'It's not that Esther Williams causing trouble again, is it?' She parted her brother and daughter, frowning at what she saw.

'At bloody last. *You* must be Enid, surely to God.'

'Don't you swear and blaspheme on my doorstep you... you... hussy. And what exactly are you wanting with me?'

A young couple, with two older women behind them, had stopped several yards down the road to peer over at the spectacle. One of the group was Florrie Harris. Just what they needed, thought Hywel, someone to spread their business around the village.

'Well look here, I'm Madog's woman, see, and now he do be in prison, I've no one to keep me.'

'Don't be so daft,' Enid spat out. 'Where'd he have got the money to keep the likes of you?'

It was obvious really, thought Hywel, what with Madog keeping most of his wages and making a good deal of money from the stolen goods. Perhaps his sister was being purposefully naïve in order to call the woman's bluff.

'How should I bloody know? But he did, see, and now you're responsible for getting him locked up and I've got no means of support and I'm with child.'

'Could be anyone's,' said Enid. 'You look like a right strumpet and a liar to boot. As for it being my fault he's in prison, you should know he pushed me down the stairs and shot my brother here, as well as abusing my daughters.' Now she'd started, she was like a horse accelerating downhill. 'And if he hadn't been so cruel to our Sara she'd still be alive for he did push her into work she wasn't well enough to do.' She took several steps towards the woman, who in turn took several steps back. 'So if anyone's responsible for him being in gaol it's him himself.'

The woman almost fell in the road as she stumbled down the pavement.

'Now get gone from my house and don't you dare come expecting money from me for I swear I'll fetch the police and get *you* thrown in gaol.' Enid walked backwards until she reached the front step. Hywel placed a hand on her shoulder.

'I think you'd better go,' he said to the woman.

'I'll go for now, but don't think you've 'eard the last of me. Oh no, for I'll make sure you'll be sick of the name Delyth Bryce by the time I've finished.'

With this she patted her belly, lifted her over-long skirt and marched back down Edward Street, all eyes on her.

When she was well out of earshot, Enid said, 'What on earth has that man brought upon us now?'

Anwen shut the door. 'It might not even be true. She seemed like a right floozy.'

Enid, making her way back down the hall, turned as she was about to go through the kitchen door. 'Of course it's true. As soon as that trollop said it, I knew it was. It explains that new suit and the other clothes he bought, and his stinking of that cologne. That wasn't for his drinking or thieving pals, was it? I thought it odd he'd stopped his... night-time attentions. And do you know what? He called me Delyth a couple of times, and I put it down to him getting me confused with my sister.'

'But he never knew her,' said Hywel. 'She died before he came to work on the farm.'

'I know, but that's how I explained it to myself. I think deep down I knew. But I didn't care.'

He couldn't help but agree with his sister. 'I also think it's highly likely this Delyth Bryce is telling the truth.'

Either way, Hywel decided he was going to find out more about it.

Monmouthshire County Gaol was intimidating as Hywel entered it. The stone bricks, arched doorway and foreboding height were like those of a castle. The illusion was added to by the fake arrow slits in the walls.

Hywel looked now at the grimy clock above the entrance of the visiting room inside. He felt uncomfortable in his suit, which he normally only wore to religious occasions, but he'd felt the need to look tidy, to separate himself from the likes of Madog Rhys.

He glanced around the room. The other visitors were a varied bunch, from a neat little man with a bowler hat, spats and a mutton-chops beard, to a woman in a loose cream dress that must have been two dozen years out of date and had seen better days. Another woman, eyeing up the other visitors nervously, held herself stiffly.

There was a barking of orders as the guards led the prisoners in. Those waiting, slumped in their various reveries, sat to attention as the prisoners were directed to different tables.

'Uh, it's you,' Madog groaned as he thudded down on the simple wooden seat.

'Aye, it's me. Who did you expect, the lovely Delyth?'

Madog's eyes darted up. 'Delyth? Who's that, then?'

'Don't give me that. She called by the house a week since, her belly inflated like a balloon, claiming she was carrying your child.' He said the last words softly.

'No idea what the hell you're talking about.'

'Claims you've been keeping her. No wonder you had no money for your wife and children. You're a disgrace.'

Madog sat forward, placing his arms on the small table. He glared at Hywel, clearly trying to unnerve him. But Hywel had no fear of him, this vile scrap of humanity, sick in the head. He never had done.

'Now you listen to me, you pitiful excuse for a man,' Madog hissed. 'I've never heard of no Delyth Bryce, you hear? And you can tell that stoopid wife of mine to come and visit next time, and to bloody bring some ciggies. She's got to be good for something. Fancy the bitch being able to walk all that time and just lying in bed.'

'Lean back there, Mr Rhys,' said a guard. 'Keep your hands down and your tongue civil.'

Hywel laced his fingers together. 'So, who is Delyth Bryce?'

'I told you, I don't know.'

'I only asked about Delyth. I never mentioned her surname though, right enough, it is Bryce.'

'What game are you playing? You bloody did say Delyth Bryce.' But Madog didn't look at all sure about the statement.

'No matter, you've answered my query well enough, which is whether she was telling the truth about carrying your child.'

Madog didn't comment, using his thumb to remove dirt from his other fingernails. Eventually, he said in a low rumble, 'You wait till I get out of here.' He smiled, presumably for the guards' sake. 'I'm going to appeal against this injustice. You're all liars, for it were *you* who attacked *me*. And when I get out I shall see to my *dear* wife and that brat Anwen, and you, for landing me in here, see if I don't.'

Hywel gave a small chuckle. He lifted his eyebrows. 'You think you have a chance in hell of appealing when you pleaded guilty?'

'It were the lawyer suggested it. Said it'd be worse for me if I did otherwise.'

'You seem to have forgotten what the judge said about you in his summing up.'

'I'll get out eventually. That Idris Hughes, he won't know what's coming to him. Insult my family, he did, discarding my daughter like she were fit only for the scavenger, then punching my lights out. I'll find him and give him what for.'

'Your daughter now, is it? She was "that brat" a moment ago. And you wouldn't have far to look for Idris, for he's in your house, being your son-in-law.'

Madog thumped his fist on the table. 'What?'

'Mr Rhys, I won't tell you again,' said the guard. 'One more incident and visiting time will be over for you.'

Madog lowered his head, his lips pinched in. 'I don't believe you.'

'Married in August, they were. Nice little wedding at the chapel, lots of the village there to wish them well. Honeymoon in London.' He didn't mention the operation.

'Idris bloody Hughes at my hearth, no doubt playing master of my bloody house.'

'No, Enid's master of the house, and no mistake.'

'A bloody woman can't be master of nothing.'

Hywel rose from the seat. 'There we'll have to disagree.'

'Always did support those bloody trouble-making Suffragettes, you did.'

'Goodbye Madog. I hope I won't see you for a good long time – if ever.'

Madog stood, knocking the chair over, hurling several insults at his brother-in-law. Two guards leapt forward, grabbed an arm each and lead him away.

Chapter Ten

'This is a surprise, to be brought to Monmouth,' said Elizabeth, as she and Ralph Tallis passed the tall Georgian and Victorian shops on the busy street. She did up the top button of her coat, having just caught the chilly wind of late October. The train journey here had been enjoyable, a change to driving the car. Ralph had met her at Rhymney station and they'd travelled together.

Shire Hall appeared just ahead. A group of people who'd been strolling across the road rushed out of the way as a black motorcar came along, a little too fast, honking its horn, causing a lot of moaning and a few calls of, 'Slow down!'

'What a maniac,' said Ralph, shaking his head. He turned his attention back to Elizabeth. 'I like getting out of the Rhymney Valley for a while, and this is a fine town.'

'Unfortunately, the last time I was here I was at the courtroom.' She pointed to the hall they were now passing.

'Not up before the beak, were you?' he joked.

'No, but sadly I was here to lend support to a friend whose father was up for attempted manslaughter.'

'My goodness, it wasn't that terrible case with Madog someone, and the men who'd set upon the carts and motorvans to steal the goods?'

'Madog Rhys. That's right. His family's relieved he's been put away.'

'I'm sorry to hear that. I read about it in the newspaper and it was the talk of the council for a while. Terrible thing.'

'I had first-hand experience of the man, and a nasty piece of work he was. Gwen was with us at the court too.'

He looked greatly confused, almost comically so. 'Gwen?'

'She was with me at the cinema,' she reminded him.

'Ah, Miss Austin. My goodness, I'd almost forgotten about her.'

Elizabeth felt happier than she should have about this. Poor Gwen. She had such a lively personality she should have been memorable. 'Anyway, the less said about that day at court the better. The family are putting it behind them. Now, where is it we're heading?'

'We're here.' He pointed to a restaurant that took up a corner plot across the side road from the hall.

'The Dorothy Café! I have heard good things about this place from Lady Fitzgerald, a friend of Mama's.'

'Not Anna Fitzgerald?' He sounded surprised.

'Do you know her?'

'A little. I know her husband, Archibald, more. We visit the same gentleman's club.'

Elizabeth experienced a little disappointment that he was the type of man who, like her father, frequented such an establishment. It was yet another sign of the patriarchy. Still, she shouldn't judge. Maybe men in his position felt they should join for the connections they could make in business.

He went ahead to open the door for her.

Inside, each table was elegantly laid out with a white tablecloth, napkins, cutlery and silver cruets. Ralph spoke to the man in a suit with a bow tie who came to greet them. He'd evidently made a reservation. Their coats were taken away and they were shown to a table beside a large mirror. The waiter pulled out one of the curved back, bistro chairs for her to sit down on. Tallis removed his Homburg and placed it on one of the empty chairs before smoothing his fair hair back and taking a seat.

Elizabeth looked round the busy café. The large lampshades dangling from the ceiling were like upside-down flowers. 'I've never been in here. It's very stylish, isn't it?'

'I suppose it is. All I know is that they do a very good steak and kidney pudding, especially considering the growing food shortages.' He breathed in deeply. 'Mm, the wonderful aroma of roasting meat. It's not French cuisine, but it's a tasty luncheon nonetheless.'

The waiter returned with a menu for each of them. She looked down the list. Roast mutton and redcurrant jelly caught her eye, with mashed swedes, sprouts and potatoes. She wondered if the vegetables would be as tasty as the ones they grew in the village.

'How is your quest for creating allotments going?' she asked Ralph, being reminded of how they first met.

'Slowly,' he replied, keeping his eyes on the menu. 'Some landowners are dragging their heels in settling for a price. We don't want to have to charge too much for people to rent. We could take over land compulsorily for the duration, but it's not as easy as it sounds.' He did now look up. 'It would probably end up costing us more than if we negotiated. You were lucky the land in Dorcalon still belonged to the coal company.'

'Yes, I think we were now I've heard the trouble other villages are having. Right, I've decided on the chicken broth to start and then mutton,' said Elizabeth. 'And a nice cup of tea wouldn't go amiss.'

'Sadly they're not doing the steak and kidney today, so I'll go for the chicken pie.'

The waiter arrived to take their order. When he left, Ralph gave Elizabeth his full attention.

'Now, tell me what you've been doing since I last saw you.'

'Well,' she said, leaning forward a little as if to impart some secret. 'I've just this morning applied for a job.'

His eyebrows met as he frowned. 'Do you need one?'

'No. That is, I'm not being forced to work by my parents. In fact, the opposite is true. At least, where my mother is concerned.'

'How so?'

'My mother has always prevented me from going out to work, one way or another. I would like to have gone to university, like my brother, Tom, but she wouldn't hear of that either. She sees me as a kind of companion, dragging me to some of her endless committees. I think she believes that, if she introduces me to some of the wealthier women, I will find a husband among the titled or the rich.'

'Ah, that kind of mother. Mine was rather like that too.' He sighed and fiddled with his fork.

'Was?'

'She died last year. Pneumonia.'

'Oh, you poor thing. I'm so sorry.' Elizabeth took his hand, holding it lightly, but regretted the hasty action immediately. What must he think?

However, he turned his hand and took hold of hers. 'Thank you. She could be irritating, but she was still my mother.'

'Of course. I would feel the same about mine should she pass on.'

They were silent for some moments.

'So, you've gone against her wishes and applied for a job?' He tipped his head and studied her with a slight grin.

'Yes. I've had this growing discontentment for a long time. It's why I started the allotment scheme with Anwen. Mother didn't really approve but she could see the sense of it. I've grown weary of this stay-at-home daughter act. I need more. And I'm tired of relying on the pocket money from my parents and only being able to buy clothes my mother approves of. I thought to myself, something has got to change.'

She felt so relieved to get this off her chest. It was something she'd have told Anwen, but she hadn't wanted to burden her friend, who she knew had other things on her mind.

'So, what is this job?'

'I saw an advert in the *Monmouth Guardian* for a temporary clerk in the overseer's office at Rhymney District Council. I meet the requirements. I'm over twenty-one and have clerical experience helping my father out at the mine when he lacked a clerk for a while.'

She'd been disappointed when he hadn't taken her on permanently. That had been down to her mother as much as anything else.

'Another stipulation was that applicants had to be ineligible for military service. I'm certainly that. Sorry, I've just realised I shouldn't be telling you this, as it also said that canvassing members of the council was prohibited.'

'I wouldn't worry. I won't tell. And it's not up to me to interview or pick a candidate. I do think they may be looking for a man, though. Not that I'm saying they should, but the wording rather suggests that.'

'Yes, I did wonder. Still, nothing ventured, nothing gained, as they say. Applications have to be in by the end of November, so it might be a while before I hear anything.'

The waiter approached and placed the tray with the tea pot, cups and jugs down, before taking his leave of them.

'Well good luck with it,' said Ralph. 'In the absence of wine, we'll raise a cup of tea to your success.'

She couldn't truthfully say it was what she really wanted. But then, she wasn't at all sure what that was.

–

The train passed Pantywaun Halt and Elizabeth sensed her lovely day with Ralph coming to an end. They had met twice since Bargoed, albeit only for coffee, but each time their conversations had become ever more familiar. They were sitting close to each other now, Elizabeth next to the window, the only people in their carriage.

'I have enjoyed today,' Ralph said. 'It's a shame it's almost over.'

'At least we have our trip to the concert in a couple of weeks.'

'Yes, I shall look forward to that.' He took her hand and she enjoyed the warmth of his touch.

They chatted about this and that, until Elizabeth recognised by the view that they were soon to reach Rhymney station, where Ralph would disembark. Her heart sank. Just an evening with Mama to look forward to, since her father had yet another meeting.

Ralph stood, drawing her up too. 'Farewell, sweet maid, until we meet again.'

The laugh she was about to engage in was stopped short by his lips on hers. She had not expected this and feared that her initial rigid response would put him off. But soon she relaxed into it, relishing the pleasure that coursed through her body as they held each other close.

It was the train braking that brought their embrace to a halt. Elizabeth wobbled and was caught by Ralph, who helped her back to her seat as he held on to the parcel rack.

'May I ring you during the week?'

'Of course you may. I will look forward to it.'

The train came to a halt. He kissed his palm and blew it towards her. Her grin was wide at this last gesture as he exited into the corridor. The smile lasted for the journey to Dorcalon.

–

Anwen shuffled out of the pew after the Sunday service and waited for her mother to do likewise. Idris had already gone ahead to have a word with Gwilym.

'I'll, um, just go and have a chat with people,' said Hywel, trying to see above the crowds. He must have spotted someone for he was soon off.

'It's parky today,' said Enid, pulling her coat more tightly around herself as she remained in the pew. 'I wasn't sure what to make of that sermon.'

'Sounds like Pastor Thomas is a conshie to me,' said Florrie Harris, leaning forward from the seat behind. 'Violet's mother-in-law, Mrs Jones, said as much at the memorial.'

'Get away with you,' said Cadi, stuck beside her unmoving daughter-in-law. 'He's just in favour of a bit of peace, isn't it? Aren't we all?'

'*Blessed are the peacemakers*, he says.' Florrie clucked her tongue. 'Not if it means surrendering to the Hun.'

'I don't think that's what he was proposing,' said Cadi. 'Come on, Enid, are you shifting or staying here all day? I'm gasping for a cup of tea.'

'All right, all right.' Enid slid across the seat. Anwen held out her hand to help her up but she waved it away. 'I'm not an invalid anymore.'

'Sorry Mam, I wasn't suggesting you were, just being polite.'

Her mother seemed to have got crosser the last couple of months. Anwen had thought her father being sent to prison, out of the way, would lift her up. She yearned for the old Mam, the perky one from before the fall, who'd always had a cheery word for everyone. Not this angry version. No doubt Delyth Bryce turning up on the scene hadn't helped.

Florrie chose that moment to leave her pew to follow them across the chapel and into the hall where they were serving refreshments. Anwen hoped she wasn't going to keep up her tirade about the pastor.

Collecting a cup of tea each from the pastor's wife, they settled into a small circle which Florrie did indeed join. Anwen felt guilty about resenting her presence. She'd had the misfortune to lose her son, Robert, in France, back in April, and was already a widow. She was now helping her daughter-in-law look after her seven young children.

'Not sure she's suitable as a minister's wife either,' said Florrie, flicking her head towards Anabel Thomas, as the others drank their tea. 'Looks a bit delicate to me.' She blew at her cup and took a sip.

It was true that she was slight and rather pale-looking, but she had a gentle manner wholly suited to her work, unlike the last pastor's wife.

'Oh, that is enough now, Florrie Harris,' said Enid, scowling. 'I'm sorry to the heart of me for the troubles you've had, but this constant gossiping you do, it's not nice. You never used to be like this.'

Florrie spilled her tea as she placed the cup back on the saucer. 'Well at least my husband, God rest his soul, was a good, honest man, not a gaol bird.'

'Florrie Harris, there's no need for—' Cadi started.

'And glad to be rid of him, I am,' said Enid, 'for he'd been a wrong'un for a long time.'

'While you sat in bed and did nothing,' squeaked Florrie. 'No wonder he looked elsewhere for his conjugals.'

'Mrs Harris!' Anwen chastised. 'That is not necessary.'

Inevitably, the chatter in the room had slowly died away as more of the congregation became aware of the argument.

'*As you sow, so you shall reap*,' Florrie quoted. 'And you've certainly reaped a situation with that Delyth Bryce.'

Enid's face went a deep red – whether from shame or anger, Anwen couldn't tell.

'Taken lodgings with Esther Williams, she has, and told her how Madog did take advantage of her and now she's carrying his child. I 'eard it off Esther herself. Says she's entitled to money but how you won't give her any.'

It was clear now by Enid's widened eyes and gritted teeth that she was livid. They'd hoped Delyth would just go away, thought she'd be too ashamed to make a fuss, despite her words, but clearly she was going to make life as difficult as possible.

'And you think that little trollop's in the right?' Enid cried.

'Calm down, *cariad*,' said Cadi. 'At least we know now what she's up to.'

'Your family seems to have brought a lot of trouble to this village recently,' Florrie countered.

Idris appeared through the throng. 'Mrs Harris, I think you should apologise.'

'Throwing your weight around are you, now you're well again?'

Idris's parents and his brother pushed through the crowds to give Florrie a piece of their minds. When Gwen appeared, the volume went up considerably.

Anwen looked on helplessly, wondering what on earth she could do. Here they all were, bickering, and the real problem was at number seventeen Jubilee Green. What had Esther been thinking? She no doubt needed the money with Edgar in prison. But more than that: it was a perfect way for her to get her own back on Anwen and Idris, after all the run-ins the two of them had experienced with her and Edgar.

Elizabeth came up beside her and touched her arm. 'Are you alright?'

Still the mayhem raged on, the spellbound audience unmoving.

'Just when you think life has taken an upturn, the devil is always there with fresh mischief,' said Anwen.

'Humans are quite capable of creating that themselves. It sounds like Esther is at the bottom of it, which doesn't come as a surprise. I just saw Anabel Thomas scurry off, presumably to find her husband. Ah, here he is. Hopefully he'll calm things down.'

The congregation parted as the minister approached the group. His attempts to be heard above the din came to nothing. They didn't even notice he was there.

'Oh dear,' said Elizabeth. 'I guess there's only one thing for it.'

She passed her cup to Anwen and stepped forward, coming between Florrie Harris and her opponents. 'Would you all be quiet now,' she said in a loud, yet unaggressive voice, one that held authority.

Anwen was surprised when they did all stop talking.

'Thank you,' said Elizabeth. 'Now I suggest we all go about our business. Florrie, could I have a word with you please. Outside.'

Florrie nodded, almost dipping her knee. 'Of course, Miss Meredith.'

After they'd left, Enid said, 'I'm not after staying here myself. Just imagine, that Delyth Bryce on my doorstep with her disgrace.' She tipped her head back to finish her tea and clattered the cup onto the saucer. 'What are you lookin' at?'

Anwen, confused at first, realised she was talking to Mrs Bowen, the dressmaker.

'Didn't mean no harm, I'm sure,' she replied, before turning her back and saying something to her husband.

'Mam, Mrs Bowen gives Mamgu work, you can't be shouting at her.'

'People should look to their own business.'

'I'll return these empty cups,' said Idris, taking them from the two older women and stacking them up. 'Then we can go.'

Enid stretched her neck to peruse the room. 'Where's Hywel gone?'

'Still in the chapel, chatting, I reckon,' said Anwen.

'Well, he can come when he wants. And you don't have to be following me around.'

'I don't feel like staying after that,' said Cadi.

'We might as well all go,' said Idris, returning. He raised his eyebrows subtly for Anwen's benefit. He was probably thinking what she was: that it could be a long day with Mam in this mood.

It wasn't until they reached the main door that they spotted Hywel, at the bottom of the steps, talking to Violet. He had Benjamin in his arms, bouncing him up and down. The little boy was giggling.

'Here you are,' said Enid. 'Hello Violet. How are you?'

'Not too bad, Mrs Rhys, thank you.'

Anwen noticed her friend's cheeks redden a little, which was unlike her. She hadn't been to visit her for a couple of weeks, being so busy at home. Yet Idris was getting better now, so she could have spared her a bit of time, what with Violet being on her own with the children and the house. What a terrible friend she was. It was odd that Violet hadn't called around their home recently though, like she used to.

'We're off home, Hywel *bach*,' said Enid. 'Not enjoying the company too much this week.'

'Why?' Hywel looked at them all in turn.

'Long story, mun,' said Idris. 'Tell you over dinner.'

'I'm going to pop round to Violet's first and fix her tap for her,' said Hywel. 'Sounds like it needs a new washer.'

'There's a kind man you are, *bach*,' said Enid. 'More of the neighbours should be like you.' She linked arms with Cadi and marched off.

Idris waited for Anwen as she said, 'I'll come and see you next week and we'll catch up.'

'That would be nice,' said Violet.

'I won't be long,' said Hywel.

Anwen nodded and took Idris's offered arm. She looked back as they walked away, to where Hywel was bouncing Benjamin once more.

'It's a shame Uncle Hywel's never married and had children of his own, for I'm sure he'd have made a splendid da.'

'Aye, I believe he would,' said Idris, 'but it doesn't happen for everyone. I believe there was someone once, back in Cardiganshire, but she broke his heart.'

'Really? How do you know that?'

'Chatting over a beer one evening, no doubt. Was a while ago now. Anyway, it's not too late for him to have a family.'

Anwen's hand went to her stomach briefly, as she tried to imagine what it would be like to fall pregnant with her own child. Hopefully it wouldn't be too long before she found out.

'I'm right, aren't I, Uncle Hywel?'

Hywel had kept his head behind his newspaper, sitting at the kitchen table as far away as possible from Anwen and Idris, in the hope of keeping out of their argument. He should perhaps have gone for a walk, but he'd wanted to finish reading the news before he took himself out.

'Ooh, don't get me involved, *fach*. I'm not about to come between a man and his wife.'

'But he only had the operation two-and-a-half months back,' said Anwen. 'You can surely see the sense of him waiting a little longer till he goes back to work. Maybe wait till after Christmas?' She was furiously rubbing the polish on the dresser as she spoke.

Idris ran his finger across his neck, over the scar of his operation. 'You know, that's exactly what my mother said when I turned up last November, after being discharged. A year ago today, that was.'

'But you didn't wait and look what happened then. Ill, you were.'

'I would have been ill anyway, you know that.'

'I just don't want you to undo the good that's been done. You're getting so much better now.'

Hywel could see this disagreement going on a long while. 'What about you get Dr Roberts to come and have a look, eh? He'd surely be the best judge of things.'

'The last time he came he was pleased with how well I was doing,' said Idris. 'That was a month ago. John Bowen says I can have the underground examiner's job back when I'm ready, but I doubt he'll keep it open forever. Always short of workers, they are, now.'

'If you're worried about money, mun, what Enid and I are earning will tide us over until after Christmas,' said Hywel. 'And Cadi's making a bit with her sewing.' He creased his brow, trying to create an expression for Idris alone that said, *for an easier life.*

'I'll think about it,' said Idris, standing to lift his scarf off the back of the wooden armchair. He wrapped it round his neck. 'I'd have thought you'd have been glad to get me out from under your feet by now, *cariad*.'

'Oh Idris, how could you say that?' Her face fell into sadness.

'Only judging by other wives I've heard complain about unemployed husbands. Right, I told Jenkin I'd go with him and Evan to visit Cadoc. Hopefully they're both bathed and dressed after their shift.'

'How are they getting on at the pit?' Hywel asked. 'I haven't seen them since I went to Cadoc's with them.'

'Bit of a shock it was for them when they first started, for all their bravado. But they seem to be getting used to it now.'

'I'm so glad the boys are visiting Mr Beadle,' said Anwen. 'For I think it has cheered him up a little.'

The scullery door clunked shut and Enid's voice called, 'Only me back.'

'Maybe,' said Hywel. 'The truth is, Cadoc is not what he used to be before the accident, and I have doubts he ever will be. I've known men in their eighties more quick-witted than him.' There, he'd said it out loud. Nobody else seemed to want to entertain the idea.

Anwen pushed a tress of umber hair off her face. 'Dr Roberts thinks Cadoc's got melancholy. He described it as being a bit like the shell shock some of the soldiers have. He took a fair battering from Edgar Williams, so I can see why he compared it.'

Enid entered the kitchen. 'He just needs to pull his socks up, if you ask me. You off out somewhere, Idris *bach*?'

'Going with Jenkin to Cadoc's.'

'Well tell him I'll be down on Sunday to collect some clothes to wash.' Despite her earlier words, she and the knitting group had taken turns to do Cadoc's washing and shopping for him.

'I'll walk part of the way with you, Idris,' said Hywel.

'Where're you off too, then?' said Enid.

He hesitated a moment, wondering whether to claim he was visiting a pal or going to the shop, but untruths never had come easily. Only when he'd been dealing with Madog Rhys. And that was only because he'd needed to protect Anwen and Sara, so he'd gone along with whatever they'd had to say to keep their father calm. 'I'm popping into Violet's. Last time I was there I noticed her picture rail was coming away from the wall in the kitchen. Thought I'd hammer it back up for her.'

He felt the pulse in his head, as if he had lied after all. It was true, but, he knew, it wasn't the whole truth, for it wasn't like he was round all the widows' houses offering to do jobs for them.

'That is mighty decent of you,' said Enid, 'for she was a good landlady to you.'

'Which is exactly why I want to help her out,' said Hywel, more to convince himself than the others.

Enid headed to the kettle, shaking it to ascertain how full it was. 'I wonder if she'll remarry. Young woman like her, a dainty face, should attract attention. And she'll need someone to keep her.'

'Mam!' said Anwen. 'I'm sure Violet has nothing further from her mind.'

'What's wrong with that? Betty King up James Street was married within six months of her husband going. Had to think of the kiddies, she did.'

'Come on, mun, let's get going,' said Idris.

Hywel went ahead. 'Get no argument from me.'

He was more than glad to escape the awkward conversation.

–

The knock on the back door was a welcome one to Violet. Anwen had said she might pop by later and it was time she put the kettle on and had a sit down. Since finishing her dinner she'd been busy with housework, needing something to keep her mind off her circling thoughts.

'Come in,' she called, putting the dustpan and brush back in its place by the sink.

She was ready to smile with a thankful hello, when the door opened and revealed Hywel. The clash between her delight in seeing him and the guilt of it, along with shame at her dishevelled appearance, must have put a discouraging expression on her face.

'I'm sorry, have I caught you at a bad time?'

She pushed the hair that had escaped her pins off her face. 'Of course not. What can I do for you, Hywel?'

He came in fully, closing the door after him. 'It's proper cold out there today, so better keep any heat in. It's got much nippier since the sun went down.'

'I was just about to put the kettle on. I thought you might be Anwen as she said she might call round.'

'Sorry to be a disappointment,' Hywel laughed. 'I wouldn't mind a cup of tea myself.' He rubbed his hands together, then looked less sure of himself. 'If you're offering, that is.'

She wasn't sure if she was or not, being in two minds as to whether it was a good idea. She didn't want to embarrass him, or herself, so said brightly, 'I need a bit of a rest and you can tell me how your job's going. Benjy and Clarice will be glad to see you too.'

'And I them. Shall I fetch the kettle and fill it up while you finish off?'

'No, no need for that now. You go and say hello to the children and sit yourself down.'

He did as he was told. Although he'd often helped when he'd lived here, it didn't seem right now. He was a visitor; that was all.

She fetched the kettle from the kitchen to fill it up. Hywel was sitting at the table, doodling something for Clarice in her book.

'Uncle Hywel is drawing me a doggie, Mam. I'm going to paint him brown and black, like next door's doggie, and Benjy says he's called Woof.'

'That's nice,' said Violet, looking from her son to her daughter, both of whom were beaming. Some of the deep sadness of losing their da had rubbed off already, no doubt with their fading memories. 'Don't pester Uncle Hywel too much though.'

Picking up the kettle and returning to the scullery, she wondered at the wisdom of getting the children to call him 'Uncle'. It had started when he'd first lodged with them, and only because they'd always called Anwen and Gwen 'Aunty'. It might have been more seemly to have gone with 'Mr Llewellyn'.

With the kettle on the stove, Violet plonked herself in one of the chairs by the fire. 'Don't feel you have to sit with the children the whole time.'

'I'm fine,' said Hywel. 'I'm enjoying myself, drawing. I'd forgotten how satisfying it is, putting pencil to paper. I'm doing a cat for Benjy now, which Clarice has suggested the name Miaow for.'

Anwen had bought Benjamin his own drawing book for his second birthday in August, as he'd always looked at Clarice's with such longing.

'Tell you what,' said Hywel, passing Benjamin's book back to him, 'Why don't you call the dog Miaow and the cat Woof?'

The children giggled.

'That silly, Nunky Hywel,' said the little boy.

'It's Uncle, not Nunky,' Clarice corrected him. She stopped colouring and considered Hywel. 'Are you going to come and live with us again? I miss you.'

The errant thought, *So do I*, invaded Violet's head before she could stop it.

'Not at the moment,' he said. 'I've got to live with my family now so I can help them.'

'You used to help us,' said the girl.

'I can still help you sometimes. Which reminds me.' He watched Violet as she made the tea. 'The main reason I came was to put that picture rail back up properly.' He pointed to the offending object in the corner of the room.

Violet brought the tea over. 'You don't have to do that.' She went back to make two milky teas for the children.

'No, I don't have to, but it needs doing and it's a bit high for you.'

She sat again with her own cup. 'I can stand on a chair. And I'm not that weak.'

'Don't be offended, *cariad*, I know you're capable. It's just you have to do all the jobs now.'

She'd been doing all the jobs on her own for a long time, but she'd let him help on this occasion. 'You know where the tools are, but finish your tea first.'

'You always did make a good cup of tea.'

She absorbed the compliment but didn't comment, not wanting to encourage him.

When he'd drained his cup, he left the children to their colouring and went out to the small shed next to the outside lavatory to fetch the hammer and some nails. She cleared up the cups, making a list in her head of what needed doing in the house next. She looked around. It was the cleanest it had ever been, yet with its scruffiness, she wondered if the effort was worth it.

Hywel was quick and efficient at hammering the picture rail back. Not that she had anything to hang up on it. Charlie had never been fond of decorations so wouldn't condone buying frames for photographs or pictures. She'd fancied a print of Barry Island she'd seen on a trip there, when she and Charlie were first married, but he hadn't liked it.

Violet tipped her head to one side, smiling at her children's sweet, chubby faces. Both had a look of Charlie, with their shapely lips and wide eyes. *Oh Charlie. If only you hadn't enlisted. You'd still be here for me and the children.* Clarice and Benjamin were almost all there was left to show Charlie had ever existed. She was beholden to them to make sure they grew up well. It was the least she could do for her late husband.

'That's that done,' said Hywel, placing the hammer and spare nails on the chair. 'The picture rail could do with a repainting. I noticed a tin of white paint in the shed. Shall I do that for you?'

'No, Hywel.' She stood. 'Please, come through to the scullery.'

'I'll put the tools away first.'

'No, don't worry about them. Please?'

She went ahead. Stopping by the butler's sink, she held onto one corner of it. It would take all her willpower to say what she had to. 'I'm grateful for your offers of help, Hywel, but I think... I think it might be better if you didn't keep calling round. It doesn't seem quite right and people might talk.'

'I'm old enough to be your da,' he joked.

'But that's just it, you're not. You're only fifteen years older, and since when did age stop people getting – together?' The implication of what she was saying had the blood rushing to her face. 'Not that I'm saying we would, no, I'm saying people will think that's the situation, and me only recently a widow. There are too many gossips in this village ready to see the worst in a situation.'

Hywel sucked his lips in and looked down at his shoes. 'That's true enough, but all the same it seems a shame to give in to them when all I'm trying to do is help you out.' He looked up at her sadly. 'I'm not expecting anything else from you, Violet, I swear.'

'I believe you because goodness knows there's not really much to admire in me.' He was about to protest when she interrupted. 'I'm not looking for a compliment, just stating the obvious. I'm also not after putting the burden of bringing up two children on anyone else. They're my responsibility. I know plenty of others remarry simply for security, but I couldn't use anyone like that.'

Why she was telling him this when he'd made it clear he had no intentions that way she didn't know. Maybe to make sure he never got any ideas in the future.

He nodded slowly. 'Thank you for making the situation clear. I understand why you don't want idle tongues wagging. It's still a shame I can't be a friend in need. It's your decision, of course. But if you ever need a friend, or someone to help you out in any way, you know where I am.'

He didn't wait for a reply before opening the door and disappearing into the darkening evening.

Violet clung onto the sink with both hands, her head hanging down. She'd managed to offend him as a friend and make a fool of herself by implying he was attracted to her. What must he think?

At least you've made your position clear. It had been a painful exchange, but a necessary one. Maybe now she'd get on with her life, without Charlie, and without Hywel's attentions.

Chapter Eleven

Elizabeth stood on the platform at Dorcalon station. There were a fair few people here to greet the soldiers, home on leave today. Next to her, a couple of young lads stood together, while a young woman peered eagerly down the line to spy the train.

Disappointment filled her as she recalled, once again, the letter that had come for her well over a week back now, to inform her that she'd been unsuccessful in her application for the job in the overseer's office at the council. She hadn't even been called for an interview. The letter had come not many days after the application closing date and she wondered, not for the first time, whether they'd even bothered reading it once they'd seen a woman's name. At least she wouldn't have to have the inevitable argument with Mama.

Today she was annoyed with her mother for not being at the station. She'd found a note in the hallway when she'd come downstairs earlier that morning. It seemed shopping in Abergavenny and having lunch with Anna Fitzgerald and her set was more important than welcoming her only son home. Elizabeth only hoped she wasn't still trying to keep on the right side of Mrs Fitzgerald in order to secure her a husband.

This would be Tom's last trip home before being sent to France. Or wherever he was being sent to. She wasn't at all sure if he'd be joining the brigade the other men from here were already in, and going to wherever it was they were going to next. She'd heard that the Welsh brigades had lost a lot of men and the numbers needed to be made up, so it was possible.

A familiar figure walked onto the platform, her blonde, curly hair pinned up under a navy hat with a small brim and striped band. Her yellowish skin contrasted with the blue coat.

'Gwen!' Elizabeth called, waving.

Spotting her, Gwen grinned and hurried to join her. 'I guess you're here to meet your brother.'

'And you yours.'

'Yes. Henry wrote that he's looking forward to the change of scenery. Anybody would think he was on an extended holiday somewhere, the way he writes.'

'At least he does write. Tom's letters have become infrequent, but then I suppose there's not much to write about when you're training. He was a keen letter writer at university, full of funny observations of tutors and fellow students. Now he simply states their day-to-day life.'

'Henry's the opposite. He talks only of capers and trips into French villages that he's not allowed to name. He gives the impression that they're hanging around in the back lines and he can't wait to get into the action again.'

'It's probably better not to know the truth.'

'No. I saw enough of that in *The Battle of the Somme*. I advised some of the girls from work not to go, but they said they wanted to see where our shells are being sent. I think they regretted it.'

Elizabeth was awash with guilt, remembering what a shine Gwen had taken to Ralph. 'That's a point,' said Elizabeth. 'Shouldn't you be at work now?'

'Yes. I'm afraid I got Mam to go to the motorbus stop this morning to tell one of the other girls I'm ill today. I know I'll be docked some money, but I'd rather see my brother.' She looked sheepish. 'Is that really bad of me? Our boys do need them shells.'

'I'm sure you do sterling work when you're there, Gwen. I can't blame you for wanting to see your brother.' *For who knows how long he has left on this earth?* It was a thought she'd had about Tom so many times, especially given his rather reckless attitude to life. 'Have you ever thought of giving it up, the munitions? I hear it's dangerous.' It was better not to draw attention to Gwen's changing skin tone.

'Not you as well.' Gwen tutted. 'I've almost fallen out with Anwen and Violet over this, and my mother. I am aware of my skin colour, for it's pointed out enough. I'm sure it will get back to normal once the war's over, for us women won't keep our jobs at the factory once the men are back. More's the pity, for it's a pretty sum to be earning.'

'I'm sorry. I don't want to fall out with you.'

'And anyway, the gentlemen certainly don't seem to be put off by my complexion. I think maybe it makes me look a little exotic.' She smiled, like someone keeping a delicious secret.

'No, I'm sure they don't.' Elizabeth didn't want to get on the wrong side of her by prying. Gwen was perhaps engaged in the early stages of courtship with a young man in the village.

'I do believe that's the train now.'

Elizabeth checked her watch. 'Dead on time!'

The chugs of the train became slower and further apart until its brakes squealed the carriages to a halt. There was a hiss and the smoke billowed around them.

It wasn't long before the doors began to click open and a variety of soldiers stepped down off the train. All were in woollen overcoats. Knapsacks were handed down before several other men alighted and repeated the performance. People ran to meet their loved ones. Elizabeth moved back and forth, trying to find Tom in the confusion. Finally, he appeared from the end of the train, just ahead of Henry and Maurice Coombes. Gwen spotted the men at the same time and both rushed off to embrace their brothers.

'Tom, I'm so glad to see you.'

'Likewise, Lizzie.'

'Henry, did you and Mr Meredith travel together?' said Gwen.

'He was already in the carriage when we got in at Newport,' Maurice butted in, in his mixture of Valleys accent and London twang, left over from his childhood. 'Filling him in on conditions out there, we were, seeing as he'll be going out soon.'

'I hope you haven't been unnecessarily ghastly,' said Gwen, frowning.

'No, not us,' Maurice laughed, slapping Tom on the back. 'And look at this.' He pointed to Tom's sleeve. 'Only gone and bloody made him a second lieutenant.'

Tom puffed out his cheeks and blew out a breath.

'Not jealous, are you?' Douglas Ramsay shouted over as he passed by.

'Nah, not me, mun. Seen what 'appens to them poor buggers what are supposed to be leading their men out and don't 'ave a bloody clue what's going to hit 'em.'

'Not in front of the ladies, Maurice *bach*,' said Henry.

Maurice bowed from the waist. 'So sorry ladies, I'm sure.' He hauled his bag onto his shoulder. 'See you 'ere in six days when we return to the bl— to the madness.' With that, he sauntered off.

'Come on Henry,' said Gwen, taking his arm. 'Mam's cooking a cawl in your honour, and even managed to get some lamb.'

'Let's go then. *Hywl fawr*,' he called back at Tom. 'Good luck if I don't see you on the journey back.'

'*Diolch yn fawr*, and thanks for the company,' Tom replied, lifting a hand in farewell.

Gwen and her brother chatted as she led him to the exit.

'She's a pretty little thing,' said Tom. 'With her blonde waves and those cerulean eyes.'

'Tom, don't you ever stop?' Elizabeth sighed. 'Maurice Coombes seems friendly towards you. I don't suppose he has any idea about the situation with Polly's baby.'

'Do you think he'd have been so civil if he had?'

'He doesn't strike me as the tolerant sort.'

'He was all right on the journey, even if he did take delight in telling me all the goriest stories about the war he could think of,' said Tom. 'Don't suppose you have the motorcar.'

Elizabeth swung round to face him, walking backwards as she spoke. 'No I don't! It's only ten minutes up the hill. I got into trouble with Sergeant Harries for "using the automobile too frequently", as he put it. There's a war on, you know.'

'Yes, I had noticed. Shame. Guess I'll have to struggle up to the house with this.' He indicated the knapsack with his thumb.

'You look fit enough to me,' she said. 'I reckon that training's done you some good after all the sitting around with the influenza. Anyway, even if I'd wanted to bring the car I couldn't have: Mama has taken it to Abergavenny to meet her friends for lunch.'

'Nice of her to be home to greet me.' He screwed his mouth up to one side.

They reached the ticket collector at this point, who waved them through with a salute and a, 'Welcome home, sir.'

Outside the station, they started on their walk round the pit.

'Was it a good journey?' Elizabeth asked.

'Very comfortable. When I saw the Pals from here get on board, I assumed they'd ignore me, but very friendly, they were.'

'That's because you're one of the gang now.'

'Whether I want to be or not.' He stopped to take a deep breath of the air. 'Despite the pit, it's good to be home in the valley.'

'Nobody wants to be in the war, Tom. It's simply something to tolerate, something to get done.'

Several women passed by, tipping their heads forward slightly and saying, 'Hello sir, hello Miss,' to which the pair of them replied in kind.

'What's the training been like?' Elizabeth asked.

'Strenuous. Not many other educated chaps in my battalion. It's no wonder they made me a second lieutenant. No damned competition!' He let out a long chuckle, finishing with an, 'Oh dear. Lord help us with me in charge.'

'I assume there'll be an actual lieutenant.'

'No idea. We're being used to fill the gaps in the 38th Welsh battalions, decimated during the Somme battles.'

Elizabeth's heart sank. 'You know nearly half the soldiers from here were killed at Mametz Wood.'

'Of course I do. A good many from other villages too, from what I've heard. Oh don't look so glum, Lizzie. They've got second lieutenant Thomas H Meredith to sort the Hun out now.'

He strolled ahead, towards the little bridge over the stream, singing a vigorous rendition of 'Pack Up Your Troubles in Your Old Kit-Bag'. Yet for all his bravado, Elizabeth could tell he'd lost some of his spark.

When Tom had finished the song, he turned back towards his sister. 'So, what are you doing with yourself these days? Sounds like, from your letters, the allotments are still going strong. You tell me so much about the village, but not much about yourself.'

'That's because there isn't much to tell. Come on, let's get a move on or we'll never get there.'

—

Hywel hadn't been so sure it was a good idea to come to the McKenzie Arms to have a chinwag with the lads home on leave. But this evening, unlike on their last leave, his erstwhile pit mates were in a better frame of mind and mixed more easily. There were some exchanges of stories of the July disaster, and the mud-filled trenches. All were told in hushed tones. Both soldiers and miners at least now had some time and distance from their pals' deaths.

'Mrs Moss has done a good job of running the public house and hotel since old Reg was put away,' said Idris.

'Aye, she has.' Hywel looked around at the larger of the two bars. The rickety chairs had been fixed and a coat of varnish applied, while the whole place was cleaner. She'd even put up a couple of pictures, of Cardiff Castle and the Brecon Beacons, though they'd not been appreciated by many of the men who preferred their sparse, plain bar.

He looked up to find Daniel Williams, Esther's oldest son, peering down at Idris. He was standing to attention in his uniform.

'I hear congratulations are in order,' said Daniel.

'How's that?' Idris looked confused.

Daniel tutted. 'What, you've forgotten already that you married a lovely girl like Anwen?'

'No, no of course I haven't. That was several months ago now.'

'I've not been here though, have I?'

Hywel noted the aggrieved tone, then remembered: Daniel had been smitten by Anwen at one time. Could be he was still carrying a torch for her.

'No, of course,' said Idris. 'Well, thank you, Daniel.'

'Thought she'd given you the elbow.'

Hywel wondered where this was going and hoped the younger man wouldn't try to start something. There was an aggression about him that hadn't been there before he'd left. He'd grown since joining the army, being broader, with a little more muscle on him. He wasn't one of the original twenty-nine to sign up; he'd been called up last April, after the conscription bill had been passed.

Idris simply smiled. 'Aye, lucky bugger I am, that she took me back.' They'd kept up the story of Anwen jilting him, rather than what had really happened.

'Indeed you are,' said Daniel. His attention was distracted by one of his fellow Pals calling over, so he took his leave.

When he'd walked away, Idris said, 'Thought he was up for picking a fight there. Anwen told me he did seem keen on her before he enlisted.'

'He might have a bit more weight on him now, but it's a brave man would stand up against your six feet. Or a stupid one. Always respectful of you the lads around here have been.'

'Apart from Edgar Williams. I don't know why the others are. It's not like I've ever been handy with my fists.'

'Just the thought you could be is enough. You've got a presence.'

Maurice Coombes strolled over next, patting Idris on the shoulder. 'How are you mun? Hear you've been down to London for an operation. You look well. Better than you did during your stint in the Pals.'

'Feeling better too, Maurice. Thank you for asking.'

'Also heard you got married.'

'That's right,' said Idris, glancing at Hywel, maybe also wondering where this was going.

'Well congratulations to you and Anwen, mun. Our Polly had her eye on you at one point. I even thought you might be – you know.'

The father of her illegitimate child was left unsaid.

'No, not me, mun.'

'Polly assured us of that, otherwise I'd have sorted you out myself.' He chuckled. 'Wish she'd told us who it was as I'd like to get my 'ands on him, I would.'

Hywel knew that Tom Meredith was the father, but very few people were aware of this. Polly had been paid off by the family. No wonder Tom had enlisted as soon as he'd recovered from the influenza. He had no doubt Maurice would have made a mess of him if he'd found out, for if Idris wasn't handy with his fists Maurice certainly was, and afraid of no one.

'Still, it don't matter now, as she met a man while staying with our aunt in London, and she married him last week. Just as well as the baby's due any day.'

'That's something at least,' said Idris.

'Aye. Well.' Maurice seemed to run out of things to say.

'You enjoying your rest from the war?' said Hywel.

'Bloody relief it is, mun. At least we haven't lost any more poor buggers from the village since Mametz Wood. We've been in the rear lines since then. Kicking our heels, we are.'

Alun Lloyd, the farmer's surviving son, came to a halt as he passed by. 'That's because there aren't enough of us left to raise a bloody battalion. As for kicking our heels, I dunno what's worse: running into the line of fire or repairing the miles of battered trenches. Trying to scoop out the slimy mud and knock in more posts to support the trenches and make them habitable. God, it's bloody endless, this war, whatever you end up doing.'

'Oh, cheer up, mun,' said Donald Ramsay, staggering over. 'Let's forget the bloody madness while we're here.'

'Easier said than done,' Maurice muttered. 'Hey, watch yourself now.' He grabbed his friend to stop him stumbling over. 'How're you so drunk? Mrs Moss only lets us have a cuppla pints each.'

'Gone out, hasn't she,' said Donald. 'Stephen is serving. He thinks we brave lads should be allowed a bit more indulgence, like.'

'You want to make sure Mrs Moss doesn't come back and catch you, for it's mad as hell she'll be if she finds out,' said Hywel. 'Very much for keeping the new laws, she is.'

Several miners in the bar muttered their confirmation. The cutting back of hours and restriction of alcohol to abide by the new rules had gone down badly with most of the public house's patrons, yet there was also a grudging respect for Mrs Moss, for keeping a better house than her husband had.

'To hell with her tonight,' said Donald.

A new batch of civilians came through the door, a rowdy group, with David Keir, the new union representative, at its centre, bellowing the punch line of a bawdy joke. The way he was swaying suggested he was already drunk. He spotted the three soldiers talking to Hywel and Idris.

'Hey, Maurice mun. Your sister had her flyblow yet?'

Hywel stretched his eyes wide, unable to believe the clumsy blunder as Idris lowered his head onto his palm.

Maurice stormed over to where David was standing. 'What's that you said?'

The two men with David told him to shush and come away, but he tottered forward to meet his adversary.

'What the hell's got into Keir?' whispered Hywel. 'He's a big mouth in the union, but keeps his trap shut otherwise.'

'Don't you remember Polly telling us, on that walk last January, that Keir had been trying to court her, but she was having none of it?' said Idris.

Hywel didn't get a chance to reply before Maurice socked David Keir straight in the jaw, knocking him to the floor.

'Hey, you can't do that, just 'cos you're a bloody soldier,' said one of the union rep's friends as he and the other man made a beeline for Maurice.

They didn't reach their target before Alun and Donald ran to defend their pal. Soon there was a scrap between the six of them. Shouts of encouragement came from both sides, miners and soldiers. Others shook their heads.

Idris scraped back his chair. 'Reckon we should do something? Stephen doesn't seem about to.'

'Aye. You go and fetch Harries the Police and I'll see if I can calm things down,' said Hywel.

Idris headed to the door into the lounge bar and went out that way. By this time, a couple more men had joined in, with the cheers and taunts getting louder.

'Right now, lads,' said Hywel, weaving his way through the baying crowd. It occurred to him Idris should be doing this, with his larger presence, but it was too late now. He stepped into a gap between the onlookers and the fighters. 'This is no way to act, is it? You don't want your time on leave spent in a cell in Rhymney now, do you?'

Alun brought his flailing arms to a halt and considered Hywel. Good, he might talk some sense into one of them at least, who might then persuade the others.

The next thing he knew, he was sprawled on the floor of the bar.

Chapter Twelve

Elizabeth stood in the hall waiting for her mother so they could take a walk into the village. She opened her handbag quickly and pulled out the letter she'd received that morning. What a relief to have got to it before her mother, who might have guessed its contents.

An interview at the council office for the job of clerk in the overseer's office: just imagine! She wasn't sure why she'd been reconsidered; all the letter said was that the job was available once more. She was to go for an interview on Thursday 21st December, only two days away. She had that to look forward to, as well as the trip out with Ralph tomorrow, to the Theatre Royal and Empire in Merthyr Tydfil. She placed the letter back in her handbag and picked up a bag of presents she wanted to drop off in the village.

When her mother appeared from the study Elizabeth called up the stairs, 'Cheerio Tom, we won't be long.'

'Shall I drive today, or will you?' Margaret asked, unhooking her umbrella from the hat stand.

'Mother, it's but a short walk, and you know the authorities are unhappy about unnecessary motorcar journeys.'

'I know, but I've been so weary recently.'

'Then the walk will do you good.' She pulled the door open, pleased to breathe in the fresh air, despite it being near freezing. It tasted like freedom after her mother's constant niggling.

The walk on the path round the colliery was filled with Margaret's chitchat about Christmas, what presents and food to buy, how they might decorate the drawing room. Elizabeth retreated into her own head, her thoughts straying to the last time she'd seen Ralph.

Reaching Jubilee Green, and about to enter the grocer's opposite the McKenzie Arms, they came across Matilda Bowen, the wife of John, the under manager at the pit.

'Good morning to you, Mrs Meredith, Miss Meredith. I suppose you heard about the spat at the public house last night, between the miners and the soldiers on leave?'

'Indeed we have not,' said Margaret.

'Well...' Mrs Bowen leaned in conspiratorially to impart the gossip. 'It seems one of the miners insulted one of the soldiers—'

'And them fighting for their country too,' Margaret interrupted.

'Yes, but the soldier hit him, and then all mayhem was let loose and the next thing you know they've all joined in, soldiers hitting civilians, civilians hitting soldiers, lots of bruises and bloodied noses. I saw that Hywel Llewellyn with a black eye.'

Hywel? He didn't seem the brawling sort, thought Elizabeth.

'So uncouth most of them are. Of course, my Tom wasn't there. He wouldn't have demeaned himself in that way.'

'Anyway, the police were fetched and several were cautioned,' said Matilda. 'Mrs Moss fair did her nut, she did. She'd left old Stephen Thomas in charge and he'd been selling more beer than is allowed.'

'They should close the pubs down completely during the war,' said Margaret. 'I can sympathise with the prohibitionists on that one.'

Matilda nodded her head enthusiastically. 'I did think of joining one of their protest marches.'

'The men need some kind of pleasure with all their hard work,' said Elizabeth. 'As long as they don't overdo it, I don't see the harm.'

'Don't see the harm, Miss Meredith? Didn't your friend, Anwen Rhys, and her family suffer because of a drunken father?'

'That's a good point,' said Margaret, her stern glance a challenge.

'But most of these men don't beat their wives. I only think—'

'You think *far* too much.' Her mother dismissed her with a wave of her hand.

Well that's me told, she thought. There was no point discussing it once her mother had made her mind up.

'What a good job your beau is—' her mother started.

'Mother!' Although she assumed that Gwen would have forgotten about Ralph by now, she still didn't want her relationship with a councillor being the talk of the village.

'Sorry, I'm sure.'

Matilda Bowen looked confused.

'I'm going to carry on with my errands,' said Elizabeth. 'I'll see you at home later.'

'I thought you were helping with the shopping?'

'I'm sure you can cope on your own.'

She marched across the road, not looking back as her mother said, 'Well don't be long.'

Hopefully she wouldn't tell Mrs Bowen anything else about Ralph. She should stay to make sure, but she'd had enough of her mother for today.

Her thoughts returned to Hywel. Surely he hadn't joined in the fracas? She'd always had him down as a peaceful man with principles. Time to be a bit nosy.

—

In the end, Elizabeth popped into Anwen's house on the pretext of a cup of tea and catching up. She didn't feel too guilty about the ruse as there were presents of preserves to drop off.

Before that, she'd dropped some off at Violet's house, receiving but cursory thanks, with the door only partly ajar. She'd likely been in the middle of something, for Elizabeth could think of nothing she'd done to offend her. There were two pots of jam to drop off at Gwen's later, although she wasn't sure jam was the right word for the gift: with its lack of sugar it was more like boiled fruit, but hopefully it would be tasty. She was sure of a better reception at Gwen's at least, which made her feel guilty, given that she had secured Ralph's affections.

'That reminds me,' said Elizabeth, taking a cup of tea from Anwen and sitting by the stove. 'I heard there was a fight at the McKenzie Arms last night.'

'Oh goodness, yes. You'd think the soldiers would have had enough of that in the trenches.'

'Was it them who started it?'

'Not exactly,' said Idris, strolling out of the scullery into the kitchen, polishing a boot. 'David Keir, the union rep, asked Maurice Coombes if his sister's *flyblow*, as he put it, had been born yet, and Maurice socked him one. Six of one and half-a-dozen of the other, if you ask me.'

'That wasn't very delicate,' said Elizabeth. More guilt was heaped upon her, given that the reason for Polly's pregnancy was very close to home.

'You talking about the fight at the public house?' said Hywel, coming in from the hall with a shirt on a hanger. His eye was vivid with shades of purple and pink.

'Oh,' said Elizabeth. 'So it's true you were involved.'

'Ah, you heard. Keir was already intoxicated when he came in. Goodness knows where he'd got that from as he'd only just arrived. And I wasn't exactly what you'd call "involved". I was trying to bring it to a close.'

He perched on the end of the chaise longue. Elizabeth was amused, yet impressed, to see him pulling the sewing basket towards him. He lifted the lid and took out a needle and thread. She could never imagine either her father or brother doing that.

Idris tugged a chair out from under the table and twisted it round to sit opposite his wife and Elizabeth. 'Alun Lloyd, of all people, punched Hywel. Not a violent man in the past.'

'Perhaps he's still angry about his brother's death,' said Elizabeth.

'Aye, that could be it.'

'So, you were an innocent party,' Elizabeth said to Hywel.

'I certainly was. Luckily enough some of the men, Alun included, told Harries this, so I wasn't cautioned.'

'I have to tell you, I'm afraid, that Matilda Bowen is going round the village telling people about it, and is mentioning your name. I swear she is going to be as bad as Esther Williams. Do you think it goes with being the under-manager's wife?'

'I do hope not,' groaned Anwen. 'The village can do without another haughty, judgemental woman traipsing around the village, poking her nose in where it's not wanted.'

Elizabeth felt awkward, given her own mother was haughty and judgemental, but at least she didn't march around the village causing arguments. And she was sure Anwen hadn't been thinking of her anyway.

There were more voices in the scullery. Violet came cautiously into the kitchen as they all greeted her. Elizabeth had the feeling, by her brief frown, that she was not pleased to find her there. Perhaps she should have a word with her about the reason. She'd like to put things right if there was a problem.

'Oh Hywel, your eye!' said Violet. 'Anwen told me what happened, but I didn't imagine it would be so bad.'

'I'm all right. It's not so painful now. Come on, sit down then.' Hywel pulled the chair out near him. 'Where are the kiddies?'

'Cadi's showing them what she's making.' She sat but looked uncomfortable.

'Did you hear about William Griffin, Violet?' said Anwen.

'No. No I didn't. He hasn't died too, has he?' Her face crumpled and it looked like she might cry.

'No, no. I saw him being brought home in an ambulance late this morning. Even though I knew he'd lost his leg in France, it was a shock to see it.'

'Was it the whole leg?' Violet asked.

'No, to the knee. He has crutches and walked into the house with them quite efficiently. His wife, Joan, was talking to the ambulance driver so I went and had a few words. Said if we could help with anything, you know. White as a sheet, she looked.'

'At least he's come home,' Violet murmured.

Elizabeth felt a profound sorrow for the young widow, but there were no words of comfort that were sufficient.

They heard the front door close and soon Enid entered from the hall, looking round at everyone. 'My, there's quite a crowd gathered here. Could do with a bit a peace and quiet to be honest.'

Elizabeth was about to rise and suggest she leave when Violet jumped up, eyes wide. 'I'll be going now.'

'You've only just arrived,' said Hywel.

'I was only popping by. I'll leave you to it.' She scurried back into the scullery and soon the back door was heard shutting.

Cadi came into the kitchen. 'Did one of you say something to upset Violet? She left rather suddenly and looked a little distressed.'

'Oh, I only suggested I needed some peace and quiet. I didn't mean to be rude,' said Enid.

'You're quite right,' said Elizabeth. 'I'm sure you've been working hard today at McKenzie House, as you always do, so I'll take my leave.'

She made her goodbyes and left via the scullery. Outside, walking down the back alley, she felt suddenly alone. Yes, there was the trip out with Ralph, but apart from that, there'd be nothing until after Christmas. Tom would be leaving in a couple of days, the day before those in the Rhondda Pals, so even he wouldn't be there to entertain her.

It was going to be a dull Christmas, but at least there were things to look forward to. She and Ralph had plenty of plans for the new year. Then there was the interview for the job on Thursday. Things were looking up.

Chapter Thirteen

Hywel stood in the kitchen drying himself after his bath, yawning. He'd been tired his whole shift, more glad than normal when it was over at two o'clock. He'd not slept well the night before, picturing the expression of hurt on Violet's face as she'd taken flight after Enid's abruptness. She'd been such a sad figure recently. It tore at his soul to see her so down. Not that he had any right to such feelings, not even now she was a widow. It would feel like taking advantage of Charlie's death.

There was a knock on the door from the scullery and Anwen's voice calling, 'Have you finished, Uncle Hywel?'

'Nearly,' he called back. 'Just getting dressed.'

A couple of minutes later he opened the door. 'I'm done now... Anwen, do you think Violet was upset by your mam's comment yesterday, about wanting some peace and quiet? The poor woman's still mourning and looked terribly down.'

Anwen brought a bucket into the kitchen to empty the bath. 'Well, I did wonder if there was a specific reason she'd called round. She didn't look herself when she came in.'

'She might have been needing a favour, or some company, or been worried about something.'

'I'll go round and have a word with her. She might think she's not welcome for Christmas dinner anymore, so I'll make it clear she is.' Anwen placed the bucket in the bath to sweep up the first of the water.

'No, I'll go round. You're busy.' Hywel did up his top shirt buttons and pulled up his braces, all the while remembering the day Violet had asked him not to go around to hers. But this would be a message from the family about Christmas. Surely that was acceptable?

'Aren't you going to have your dinner first? Mam managed to get a little bit of ham at the butcher's to put with the bread and dripping.'

'I'll go to Violet's first, make sure she's all right.'

Anwen took the bucket to the scullery to empty it down the sink. As Hywel followed her in, she pointed out of the window at the wind and rain. 'There's a real squall out there. Do you want to wait?'

'No time like the present.'

Two minutes later he was out, head down against the blowy shower. The clean jacket and cap he'd fetched from his room were not equal to the weather. He soon turned onto Bryn Road, glad Violet only lived round the corner.

Knocking twice, he almost gave up, thinking it was a little early for her to be fetching Clarice from school already, when the door opened. Violet stretched her eyes and blinked. Her hair had come a little loose on one side.

'Oh, Hywel. Hello. Sorry, I must have dozed off in the armchair, reading this letter from my father.'

'Can I come in please?' He pointed up at the sky.

She hesitated, probably wondering what he was doing there when she'd made it clear he should stay away. It might have been a better idea for Anwen to come after all.

'Yes, all right.' She stepped back to give him room.

'Benjamin and Clarice are both napping,' she whispered as she led him to the kitchen.

'Clarice? Oh, of course, it's the Christmas holidays... You say the letter's from your father. Is your mother all right?'

'She's gone down with a heavy cold, he says.' She sighed deeply. 'They go straight to her chest since she had the influenza. They'd been hoping to pop over for a couple of days between Christmas and New Year, but it doesn't look like they'll be able to now.' She placed the letter on the table with a further sigh.

'That is a shame.'

'What can I do for you, Hywel?' It was said in an official way, her neck stretched and her chin jutting out. She stood with her back to the fire. On the stove was a black kettle, steam issuing forth from the spout.

'I've come to apologise about yesterday. You'd only just arrived before Enid indicated she wanted people to leave.'

'I see.'

'And we never asked why you'd come in the first place. It might have been something important.'

Violet's posture slumped a little and he saw her chest rise and fall as she blew out a large breath.

'Sit down, Hywel. I'll make you a cup of tea.'

'I don't want to be any trouble.'

'I had the kettle on anyway.'

She busied herself filling the teapot, placing a knitted cosy on it then fetching two cups. He'd never known Violet have any saucers and there wasn't one cup without a chip in it. He knew she'd sold much of the furniture in her front room. This made him deeply sad. It also filled him with guilt, for at least his lodging rent had given her a little extra money. He glanced round the room, taking in its shabby appearance. Yet it was always spotless, for all that.

'Have you thought of taking in another lodger?' he asked.

She looked at him sharply. 'I only took you in because of Anwen, and knew you were a decent sort, not about to, to try anything… unseemly.'

Hywel was tempted to chuckle at Violet's prim face and pursed lips as she related that. Yet she was right to be cautious, a young woman on her own.

'Anyway, I didn't visit yesterday for anything in particular. Just for a bit of company, I suppose.' The prim face slipped a little, betraying a smidgen of hurt.

'I'm sorry, it must get lonely here, even with the children. It's not like having adult company.'

'I manage well enough,' she said, the prissy mask back in place.

'Anwen said to tell you you're still invited to dinner on Christmas day, just in case you thought you weren't welcome.'

'I hadn't really thought about it.' She placed two cups of black tea on the table. 'I'm sorry, I've run out of milk and I don't remember the last time I had some sugar in the house.'

'Black tea's fine. I've made myself get used to no sugar so the little we have can be used for the odd bit of baking.'

Violet joined him at the table, sitting at the other end.

'What have you got the children for Christmas?' he said, trying to find something to say. They'd never been short of conversation when he'd lived here. She'd been good company and he liked to think he had been too.

'A rag doll and skipping rope for Clarice and a spinning top and pull-along soldier beating a drum for Benjy.'

'They'll enjoy them, I'm sure. I had a spinning top when I was little and played with it all the time.'

'I have to admit I was a little put out by Elizabeth's presence yesterday. She's become a good friend of Anwen's and sees her far more than I do these days. Or at least she did when Anwen was still helping her run the allotments.'

'I can understand that. But I think she'd like you all as friends, Gwen too.'

Violet picked up her cup but didn't take a sip. 'I know that, for Gwen went to the pictures with her back in August, while Anwen and Idris were away. I have wondered why she would bother with the likes of us. She must have much more sophisticated friends.'

'Maybe… oh, I don't know. Perhaps she thinks you're nicer than them. She's not snooty like some of the middle classes, so perhaps she doesn't like snooty people either.' He was making this up as he went along, not having thought too deeply about it until now.

'You could be right. When she called at my house yesterday, with the jams, I felt ashamed. If she'd been anyone else, I'd have invited her in for a cup of tea.'

He frowned. 'Ashamed of what?'

She lifted her hand and made a circle with it. 'All this. I have other things I have to spend my widow's pension on. There's not enough to decorate.'

Hywel thought for a while. Should he make this offer? He had nothing to lose. 'If you need to borrow a bit of money, I have some put by. It's not much, but it would tidy up the walls a bit.' She was already shaking her head as he added, 'And we're managing all right at Enid's, what with my and Enid's wages, Cadi's bit from sewing and Idris will be—'

'No, Hywel. That is very kind of you to offer, but I couldn't possibly. I doubt I'd ever be able to pay you back.'

'Then take it as a gift.'

Tears welled up in Violet's eyes. 'You are a good man, Hywel Llewellyn, but you have your own family to think of. When Benjy goes to school, I will find work, even if it's screening coal at the mine. I'm afraid I'm not much good at practical skills, so it's not like I can take in sewing, but, there it is.' She shrugged.

Hywel was about to tell her about Mrs Jenkins two doors away from them, who took in washing, when there was a knock at the door.

Violet pulled herself up from her slumped position, sniffing. 'My goodness, who is that now?' She rose and made for the door, saying as she went, 'I am popular today.'

Soon there was a new voice coming from the hall, much louder than Violet's. Hywel recognised it from somewhere.

'Well, I told Brynmore, our Violet can't spend Christmas on her own, can she? But he didn't want to—' The door from the hall opened and through it appeared Olwen Jones, Charlie's mother. In her hands were a purple carpet bag that had seen better days and a large sack bag. 'Oh! What are *you* doing here?' She twisted her head towards Violet, her eyes narrowed in accusation. 'I thought you'd got rid of your lodger.'

Hywel sat forward, hovering between feeling that he'd outstayed his welcome and concern about leaving Violet on her own with this woman.

'I didn't get rid of him. I told you he'd had an accident and was also supporting his own family.'

'What's he doing here then? And look at that eye. Been brawling, has he?' Olwen now had her back to him, talking about him as if he wasn't there.

Violet's hesitation was cut short by Hywel. 'I got thumped trying to bring a brawl to an end, if you must know. And I came round to ask what we can get the children for Christmas, seeing as they're coming to us for dinner.'

Olwen pulled her gloves off and slapped them on the table. 'That won't be necessary. *I'm* here now and so we shall be having our own *family* Christmas.'

'But I've already said we'll go, and it would be rude—' Violet started.

'We'll discuss it when *he's* gone.' She nodded her head to indicate Hywel.

'He hasn't finished his tea yet,' said Violet.

'It's all right,' said Hywel, stretching the injured leg before standing. It still gave him the odd bit of trouble, especially when it was cold. 'I need to get back and have my dinner. Wasn't hungry when I came off shift.'

'If you're sure,' said Violet. He fancied he saw an appeal in her eyes, but what could he do? Olwen Jones might well see him as a single man sniffing around a poor young widow woman.

He walked towards the door, limping ever so slightly. Olwen removed her coat, slung it over the nearest chair and filled his vacant seat with her pencil-thin body. She still had on her hat, a stiff, black felt one with no adornment.

Before entering the hall, he said, 'The invitation's still open, if you change your mind.'

'Goodbye,' said Olwen. 'See yourself out.'

So he did, concerned it was the wrong thing to do but at a loss to know what was the right thing.

Anwen woke up Christmas morning with a weight on her heart. It was a year today that Cadi had found Sara, passed away in her bed. It had been Mumgu's long lament of grief that had alerted Anwen to something being wrong. Sara had evidently died during a fit of coughing, judging by the blood on the sheets. Anwen squeezed her eyes shut now, trying to dispel the memory of it. Even her father had looked shocked, though he'd disappeared for the rest of the day, leaving them to deal with it.

Idris emitted a low, rumbling hum and stretched as he awoke. 'Morning,' he croaked, pulling himself up to kiss her cheek. 'What's wrong, *cariad*? It's sad you look. Is it Sara you're thinking of?'

'Yes. I had such hope for last Christmas Day, to make Christmas special for her.'

'I can understand why it still hurts, but Sara wouldn't want us to be sad all day.'

'I know.' Anwen flicked back the blankets and sheet. 'It's going to be a very different Christmas here to one we've ever had, what with my father gone and you here. And Mam walking and doing things for the first Christmas in a while. And Uncle Hywel here too. What with Mamgu, it feels like a proper family again.'

There was only one thing that would have made it even better, she thought, and that was a little one of her own. She didn't share her disappointment at not yet falling pregnant with Idris. She knew what her mother and Mamgu would have said, about it only having been four months since they'd married, but Violet had fallen pregnant straight away with Clarice after her marriage. And look at how many women got pregnant before wedlock, like Polly Coombes and, of course, Delyth Bryce. She was one person she *was* going to forget today. It couldn't be too long before she was due. It would be strange, having a half-sibling, one she'd unlikely be allowed to get to know. And would she want to anyway?

'You look miles away,' said Idris, clambering out of the bed.

'Just thinking how I might have a new brother or sister soon.'

'Let's put that thought to one side for today, for we don't want to upset your mother.'

'Don't worry, I will. I'll go and fetch some hot water to wash. I dare say Mamgu's already up and got the fire going.'

'It's all right, I'll do that.'

He got partly dressed, putting only a vest on above his trousers, and left the room. Despite the anniversary of Sara's death, Anwen felt immensely fortunate at this moment in time. It wasn't everybody who had such a considerate husband. No, as sad as she felt, she knew she had to count her blessings.

—

Cadi had put on a large Christmas breakfast, with bacon and eggs and homemade bread. They'd gone without some things the last few days to save up money for them. She now put out the jams that Elizabeth had given them, which they tucked into eagerly.

'I'm so glad to be able to join the family properly this year,' said Enid, buttering a second piece of toast.

'You could have done last year, if you'd let anybody know you could walk,' said Cadi.

'You know why I didn't. I was afeared what Madog would do to me.' She put down her toast and closed her eyes.

Cadi took her hand. 'Aye, I know, *cariad*, it wasn't as we'd have wanted it.'

'Are we going to open our presents after breakfast?' said Hywel, toasting a slice of bread on a long fork by the fire.

'Why, *bach*, you're like an excited child,' said Cadi, grinning indulgently at him.

'It's only Christmas once a year, isn't it? And I've spotted something under the tree with my name on.'

Although Hywel called it a tree, it was not much more than a large conifer branch that Anwen had found in the woods behind

McKenzie Cottages. It was sitting on an occasional table from the front room, propped up against the wall. She'd decorated it with some old baubles they still had from a childhood trip to the arcades in Cardiff. On the table around it were lots of small presents. Anwen felt a swell of excitement, as much looking forward to seeing everyone else's faces as their presents were revealed as she was to opening her own.

'We'll open them after dinner, like we've always done,' said Enid. 'Then we can do it with Violet and the kiddies, for she's bringing their presents round. First, we've got to clear the breakfast things away and get ready for chapel. If everyone helps, we'll get it done all the quicker.'

Cadi rose and filled everyone's teacups from the pot before filling it again from the kettle. It was then there was a hefty knock on the front door.

Enid tutted. 'Who on earth is that on this holy day? And so early too.'

'I'll get it,' said Anwen, rising. 'I've finished my breakfast now.'

She was soon in the hall, almost skipping to the door. Opening it, she was confused to find Esther Williams standing there in a much too long coat, face like thunder. What on earth could she have in mind to spoil their day?

There were no pleasantries, no *Happy Christmas*, but she launched straight in with a strident, 'Delyth has given birth. Had a girl, she has.'

By this time, Idris was standing behind Anwen, maybe afraid it would be bad news.

'Had it early this morning she did, screaming the house down while Hatty Kelly, the midwife from Walter Street, delivered it. *I* had to go and fetch her at two-thirty in the morning, mind, so I've not had much sleep. Don't charge enough rent for those kind of services.' She sniffed and tucked her hands around her coat.

'I'm not sure what you want us to do about it,' said Anwen.

'The baby's your half-sister, isn't it?'

'Strictly speaking, yes, but it's nothing to do with our family.'

'You can't even be bothered to come and see her? And look you, I'm not Delyth's mother, and I'm not about to go fussing over her. She needs a bit of looking after, and it's not my job.'

'Nor is it *our* job,' came Enid's voice as she stamped down the hall. 'That harlot has nothing to do with us, and that baby is no part of our family.'

'Well, there's heartless,' Esther huffed.

Enid pushed past Idris and Anwen. 'Don't talk to me about heartless, for it's not me who tied my son to his bed to stop him enlisting. I didn't cover for a husband who knocked six bells out of Cadoc Beadle. You want to look to yourself before you go criticising others.'

'Hm! What's that got to do with a new baby and its poor mother? I should have known better than to expect any sympathy from you lot.'

She turned to leave, propelling Enid onto the street. 'Don't you act the high and mighty with me, Esther Williams, for your husband is in prison, the same as mine.'

Esther kept walking, offering no retort.

'Everything all right here?' said Rachael Owen, from her step two doors away. Her son, Gwilym, stood behind her, hand on her shoulder.

'It will be now she's gone,' said Enid, turning abruptly to go back inside.

'She came to tell us that Delyth Bryce has given birth,' said Anwen. 'Seemed to think we should look after the pair of them.'

'Of all the cheek,' said Rachael. 'If she can't look after herself, there's always the workhouse. Anyway, *Nadolig Llawen* to you all. Are you and Idris's parents still coming over for some supper this evening?'

'Of course,' said Anwen, smiling. 'We're looking forward to it.'

Rachael hesitated. 'It, it feels a little odd, the first Christmas, you know, without Earnest.' She pulled a handkerchief from her blouse sleeve and dabbed her eyes. Gwilym nodded and rubbed her arm.

'I can understand. It does for us, without Sara.'

'Yes of course, it would do.' Rachael tipped her head to one side and pressed her lips together. She shivered and wrapped her shawl around herself. 'We'll see you later.'

Anwen and Idris watched them go inside. They could hear Enid raving to Cadi and Hywel in the kitchen about Esther Williams.

'I hope she doesn't keep that up all day,' said Idris.

'Me too,' said Anwen, 'especially with Violet and the littl'uns coming for their dinner. Oh, and Mrs Jones.' But her eyes were on the disappearing figure of Esther as Rachael's words about the workhouse came back to her. However much she disliked the situation, she hoped it didn't come to that for Delyth and the baby.

—

Violet had known this would be a mistake ever since Enid had popped round to extend the Christmas dinner invitation to Olwen. At first she'd declined, saying they'd be fine on their own, but Enid had gently persuaded her, over a cup of tea, that it would take the work out of the day for them both.

Violet had been placed next to Hywel, who was at one end of the table, a circumstance that she would ordinarily have been happy with, since she'd always enjoyed his company. But the moment he engaged her in conversation, Olwen peered, narrow-eyed, at the two of them, from her seat at the other end. Hywel seemed unaware of her mother-in-law's scrutiny, regaling all with tales of his old hewing butty being cautioned by Sergeant Harries.

'You should have seen him, mun,' laughed Hywel. 'Could barely stand as Harries the Police dragged him out of the public gardens, brandishing a branch of the one holly tree there. Drunk as a lord he was, whining about how he only wanted to give the house a bit of colour for Christmas, for the kiddies, like.'

'I've never seen him get like that,' said Idris. 'He's never been much of a drinker.'

'Maybe that's why he was three sheets to the wind. It doesn't take much if you're not used to it.'

'He should have walked up to the forest, like I did,' said Anwen, indicating the holly sprigs decorating the table and the mantelpiece. 'Hope his wife gave him a good talking to.'

'Hmmph!' said Olwen, poking gingerly at a roast potato. 'I'd have had him in gaol if it had been up to me. Can't be doing with his sort, ruffians. Like those miners what striked in July last year. My Charlie wouldn't never have done nothing like that.'

Violet noticed a glance flick between Idris and Hywel. A flush crept up her neck and she was glad of the high-necked blouse. Her head went down as she attempted to eat a piece of the beef Enid had managed to get hold of. Glad she was of it, having not had any in over two years, but it stuck in her throat as she swallowed. If only Olwen had stayed at home in Bargoed. What must Brynmore be thinking, left to go to his cousin's for Christmas on his own?

She glanced at the children. They were happy and that was the main thing. She should try to cheer up too, for surely this was better than being stuck at home, coping with Olwen on her own.

'This is lovely, Mrs Rhys,' said Violet. 'The roast potatoes are particularly tasty.' She took in a deep breath of the meaty aroma that filled the room.

'I put them under the beef when I roasted it, with some herbs, that's the trick. I was grateful for you all putting in a few coins towards the meat. And haven't the allotment workers done us proud with the veggies? They've worked hard considering the bad weather we've had. Such tasty parsnips and leeks.'

All the adults nodded and agreed, apart from Olwen.

'Of course, growing up on a farm we had turkey and goose a few times for Christmas,' said Enid. 'Much more festive, and a nice change, but a bit expensive these days.'

'If you could even get them,' said Violet. 'Haven't seen them for a few years in the butcher's here.'

'True enough.'

'Can't seem to make its mind up out there, the weather,' said Anwen, leaning back in her chair to peer out of the back window. 'One moment blue sky, then cloud, then a passing shower. Too mild for snow, sadly.'

'Snow's no good for man nor beast,' said Olwen. She placed a tiny forkful of parsnip in her mouth and chewed with her lips scrunched up.

'It's nice for the kiddies,' said Cadi, 'but it does play havoc with the delivery wagons and motorvans, that's true enough. I'd like it if it came one day and then disappeared overnight. That way we wouldn't get all the slush, especially when it's mushed up with the coal dust.'

'I like snow,' Clarice's reedy voice piped up. 'It's fun to play in.'

'Yes, it fun to playing,' Benjamin tried to repeat. 'When we open pressies?'

'Hush now,' said Olwen. 'Children should be seen and not heard at the table.'

Anwen pulled a sorrowful face at Violet, who raised her eyes slightly.

'In my house, children can speak as much as the adults,' said Enid. 'And quite often they have far more interesting things to say, in my experience. We'll open the presents after dinner, Benjy *cariad*. Now, please excuse me while I see how the pudding's doing.' She rose and went to the stove to lift the lid of a large saucepan.

Hywel knocked Violet's forearm with his elbow. 'What's the matter with you, *fach*? You're not eating much.' He gave her an encouraging smile. Her stomach fluttered, disorientating her for a moment.

'I'm fine, just taking it slowly.' She started on the beef once again, determined not to let her mother-in-law spoil the meal for her.

'I'm sure I won't be wanting pudding,' said Olwen, shoving the rest of her potatoes and parsnips to one side of the plate and placing her knife and fork together in the middle.

'Get away with you,' said Enid, 'You can't miss this pudding. Been saving up the dried fruit for months, and the flour. I saved some eggs and Miss Elizabeth even gave us a little drop of brandy to put in it. There's not as much sugar as there should be, but I'm sure the fruit will make up for it.'

'And I managed to get a couple of cans of condensed milk to pour over,' said Cadi. She rubbed her hands together. 'I'm so looking forward to it. I'm sure you'll enjoy it, Olwen.'

'My name is Mrs Jones,' was the only reply she gave.

'This is the best meal I've had all year,' said Hywel. 'Always look forward to a bit of Christmas pudding.' He smacked his lips together.

'I'm not a self-indulgent person,' said Olwen. 'In my opinion, this war's at least been good for stopping people's gluttony. It's one of the seven deadly sins.'

Hywel widened his eyes but said nothing. Violet reflected that pride too was one of the seven deadly sins, and Olwen was brim-full of it.

'Can I have puddin' too?' said Clarice. 'And Benjy?'

'Of course you can,' Violet said quickly, to get in before Olwen said the opposite.

'Well I can do without,' she said.

An idea occurred to Violet. 'Olwen, if you'd rather go home and rest, I don't mind. You seem tired. We'll follow on later.'

Olwen looked from Violet to Hywel, her lips pinched in. 'No, I'm not at all tired. I shall stay and partake of a cup of tea instead of pudding. And I want to see my grandchildren undo their presents.'

'Good idea,' said Cadi, rising. 'I'll get the kettle on. Though I'm going to have both.'

When Violet finally put her knife and fork down, Anwen said, 'Help me clear the plates, would you?'

'Of course.' Anything to get a moment's respite from Olwen's disapproval of everything.

In the kitchen, as they placed the dirty plates on the table, Violet murmured, 'I'm sorry about my mother-in-law.'

'It's not your fault she's so rude.' Anwen looked round and lowered her voice to a whisper. 'Delyth Bryce had the baby this morning. Esther Williams came banging on our door, telling us we should come and help out.'

'The cheek of it. What are you going to do?'

'Nothing. Do you think Delyth would even appreciate it if we did?'

Violet laughed briefly. 'No, I very much doubt it from what I've seen of her. She's a loudmouth and so offensive to people.'

Anwen looked thoughtful for a moment. 'But it did occur to me... I know it's silly...'

'What is? You can tell me.'

'Well, she had a girl, see, and I thought, it's strange, what with Sara going a year ago today. It's almost like she's been born to replace her. No, not replace, for no one can replace my lovely sister, but, oh, I don't know.'

Violet put her arm around Anwen's shoulders. 'I know what you mean, *cariad*. It's like she's sent a little Christmas present.'

Cadi strode in at that moment, and, judging the situation correctly said, 'You've told Violet then, have you?'

Anwen nodded, taking Violet's hands and squeezing them in thanks. 'I knew you'd understand.'

'Right, you two get the bowls. I'm going to make a hole in these condensed milk cans.' Cadi headed towards the table. 'How long's *Mrs Jones* staying then?'

Violet let out a deep breath. 'Hopefully only till the New Year. I'm sure my father-in-law will have something to say otherwise. He's spending Christmas with a cousin who lives alone. Apparently, Brynmore promised they'd go there back in

November, so he felt at least one of them should keep to the promise. It still doesn't seem right, her leaving him to go on his own. She had a letter from him, but she wouldn't tell me what was in it.'

'Well you know where we are if you need us.' Cadi patted Violet's arm.

'Thank you, Mrs Rhys, that's very kind of you.'

'What's all this "Mrs Rhys"? It's about time you called me Cadi. Come on, I want my pudding.'

Violet's mood lifted a smidgen. Olwen would be gone in another week and then she could get back to normal. Normal. Currently that involved mourning and guilt at being inadequate – very unappealing companions. She tutted at herself and followed Anwen back to the kitchen. For now she would banish those thoughts.

–

'*Siôn Corn* gave me a – a – I dunno,' said Benjy, holding up his first present from Santa Claus.

'It's a spinning top,' said Violet, leaning over to show him how to work it.

Despite Olwen's brooding presence, Violet was really enjoying the afternoon. It was like a proper family Christmas.

'My turn, my turn,' Clarice chanted, picking up a parcel for herself, wrapped in newspaper but with a Christmas tree painted on.

All of the presents Violet had brought were wrapped like that, but with different seasonal pictures.

'Did you do those?' Hywel asked, pointing at a painting of Santa Claus.

'Um, yes, I did. I used the children's paint boxes.' She went a little red, hoping she didn't sound like she was boasting.

'They're very good.'

'She was always the most artistic of us at school,' said Anwen.

'Oh, I dunno about that,' said Violet.

The little girl pulled the string free and tore off the paper, revealing a rag doll. 'Dolly!' she called, holding it up before clutching it to her chest. 'I'll call her Elin.'

The children had another turn each, revealing the skipping rope and pull-along soldier. Anwen pulled out another gift from under the makeshift tree.

'This is for both of you, from me and Idris.' She handed them a parcel wrapped in brown butcher's paper with what looked like a hair ribbon.

They undid the wrapping between them. Clarice called 'Skittles!' grabbing two of the six of them while Benjy took hold of the ball.

Violet hunkered down next to them. 'What do you say to Aunty Anwen and Uncle Idris?'

'*Diolch yn fawr*,' they chanted together.

The next presents were a sailor-style shirt and britches for Benjy and a dress with a sailor collar for Clarice, made by Enid and Cadi. Anwen noticed Olwen pinch her lips in as she went to fetch her presents, done up in proper wrapping paper, which she'd already told them she'd got from the department store in Merthyr Tydfil. When the children undid them, treating them no better than the newspaper, it became evident why she was annoyed. There sat another dress and britches with a top.

'You can never have too many clothes,' said Cadi.

'*Mine* were from R.T. Jones,' she said. 'Not homemade.'

'Well we're not all blessed with the gift of sewing,' was the older woman's retort.

Violet noticed Anwen glance over at her, as she had many times today.

'Time to move on to the grownups presents now,' said Enid.

'Ohhh,' the children sang as a disappointed duet.

Hywel got up from the table. 'One moment there.' He picked up a parcel from the floor, where the ones that didn't fit on the small table had been put. 'Here you go, children, one more present each for you.'

Clarice jumped up and down in excitement, grabbing at hers before Benjy had even reached Hywel.

'Now open them nicely,' said Violet.

Olwen glowered at him. 'Well, I'm sure that wasn't necessary.'

Everyone ignored her as the youngsters tugged at the brown paper. Clarice got through first, pulling out a stuffed toy and exclaiming, 'Pussy cat!'

Benjy followed on quickly with, 'Doggy!'

'It's Miaow and Woof!' Clarice announced. 'Thank you Uncle Hywel!'

When everyone looked confused, Violet explained about the drawings Hywel had done for the children the month before.

'And what was he doing around your house?' asked Olwen, eyes narrowed.

'Just fixing the picture rail,' Hywel said lightly. 'It was a bit high for Violet. But the question is, which one is Woof, and which one is Miaow?'

The children giggled.

'They're stoopid names anyway. I'm sure we can think of something better,' said Olwen.

'Never mind that,' said Enid, 'let's get our own presents open. I know Hywel's been waiting since this morning.' She tapped his arm playfully.

Chocolates, homemade biscuits, handkerchiefs, a second-hand pomander and hand-knitted gloves made up the bulk of the remaining presents.

'Can we play the games now?' chirped Clarice.

'Of course,' said Anwen. 'I've already hidden the thimble in the front room, and I've got a large donkey drawn on some butcher's paper that needs a tail. Then there's a pack of snap cards we can have a go at too, if you like.'

'Can we find the thimble first?' Clarice jumped up and down while turning a circle.

'Stop all that nonsense now,' said Olwen. 'Otherwise we'll be going home.'

Violet felt the fury rising inside her. When did Olwen get to decide when they did things? She swiftly directed the children towards the front room. 'Off you go now. I don't know where it is either, so I'll be having a look, so you better be quick if you want to beat me.'

The games were a big hit with the children, with all the adults joining in – except her mother-in-law. After a third game of snap, Benjy yawned and his head lolled onto the table, where he was sitting on Violet's lap.

'Bless him,' said Cadi. 'Why don't you lay him on the chaise? There's a blanket over the back you can pop over him.'

Violet shuffled round carefully, struggling to stand with him in her arms. Hywel came to her rescue, taking Benjy from her and placing him on the chaise longue, on the other side of the table against the wall. She sat for a while, watching the fire in the range. The usual coal had been replaced by logs today, with cones added, lending a hint of pine to the familiar scent of burning wood. It was a winter smell that took her back to the bonfires of her childhood, filling her with contentment. If only today could last forever. Preferably without her mother-in-law.

'I think that signals time for the sing-song,' said Idris.

'You'll wake Benjamin up,' said Olwen, with a little shiver of indignance.

'Not if we're in the front room with the door pushed to,' said Violet. 'When he's worn out, he can sleep through a thunderstorm.'

'I don't want to sing anyway. There's already too much frivolity for the day of the Lord's birth.'

'Give over,' said Cadi. 'It should be a day of celebration.'

'I'm going to sit next to Benjamin and read my psalm book.' She pulled out a small volume from her skirt pocket and changed seat.

'As you wish.'

Violet was the last in the room, looking back at Olwen as she opened the book and peered closely at the words.

In the front room, Anwen sat at the piano. 'I'm a bit rusty. I hardly ever play now. What shall we sing first?'

'How about "*Dawel Nos*"?' Idris suggested.

With a murmur of agreement, Anwen started playing the tune to '*Silent Night*', and they sang the words in their native tongue.

Violet was standing next to Hywel, his melodic voice introducing a harmony, while Idris's created another. *Sleep in bliss and peace*, they all sang in Welsh.

Bliss and peace. How she wished she could find that in her life.

There was a cry of dismay from the kitchen. Violet ran out of the room, knowing it was Benjy. He was sitting up, being comforted by Olwen. It wasn't like him to awaken like that when he'd just gone to sleep. It was almost as if... Of course. She'd have laid good money – had she been well off and the gambling sort – on betting that Olwen had awoken him.

'Poor lamb. He must have had a bad dream,' said Olwen, looking at Violet accusingly.

That was certainly the end of her bliss and peace for today.

–

Anwen woke up early, shivering. She felt colder than she had done the past few mornings, despite being squashed up close to Idris. He was sound asleep, his breathing slightly noisy. Something was bothering her; she thought hard to remember what it was.

The dream. It was about Delyth and the baby going to the workhouse. How she wished Rachael hadn't mentioned that establishment yesterday. She turned on her back and lay there a few minutes, trying to think of nice things to lull herself back to sleep. It was no good. All she could think of was the new arrival.

She slid out of bed, noticing the dim light peeking through the gap in the curtains, before putting on her dressing gown and slipping downstairs. In the kitchen she glanced at the clock on the dresser. Five to eight. The fire was already burning brightly.

'You could have had a bit more of a lie-in today,' said Enid, coming through the door with a loaf of bread. She placed it on the board, end up, and started sawing it horizontally with the knife.

'You're up.'

'I always wake up early and can't get back to sleep these days. Would you like some bread and dripping for breakfast? I've run out of the eggs now, I'm afraid.'

'No, I'll get washed and dressed first. Is there any water in the kettle?'

'Yes. Why the hurry?'

'I want to get on with the day and enjoy it, while Hywel's still on holiday and before Idris returns to the pit. I'll get on and wash now.'

She managed to get ready without disturbing her husband. Her mind was in turmoil, all the possible outcomes to what had happened recently going around in circles. By the time she'd got back downstairs, she'd hatched her plan.

'I'm going to pop to Mrs Harris's for some tea. You said we were running out yesterday.' Thank goodness she had a genuine excuse.

'Let's hope they have some as there wasn't a lot before Christmas. You could see if they have any more eggs too, though I doubt it. Most are being sent out to France for the wounded soldiers, Mrs Harris told me.'

'I'll see what I can do.' She picked up the sack bag to put her purse inside it. 'I might call round at Violet's, make sure Olwen's behaving herself.'

'Goodness, what a character she is! Don't be too long.'

The cold air hit Anwen as she stepped outside. The puddles in the road were icy. It wouldn't take long just to make sure

Delyth and the baby were well, then she'd get on with the other tasks. She didn't want to see either of them, just to check. Giving birth was such a hazardous thing when there wasn't really anyone there to take care of them. She doubted Esther was doing much.

Outside number seventeen Jubilee Gardens she hesitated. She took a deep breath before pushing the metal gate open and taking the four steps along the short path. After another pause, she stepped into the tiny porch and gave two taps of the door knocker. It was then she heard the raised voice from inside getting louder as a figure appeared through the glass.

The door swung open and there stood Esther, prim in a full-skirted dress from well before the war. It was clean but a little threadbare in places, not like her usual fashionable clothes. Her hair, however, was neatly pinned up.

'Well, there's timely,' Esther snapped. 'Conscience got the better of you, did it?'

'I only want to find out how they're doing. I have no desire to step over your threshold.'

'It's a bit late for that.'

Behind her, Anwen spotted the tall, thin figure of Sergeant Harries coming down the stairs, his hair considerably greyer than it had been at the start of the war.

'What's happened?' said Anwen, grasping her coat lapels. She pictured a grim scene, of Delyth and the baby, dead in their bedroom. It wasn't unlike the unforgettable image of her sister Sara. She sucked in the urge to holler.

'She's only gone and run away,' said Esther.

'So she's left with the baby.' Anwen shrugged. At least that would keep her out of their way, particularly her mother's.

'No,' said Sergeant Harries, poking his head round the door. 'She's left the poor babby here.'

'She's probably gone out to the shops.'

The policeman stepped into the doorway, causing Esther to step back. 'No. Her bag and all her possessions have gone too.'

'What?' She quickly dismissed the obvious interpretation of what Sergeant Harries was saying. 'I don't understand.'

He rose on his tiptoes and came down again. 'Mrs Hughes, I'm telling you that the babby has been abandoned.'

She felt dizzy, clutching the edge of the stone porch wall.

'Are you alright?'

'I just can't understand how anyone could abandon their babby. Where is she?'

'Upstairs. I understand, from Mrs Williams, that she's your half-sister.'

She felt a moment's shame before realising it was pointless. The whole village would know by now and it was hardly her disgrace, but her father's. 'That's right. Can I see her?'

'Take your opportunity while you can.'

He stood to one side to let her in, then led her upstairs to the small bedroom where they'd found Esther's son Christopher tied up last July. It was considerably untidier and had a pungent whiff about it. She wondered where the lad was.

Constable Probert, who'd come out of retirement when young PC Davis was sent off to war, was holding the baby, jogging her up and down as she whimpered. She was covered in a large sheet that had been wrapped around her several times. It had yellow and brown stains.

'Can't you get another sheet, Mrs Williams?' said the sergeant. 'Or something else clean to wrap her up in?'

'And where's the money to provide such things? I noticed a ten-bob note in Delyth's purse when she paid the midwife, and plenty of change, though she was always late paying me. She should have left some money here to help with looking after the babby. Lord knows where she got that money, for she wasn't working.'

'Maybe profiteering along with Madog Rhys, since she was his fancy woman?' Probert suggested.

Now there was a thought. So much for Delyth's claim that she needed money, thought Anwen.

'Now if you don't mind getting that sheet, Mrs Williams,' said Probert.

She stomped off, complaining.

'You should know,' said Harries, 'that we're going to contact the Guardians to get this poor mite into the workhouse. There's no other choice for an abandoned babby, and one that is a… you know.'

'A bastard,' said Esther, returning with a folded sheet.

'There's no need for that language,' said Anwen.

She thought quickly, peering at the small soul who was being wiped clean on parts of the old sheet. Her eyes were large, a dark blue, her hair a shock of pale brown. She recalled being a six-year-old, peering over the blanket at Sara after she'd been born. They looked very similar. Her eyes were crinkled as if she was confused about why she'd been left. Anwen sniffed back the tears as a small whoosh of emotion stirred inside her. It was a little like falling in love.

'Yes, there is an alternative. She's my sister and she deserves a proper family.'

'You've changed your attitude,' said Esther.

'Are you sure about this?' said Harries. 'Often these days the Poor Law authorities organise for young children to be fostered, or even adopted.'

'And often they don't.' Besides, she didn't like the idea of her sister, half or otherwise, being brought up by strangers.

'I'm not sure how we'll proceed with this,' said the sergeant. 'We'll still have to contact the Guardians, and a decision will be made. I think Dr Roberts can help you with that. In the meantime, would you please get some warm water in a bowl, Mrs Williams, so we can give this babby a proper wash before she goes to her new home, temporary or otherwise.'

-

Outside her front door, Anwen hesitated. She was carrying the sleeping baby, now swaddled in a blanket that Dr Roberts' wife had found in their own home. That wasn't all she'd found, having sorted through a box of baby things she'd kept in their spare room. With the items Mam had kept from Anwen's babyhood, there should be enough to get them going.

'My mother is not going to like this,' she told Dr Roberts, who was standing next to her with his leather bag.

'I grant that it's an odd situation and not one that most people would relish, but it's a good deed you're doing, Anwen, for I know the orphans in the workhouse do not have good lives. And you're right that there's no guarantee this little one would be adopted.'

'I'm not sure what Idris will make of it either.' Would he want her looking after someone else's *flyblow*, as Maurice Coombes had put it?

'We're not going to find out standing on the doorstep, are we?' The doctor opened the front door. 'I'll go ahead and prepare the way.'

She walked inside slowly, hearing her mother call, 'You took your time,' followed by a panicked, 'Oh, it's you, doctor. What's happened?'

She waited in the hallway as Dr Roberts told her family of the abandonment. He ended with, 'And so the only decent thing to do was bring the baby here.'

Anwen stepped in the kitchen at this point, looking round at the four shocked faces.

Enid stood up from the armchair near the fire. 'What! I'm not having that, that illegitimate spawn of my philandering, criminal husband anywhere near me.' Her voice reached a crescendo as she hollered, 'You don't want that baby here, do you, Idris?'

Idris looked at Anwen, eyes wide, before Hywel jumped up, saying, 'Calm down. Let's not fly off the handle, eh? We need to sit and talk about this.'

'What's to talk about? It's my house, and I say it's not staying.'

'I've never been bothered about being man of the house, but if you keep on like this, Enid, I'll have to take a stand. We're all adults. We can talk about this and work something out.'

'*You* can all talk about it. I'm going to Rachael's for some civilised company.'

'Enid!' Cadi called, as her daughter-in-law grabbed her shawl off the back of the chair and escaped via the scullery.

When the back door had slammed, Dr Roberts shook his head. 'I didn't think she'd take it well. What do you want to do?'

Anwen looked over hopefully at Idris sitting at the table, an empty plate and a mug of tea in front of him. 'I'm sorry, Idris. I should have talked to you first.'

'It would have been nice to be consulted, aye. However, I don't like the idea of anyone going into the workhouse, let alone a little scrap of a babby. And she is your sister. Let's have a peep then.' He got up and walked over, peering down at the little girl who was moving her lips as if sucking.

Hywel came over next, pulling back the top of the blanket to reveal a little of her hair. 'She reminds me of Sara as a baby. Has she got a name?'

'Mrs Williams wasn't aware that Delyth had named her, so no.'

Cadi was last to inspect the new arrival, pulling herself out of the other armchair. 'She is like Sara. I understand how Enid feels, for this little one is no blood relation of hers, but she is my grandchild all the same. Can I?' She held up her arms. Anwen handed the baby over to her.

Dr Roberts undid his bag to remove the bits and pieces his wife had found, including two double-ended, curved glass feeding bottles. 'If Miss Bryce doesn't return, there'll be the matter of registering the baby. I can help you with that. At least you know who the father is.'

'We don't know all Delyth's details though,' said Anwen.

'I'll ask my wife to glean anything she can from Mrs Williams. Miss Bryce was having meals there, so they might have talked. She must be fairly local. In the meantime, you'd better see if you can beg, steal or borrow a crib. Preferably not steal though,' he chuckled. 'I'll be back tomorrow to give her another check-up. I don't know how long she was left alone, but she doesn't seem to have come to any harm at least.'

'I don't suppose Delyth had been gone long,' said Idris. 'Babbies aren't known for keeping quiet for any length of time.'

'Talking of which, I dare say she'll be wanting some milk soon. Do you have any?'

'We got some fresh from Morgan the Milk this morning,' said Idris. 'It's in a tin bottle under a wooden crate in the back yard.'

'Make sure you boil it and cool it down till it's nicely warm. And get some more when Morgan comes back round later. And if you have any evaporated milk in the house, that will do the job too. You know where I am if you need me. And Miss Kelly can help you out too. She's a certified midwife, not one of those untrained ones, like that old Mrs Kent on Bryn Street.'

'Thank you for all your help,' said Anwen.

The doctor smiled and took his leave.

'It's a good job we pay subs for our medical care here,' said Idris. 'Otherwise getting so much of the doctor's time could work out expensive.'

Anwen had a sudden thought. 'Oh Idris, what about your family? We were supposed to be having dinner with them.'

'Don't worry,' said Idris, 'I'll get Jenkin to help me carry their food over to us, then Mam can come and cook it here. I'm sure she won't mind when she finds out what's happened.'

'Well, I'd say we had our work cut out for us today,' said Hywel. 'This is certainly not what I expected on Boxing Day.' He rolled up his shirt sleeves. 'Come on then, let's get on with it.'

Chapter Fourteen

Violet came down to the kitchen New Year's Day to the sight of her children at the table with toast and jam in front of them. It had to be from the jars Elizabeth had brought round, for she had no other. Olwen had used the crockery service she had carried from her own home as a Christmas present for Violet. It was an old one, having belonged to Olwen's mother. It wasn't a pattern or colour Violet would have chosen, but at least there were fewer chips and cracks, and the cups all had saucers.

She yawned widely, having not had a good night's sleep. Clarice was singing '*Calon Lân*', in her sweet little voice. As he often did, Benjy tried to join in, only to be told off by his sister. He went back to eating his breakfast, his bottom lip sticking out.

'You can sing to me later, Benjy,' Violet said to cheer him up.

He gave her such a cute grin she felt compelled to give him a big hug. She hugged Clarice next, so she didn't feel left out.

'You're late down, my girl,' said Olwen, striding in from the scullery.

'It's barely seven o'clock. I thought, since it's New Year's Day—'

'It's not a public holiday, you know. If my Charlie were still here, you'd have been up two hours since, getting him ready for work. No excuse for lazing around in bed. And what about the children?'

She wanted to say, *but Charlie's not here to boss me around anymore. And why are you still here?* Instead she said, 'They don't tend to wake before I do. They play in their bedroom when they do.'

'You're getting into bad habits, look you. It's a good job I'm here to put you straight.'

'About that, Olwen. Brynmore must be feeling a little lonely now he's back from his cousins. When were you thinking of going home?'

'He's perfectly capable of looking after hisself for a bit, while I'm here. You and the babbies need looking after for a while. You've become rather morose and you need to snap out of that, my girl, else they'll be carting you off to the—' She looked round at the children, then whispered, 'Asylum.'

A jolt of shock went through Violet. Why would her mother-in-law say such a thing? 'I'm not – "morose" – as you put it. I'm mourning my husband.'

'Are you?' She plodded back to the scullery.

Violet followed her through. Goodness knows what time Olwen had got up, but it looked like she'd scrubbed it from top to bottom. It was the second time she'd done that since arriving. Was she trying to say something about Violet's cleanliness? She'd also rearranged the items in the larder, few as they were these days, swapped round items of crockery on the dresser shelves, reorganised her pans in the dresser cupboard and switched the washing tub and mangle with the tin bath. Violet was afraid she'd start with the furniture next, such as it was.

'I don't know why you said that, but yes, I am mourning Charlie.'

'You seemed very cosy with that Hywel Llewellyn on Christmas Day, sitting next to him and gossiping.'

'I was placed there. Besides, I've known Hywel for a long time, him being Anwen's uncle, see, and then my lodger for a while. There's no point being unfriendly, especially on the day of the Lord's birth.'

'Does he know that, though? Men only need a little encouragement to do something inappropriate.'

'Do you always have to see the bad side of people? You were quite rude to Anwen's family, especially considering they invited you to dinner.'

'Hm! I didn't want to go, I'd already made that clear. Forced I was, by Enid going on and on. Is it any wonder she drove her husband into the arms of another woman?'

It was on the tip of Violet's tongue to say something she knew she'd regret. Better to do something, keep busy. She lifted the teapot from its place on the table. It was light. 'I'll make some more tea. You sit and have your breakfast now. And thank you for getting the children theirs.'

'We're nearly out of tea. You'll need to get some from Mrs Brace later, when you go and do the shopping. We're short of a few bits and pieces.'

Violet thought about the few pennies in her purse. 'I'm not sure I have much money left until I collect the next bit of widow's pension, after the extra bits I bought for Christmas. You don't have a few coppers you could lend me, do you?' Give her, more like, seeing as she was eating their food and not paying a farthing.

'You shouldn't have been so extravagant. It's Brynmore what looks after the money, and I didn't bring a lot with me.' Olwen sniffed.

Violet went about refilling the teapot while her mother-in-law told Benjamin off for talking with his mouth full, poor little lamb.

Having made the tea, Violet put the pot on the table and fetched an extra cup and saucer for herself.

'Sounds to me like you need to get a job, my girl,' said Olwen. 'There's plenty to be had at the screens, sorting the coal.'

Violet had done this work before marrying Charlie and had hoped never to repeat the experience, despite what she'd said to Hywel a few days back. 'Maybe when Benjy goes to school, but I couldn't leave him with anyone now. I suppose I could get another lodger.' When Olwen looked at her askance, she added, 'A single woman. Or a widow with a child.'

'Why do you need to? I'm here to look after Benjamin, and collect Clarice from school if need be. I'm not just anyone now, am I?' She turned to the children. 'Wouldn't you like that, *cariadon*? Your mamgu here to look after you?'

'Are you staying forever?' Clarice asked, wide-eyed.

'For as long as you need me. So, your mam can take a trip to the colliery while she's out shopping.'

Violet nodded, not knowing what else to do. She couldn't last forever on the pittance she received each week, so she'd have to do something. Not having the energy to fight Olwen on this, she gave herself up to the inevitable.

–

Elizabeth's Morris Oxford stopped near the end of Edward Street and Dr Roberts got out of the front passenger seat. He opened the back door for Anwen, who passed the baby to Idris.

Before getting out, Anwen leaned forward, to poke her head towards the driver's seat. 'Thank you, Elizabeth. It was a great help going in the car. And having you and Dr Roberts there was very useful.'

More than useful. She didn't know how she and Idris would have persuaded the registrar to register the baby without them. On their own, telling the story of an unmarried mother and a father in gaol, she and Idris would have sounded far less convincing.

A week had gone by since Delyth had disappeared, with no signs of her coming back. How anyone could leave a poor, defenceless little babby on their own was beyond her. She hoped now she never came back, for who knew what kind of life the little girl would have with such a mother.

'I'm glad we could help. I'll leave you here, if you don't mind. I want to make sure I've got suitable clothes for the start of my new job tomorrow. Hope it goes well with your – family.' She meant, of course, with Mam.

'Thank you. And good luck with the job. I'm sure you'll do better than the man they've just sacked. It sounds like he'd no idea how to do the job.'

'I jolly well hope so.' She smiled, clearly excited, before a cloud passed over her face. 'Though I've still got to tell my parents. I've been leaving it to the last minute, so my mother doesn't interfere.'

'Good luck with that too, then.' Poor Elizabeth, she thought. There was she and Sara who'd been thrown into work they didn't want to do by a parent, and Elizabeth who was threatened to keep away from it when she was desperate to do it. What a strange world it was.

Anwen shuffled out of the car and leaned in to take the baby from Idris, who picked up the sack bag with a baby's bottle and a tin full of milk. She'd been as good as gold for much of the journey, the movement of the car lulling her to sleep.

They all watched as Elizabeth turned the car round and drove off.

In the kitchen, Mamgu was sitting at the table, sewing a hem on a dress. Uncle Hywel hadn't arrived back from the pit yet.

Cadi stood up. 'Hello *cariadon*. How did it all go?'

'It's done,' said Dr Roberts.

'So, will they be able to adopt her?'

'It's a bit early to say, Mrs Rhys. We'll have to see if Delyth comes back to claim her.'

Anwen's stomach rolled at the thought. After only a week she'd grown fond of the dear little scrap. 'I suppose it's a kind of fostering for now,' she said. 'But we'll have to go through the authorities to make it official.'

'That's right,' the doctor confirmed. 'Where's Enid? She told me she didn't work Mondays.'

'Been out all morning, she has,' said Cadi. 'Claimed she was visiting Rhonwen Evans. Very snappy she was before she left.

I've never known her like it. Always been an even-tempered soul, has Enid. I can understand her being upset about Delyth being pregnant, but it's not the babby's fault, is it? Help yourselves to tea. There's plenty in the pot.'

'I'll get some cups,' said Idris.

'I was hoping to have a word with her again,' said the doctor. 'Try to get her to see sense. No point crowding up the workhouse with yet another poor foundling when there's a good home here for her.'

'I'm sure she'll come around eventually,' said Cadi. 'She's a sweet little thing, the babby, looking out at the world with those big, confused eyes of hers. Makes me want to shed a tear, it does. It's as if she knows.'

It was odd Cadi should say that when Anwen had thought the same the moment she'd laid eyes on the baby. As for her mother coming around, she had grave doubts. Enid had barely talked to them all week, not taken one bit of notice of the baby and had been in a quietly foul mood.

The back door slammed and Enid was soon in the kitchen, undoing her coat with determination. 'Spotted Miss Elizabeth's car so I thought you'd be back.'

'Mam,' Anwen started. 'Don't be angry, please. She's only a baby.'

'Yes, Madog's baby. Not mine. Not his wife's. Not that I'd want the bother of another at my age, like Mrs Mitchell on Bryn Road. Forty-six she is, a year older than me, and tired out with a two- and a four-year-old, after a gap of eight years.' She tutted as if the very idea was detestable.

Dr Roberts took the cup offered by Idris and sat at the table. Enid had great respect for him, being a *learned man*, as she would put it, so if anyone was likely to talk her around it was him.

'Enid, sit down please,' he said.

She removed her coat, throwing it onto the chaise longue, and sat reluctantly. Cadi sang softly to the baby, while Anwen and Idris stood together near the stove.

'Would you like to know what the baby's been called?' said Dr Roberts.

'No.'

He drew a breath and let it out slowly.

'Idris and I decided on Sara Cadi, Mam. That's nice, isn't it?'

'You called her middle name after me?' said Cadi, her cheeks bulging with such a large smile.

'Well you're her Mamgu, aren't you? And since she was born on Christmas Day, exactly a year after dear Sara left us, it seemed like—'

Enid scraped her chair back, her hands crunched into fists that she held in front of her. 'She is *not* a replacement for my Sara. And that's stupid, that is, two sisters with the same name. How dare you?'

'Mam, I—'

'Don't you *Mam* me. If you want to keep that – that *thing*, I suggest you live elsewhere.' She grabbed her coat and shoved the door to the scullery open. Soon the back door was heard to slam once more.

Dr Roberts shook his head. 'I really don't know what's to be done.'

'Maybe we have been unfair,' said Anwen. 'After all, look what my father did to her, and now we're expecting her to accept his child by another woman into the family.'

'No,' said Cadi. 'As we've all said, it's not the babby's fault.' She rocked her as she spoke. 'No, not Sara Fach's fault, is it, *cariad*?' Cadi sung a hastily made-up version of '*Sosban Fach*', changing the words to *Sara Fach*.

The baby's eyes fluttered as if not used to the light. Her chin wobbled and her lips pouted a moment before the first mewing cries started.

'Looks like I need to get some more milk ready,' said Anwen, heading to the scullery. This would be her life for a while, and though she wasn't displeased with it, it could be better.

Chapter Fifteen

It was the second day Violet had arisen at five for her new job, screening at the pit. Olwen was already sitting at the table by the time she got to the kitchen, a pot of tea and two cups in front of her.

'You see, it's not so hard when you get used to it, is it?' said Olwen, looking smug.

'I did it for years with Charlie, and before, when I used to work on the screens.' Though it had never really got any easier she thought, but did not say.

'But you've got lazy since Charlie passed. That won't do. Good job I'm here to put you right.'

Violet sat and poured herself a cup of tea without commenting. It wasn't as if there was anything for breakfast, not for her, since the grocer's was almost bare yesterday. There wasn't even any of that *newfangled cereal from that America*, as Olwen had put it. What they had in the larder they mostly had to save for the children, and for supper.

'I'll give you some money before I go, so you can visit the shops later. Hopefully there'll be some deliveries today,' said Violet.

'We can hope. You won't get as much money doing four days a week. You were doing the usual six days when you met my Charlie.'

'Yes, but I didn't have little children then.'

She hadn't told Olwen her idea to do only four days before she'd left to get the job. She knew she'd somehow persuade her otherwise. She'd got the idea from Enid, who was only doing

Tuesday to Friday at the Big House. Bosses were desperate for workers and accepted any hours they could get out of people. That she was missing any of Benjamin's young years tore at her heart. At least the shift finished before Clarice got out of school; that was the advantage of doing an early one. She should be grateful to Olwen, she knew, for she'd given her the opportunity to earn a few more shillings to add to the meagre widow's pension, and yet, if she could have had a lodger instead, she'd have had the best of both worlds.

Violet's stomach rumbled. 'Is there any spare bread left, even half a crust?'

'No, only two slices there are, and them not very fresh, but they must go to the babbies.'

'Yes, they must.' She turned away.

'I'll see what I can fetch for your dinner when you return, and I 'eard someone from the allotments say yesterday that there might be some kale, cabbage and parsnips at the greengrocer's today.'

'It's best to go early, even if there is a queue. There have been a lot more recently, since winter set in.'

'What do you expect, with the boats not getting to Britain? Those allotments aren't enough to fill the gap. And when there are food shortages it's always the young, the old and the ailing what go first. So the babbies and me need looking after.'

Violet felt sick at the possibility of her children becoming ill. Any food they managed to buy would go to them first. Olwen was neither old nor ailing. And hadn't she come to help look after *them*? Yet Violet seemed to be looking after her.

She finished the tea. 'I'd better get going.' She picked up her old, thick shawl from the chair and tied it around herself. She'd rather have worn her coat, it being so cold, but it would get too grubby for going out in if she wore it to the pit. And once she got started on the endless work of sorting coal from stone, she'd soon warm up.

'I'll see you later then,' said Olwen, pouring herself another cup of tea. 'Don't forget your tea tin.'

Violet nodded, picking it up. Her stomach rumbled once more.

Outside her front door, stepping into the dark, she rearranged her shawl to place it over her head. She'd only gone two steps when a voice behind her said, '*Bore da.*'

Hywel, just visible in the lights from the houses, lifted his cap. Idris and Gwilym, beside him, greeted her also.

'First time I've seen you since you started screening,' said Hywel.

She fell in step with them, comforted by Hywel's presence. 'It's only my second day.'

'I was surprised when Anwen told me you were starting there again.'

'I'd rather not be doing it, but Olwen has been kind enough to stay on to look after the children, so I should take advantage.'

'She's not staying permanently though, is she?'

Please God, no. 'It's just until I get myself sorted out.' She wasn't even sure what that meant. It was only a way of stalling Hywel's questions. The growling in her stomach was more than hunger, it was a gnawing stress at what the future held.

'Well, here we are.' Hywel pointed to the gate up ahead. 'Maybe see you on the way out at two.'

'Maybe.'

—

Far from passing quickly, the day had gone exceedingly slowly for Violet at the screens, sorting through the coal, her arms wearied by lifting the heavier bits of rock and her hands scratched by the shingle.

Her heart warmed when she entered her kitchen to see Clarice and Benjamin on the floor, playing with the spinning top.

'Mam!' Clarice jumped up and ran to Violet. Her brother wasn't far behind, hollering a greeting.

Olwen pushed the door from the scullery open. 'What's all this noise? Sit down, children.'

'It's all right,' said Violet. 'For it is lovely to have such a welcome.'

'Undisciplined they'll be if you let them run wild.'

Violet bent down to the children, who attempted to hug her. 'Let me get a wash and changed first, *cariadon*, for you don't want coal smuts all over you.'

'Spoilt, they are. Now sit down and let your mam get washed. I've just prepared the bowl and put some clean clothes out by the fire to warm. They dried well today, in the wind. And I managed to get some bacon scraps to have with the small loaf I found for dinner. There were queues at both shops. Then I took the children for a walk in the woods by the stream and found some turkey tail mushrooms to put with the veg at supper. The food's there for those what look for it. Even in winter.' Her sniff was followed by a 'Hm!' before she went back to the scullery.

It was then Violet noticed the letter, addressed to her, on the mantelpiece. The writing was her mother's. She lifted it off and turned it round to find it had already been opened. Her face puckered with annoyance as it became obvious her mother-in-law had read it.

Olwen appeared once more. 'Oh yes, I found that on the front mat and misread the initial. Thought it was an O but realised too late it was a V. Easy mistake.'

Violet considered her mother's writing. It was very precise. She'd always prided herself on being able to read and write well. She took it with her to the scullery.

Left alone to wash, she lifted the letter out and was soon involved. Her mother was upset. It seemed she'd come across Brynmore in the High Street at Bargoed one afternoon, and he'd complained of his wife being stuck in Dorcalon, feeling she had to look after Violet and the little ones.

She wasn't sure if her mother was upset that she'd 'chosen' Olwen to look after her over her *own mam*, or annoyed that

Violet had 'put upon' *poor Mrs Jones*. Violet shook her head. But she'd been too unwell to come over the Christmas period, according to her father's letter, and too tired to cope with little children. She couldn't have it both ways.

Her own mother staying would have been preferable, for she didn't boss people around or make them feel ungrateful or stupid. She'd suggested her parents move back to Dorcalon a couple of years before, knowing Charlie would never have agreed to move to Bargoed. What was stopping *her* from moving there now though? The thought of finding a new house to rent, of all the upheaval, depressed her. Her good friends were here. And so was Hywel.

She shook the last thought away. Brooding wasn't getting her washed and changed. Her mouth salivated, anticipating the salty bacon and bread. She'd only had tea so far today. After, she'd have to write an appeasing letter to her mother. As tempting as it was to admit that Olwen was unwelcome, she didn't want to cause bad feeling. The last thing she needed right now was any trouble.

Chapter Sixteen

Violet couldn't believe that at last she had some freedom. It wasn't the trip she'd planned; she was supposed to be walking into Rhymney with Anwen, who was also to have enjoyed a couple of hours of liberty. Cadi had willingly volunteered to look after Sara Fach, but the little girl had since come down with the sniffles. Since Cadi had now done the same, Anwen felt uncomfortable at the thought of leaving the pair of them.

Violet had worried about her friend taking on a baby so suddenly like that, but she seemed to be thriving on looking after little Sara. It was a shame Enid had taken against the babby and refused to have anything to do with her. Still, Anwen's mother worked at the Big House on a Friday, so wouldn't have been around to look after her anyway.

So here she was, early Friday afternoon, on her own, passing the last house on Mafeking Terrace. The pit was already behind her. She was cheered by the February sun and brilliant blue sky as it shone on the green valley to her left. Beyond that she could make out the pit at Pontlottyn. The air was more chilled than it had been of late, but the walk warmed her up, even in her worn coat and thin scarf. She'd make the most of her time, looking in windows at items she couldn't afford, maybe fetch a little sweet treat for the children, if she could find one. The sweet jars in Mrs Davies's shop had largely been empty of late. Providing she had enough pennies left, she'd buy herself a cup of tea in a pretty café. It was the most personal pleasure she could hope for in life now.

From behind came a *clip-clop* sound. She turned to see Samuel Lloyd, from Dyffryn Gwyrdd farm. He announced a 'Whoa!' and brought his horse and cart to a halt just ahead of her. He leaned back and looked at her.

'Hello, it's Violet Wynne, if I'm not mistaken.'

'Hello Farmer Lloyd. Yes, and I'm Violet Jones now.'

'Of course,' he said, removing his cap. 'Your husband was with my sons in the Rhymney Pals.' His face displayed the unspoken words, that his late son, Bryn, was killed with Charlie. 'Are you walking into Rhymney, for I'm going in myself and could give you a lift.'

'That would be very kind, thank you.'

His tall, lean frame leapt from the cart and he gave her a hand getting up on the other side. As it set off once more, she gripped the sides, wondering if she'd been wise in agreeing to this. In her childhood she'd had trips in the cart itself, around a field, with the Lloyd children. She'd been braver then.

He dropped her off outside the Imperial Cinema, waving as he set off once more. She looked around, wondering where to start. The cinema was as good a place as any. She examined the posters for the pictures it was showing. There was a Charlie Chaplin film, *The Floorwalker*. She'd never seen one of his, though both Gwen and Anwen had spoken of how comical he was. She moved on down the row, examining the large selection of shops, so many more than in Dorcalon. Mainly, she concentrated on the drapers and outfitters, picking out dresses and fabrics she would have bought, had she been able to afford them.

So taken by her reverie was she, that she didn't spot Hywel until he was right next to her. She started, seeing him there, the green in his hazel eyes more obvious in the sunshine. The shock was followed quickly by a wave of guilty delight.

'Why Violet, I didn't expect to see you here.'

'Didn't Anwen mention we were supposed to be having an afternoon out?'

'She did, but I didn't imagine you'd come on your own. Or that Mrs Jones would allow it.' He gave a chuckle until he saw Violet's serious face.

'I didn't tell her Anwen wasn't coming.' She bit her bottom lip like a naughty child, until it occurred to her just how funny it was. When she giggled, the wide smile he gave in return showed off his dimples.

'I shan't tell.'

'If she knew I was talking to you she'd be very cross. She thinks you're quite the ruffian, isn't it.' She couldn't keep a straight face at this thought. Hywel, so kind and gentle, roused to a passion only when he felt something was unfair or simply wrong.

'Huh! It's a good job she wasn't in the village when Madog Rhys was around then.'

'What are you doing here, anyway?' The thought briefly crossed her mind that, despite his words, he'd visited Rhymney on the off chance she'd be here. No, she wasn't interesting enough for him to bother doing that. Relief entwined with regret, followed by more guilt.

'Having my hair cut. Came straight from my bath, didn't even have dinner. Mr Connor, the hairdresser in the village, has gone away for a few days, see.'

She looked curiously at his dark brown mane. 'I don't see any difference.'

'I haven't had it done yet!' he laughed. 'You planning on a new spring wardrobe?' He pointed at the shop window.

'I'm sure you know the answer to that, Hywel. Just dreaming.' She looked longingly at the blue dress with its wide pointed white collar and long sash belt.

'Ah, we all need dreams.' He cleared his throat. 'I was thinking of popping into Perilli's café for a beverage and maybe a piece of cake after the haircut, treat myself, like. Could I treat you too?' He tilted his head to one side a little, looking hopeful.

It was on the tip of her tongue to say no, better not, but then she thought, *why not?* What harm would it really do to have some adult company for a change, the sort that didn't make you feel you were inadequate at everything you did?

'Yes, Hwyel. That would be nice.'

'I'll meet you outside there in, say, half an hour?'

She nodded. He patted her arm, perhaps for reassurance, but the tingle that went down it brought her whole body alive. It confirmed her initial reluctance but the excitement at spending time in his company was too much to resist.

He grinned broadly, showing some of the pleasure she felt but couldn't quite display.

—

Hywel spotted Violet five minutes after he reached Perilli Bros Refreshment House. The look of relief on her face matched what he was experiencing. He'd half expected her to have second thoughts, to have bolted back to Dorcalon. And who could have blamed her?

'Ah, now I can see you *have* had your hair cut.' She gave his head the once-over. Her deep brown eyes crinkled at the corners. He noticed her black hair was in a neat plait wrapped around her head like a band. It was a style she normally only adopted on high days and holidays. He'd always thought it a little austere for her slim face with its high cheekbones.

'Does it meet with your approval?' he said.

'Of course.'

'Shall we go in?' He pointed at the shop. The window was not rammed full of merchandise like it had been in the past, having but few examples. He opened the door and allowed her to go in first.

'Oh my goodness, it is fragrant in here.' She looked around at the shelves and displays of cigars, tobacco, pipes, jars of sweets and chocolates. As in the windows, there was less than half of what he'd seen here previously.

'Haven't you been in here before?'

'Never. I haven't been to Rhymney in a long while.'

A deep sorrow inhabited him. As far as he was aware, she'd barely been out of the village since she'd married Charlie. He'd never been one for spoiling his wife, from what he could tell. She'd been such a happy soul when she was younger. Now a shroud of despondency always seemed to surround her. Poor, sad Violet, enclosed in her tiny world.

'Good afternoon to you,' said a stout man with an Italian accent. He had a spotless white apron wrapped around his middle. 'How may I 'elp you?'

'We'd like afternoon tea, please,' said Hywel.

'If you'd like to queue by the menu stand, you will be shown to a table.' The man bowed slightly and indicated the place with his hand.

They stepped over to the stand, looking into the tearoom area with its stiff white cloths, red napkins and little vases of greenery.

'This is very smart.' Violet bit one side of her bottom lip and looked worried. 'The waitresses look like maids with their black dresses and white pinnies and caps.'

A waitress came towards them. On her badge was written the name 'Assunta'. She showed them to a table by the window and handed them each a menu.

'We don't have the variety of cakes and pastries we used to, I'm afraid, especially since so many of the boats with sugar on board have been sunk. Just scones, fruit buns and Garibaldi biscuits.'

They both chose tea and a bun. Violet leaned back and seemed to relax at last.

Hywel went to speak, then thought better of it.

'You were going to say something?' Violet asked.

'It's just, I was wondering, how you're getting on with Charlie's mother now.'

She looked at the table for a while then out of the window as two young lads went scuttling by. 'I'd rather she wasn't there, but... needs must as the devil drives, as they say. The devil has driven me to a widow's pension, so I need to work. Having Olwen there allows me to do that.'

His heart sank. It was as if she expected life to get ever harder and had little fight left against it.

The waitress returned with a tray full of tea things and the buns. 'I'm afraid we have to ask our customers only to have one spoonful of sugar with their tea, as we might run out otherwise.'

'That's all right,' said Hywel. 'We both gave up sugar in tea a while back.' He grinned at her to relieve her worried face. No doubt some customers had complained about this. It worked and she went off with a smile.

'Has Charlie's mother *left* his father?' He knew he shouldn't pursue this again, but it had popped out of his mouth without him thinking much about it.

Violet looked weary, closing her eyes for a moment. 'I really don't know what's going on. He keeps writing to her, but I don't know what the letters say or if she replies to them. I just recognise his untidy scrawl. I've tried to ask her a couple of times, but she tells me only that things will work out, whatever that means. In a way, if she was going to live with me, I wish she'd brought Brynmore too. He's a funny soul and much more reasonable.'

'Perhaps you should suggest it? What about your mother. Has she recovered from her cold at Christmas?'

Violet seemed a little happier talking about her own parents. 'She's taken a while but is apparently much better now. I had a letter from her yesterday. It's a shame really.' Her face fell into a frown once more.

'What is?'

She took a sip of the tea before replying. 'That they moved away from Dorcalon. They went to Bargoed to help Ivy when she was unwell after the birth of her fourth baby.'

'Aye, I remember Anwen saying.'

'Then Ivy went and moved to Hereford anyway, so she wasn't there to look after Mam when she had the influenza. If only my parents hadn't moved in the first place.'

'Perhaps they'd consider moving back if you asked them. There's jobs going at the mine here that'd suit your father.'

'I asked them a couple of years back, but they said they were settled where they were. Come on, eat up your bun.'

He had no doubt that this was a polite way to tell him to mind his own business.

After a period of silence, Violet said, 'I'd rather have had a Victoria sponge, but this is nice too.'

'It is,' he said, though he'd barely touched it. 'So, what are your plans for the future?'

'Plans?' She blinked a couple of times and widened her eyes. 'What plans do there need to be? I – I have to bring the children up, put food on the table and clothe them. What else is there?'

Her lack of any hopes depressed him further. 'Well, take me, for instance. I thought I'd muddle along being a hewer for the rest of my life, lodging in houses. It had never occurred to me to do anything else until the accident. Now I'm a deputy fireman and training up to the job, see. It's given me the idea that I can do better for myself, train for something else later, maybe afford to rent a small place of my own eventually.'

'You're an intelligent and hard-working man, Hywel, so that doesn't surprise me. I'm just a housewife. Or widow, now.' She looked down at her lap. 'What are the likes of me supposed to do?'

'All right. Let's say you could do anything you wanted. What would that be?'

'Well… Sitting in McKenzie House with nothing to do but arrange flowers and have afternoon tea would be nice.' She smiled to show she wasn't serious.

'I see, fancy being the manager's wife, do you? I'm sure Mrs Meredith would have something to say about that.' He laughed as he shook his head. 'I can't say she's my favourite person, not friendly and easy-going like Elizabeth, but I've heard she's a hard worker on the various committees she sits on.'

'I wouldn't want to be her anyway, having to keep up appearances and boss staff around. I would quite like…' She stopped to look out of the window, as if deciding what to say next.

'What would you like?'

She turned her attention back to Hywel. 'I admire Mrs Bowen, running her own business. I wish I could sew like her and be able to work for myself. Even Mrs Rhys does bits of sewing for money. I could do it at home, with the children, be independent, like.'

'Why not?'

'Oh Hywel, you've seen my attempts at darning. I'm 'opeless!' She covered her mouth as she giggled.

'Mrs Bowen doesn't only sew. She buys second-hand clothes and sells them on at a profit. Anyone could do that.'

'Usually after she's mended or altered them though.'

'Then there's Mrs Jenkins, two doors up, who takes in washing. You're good enough at that. I was going to suggest it before but didn't get the opportunity.'

'As if anyone would bring their washing to me. Look Hywel, I've got enough on my plate at the moment.'

'Mrs Jones could take in washing while you're at work.'

'Oh yes, I can just see her doing that.' She raised her eyes.

'No, I suppose not.'

'Enough of me. What have you been doing with yourself lately, apart from studying? Anwen says you're hard at it.'

'I'm determined to pass the course. Other than that, I've been to a couple of union meetings with our new rep, David Keir. He's a mad fool in some ways, but a better representative than Philip Hubbard was, God rest his soul.' Hywel quickly brushed from his mind Idris's description of finding Philip after the mine explosion, and how he'd died as they were trying to help him.

'You used to like going to talks and concerts when you were lodging with me. Have you been to any lately?'

He was sure she wasn't really that interested but was trying to keep the conversation away from herself. Fair enough. 'Yes.

I went to that concert in Rhymney a couple of weeks back, with Twm Back and Mr and Mrs Schenck. Lovely playing and singing there was. And a coupla days ago I went to see Charlie Chaplin at the picture house here.' He pointed up the road.

'I do envy you,' she sighed. 'I was thinking as I passed the Imperial that I'd never seen a Charlie Chaplin film.'

'You're joking.'

'I'm not. And I don't remember the last time I went to the picture house. Before the children were born, certainly. And I miss the dramas and operettas at the Workmen's Institute, like *The Bohemian Girl* that was on a while back now. And the talks. They were so interesting.'

'I don't think you'd have enjoyed the last one I went to: "The Humour and Pathos of the House of Commons".'

She shook her head in bemusement. 'Probably not. But if you're asking what I'd really like to do, I'd say it's to get out sometimes, without the children, however much I love them.'

A heavy weight hung on his heart. He had the urge to place his hand on her arm and stroke it, like Enid and Cadi did when people were upset. He daren't though. He took a bite of his bun instead.

'Well, there it is,' she said. 'You did ask.'

'Hmm,' he replied, his mouth full. When he'd finished chewing he said, 'Violet.'

When he didn't continue, she said, 'What? What is it? You look serious.'

He put the bun down. 'I know you said, back in November, that we shouldn't see each other...'

'And yet here we are. I actually said you shouldn't keep popping round because people might talk.'

'Didn't you think they might talk when I was lodging there?' He took a long draught of tea.

'That's different. Lots of men lodge in houses. It's not the same as popping round for no good reason.'

'I'm sorry if you felt that.'

Violet looked him squarely in the eyes. 'Don't take it the wrong way, Hywel. I'm not saying that your company wasn't welcome. I missed you when you went back to Anwen's. You've always been interesting to talk to and are good at helping. Charlie was never really either – oh dear. I shouldn't say that. It's true, though. We had fun together in the early days, and he liked the picture house like me, but always made fun if we went to a drama. And I couldn't get him near a talk. Always was more of a man's man, was Charlie. Women were just silly creatures to him, there to do the, the—' She took out a handkerchief from her pocket and dabbed her eyes.

Hywel placed his hand on her arm and rubbed it once. 'Oh Violet, I'm sure Charlie thought more of you than that. He just wasn't good with words. You mustn't think he didn't care though.'

'If he'd cared, he wouldn't have left us to go off to fight. And he'd have made sure I had more money to buy things for the house, instead of putting it on bets and going to the McKenzie Arms so many nights.'

'I'm sorry he kept you short, Violet. I guess some men think they're entitled because they've earned the money.' When she looked up sharply he added, 'Not that I agree. The women work equally hard and usually longer hours. They look after the home which means the men don't have to worry about it. It's a partnership.'

She looked at him in surprise now. 'I wish more men thought like you, Hywel. You'll be saying next that women should have the vote.' She smiled, looking up under her eyelashes.

'Are you bating me, Violet Jones? You know I agree with women's suffrage. And it'll happen. Just this morning I read in the paper that married women over thirty or thirty-five are likely to be given the vote soon.'

'Good. But I'll still be eight years too young to vote, even if it's thirty. And do widows count as married women?'

He pulled a face and shrugged. 'I've no idea.' At least she'd cheered up now. This was the most spirited he'd seen her in ages. He lifted his cup to take another drink to find it was empty. 'More tea?'

'Yes please.'

He poured the fragrant amber liquid into both cups. 'It would be nice if we could do this once in a while. I reckon it's done you no end of good.'

'It is a nice change. I'm not sure how easy it will be to get away in future. Let's play it by ear, shall we?'

He nodded, adding a little milk to each cup.

'The sun's getting low. We'd better not be too much longer,' she said.

'I'll walk you back—' She was about to protest so he said quickly, 'Just to Mafeking Terrace. Then you can go on ahead and it will be like we'd never met.'

He'd have liked to have told his family about the chance meeting, being so pleased that it had happened and not inclined to keep things from them. But even though it was innocent, it might accidently get back to Olwen. He didn't want Violet in any more trouble. His family would wonder why he'd taken so long when he'd only gone out for a haircut. He'd say something vague about wanting to take a walk as it was a sunny day.

'Thank you for being so understanding, Hywel.'

About what, he wasn't sure.

How much did Violet enjoy his company? As a friend or even a kind of uncle? Or was there more to it? It wasn't appropriate to ask. He'd concentrate on enjoying the rest of their time together instead.

—

Violet's trip into Rhymney the day before filled her mind as she strolled up the road to James the Veg. Luckily Olwen had not asked too many questions about the trip, only about whether some products were available. Violet had managed to pick up some fruit gums for the children and a few toffees for her mother-in-law, purchased from Perilli's before she'd left, since it had slightly more choice than Mrs Davies's shop.

As she reached the end of Edward Street, she glanced briefly down towards Hywel's house before entering the greengrocer's. The heat of guilt swept over her, afraid as she was of giving herself away. Mr James looked up, as did Molly Prior, the mother-in-law of Harold Prothero, one of the men killed along with Charlie. Violet was tempted to back out of the shop once more, weary of the mutual sympathy and looks of understanding all those who'd lost men in the war gave each other every time they met. She guessed it was comforting to some, but it had never afforded her any solace.

'I'm sorry,' the greengrocer was saying to Molly. 'There just isn't much available now, and certainly not much variety. Most of what we had was bought earlier in the day. That's when you need to come. I know there's queues, but better that than missing out. It's the continual cold, see. Not conducive to even the winter veg...' He shook his head. 'So it's the caulis, potatoes or onions that I can offer you. I dunno, I'll be closing at this rate. A man can't keep a roof over his head with such slim pickings.'

Mrs James's voice called something from the back.

'What's that?' He opened a door behind him to have a brief conversation. 'Ah, that's something.' He turned back to his customer. 'It seems you're in luck, Mrs Prior, for Mary Jones has brought down some savoys and a few carrots from the allotment.'

'That's better, for it's sick of cauliflowers and onions I am.'

'Who knows, with America cutting ties with Germany now maybe they'll join in the war soon and help us end it. Anyway, the veg are out the back so I'll have to go and fetch them.' He went through the door.

'Oh, hello Violet dear,' said the older woman, noticing her. 'Getting tired of these shortages I am, especially the meat, the sugar and bread. All things I like.'

'It is worrying. My mother-in-law was supposed to come earlier, but she's been coughing today and didn't feel up to it.' Violet wasn't convinced, for she'd found Olwen had quite a lazy streak about her after her initial cleaning spree. Often things around the house were not completed and Violet ended up doing them herself when she returned from work, or on her days off.

Mrs Prior came towards her, tipping her head to one side and displaying the sad expression Violet knew so well. 'How are you both, dear?'

'Getting on with it,' Violet said lightly, in no mood to be maudlin.

'My poor Brenda do pine so for Harold. I don't know why after what she found out.' She tutted several times.

'I hear she's been unwell.'

'Aye, she is, and I need to speak to you about that. I've spoken to some of the other soldiers' wives already.'

Violet was confused. What had it to do with her and the other wives?

Mrs Prior looked to make sure Mr James wasn't returning. 'This is not to go round the village, but you need to know so you can get tested too.'

'I don't understand.'

'She has the pox.'

'What, chicken pox?' Why would the soldiers' wives in particular need to know that?

The older woman's eyes lifted heavenward. 'Oh you are an innocent. No dearie, syphilis, you know, what men do get when they cavort with,' she leaned in and whispered, 'Whores. Was probably going with French harlots, was Harold, according to Dr Roberts. Not that he put it like that, but that's what he meant. Then passed it on to my dear Brenda. She might not even have known if she hadn't just lost the babby. It was the midwife what noticed the ulcer on, you know, her birthing area. And they do say a lot of the soldiers, missing their conjugals, do be going with the ladies of the night. As if we haven't

199

got enough to contend with in this bloody war. Oh! Excuse me. But it do make me cross.'

Violet felt queasy. It was an awful thing to happen to poor Brenda, who was a kind soul. And what if Charlie had been *cavorting* as Mrs Prior had put it?

'I don't know what to say. Do give Brenda my best wishes. Is there a treatment?' She knew little about the disease except that it could be fatal. She shuddered.

'One developed a few years ago, the doctor said. Injections. Don't know what of, but Dr Roberts do give them to her. Make her nauseous they do, but if they cure her, she can put up with that. This is for your ears only, mind, so you can be checked out too.'

'Thank you, Mrs Prior.'

Mr James returned at this juncture, which Violet was grateful for. As he served the other woman, she considered this startling news. Charlie had certainly been off with her on his last leave. Had he gone to brothels and been more satisfied with what they'd provided in that way? Or had he been unwell and suffering?

Her stomach churned with the possibilities. She'd need to see Dr Roberts straight away, and she needed to work out how she could achieve that without Olwen suspecting anything.

–

'So, what is this about?' Dr Roberts closed the door of his consulting room in the cottage hospital and invited her to sit down. 'You seemed very agitated earlier.'

What a fool she'd felt, waylaying the doctor as he'd left someone's house. At least it had saved her from knocking on his door and trying to keep her concerns private.

'I'm so sorry, doctor, for I don't want to waste your time, it's just...' She took a deep breath. This was highly embarrassing but in his job he'd probably heard most things. 'I bumped into

Brenda Prothero's mother last week...' And on she went, at a pace, relating all that Mrs Prior had said to her.

'I won't lie to you, Mrs Jones, it is true that cases of venereal diseases have gone up dramatically since the war began. We shouldn't assume that all men on the Front use these... bordellos, though. Do you have any symptoms?'

'No, but Mrs Prior told me her Brenda didn't either, and that they only discovered—'

'Yes, yes, I know that. Did your husband have anything on his private parts when he returned, ulcers or wart-like growths? A rash on his palms or soles of his feet? Did he complain about tiredness or painful joints, or of being feverish?'

Violet blushed at the doctor's reference to Charlie's *private parts*. 'No, in fact I'd say he seemed fit. As for any growths, I, um, wouldn't know. You see, we, you know, we didn't, he didn't touch me while he was home, not like that.' Not like anything, as she recalled. He hadn't even kissed her.

The doctor's eyes widened as he stared at her. 'Are you telling me, Mrs Jones, that you and your husband were not at all intimate in any way when he was home on leave?'

She blushed, lowering her head to consider her hands. 'That's right.'

'Then you need have no worries about syphilis. Did you not realise this?'

He must think her terribly ignorant. 'I suspected that was the case, but I wasn't sure see, how exactly it was passed on.'

'I suppose there's no reason why you would know. But you mustn't listen to the scaremongers, though I dare say Mrs Prior had your welfare at heart.'

'She did say she was telling the other wives about it too.'

He huffed out. 'Then I shall expect more worried wives on my doorstep in the next few days.' By the time he'd finished the sentence his voice suggested he'd come to terms with this situation.

Violet rose. 'I'll take up no more of your time, doctor.'

'Good day to you, Mrs Jones.'

She left the consulting room much relieved, as much to be out of there as for knowing that she couldn't be infected.

Chapter Seventeen

Anwen joined the end of the queue for the butcher's on Jubilee Green. She strained to see what was left on the slabs, cradling Sara Fach who was awake and taking in her surroundings hungrily. Cadi's diminutive yet stout body stood next to hers.

'I do so fancy a bit of pork,' Cadi said forlornly. 'But it's been a while since I've even seen any.'

'It said in the paper that it's expensive now as there isn't much. If it has to be rabbit or pigeon yet again, that's better than nothing.' She jiggled the baby as she cooed.

'Hello,' said Gwen's mother, coming up behind them. 'I hope there's something decent left.'

'Hello Ruth. That's just what we were saying.'

'It's all very well saying we have to ration ourselves to two and a half pounds of meat a week, but we're lucky even to get that.' Ruth stretched up, trying to look into the butcher's, as Anwen had done. Next, she put out her finger for the baby to grab. 'My, she's growing fast. And such a pretty babby she is.'

'I haven't seen Gwen in a couple weeks,' said Anwen.

'Been out and about of an evening, and Sundays too. She says it's with some of the girls from work, but I reckon there's a young man involved. She's always been careful about her appearance but seems even more so now. You probably know more about it than I do,' she laughed.

'No, can't say I do.' She felt hurt that Gwen wouldn't have confided in her.

'Not another queue,' a voice complained. They all turned to see Olwen, trudging up past the bookshop. She stood behind Ruth Austin.

'Don't know why you'd expect anything else,' said Cadi, who'd taken against her since her rudeness at Christmas.

Two women came out and the queue shuffled forward enough to get them into the shop. The pungent odour of blood and flesh made Anwen wrinkle her nose.

'Oh dear,' said Ruth. 'I guess one of those sheep heads will have to do. It'll make a nice stew with the bits of vegetables we've got left. Might go and see what's in the woods to make it go further.'

'Next!' called Stanley Pritchard.

Before Anwen and Cadi had a chance to step forward, Olwen started moaning loudly. 'I don't know how you expect the village to live on this. There's hardly anything here. You'd think there'd be a bit more lamb at least.'

Gertie Pritchard, standing next to her husband, called over, 'You should have come in this morning. The early bird it is what gets the worm. Or lamb.'

'I bet you puts by enough for the nobs of the village, like the doctor and them at the Big House. Like I'm told that Prosser used to.'

Gertie gave Olwen a thin-lipped glare while wrapping up a rabbit in paper. 'Not likely. I wouldn't put a sparrow under my counter for that hoity-toity Mrs Meredith, not after she sacked my poor Rose. Innocent of those thefts, she was. She can queue up for her meat like everyone else.'

Anwen felt the heat spread across her face. This could turn very nasty given that Rose had initially accused Anwen of stealing food from the Merediths' pantry.

'Oh, don't go on about that now,' said Stanley. 'That's all water under the bridge. Now ladies, what can I get you?'

While Cadi chose a sheep's head, Ruth stepped up to be served by the assistant. It wasn't long before Gertie was serving Olwen.

'Hello Mrs Jones. Wanting something special today is it, since you were asking about lamb? Oh, don't tell me, your Violet's getting married to that Hywel Llewellyn and want's something for the tea? They've been seen walking home together after work, so it makes sense.'

Anwen glanced at Cadi and Ruth, who were regarding each other. Gertie's comment had not been conveyed in a pleasant tone, more one that was bent on causing trouble.

'I will have you know that Violet is not involved with Mr Llewellyn. He was pestering her and has been sent packing.'

'I was only joking, Mrs Jones. You shouldn't take things so seriously.'

Olwen's face was grey with fury, causing Gertie to display a smile which was almost a sneer. She clearly thought she'd won this battle.

'I will have this sheep's head.' Olwen pointed to the second to last one, her words forced out between partly clenched teeth.

'I've a good mind to—' Anwen started to whisper to Cadi.

Stanley must have picked it up for he said under his breath, 'I'll have words later.'

When Anwen heard a voice asking people to excuse her, she realised her mother had caught up with them. She'd been to the grocer's to get a few items there.

'Here you are. You've managed to get something, good. I was going to say there's some tinned mutton at Mrs Brace's if you hadn't.'

Sara Fach let out a particularly loud gurgle that made those around her laugh, even Gertie. Olwen and Enid alone were unmoved. The baby looked round as if to see where the noise was coming from, her eyes, now darker than they'd been at birth, wide with wonder.

'Well, there's a pretty granddaughter you have, Mrs Rhys,' said Gertie, peering over.

'Why thank you,' said Cadi. 'She's a joy and no mistake.'

'Oh, yes, of course, but I was talking to the other Mrs Rhys.' She pointed at Enid, who twisted round as if she'd been poked by someone. 'Though of course, as her great grandma, you must be very proud too.'

Was this an innocent mistake on Gertie's part or more mischief-making? It was hard to know how much she'd heard. Either way, her mother's face was stiff and she gritted her teeth. She quickly composed herself to reply, 'Babies are babies at this age. They all look the same to me.'

Gertie was soon distracted by Olwen handing over some coins and the incident was over. Except Anwen knew it wouldn't be. She cuddled Sara Fach closer, sore to the heart that she was being used in this spiteful way.

The three women stepped outside the shop at the same time as Olwen, who announced, 'As you sow, so shall you reap,' before heading off back down the hill, her sack bag draped over her arm.

'Whatever that's supposed to mean,' said Enid, twirling on one foot and heading upwards. Anwen and Cadi rushed to catch her up, the older woman struggling with the heavy shopping sack.

'Mam, thank you for not making a fuss about Gertie's comment. I think she just doesn't know.'

'You'll have to accept Sara Fach at some point, *cariad*,' said Cadi, panting. 'For when she grows old enough to understand, she'll be hurt by something that's not her fault.'

Enid came to a standstill, hands on hips. 'You should have all thought of that before you brought her into my house. By the time she's older, I imagine Anwen and Idris will have a place of their own.'

'That's not a solution,' said Cadi.

Enid's reedy body turned back and raced even further ahead. Anwen and Cadi slowed down, both sighing at the same time.

'She'll never come round.' Anwen felt the years of gloom ahead fall on her like a great weight. She kissed the baby's head.

'We'll see,' said Cadi. 'We'll see.'

Violet spotted Hywel exiting the colliery gate just ahead of her. Her heartbeat increased, seeing him there, even though he was covered from head to foot in a sooty grime. As if he'd felt her presence, he glanced round at her before walking ahead with Gwilym and Idris. At the turning for James Street he halted outside the grocer's, saying something to the other two. They headed off whilst he lingered by the shop window.

When she caught him up he said, 'Can we walk the long way home?'

His bright eyes were a startling contrast to his grubby face. His expression stole her breath away, leaving a few seconds before she replied. 'The long way round could mean anything.'

'The least conspicuous way, then.'

A group of miners passed them, causing the pair to look in the window as if trying to locate something.

When they'd moved on, Violet said, 'I'm not sure there is one this time of day.'

A sudden gust lifted the strands of hair that had loosed themselves from her rather severe bun. She wrapped her shawl more tightly around herself. Above, dark clouds raced across the blue sky, slowly devouring it. The workers leaving the shift began to hurry, taking no notice of them.

'We could take the length of James Street and go up round the back, past the allotment up onto Edward Street. Then you could come back down Bryn Road, as if you'd gone up past the shops on Jubilee Green, just to see what was in the windows like.'

'You have it all worked out, don't you?' She frowned but she wasn't displeased. Even a brief time in his company would set her mood up for the rest of the day. 'I have to warn you that Mrs Pritchard told Olwen she thought we were courting and so I have been warned to keep away.'

'Anwen told me about the conversation at the butcher's. Would you rather go straight home?'

'No. I'm not giving in to tittle-tattle.'

'Then I'll go on ahead a little, till we get to the end. Just in case Olwen decides to come down to meet you.'

He grimaced and she couldn't help but laugh. The sound was whipped away by another gust of wind.

'We'd better be quick,' she said, 'for that sky doesn't look too promising.'

He went ahead and she followed on. A thrill coursed through her, due not only to his presence but to the idea of doing something daring, something *naughty*. She'd never been one for disobeying her parents as a child, not like her sister. No, not obedient little Violet Wynne. She wondered now if she'd been missing something.

Passing the bottom of Bryn Street, she glanced up to make sure Olwen wasn't there with her beady eyes. No, only the backs of two screeners could be spied, their shawls flapping in the breeze. She found Hywel next to the side wall of the end house on James Street, hunched over, with his hands in his jacket pockets. He pushed himself away from the wall and they walked up the hill together, along the edge of the village, sheltered by the houses.

'When I was in Rhymney a coupla weeks back, before I met you, I saw a lovely embroidered Saint Valentine's postcard.' The words tumbled out as if he were in a hurry to say them. 'It had roses and a heart. I'd so loved to have bought it for you.' He let out a long huff of breath.

Despite the soaring sensation of delight she said, 'You shouldn't be telling me that, Hywel. For it's only seven months since Charlie passed.'

'I know Violet, I've been telling myself not to, but it's been burning away inside me. I know we can be no more than friends. I just want you to know there's someone who cares about you.'

The revealed passion made his steps quicker. She had to run to keep up.

Before they reached the end of the wall of the last house on Lloyd Street, she called, 'Stop a minute, will you, for it's out of puff I am.' It was an emotional weariness more than a physical one.

He slumped his back against the wall. 'I'm sorry for speaking out of turn.'

'Don't be, for I'll tell you the truth, Hywel. It's...' She searched for the right word, 'nice' not being adequate to what she wanted to convey. 'It warms my heart to know that another cares for my wellbeing, for whatever Olwen says, I don't believe she does. Anwen has her own worries. Gwen is never around. I can't talk to them the way I used to for I don't want to put any more burdens on them.'

He pushed himself away from the wall and took the three steps to reach her. 'I care about you, Violet, and you can talk to me about your troubles anytime you want to. I'm always there for you.'

'Thank you, Hywel. I do appreciate that. And I hope you know you can talk to me anytime too.'

'Oh, I've not many complaints currently, not with Madog Rhys locked up. Though I wish Enid would accept Sara Fach. My main problem is, well, it's not being able to see you whenever I want.'

Violet felt the blush bloom on her face and neck, for didn't she feel the same way?

'What was that?' Hywel looked around the area. 'I thought I heard something. Must be the wind rustling.'

'I'd better get back before Olwen comes searching for me.'

They left the shelter of the last house and headed across the edge of the Edward Street allotment, the wind gusting more vigorously than it had a few minutes before. There were a few drops of rain now too.

'How are you finding screening?' Hywel shouted against the squall. 'Have you got used to it again?'

'As much as I ever will. I hated it when I was a girl. It's not got any better.'

'I read that the government are allowing women to become taxi drivers. Perhaps you could do that instead,' he joked.

She laughed. 'I can't imagine myself driving a motorcar at all, not like Miss Elizabeth does.' Out in the open, Violet became nervous about being seen. 'You carry on, Hywel, I'll head across the allotment. *Hwyl fawr.*'

'*Hwyl fawr, cariad.*'

The rain got fiercer as she found the path between the rows of tatty vegetables, the worse for wear because of the harsh chill they'd experienced that winter. She shivered in her insubstantial outfit, considering briefly what it must be like to sit in a trench all day and night in this weather. But the thought soon dissolved. Despite the wet, icy gusts, inside she was as warm and content as if she were sitting by the fire.

–

Violet walked towards the gate of the colliery after her shift on Monday, looking round for Hywel. Surrounding her was a heavy fog, making it difficult to see who was there. She'd put one of Charlie's old vests on over her corset that morning, having felt the chill as soon as she'd got out of bed. It would be nice, if possible, to walk back with Hywel today; the fog would make it harder for anyone to spot them. It had been a day of bone cold sorting, but at least her imagination had kept her warm.

She hadn't spoken to Hywel since the Thursday before, only spying him from afar at the chapel. Olwen had stuck to her like a piece of goosegrass. Which reminded her that she'd planned to have a look in the small woods beyond Lloyd Street to see if she could find some to bulk out the meagre ingredients they had for supper that evening.

Reaching the gate, a familiar figure came into view. It wasn't dear Hywel, but rather Olwen, standing with one hand holding Benjamin's, the other tucked around the waist of her coat. Her lips were pinched in, leading Violet to suspect bad news.

When Benjamin spotted her, he tried to pull away to run to her, but Olwen held him fast.

'Mam!' he called instead, jiggling on the spot.

Going straight to him, she went to pick him up, only to be stayed by Olwen.

'Don't go making him all sooty now,' was conveyed in a grumpy voice. 'Come along. It's much too cold to be hanging around.'

'You didn't have to meet me from work,' Violet replied, annoyed at Olwen's implication that she'd left them waiting.

'Oh I think I did, madam.' She went a little faster, pulling the boy along, who was whimpering with the effort.

'I don't understand. Has something happened?' A sudden thought struck her, from where she had no idea. Had Charlie turned up at home, alive after all? Had someone mistakenly thought it was him shot in Mametz Wood? She'd heard that some men were never found, that it was only assumed they were dead. How many would turn up by the end of the war, to the surprise – or shock – of their families?

The brief, illogical notion melted away. She'd gained some relief from an idea that would have solved the problem of Hywel. Regret fought with relief, which again became guilt. And anyway, Olwen would surely have been in a good mood if that had happened.

'I'm not one to wash my dirty linen in public, even if you are.'

Whatever this was about, an evening of reproach beckoned. She looked back to the gates of the colliery, if only to steal a glance at the person she'd not be walking back with this afternoon. When she turned back, Olwen and Benjamin had almost disappeared into the fog.

In the house Olwen still said nothing, leaving Benjy to play with his pull-along soldier. She stomped into the scullery with the kettle she'd boiled before leaving the house. After filling a ceramic bowl of water, she fetched the clean clothes in. She left Violet to wash.

As she did up her clean blouse, Olwen knocked on the door, coming in before Violet had a chance to invite her. She closed the door behind her.

'I'm going to say my piece before we go to fetch Clarice from school.'

'I can do that. No need for you to go out again,' she said lightly, trying to lift the mood.

'No, we'll go together, for I now know I can't trust you to go out on your own. Like a female dog on heat, you are.'

'I beg your pardon?' Violet dreaded what was coming next.

'You assured me last Monday, after that embarrassing conversation I had at the butcher's with Gertie Pritchard, that you hadn't been walking home after work with Mr Llewellyn. But today I had her disagreeable daughter telling me she saw you and him on Thursday, secreted away at the end of the village. Thought you wouldn't be seen, I suppose, especially in the drizzle. Said you were no doubt there for a private kiss, she did.'

'We most certainly were not there for a kiss!' It was one thing to be caught out, but quite another to have untrue accusations levelled at her. Nevertheless, she needed a credible cover story. 'I didn't say I hadn't walked home with Hywel before, I said we were not walking out together. On Thursday Hywel was showing me the disappointing winter crop and telling me what they were planning on doing next.'

'I don't really care what he said he was doing, for that won't be what was really on his mind. I know men better than you do, my girl, and they're not to be trusted. From now on I will accompany you back from work every afternoon, and to the school to collect Clarice. I'm certainly not leaving you at home on your own, for if Mr Llewellyn gets wind that you're there, he'll be sniffing around.'

Violet felt the walls of her private gaol close in. An overwhelming sensation of being suffocated assailed her and she found herself fighting for breath. It was the all too familiar panic she'd experienced lately. Breathe slowly and deeply, she told herself. Where on earth had Rose seen them? Then she remembered: Hywel had heard a sound which he'd decided was the wind rustling. Perhaps Rose had even spotted them on the street and followed them round to make mischief. They'd have to be a lot more careful.

'What's for dinner?' she asked, hoping to change the subject.

'Never mind that for now. There's another matter.'

Oh, what now?

'Florrie Harris waylaid me in the grocer's to ask if you were well now. It seems her daughter saw you coming out of Dr Roberts's consulting room at the hospital. Now why would you be there, unless maybe you're pregnant with Mr Llewellyn's baby?'

It took a huge effort to calm herself. She'd never been given to a temper, in fact, her mother had always said she was too mild. But this slur was unacceptable.

'I most certainly am not! And maybe it would help if people in this village minded their own business, for it was for women's troubles that I went to see the doctor, not wanting to ask him here with you and the children around.'

'You shouldn't go bothering the good doctor with women's problems. Got better things to deal with, he has. We women just have to put up with these things.' She gave her head one sharp nod, emitting a 'Hmph!' at the same time. Her expression changed from affront to curiosity. 'Though, maybe those problems would account for your unacceptable behaviour. I knew a woman in Bargoed, got sent to the asylum because her women's problems made her insane. It happens, you know. Such a shame, for she'd three young babbies and wasn't able to see them grow up. The father couldn't cope, so the grandparents are bringing them up now.'

Within the innocent-sounding account Violet detected a threat. Would Olwen attempt to get her committed, using her relationship with Hywel as proof of madness? It was surely far-fetched, but the possibility of it was like a hand squeezing her heart.

'As for dinner, there was no meat at the butcher's for supper again, just some bones to make a stock. That will have to do, with the bits of veg what's left in the larder and some bread and dripping.'

Olwen marched back to the kitchen, like a soldier going to war.

Hywel, oh Hywel. She'd have to find some way of letting him know that their relationship, such as it was, had to end. The very idea cut to the core of her, but there was no other choice. Whatever had made her think it was acceptable with Charlie barely cold? No, it was just as well that Olwen was there to keep her on the straight and narrow.

Chapter Eighteen

Anwen and Idris joined the crowd outside the Workmen's Institute, which sat majestically at the top of Jubilee Green. Like many in the queue, they were sporting daffodils on their lapels, though there were also plenty with leeks too. Cadi stood beside them, proudly carrying Sara Fach, who was smiling at people and blowing bubbles. Hywel stood behind, chatting to a couple of work colleagues. Both the Union Jack and the Welsh flag – white with a small red dragon in the centre – were draped along the iron railings on both sets of the Institute steps. Anwen stared up at the blue sky, enjoying the warm air.

'Well hello there,' said Idris's mother, Meg, joining the end of the queue with his father, Isaiah. She hugged her son and daughter-in-law. 'Where's Enid?'

Anwen glanced at Idris. 'She, um, didn't feel too well.'

'She looked fighting fit yesterday when I saw her. Never misses the St David's Day festivities normally.'

'These things happen sometimes.' Anwen didn't want to admit her suspicions; that her mother didn't want to be seen with 'her husband's disgrace', as she'd heard Enid refer to the baby. It made her sad each time she recalled it. She stroked Sara Fach's face and the little girl beamed at her.

Violet appeared through the crowd, walking along with Benjy and Olwen. When the older woman spotted them, she steered a confused Violet away, scowling in their direction. Anwen could only imagine Olwen was still obsessed with keeping her away from Hywel. She almost wished there was something going on between them. Perhaps she'd worry less about them both.

The crowd looked towards the other end of the park, where the village children were being gathered by the gates. She spotted Jenkin and Evan, in their uniforms with their fellow scouts, helping to organise the younger ones. Finally, they were all in line. The two lads hoisted the British and the Welsh flags between them. The children duly saluted them and so began their procession.

They commenced their first lap of the park, to cheers and salutes from the adults. Little Clarice waved madly at Anwen as she passed by. After the second lap, the crowd stood to one side to allow them into the Institute. They took the left set of steps up, chattering like a field full of birds to each other. After the last one had disappeared, the crowd surged forward, all eager to be as near to the front of the queue as possible to get good seats.

Anwen's family ended up between Gwen's family and Rhonwen Evans, who was standing with her daughter Mabel and granddaughter Lily.

As Gwen made a fuss of Sara Fach, Anwen said to her, 'Bet you're glad to have a day off.'

Her friend had on what must be a new dress – or at least, a good second-hand one. As usual, her hair was perfect along with her rouge and lip stain. But she looked tired.

'I could do with a few more. It's exhausting, getting up so early every morning to catch the motorbus to Ebbw Vale, and the work seems to get heavier and heavier.'

'I, um, hear you've possibly been walking out with someone?' Anwen asked tentatively.

Gwen tutted, but good-naturedly. 'I bet that was my mother with her speculations. I can't say a lot at the moment. I'm seeing Ralph next— oh, I mean, seeing *him* next week.'

'Ralph, is it? I won't tell anyone, don't worry.' Not that there was anything to tell, since she had no idea who he was.

'Thank you. I want to keep it to myself for a while. Which reminds me, I'd have thought Elizabeth would have found us here by now.' She looked out among the crowd.

'I believe she was going to an event somewhere else.' She'd said something vaguely about it when Anwen had seen her at chapel on Sunday. 'I don't see her so much now she's working. Why did you having a suitor remind you of—'

Her enquiry was interrupted by Mabel calling over, 'Have you heard from your Henry recently?'

'Had a letter a week or so back,' said Gwen. 'It sounds like they're still in the back lines, after the battalion getting the hammering it got.'

'That's the impression I had from Maurice. He says it's boring and dirty, clearing up and repairing, but it's a relief, I can tell you.' She looked down at three-year-old Lily, whose hand she was holding. 'I just hope they stay there until the end of the war.'

Gwen's expression conveyed the unlikelihood of that, but she said nothing.

'My niece's husband is still in the thick of it in France,' said Rhonwen. 'Doesn't sound like it's about to be over to me. Did you see in the paper what that General Haig said about breaking the German front and destroying them? Revenge and complete victory, he's after. I can see a lot more of our boys coming to a sad end.'

'Oh don't say that, Mam.' Mabel looked like she was about to cry.

Anwen shook her head. It all seemed so hopeless. 'Let's pray it doesn't come to that.'

Ahead, there was a raucous laugh and some overloud chatter. Anwen didn't recognise the people it was coming from.

Rhonwen pulled herself up to look round the crowd, then leaned forward towards them. 'Did you hear about Maurice's sister, Polly, turning up with her new husband and family?' She tossed her head back to indicate the noisy group.

The women all gathered in to hear what Rhonwen had to say. Idris, Hywel and Gwen's father were chatting instead about the last union meeting.

'I can't see Polly there,' said Anwen, looking again to make sure.

'Look, there she is, just joining them now with that strapping baby.' Rhonwen pointed surreptitiously with her thumb. 'As gaudy and cheap as ever. I heard they turned up a week ago and took the vacant house on James Street, four doors up from Polly's parents. Her husband's called Gus Smith. His mother, sister and brother-in-law, Frances, Hilda and Vic have moved in too. Right noisy lot they are, I've been told. And how he's not in the army I don't know, rather than swanning into a reserved occupation.' She bristled and huffed.

'I hear the reason Polly got packed off to Surrey was because she was expecting,' said Cadi.

'Yes, five-month-old that babby is, so Gus is clearly not the father. Must be someone in the village. Suppose you have to admire him, being willing to take on someone else's mistake.' Rhonwen sniffed.

Anwen knew a lot more about Polly's predicament than those here. She'd not told anyone but Idris and Hywel about it and she wasn't about to now.

'What did she have?' Gwen strained her neck to see more clearly.

'A boy. Herbert. A bit too distinguished a name for the likes of her, if you ask me.'

Anwen only just stopped herself from exclaiming. *Herbert.* That was bold, naming the baby after the father's father. It might have been even more obvious if she'd named him Thomas, but then it was such a common name it was unlikely anyone would question it. It must surely have been done to annoy the Merediths. She wondered if Margaret had come across Polly and the baby yet. It could only be a matter of time, especially as she was one of the organisers of today's *eisteddfod*. Yet it wasn't such a different situation to Sara Fach's. Cadi had accepted her granddaughter, despite her inauspicious introduction to the world. The same was not likely to happen to baby Herbert and his grandparents.

The queue started to move, prompting the women back in order. It wasn't long before they were inside, picking up their children and finding seats. Anwen and Gwen's families settled themselves in the fourth row back. She spied Violet being dragged along to one end of the second row, where she and Olwen settled down with a child on each lap. In the very front row, Polly's new family had taken up prime position in the middle, cawing loudly about their success.

'Here, Mamgu, I'll take Sara Fach now. You must be worn out carrying her.'

Cadi looked disappointed, but handed the baby over. Anwen settled her on her lap. The baby leant against her and sucked her thumb. Idris gently held the tot's tiny arm. Anwen wouldn't be at all surprised if she dropped off to sleep. She looked so sweet, with the shock of brown hair sticking up and her chubby cheek squashed against her chest. She felt the tingle of love she'd experienced from the first day she'd laid eyes on her.

Wandering round by the small stage, Mrs Meredith was consulting with Dr Robert's wife and the under-manager's wife, Matilda Bowen. All were on the parish church council for St Peter's, the Anglican church on Gabriel Street. Anwen watched as Mrs Meredith came down the three steps off the stage. Nowadays she looked even more austere than she had done when Anwen had worked for her. Halfway down the steps she stopped, looking into the audience. She had clearly spotted Polly bouncing the baby on her knee. Her eyes widened for an instant before she rushed from the hall.

The voices gradually hushed when Pastor Thomas came on stage with Reverend Banes, the Anglican vicar. The pastor started with a prayer and a profuse welcome in Welsh. It wasn't long before a grumpy London accent at the front was yelling, 'Talk in the King's language, will you?' It was Gus Smith.

'What, German?' some wag called from the middle of the room.

The audience laughed, with a couple clapping.

'I knew he'd be trouble,' Cadi muttered.

Gus stood and faced his critic. 'What's that supposed to mean?'

Someone else in the crowd called, 'Look at the surname, mun. Saxe-Coburg-Gotha. Not very British now, is it?'

'Ah, shut your trap. Treason, that is, talking against our King.' Gus flung his hand towards the audience as if to dismiss them.

Reverend Banes coughed. 'Could you sit down please sir, so we may begin.' When Gus had plonked himself back in the seat he continued. 'The concert today will be conducted in *both* languages, as is the custom.' He gave Mr Smith a hard stare. 'The proceeds will be going to the Welsh Soldiers' Fund, as it has done the last two years.'

Anwen had never had much time for Polly, what with her being mean to the younger children when they'd been at school, but she felt sorry for her in that moment. What a brute of a man Gus Smith seemed. The contrast between him and Tom must surely have occurred to Polly. Yet, deep down, behind his fine manners and easy charm, was Tom any more enlightened where women were concerned?

The afternoon began with harp music, followed by performances from the choirs of the church and various chapels, voice soloists and the school choir. There were addresses delivered on St David and '*Islwyn, His Life and Poems*'. Sara Fach fell asleep. The children in the hall shifted, whispered and napped. Tomorrow would be their day, when the school would have its traditional *eisteddfod* back in this hall, with relatives looking on proudly, cheering them on to win in their music, speech and drawing contests. She'd already asked Cadi to keep an eye on the baby, so she could watch Clarice perform '*Ar Hyd y Nos*' as a soloist, with her pretty, piping voice.

When it was all over, the audience applauded, some standing when the performers came on stage together to bow. The Smiths, however, took this as their cue to vacate their seats.

Anwen and her family got up to depart, taking the steps to the exit. Sara was awake now and fascinated by the people passing by. Down the bottom of the steps, the Smith family were still gathered and looked, if their expressions were anything to go by, to be having an argument.

'You didn't mention nuffin' about it being in Welsh,' Gus was saying to Polly, who was half turned away from him, holding the sleeping tot.

The mother and sister stood close by, arms crossed, for all the world like Cinderella's stepsisters.

The four relatives walked off, leaving Polly looking despondent, leaning against the wall. She didn't know what compelled her, but Anwen felt she should stop to talk to her.

'Hello Polly. How are you?'

'We'll go on and meet you at home,' said Idris, passing by with the others. 'Shall I take Sara Fach?'

'No, it's all right.' She smiled up at him as he stroked her face.

'Fell on your feet, didn't you,' Polly said as Idris walked away. 'Thought you'd broken up with him?'

'We got back together. Got married in August.'

The other woman raised her eyebrows and smirked. 'Looks like you had no choice either. You're not so different to me.'

'Sara Fach's my sister, not my daughter.' The lack of her own baby hit her anew. Each month she hoped her flow wouldn't arrive, but it always did.

'What, your *mother* had another baby? She's past it, isn't she?'

'No, she's not the mother.' She wished now she hadn't bothered stopping, though Polly would hear rumours around the village sooner or later. Better she got the truth. 'My father had a fancy woman what got pregnant. But she ran off the day after she had the baby. My father's in gaol, as you may already know.'

'I had heard something of it. Sounds like you had a good deal to put up with, from what my mother told me.'

'Where is your mam, by the way? I didn't see her today.'

'Oh, she, um, isn't well. Bit of a chest, you know. My sister's looking after her.' She jiggled the baby a bit more, though he was quite content.

'That's a shame. I hear you've called your boy Herbert.'

'Gus chose it. We call him Herby for short. I was lucky to meet him, I suppose. Neighbour of my aunt's, he was, him and his family. Funny really, because he's from Hackney originally, not far from where I was born, in Whitechapel.' She sounded wistful.

The places meant nothing to Anwen. She gathered only that they must be in London because that's where Polly had moved from as a child.

'I'd better get going,' said Anwen, having run out of things to say. There was a lot she'd have liked to ask but it didn't seem appropriate. 'Mam's been putting together a tea, as much of one as you can now.'

'Your mother wasn't here either, then?'

'Felt a bit under the weather, she did. I hope you all settle in quickly.'

'Me too.' Polly didn't look hopeful.

Anwen smiled before she walked off. Despite the less than warm relationship they'd shared over the years, she felt a strange affinity with Polly. Goodness knows why. 'We've nothing in common, have we, Sara Fach?' she whispered to the baby, then kissed her woollen hat.

Chapter Nineteen

Violet's parents had only been at the house three days, since Good Friday, and already she was wishing they'd go home. She'd longed for their arrival, thinking it might make the days with Olwen more bearable. Instead, the two mothers had sniped and endeavoured to outdo each other in helping out, like it was a competition. Her father, too tolerant, had simply raised his eyebrows and smiled.

'All I'm saying is, the Russian people might be better off without a tyrant like Tsar Nicholas ruling them.' Her mother, Doris, was spreading margarine and the last of Elizabeth's jam on thin slices of bread for the children's early dinner. 'They don't have a democratic government over there, like we do, and my understanding is—'

'*Your* understanding? We women don't need no understanding of it. We should keep to what we do understand, and that's looking after the home.' Olwen eyed Doris's activity closely, looking ready to jump in and grab the knife to take over the spreading. 'I'm sure Ioan will agree with me.' She looked towards Violet's father.

'Doris is more informed about such things than me,' he said. 'Her father was involved in the establishment of the Miners' Federation back in the late 'eighties. She was brought up with the politics.'

Olwen humphed as she placed herself behind Clarice. She pulled a brush out of her apron pocket and started tidying her hair, at which her granddaughter started whining.

'And since Mr Lloyd George has just announced a bill to enfranchise married women over thirty, it looks like he agrees with me too.' Doris placed the pieces of bread on the children's plates. 'Now eat up, *cariadon*, for the Sports Day do start soon and your tadcu do be keen to see the seven-a-side football.'

'Why don't you go now, Da, since you've finished your dinner?' said Violet. 'The tournament's already started. It's taking place on the field at the end of West Street. Idris, Gwilym and, and, Hywel are playing in a team called the Dorcalon Rovers.' She longed to see the matches herself, though not out of any fondness for football.

'I'd like to go and support them. I think I will.' He headed off to the hall, calling, '*Hwyl Fawr*,' as he went.

'Sports Day on an Easter Monday,' Olwen mumbled. 'What's that got to do with the Lord's resurrection?'

'It's a celebration of the wonderful miracle,' Doris countered, preparing more slices of bread.

'While our boys fight and die.'

Violet sat to eat her lunch. 'They do such things in the front lines too, for I recall Charlie mentioning a sports day of sorts in one of his letters.' It had been the only communication from her late husband that had displayed any kind of enthusiasm.

'Who's dying, Mam?' Clarice asked, her little face puckered with worry. Since being told of her father's death she had picked up on the word in all sorts of overheard conversations, worrying about those who had passed on.

'No one is, Clarice. Eat up, there's a good girl. You can enter some of the races this afternoon. You'll enjoy that.'

This information soon put a smile on her face.

'Can I go in races?' Benjamin asked, his eyes wide with hope.

'You're still a little young, I'm afraid, *cariad*. But I think there might be a couple of stalls selling treats.'

That cheered him up and both children ate quickly, eager to get out to the fun.

'Well done, Clarice!' Olwen had her arms open ready to receive her granddaughter as she rushed back from coming second in the under-seven's race. But Clarice managed to bypass her and go to her mother first, throwing her arms awkwardly round her coat. Violet experienced a great deal of satisfaction at that, scolding herself for being petty.

'What a fast girl you are.' Violet picked her up, though it was an effort these days, and hugged her tight. Their puffs of breath met in the cool air, for the sun lent little warmth to the day. 'You were one of the younger ones too.'

'I was only beat by Willy Harris, and he's *very* fast.'

Benjamin jumped up and down. 'Clary won, Clary won.'

'No, silly,' said his sister. 'I was second.'

'Come here, lovey,' said Olwen, getting to her granddaughter before Doris did.

'I think that deserves a treat, don't you?' said Ioan. 'It can also serve as a celebration for the Dorcalon Rovers winning the tournament. Mrs Davies must have been saving the sweets up for this, for there were near empty jars when we went in the tobacconist Saturday.'

'Yes, and a pretty penny she'll no doubt be charging for selling them on a stall,' said Olwen.

'Half of which is going to Netley Hospital,' Violet countered.

'Why don't you have a go in the widows' race?' said Olwen.

The word 'widow' hung in the air, at least for Violet. It didn't seem right that she could be one, not at her age, though it happened to plenty of others. She felt suddenly old, past her best. What was left in life for her now, but to work for ever more with her mother-in-law in the house to look after the children? At least for the next ten or so years.

'You gone deaf?' said Olwen.

'I'm sorry. No, I won't go in for the widows' race.'

'Quite right,' said Doris. 'As if you need reminding. Tug-of-war would be fun. You might be slim but you're strong. Get that from my family, you do. I think Clarice is going to be just like you.'

'I'm going to enter the egg and spoon race, over there,' said Olwen. 'Much more ladylike.'

'Well let's come and watch you then,' said Doris. 'Always a laugh they are.'

As they all headed off, Ioan took his daughter's arm. 'Why don't you go and find your friends? There's three of us to look after the babbies. I saw Anwen and Gwen just now.'

'Can you keep an eye on Mam and Olwen? They seem determined to be in competition about everything.'

'Aye, of course. When is she going home? I don't wish to pry, but she seems to have got her feet under the table. I thought she was only coming for a bit to help you out over Christmas. And what does Brynmore think?'

'I've asked but Olwen only says it's not my business. I'm wondering if she's left him. And the thing is, Da, her being there means I can do some work, for the widow's pension isn't up to much.'

'Mm. Brynmore didn't say much when we saw him, but he didn't seem pleased about the situation. It's such a shame you had to go back to the screens, but as long as you're sure. Nice-looking girl like you should be able to get another husband.'

'Oh Da! Charlie's only been gone eight months. And I wouldn't take on another man just for his wages. What kind of woman would that make me?'

'Plenty do. There's no shame in it. Got to survive, haven't you? I wish we hadn't moved to Bargoed, especially now our Ivy's moved to Hereford. Anyway, you go and find your friends.'

'Thanks, Da. I haven't got to see them much recently, what with Olwen always keeping— that is, Olwen being around.' She was about to say *keeping an eye on me* but didn't want to cause any more friction in the family.

Violet walked through the crowd, her neck stretched, searching for Gwen and Anwen.

'Violet! Wait up.'

She wheeled round to see Hywel dodging past Polly and Gus and his family. Turning her head this way and that, she made sure Olwen wasn't around. By this time he'd caught her up.

'I haven't seen you in a fortnight.'

'No, it's better that we don't see each other, Hywel. People are talking and we don't want them getting the wrong impression.'

'Why? We haven't done anything wrong.' Hywel looked like he was about to take her hands but thought better of it.

'People will jump to their own conclusions, you know that.'

'Is it Olwen you're worried about? Surely she'll be leaving soon, she's been here long enough.'

'I think it might still be a while yet. I need her help, Hywel.' She kept looking into the crowd, making sure neither her mother-in-law nor anyone else bent on trouble was around.

'Maybe… maybe there could be some way I could help you. Eventually. When the time is right.'

She wasn't sure what he was getting at and she didn't want to explore it too deeply. Her next-door-but-one neighbour came close by, causing Violet to say loudly, 'I hear your team won the tournament. Well done.'

'Oh, aye.'

He looked confused until Violet said, 'Hello Mrs Prowse, enjoying the games, are you?'

'Goodness yes. It's nice to be out, even if it is a tad chilly.'

She soon passed by, much to Violet's relief.

'Look, if you need the money and want to get rid of Olwen, I know of an older gentleman who's looking for new lodgings as he's just retired and his wife's not long passed.'

'Thank you for thinking of me, Hywel, but no, I'll keep things as they are.' It was easier, and she needed a quiet life for now. Battling Olwen was exhausting, and she'd simply run out of puff.

There was the sound of music. Violet realised that the Dorcalon Silver Band, such as it was with its eight instruments, had started up again. It had only been formed recently, by Gwen's father, who played the euphonium. The band included Mr Schenck's nephew, Noah. The musicians were standing on the road overlooking the field. Everyone stopped to look. Herbert Meredith, who'd opened the event earlier, had also returned with his wife. Everyone moved in as it appeared he was about to say something. The band's short tune, clearly an introduction to get their attention, came to an end.

'Ladies and gentlemen,' Mr Meredith began, his voice clear and carrying well across the field. 'My good lady wife and I received a telephone call, not fifteen minutes ago, from one of the counsellors to say they'd heard that the United States has officially declared war on Germany.'

A cheer went around the field. Violet's neighbour, now close by again, called, 'Perhaps this war will come to an end a bit quicker and we can get our boys back.'

Mr Meredith held his hand up to silence them. 'Furthermore, there is news that Cuba and Panama have also joined the allies against the German and Austro-Hungarian forces.'

A further cheer went up.

'Now, please, return to your afternoon of fun.'

The Silver Band started up once again, with a rendition of 'Pack Up Your Troubles in Your Old Kit-Bag', prompting much of the crowd to join in. Singing louder than anyone else was Gus Smith and his brother-in-law, Vic. The tune came to an end and the crowd headed to the next set of races, chatting more happily even than they had done before the announcement.

At last Violet caught sight of her friends. She rushed to them, dodging various people as she went.

'Violet!' called Gwen, holding out her hands to her friend. 'Your da told us you'd be looking for us. Let off for good behaviour, is it?' She laughed. She had on yet another dress that Violet hadn't seen before, daringly calf-length, with a felt hat sporting a narrower brim than normal.

'How are you getting on?' said Anwen, putting one arm through Violet's.

'Oh, I'm fine. It's nice having Mam and Da to stay.' She wasn't about to burden her friends with her problems.

'Let's go to the women's under thirties race,' said Gwen. 'One of you should have a go.'

'You were always the fastest of us,' said Violet.

'I'm too exhausted these days. Don't even think I'll manage the allotments this spring.'

'No wonder when you're always out,' said Anwen. 'It's that young man who's getting the benefit of your company these days.'

It was the first Violet had heard of it. She felt left out.

'Now now, don't pry,' said Gwen, grinning. 'I wonder where Elizabeth is today.'

'Mam overheard that she was going off to a concert somewhere,' said Anwen. 'She had the impression it was some suitor or other. I'd have thought she'd have mentioned it though, if that were the case.'

'Well well,' said Gwen. 'That's something.'

'Why's that?' asked Violet.

'Oh, no reason in particular.'

'I'm going to have a go at this race.' Anwen surged ahead.

They arrived as the women were lining up. Rose Pritchard was among them, along with Polly's sister-in-law, Hilda.

Violet considered them all for a second. 'Oh, do you know what? I think I will have a go. Why not?'

She just registered Gwen's eyes widening when she headed off. She'd never been the bravest of the three of them, liking what she knew, not feeling herself capable, but she wanted, on this day, to have a small adventure. She lined up on the opposite side from Anwen, not wanting to be obvious competition. On the side lines she caught Hywel's eye, his face registering the same amazement as Gwen's.

Soon they were off. Violet didn't mind if she didn't win, providing she wasn't last. This thought propelled her forward. To her surprise, she was soon fourth, with Rose and Hilda battling for first position. She looked behind to find Anwen two people behind her.

As they raced to the finish it became clear there was some trouble ahead. Rose and Hilda seemed too close together, almost touching. No, they *were* touching, and not by accident. They were pushing each other! There were cheers and cries of disdain from the crowd. Only yards before the end, Hilda pushed Rose so hard she fell over. Initially triumphant, she went to spring ahead, only to have her heel grabbed by the prostrate Rose, causing her to tumble over. The woman in third place had to dodge to avoid them, leaving Violet to take first place.

Over the finishing line, she bent over, clutching her knees. She registered the cheers for her among the booing for the troublemakers. Looking back the way she'd come, she saw Anwen come in next. Behind her it was chaos, with Gus and Rose's mother helping their own family members up whilst shouting at each other. Vic and Frances joined the fray which soon included Rose's father and James the Veg.

Inevitably, Sergeant Harries turned up on the scene with PC Probert, ordering the quarrelling groups apart and telling them to go about their business.

With the brawl ended, Violet was awarded her rosette by Mrs Meredith. Clarice and Benjamin ran over to cuddle her. Her parents weren't far behind with enthusiastic praises, along with her friends. Olwen skulked at the back, saying nothing. A few yards away Violet spied Hywel, waving to her in congratulation. She couldn't help thinking she didn't deserve it. If it hadn't been for the scuffle, she'd have come in fourth.

Gertie Pritchard went by with Sergeant Harries, bending his ear with a constant stream of words.

'We shouldn't be surprised it was them what caused all the fuss. Look at the way they treated Esther Williams when she did that sewing work for them, saying it was shoddy and refusing to pay her, but I'll tell you, Sergeant, she's done plenty of work for me and neat as a pin she is and say what you will about her gossiping and interfering, but she has a steady sewing hand, does Esther.'

The diatribe faded as the two of them walked away.

'Gertie Pritchard sticking up for Esther, now there's a match made in heaven,' said Gwen, laughing. 'Come on, let's buy some sweets while there are still some available. No doubt Mrs Davies will sell out and the jars'll be empty in her shop next week.'

She led the way followed by Anwen and then Violet, who took a last look around to see if Hywel was there. He wasn't.

—

Violet and her friends got to the end of the field closest to the back of the school a couple of minutes before the men's under thirties race was due to begin. It was Margaret Meredith who was to start this race.

'Look, there's Idris and Gwilym, with Noah Schenck!' Anwen pointed at them as they took their places.

'Oh Lord, and that Gus and Vic are taking part as well,' said Gwen. 'I see more trouble ahead.'

'They've been warned,' said Violet, 'so hopefully they'll behave.'

The race began. It was soon clear that Gus and Vic were not bothered about what the local constabulary thought. Their elbows were flying left and right, knocking their opponents out of the way.

Gwen threw her hands up. 'Unbelievable!'

Margaret Meredith's voice called warnings to the men, as she hurried along the line of the race, trying to keep up. Her voice became shriller with orders. By the middle of the race, the union rep, David Keir, who'd had a spat with Maurice

Coombes and the other soldiers in the pub before Christmas, had taken umbrage. He started pushing Vic back. He was soon joined by his pals, which in turn brought Gus back when he'd been speeding on ahead. The rest of the men, Gwilym and Idris included, stopped racing and looked on, shaking their heads in disbelief.

'Not again,' said Gwen. 'And what does Mrs Meredith think she's going to achieve?'

Margaret was running in dainty little steps across the race-track, all the time demanding that they *stop this minute*!

'She's brave,' said Violet, just at the moment the manager's wife reached the rabble.

The next thing they knew she was screaming, her hand pressed against her cheek. By this time, the two policemen had turned up again with Mr Meredith.

'Someone hit me,' Margaret cried. She looked around at who was close by. 'Him, him there.' She pointed towards Vic.

'It weren't me. And you were only clipped. Serves you right for getting in the way, you silly bint.'

'I *beg* your pardon?'

Several of the other racers went to speak, but Noah got in first. 'It was Gus Smith.'

Gus folded his arms, showing off the muscles through the thin shirt. 'People are picking on us because we're English.'

'Are you sure, Mr Schenck?' asked Sergeant Harries.

'Schenck?' Vic screwed up his face and glared at Noah. 'Bloody German are you, like that bookshop owner? Your father, I bet.'

'He's my uncle, and I'm Dutch, actually,' he said in a Welsh accent. 'But I don't even remember the Netherlands much.'

'Anyway, we all saw it,' said Gwilym, butting in.

The other racers agreed.

'You would bloody say that.' Gus slowly turned, taking them all in. 'You'll regret turning on us.'

'Now, Mr Smith, I'd be careful what you say,' warned Harries. 'I'll assume for now it was an accident. But we'll have no more being rude to the manager's wife. This race is at an end. Move on to the next one please. And no more trouble, for I'm not inclined to arrest anyone on this happy day, but if I have to, I will.'

A strident voice alerted Violet to her family, a few yards away. Olwen was pointing her finger at Polly Coombes, or Smith, as she now was.

'What have you brought with you to our village, eh? I've 'eard about you, cheap piece of nothing.'

Anwen went over to them. 'I think that's enough now, don't you? It's not her what's had the argument.'

Polly looked close to tears, holding baby Herby to her as she shuffled away. With her victim gone, Olwen turned on Violet. 'See the kind of company that ruffian Hywel keeps?'

Violet was confused. 'But it was Gus and Vic who started the trouble. Hywel wasn't even in the race, being over thirty.'

'The Smiths were egged on by Gwilym and Idris, I saw it. And they're all friends.'

Anwen squeezed her lips in. 'Do you mind, Mrs Jones, but you're talking about my husband and my uncle. And I can assure you that neither Idris nor Gwilym had anything to do with the fight, and they, along with Uncle Hywel, are peaceful men.' She turned towards her friend. 'I'm sorry Violet, it's not your fault, but I'm joining my family now.'

As she walked off, Gwen said, 'I'm going to find my parents and mamgu too. Take care.'

And they were gone. Violet had never felt so alone. She knew her friends didn't blame her, but she was the one hosting Olwen at her house.

She wanted to shout at her mother-in-law, but all she said was, 'Where are Clarice and Benjy?'

'With your mam and da. I needed a rest from them, spending all day with them like I do.'

'I'm going to find them.' She'd console herself with cuddles from her babbies and they could watch the rest of the races together. The tug-of-war was due soon, which was always entertaining. These cheerful thoughts she used to dampen the tears stinging her eyes. Anwen would almost certainly tell her family what Olwen had said. Not that Hywel would be surprised.

She spotted her family and put on her biggest grin as she hurried to join them, but inside she was hurting.

–

Hywel closed the front door and ran across the road, to where Gwilym was bashing a hammer against a piece of wood.

'So what is it you'd like me to do then, mun?' He raised his voice above the din.

Gwilym stopped and looked up. 'Is Idris coming to help?'

'He and Anwen have gone for a walk up Twyn Gobaith. They're taking advantage while the sun's out, so Cadi's in charge of the babby.'

'I guess he has a wife and family to think of now.'

'Aye, he does that.' Hywel sighed thoughtfully.

Gwilym put the hammer down on the box of tools beside him and hunkered down on a mound of grass that edged the allotment. 'We can't all be so lucky, to meet the love of our lives.'

'It's not the meeting that's the problem, though, is it? Not for me. Have you never met anyone you'd like to settle down with?'

'Had a slight crush on Gwen years ago, but, no.'

'Well, you're only twenty-five. Plenty of time.'

'Have you talked to Violet recently?'

Hywel was beginning to wish he hadn't confided in Gwilym. That's what having a pint at the public house with a friend when you were feeling low did for you.

'What, with Mrs Nosy Parker ruling her life? I've begun to wonder whether having Olwen there is a convenient way of keeping me at arm's length.' There, he'd said it.

'And maybe with good reason, for it sounds to me, from what you've said, that she is fond of you, but still mourning Charlie.'

'Oh what's the point of going over and over the situation? It doesn't alter anything. Change the subject, shall we?'

'Whatever you want.' Gwilym picked up the hammer, turning it in his hands.

'You'd think you'd have enough to do with work and running the allotments without taking on the chickens too.'

'I like to have plenty to occupy me. It would probably help you too, to keep busy.'

'When are these chickens coming?'

'In a fortnight or so, a coupla dozen. We were supposed to get them last year, but Mr Lloyd found he was short in the end. He's managed to get a load more this year as he's being encouraged to send eggs to the Front.'

Hywel sat down beside his friend. 'Thought he was a sheep farmer, not a poultry one.'

'I guess the government's trying to get as much out of the farmers as they can. Though I dare say Lloyd will be paid well enough for them. Still, it's kind of him to set us up with that many. It'll help out a bit, even if they're only for the children. Ah, here are Evan and Jenkin. They said they'd help too.'

'How was Mr Beadle?' Hywel called, knowing they had paid their customary Sunday afternoon visit to him.

The lads had caught up before Jenkin said, 'He seemed a bit brighter.'

'He even talked about coming back to lead scouts again,' said Evan.

'He shouldn't get ahead of himself, though it's good he's thinking positive. Been too down in the dumps recently,' said Gwilym.

Hywel worried about Cadoc's ongoing memory losses. He doubted now he'd ever be back to normal.

'So, you gonna help with this then?' Gwilym pointed to the planks of wood and the wire on the ground.

'Of course,' said Evan. 'Cyril and Emlyn did want us to go up the woods, but I said we were going to help you seeing as we're working men now.' He stretched to make himself taller and folded his arms.

Gwilym cuffed him lightly across his head.

'Hey, don't do that, mun!' He straightened his hair so the middle parting was back in place. The new hairstyle was a little too grown up.

'You wait till you're hewing coal, then you can call yourself a working man.'

'I'm looking forward to the chickens coming. They're funny creatures,' said Jenkin. 'Especially those Houdans Farmer Lloyd has. All mottled with funny furry hats on. That's what it looks like, anyway.'

'If we look after them properly and keep them looking good like, maybe we could even enter them into a poultry show in Aberbargoed.' Evan looked hopeful.

'We don't want to be running before we can walk, eh *bach*?' Gwilym passed his brother a piece of wood and a saw. 'Now let's get on with it.'

Chapter Twenty

It was a pleasant day when Hywel, Gwilym and Idris climbed Station Road after their shift. They headed away towards Jubilee Gardens, Hywel lapping up the cheery brilliance of the May sunshine as it peeped out from behind a cloud. It had been playing hide-and-seek the last couple of days.

As they approached Schenck's bookshop, they became aware of a loud rapping. The mine manager's wife was banging on the door of the baker, next door to the book shop. Mr Schenck was already there, talking to her.

'I'm afraid, Mrs Meredith, that the baker's has closed,' he was telling her.

She turned to look at him, pursing her lips. 'Why is that? It's only half past three. It's supposed to be open until six o'clock.'

Hywel stepped forward. 'No, what Mr Schenck means is, it's closed down, coupla days ago now. Mara Pane's been losing money since flour's become scarcer and she's had fewer loaves to sell. And that was before King George told us to eat a quarter less bread. She's moved in with her sister in Deri.'

Margaret stepped back from the door. 'Well where is one supposed to acquire bread then?'

'Mrs Brace the grocer is now selling it,' said Mr Schenck. 'I believe it's coming from a baker in Rhymney. I doubt they have any this time of the day, but it's worth a try.'

The bookshop owner was not his usual jovial self, his posture being somewhat slumped and his hair not as neat as it was normally.

'Really, it's bad enough that one has to buy one's own bread.' Margaret put the back of her hand to her forehead and closed her eyes.

Hywel glanced at Idris with a slight smirk. It would do Mrs Meredith good to see how the other half lived, though it was more like the other ninety percent.

'It's what everyone else has to do,' Gwilym said.

They didn't notice Esther Williams until she said, 'Being disrespectful to Mrs Meredith, are you, Gwilym Owen? Don't know why I'd expect anything else. They're nothing but troublemakers are the Rhyses, Hugheses and the Owens.' She gave the three men an unflattering once-over.

'Well I'm in the clear then,' Hywel quipped, 'for I'm a Llewellyn.'

He realised it was an ill-judged attempt at humour when Esther replied, 'You're the worst of the lot, you are, sniffing around a married woman.'

'If you are referring to Violet Jones, then she's a widow,' said Hywel, attempting to keep calm. 'Oh yes, I know that Olwen Jones has been spreading rumours about me, as have Rose and Gertie Pritchard. But I have simply been a friend to Violet, who used to be my landlady, and—'

'That wasn't right, either,' Esther interrupted. 'Mucky goings-on with young married women taking in men as lodgers. No, you're all the same, a Rhys by blood or not.'

'Well there I have to disagree with you,' said Margaret, looking down her nose at Esther. 'Anwen was an excellent maid and Mrs Rhys has been an invaluable worker, albeit part time. And if Rose is involved, it's bound to be a lie. I wouldn't believe a word she tells you.'

Her voice got much louder during the last two sentences. It was soon clear why. Rose had appeared around the corner.

'What are you saying about me now, you old cow?'

'Please, Miss Pritchard, some decorum please.' Mr Schenck did his customary slight bow.

'Oh bugger off, you silly fool,' said Rose.

'Please, do not be talking to my husband in that manner.'

They all turned to see Mrs Schenck standing by the book-shop window nearest the door, her fair hair piled high on her head. Her clothes, a cream, high-necked blouse and a brown skirt, were plain but neat. Under her arm was what looked like a closed ledger.

'It's all right, Mirjam,' Mr Schenck said, kindly. 'I will deal with this.'

'But it is not all right. Already we have suffered misfortune today, and you do not deserve this woman's words of censure.'

'Why, what's happened?' Hywel asked.

'It is nothing to be concerned about, just, just—' Mr Schenck stuttered.

'A break-in,' Mirjam finished. 'Last night. Some books stolen, and a little money.'

'Have you told the police?' said Idris.

'Yes, yes, though it's a paltry matter.' The shopkeeper flicked his hand to demonstrate how unimportant it was.

Margaret let out a loud, 'Hm! Well, we all know who's the thief around here.'

Rose returned her glare, jabbing a finger in her direction. 'Are you referring to me, you old hag?'

Her skinny frame leapt forward, almost knocking Esther off her feet on the way. Her hands were thrust out, as if to attack Margaret. Hywel and Idris threw their arms out to grab hold of her but missed, while Mr Schenck stepped firmly in front of the older woman.

Rose came up short. 'Protect her, would you? More fool you!'

Esther steadied herself and felt her hat to make sure it was straight. 'I shall be fetching your father if you don't go home immediately, you silly young woman!' A little of the former, authoritative Mrs Williams 'the Guardian' was back.

'And you can bugger off too, you bitch.' Rose's voice reached a piercing crescendo. 'You can all bugger off. And you, you gawpers.'

She was glaring at the crowd starting to form at a safe distance, some of them fresh out of the pit, when Stanley Pritchard's stout form rushed around the corner.

'What on earth are you doing, girl?' he hollered. 'It comes to something when a customer comes to tell you that your daughter's acting like a hoyden!' He grabbed hold of her arm. 'Now get indoors with you and get on with your work. You were only supposed to be getting me some baccy. You're a damned liability.'

'I hate bloody working in that shop,' she yelled.

Stanley pulled her more roughly. 'Don't you swear at me else I'll dock your wages. And you're not too old for a clip round the ear, either.'

The noise faded as he dragged her back round the corner to the butcher's. Mirjam slipped back inside the shop.

'I've never seen such an ill-bred brat in all my days,' said Esther. 'And for her to pick on the manager's wife. Well!'

Margaret came forward two steps. 'I hardly think you're in a position to speak when your husband is in gaol.' When Esther started to interrupt with Enid's name, Margaret raised her hand to silence her. 'If you're about to say that Mrs Rhys's husband is in gaol too, at least she was a victim and did not know what her husband was up to.'

'Neither did I! I knew nothing of the hoarding and profiteering.'

'We only have *your* word for that. So please, just go away. I did not ask you to jump to my defence and consider you worse than useless as an advocate.'

Esther looked at each of them in turn, her final gaze, tight-lipped and pinch-faced, resting on Margaret. 'You'll all get your comeuppances, mark my words.' Looking up at the sky, she wrung her hands. 'Oh Lord, how long shall the wicked exult?'

At which she turned on her heels and walked off towards Jubilee Green.

At the same time, Mrs Meredith walked off in the opposite direction.

Mr Schenck looked left and right at the departing women and shrugged. 'Good day to you, gentlemen.' He bowed his head before ambling towards his shop.

The men carried on up Jubilee Gardens. Everyone seemed to be falling out with everyone else, thought Hywel. 'Who needs enemies abroad?' he said, thinking of Olwen Jones more than anyone.

'When we've got them on our own doorstep?' Idris finished.

'That's worrying, that Mr Schenck should have been robbed,' said Gwilym. 'I wonder who is responsible this time. The last lot of thieves from here are all locked up.'

Idris walked backwards just ahead to look at his friends. 'It could have been worse. At least no one was hurt.'

'Until the next time,' said Hywel, who had the feeling this was just the beginning of more trouble.

—

The bell of the grocer's door tinged and Hywel turned his head to see Violet entering with a shake and a small exclamation of 'Oooh!'

Even in her soggy, bedraggled state his heart leapt at the sight of her. She was a sorry sight indeed, yet, if anything, more beautiful to him.

'Still drizzling then?' He looked out the window at the foggy air.

Violet looked up with a start. She'd been avoiding him since Sports Day, when she'd declared that they shouldn't see each other.

Mrs Brace was weighing some cheese on the scales. 'Fog and rain in the middle of May. Where's the sun and warmth gone?'

'At least that would make up a little for the lack of food,' said Hywel.

'Not my doing,' said the grocer, following her comment with a tut and a shake of her curly grey hair. 'It's this war, robbing us of necessities – and young men.'

Hywel realised she was thinking of her two sons, both of whom had lived in Merthyr Tydfil before being conscripted.

'Anyway, good afternoon to you, Mrs Jones. If you can call it good.'

'Good afternoon, Mrs Brace.'

'We were just talking about the bus drivers' strike. Taking advantage during a war too. Whatever next. Of course, Mr Llewellyn here has a different viewpoint to me.' All the while she kept her eyes on the cheese she was wrapping.

'It's the government what takes advantage, Mrs Brace. We can't allow that either,' he said.

She grunted and placed the item in a sack bag. 'Last of the cheese that was, so I 'ope you weren't wanting some too, Mrs Jones.'

'Not especially, though it would have been nice.'

'Need to come in earlier then, you do. Of course, you're working, but your mother-in-law could have popped round.'

Violet looked crestfallen. 'She was, um, feeling under the weather, apparently.'

The addition of the last word made Hywel suspect she was nothing of the sort. More like being lazy and taking advantage. Anwen had told him she believed that Violet was having to do things in the house after work that Olwen could have done.

'That's a shame,' said Mrs Brace. 'Now, is there anything else, Mr Llewellyn?'

'That loaf of bread, please.' He pointed to the last one in the basket.

Turning around to regard Violet once more, he saw the look of disappointment as she followed the bread's journey to the counter.

'Did you want some bread?' Hywel asked.

'It was one of the items, but if that's the last one, you were here first.'

'I'm afraid it is,' said Mrs Brace. 'I don't get as much delivered from the baker in Rhymney as Mrs Pane used to make though—'

'You must have it,' said Hywel, his tone insistent, knowing she'd turn it down otherwise. Already she was shaking her head. 'Yes, you have little ones to feed. That's far more important.'

'Very well,' said Violet. 'Thank you, Hywel.' She looked at the ground like a child who'd been told off.

'I was going to say,' Mrs Brace carried on, 'that I do have some homemade potato bread rolls that my daughter's been baking in the back, if you can wait five minutes or so.'

'Potato bread?' Hywel didn't like the sound of that.

'No need to turn your nose up till you've tried it. My daughter found a recipe in a magazine. We baked some and very nice they were. You do know the bread we sell has rye, barley and oats and even potato flour added now, don't you?'

'Does it?' said Violet. 'That would account for why it's not as good as it used to be. And it's more expensive.'

'I had read that somewhere,' said Hywel, omitting that he'd also read that it sometimes had chalk in it.

'It's up to you, of course.' Mrs Brace looked put out.

'Oh, go on then. Might as well give them a go,' said Hywel.

'Righty ho. I'll go and see how they're doing.' She disappeared through a door behind the counter.

Violet was examining the stack of tins of corned mutton and corned beef.

'The butcher's had some chicken in earlier, and a bit of beef,' he told her.

It was a few seconds before she replied, 'This is cheaper.'

'Ah. How are you and the children then?' He purposefully didn't mention Olwen the Ogre, as he'd recently nicknamed her, having remembered the fairy tales he'd read as a boy.

'We're fine, thank you.'

He carried on staring at her, so she added, 'Clarice is doing well at school. Benjy is growing at a pace. He'll be three in August. It's hard to believe.' This was all delivered as if he were merely a neighbour she occasionally passed the time of day with.

He knew he shouldn't, but he couldn't stop himself from asking, 'And is there any sign of Mrs Jones going home?'

She let out an impatient sigh. 'Hywel, I've already explained this to you.'

'But she's a controlling busybody who isn't allowing you to lead your own life.' He was going to say it, even if she no longer wanted to hear it.

'I've said all I'm going to on the matter.' It could have been his mother talking to him. Or Enid.

He racked his brain for some other way to engage her in conversation, to stop her looking ahead with that scowl that made him sad.

'Did Anwen tell you about the argument between Mrs Meredith, Esther Williams, Rose and Mr Schenck, a week back?'

She did now consider him. 'Yes, she did mention it. The day after the Schencks were robbed.'

'That's right. It's a rum do when people are fighting their neighbours during a war.'

Violet didn't seem impressed with this thinking. 'Perhaps Mrs Meredith shouldn't have accused Rose of the theft when she had no evidence.'

He was surprised at her taking Rose's side, but even more so by the tone she used. She turned away and he stared at her until the ting of the door's bell announced a new customer. They both looked round to see Olwen enter with the children.

'I wondered what was holding you up, and now I see it.'

'We're waiting for Mrs Brace to—' Hywel started.

'I don't want to hear from you. Why are you still here, Violet?'

'Mrs Brace has gone to fetch some potato bread that her daughter has made. I popped into Mrs Davies's first to see if she had any sweets for the children.'

'More likely you arranged this meeting.'

'Olwen, the children!' Violet hissed. But they'd wandered off to look at the empty tubs that normally held loose biscuits. 'How could I have arranged this when I didn't know I'd be coming to the shops?'

'Aye,' Hywel agreed, growing angrier by the second. 'And I thought you hadn't been shopping because you were unwell. Not unwell enough to come spying though. Is that why you sent Violet out, to follow her? And how would we have arranged this when you come to meet her from work every day?'

'You could have sneaked up to her *during* the shift and arranged it.'

'What, leave the mine shaft just to talk to the women? The overman would have something to say about that.'

'Please, I will handle this,' said Violet with some annoyance. 'I can assure you, Olwen, that I came across Hywel by accident. I can't predict who is going to be in the shops when I go out.'

'Well it seems mighty suspicious to me.'

'Here we are,' said Mrs Brace, coming back through the door with a basket of rolls. 'They've cooled a little now. I can only let you have two though, I'm afraid. Oh, hello Mrs Jones.'

Olwen didn't reply, going instead to fetch the children back and holding onto them.

'That's all right,' said Hywel. 'I wouldn't want to deprive others of a share.'

When Olwen came back to the counter, she noticed the one loaf of bread. 'Trust you to get the last loaf. That's not fair. We've got children.'

'Which is exactly why Mr Llewellyn gave up the loaf to your daughter-in-law,' said the grocer. 'Very kind thing to do, that was.'

'Hmph. The least he can do,' was Olwen's reply. 'Has he finished now? It's about time, holding up the proceedings.'

Hywel paid Mrs Brace and she passed over the sack bag.

He was loath to leave but knew there was nothing else for it. '*Hwyl fawr*,' he called as he walked towards the door. Only the grocer replied.

Outside on the street, the drizzle had halted though the fog was as thick as ever. He crossed the road and trudged up the hill. At the top he stopped, looking back down Jubilee Gardens. He wouldn't have spied them even if they had come out, the shop having disappeared in the fog. He trudged home instead.

Chapter Twenty-One

'Will you keep this – this – *child* out of my way!' Enid stood and threw her sewing onto the table, dashing away as Sara Fach once more made a wobbly beeline for her.

Anwen wasn't far behind, scooping the crawling tot up and cuddling her. 'It's not her fault, Mam. Maybe she likes the look of you,' she said hopefully, to no avail.

'I've never known a babby crawl so early. Not natural, it isn't.'

'She's nearly five months old. It's not that unusual. Violet told me Clarice wasn't quite six months when she crawled.'

'I don't want a discussion about it. Just move it.'

It. Always 'It'. Never she. Anwen sniffed back the tears as she picked her sister up. Poor little mite. A happy little soul she was too, but Enid could only take her for what she was, not who.

Anwen carried the baby to the scullery and looked out of the window. The sun had finally come out, after days of an overcast sky.

'Shall we go to the park on Jubilee Gardens, *cariad*?' She kissed the baby's head. It would get them out from under Enid's feet for a while.

Idris came into the scullery, heaving the box of tools with him. 'We've fixed the drawer in Hywel's room. Reckon all those heavy bottles your father kept in them dislodged the back panel.'

'I thought I'd take Sara Fach to the park since the weather's improved.' She didn't mention the incident with her mother.

'Aye, might as well take advantage. Been a terrible spring so far. Thought I'd pop over to the McKenzie Cottages allotment with Hywel to help out. Could do with some fresh air too.'

'Getting involved again will do you the world of good. As long as you feel up to doing it alongside your job.'

He stopped on his way to bend down and peck her lips. As he did so, Sara Fach grabbed his chin and giggled.

'Hey, you cheeky girl,' he laughed. 'I've never felt more up to it. I realise now how many years I must have had this thyroid business. I'd better get these tools to the lean-to before my arms drop off.'

Five minutes later she left the house through the front door, almost bumping into Gwilym as he went past. He lifted his cap to greet her and the baby, who giggled.

'Hello,' said Anwen. 'You working on the allotments today?'

'Aye, just heading over to the far field, see how they're getting on.'

They chatted about the vegetables, which were still not impressive, due to winter's long fingers creeping into April and May.

'What with all the other shortages it's not going to be hard to self-ration, as the government's told us to do,' said Gwilym, slouching along with his hands in his pockets.

'At least the chickens are doing well,' said Anwen, trying to bring some cheer to the conversation.

'Aye, they are that.'

When they reached Jubilee Gardens they saw Sergeant Harries plodding up with Constable Probert.

'Oh Lord, I bet some poor soul's in trouble,' said Gwilym. 'I know that look.'

'Maybe they've found out who broke into the bookshop.'

'Let's hope they've got the right person this time then, for they've not got a good record on that score.'

He carried on down the road. Anwen entered the park through the top gate, singing softly to Sara Fach as she went.

Halfway down the path through the centre of the garden, little Clarice came running out from one of the bushes, having spotted them. Benjamin soon followed on. Violet must have brought them home this way from school.

'Aunty Anwen and Sara Fach!' Clarice called, skipping up to them with Benjamin.

'Hello there,' Anwen replied. 'Having a nice time?'

'We been collecting blossoms.'

Violet appeared from round the bush, remaining several yards away, watching the scene.

'Look what I've got, Sara Fach.' Clarice lifted her hand to show her the blossoms. Benjy copied.

The baby stretched her arm out, trying to touch the offering that was just out of reach.

'Hello, Violet,' Anwen called. 'I fancied a walk with the littl'un.'

'Hello.' Violet seemed nervous, looking out of the park and across the road.

'I'm glad I've seen you, for I'd like some advice about this cradle cap of Sara Fach's.'

At that moment, Olwen came in through the bottom gate. She marched up the path. 'Just saw the police walking up the road, looking like they meant business. No doubt arresting some villain.'

Anwen tucked the blanket back round Sara Fach from where she'd stretched out of it. 'Could be.'

Violet and Anwen sat on the bench to discuss the cradle cap. Mrs Jones was constantly in a bad mood, thought Anwen. And she really seemed to dislike Hywel. Why did she continue to assume there was something between him and Violet when he'd insisted there wasn't? But what if there was and he simply didn't want to admit it? Wouldn't Violet have told her, if that were the case? Yet her friend seemed to reveal little of her private life these days.

Clarice was talking to Sara Fach, showing her the rag doll that she'd tucked under her arm, the blossoms now on the seat beside Violet. Benjy was singing a nursery rhyme to her, not quite getting the words right. The baby treated them to a wide, toothless grin, all the while gurgling at the back of her throat.

'She's a chirpy one, isn't she?' said Olwen.

'Always has a smile for everyone,' Violet confirmed.

Even if they didn't always have a smile for her. Anwen thought about her mam once more with a sinking heart.

'So, have you heard from the mother – Delyth, isn't it?' said Olwen.

'No, we haven't heard from her at all.' That the baby's mother might turn up was a recurring theme in her nightmares.

'Violet says you've fostered her officially now.'

'That's right. And we'll hopefully be able to adopt her soon.'

Olwen looked at the seat, then at the two young women. The look implied they should shift up to let her sit too. Why couldn't she just ask nicely? It was like she was determined to get on the wrong side of everybody. Anwen shuffled up a little, which the baby thought very funny. Violet soon got the idea and did likewise, picking up Clarice's blossom.

Olwen sat and leant her umbrella against the seat. She undid and retied her bonnet, a black affair that looked like it would have been worn at a funeral thirty years back.

'So, you've not fallen pregnant yourself yet?'

'Olwen, that's none of our business,' Violet muttered.

'I'm sure it's a perfectly natural enquiry.'

Anwen always dreaded this question. Why did people think it was any of their business? By now she had a standard answer, which she always delivered with her head to one side and a slight smile.

'These things happen in their own time, don't you think?' Before Olwen had a chance to give an opinion, she added, 'The good Lord clearly wants me to see to Sara Fach first. Imagine if I'd had a baby at the same time she was born.' She gave a little laugh.

'People have twins,' said Olwen. 'And look at that Jane Harris with her seven babbies under nine, and her a widow.

They just have to get on with it. It's a shame Violet won't have any more though,' she added.

Anwen was about to ask how she knew Violet wouldn't have any more when it occurred to her. If Olwen had anything to do with it, she wouldn't have the opportunity. She glanced at Violet who was staring ahead, expressionless. What did she think about this? She'd spent so much time making excuses for Olwen and her distress at losing her son, had she realised this woman simply liked being in charge? It was as if Violet had given up and had let Olwen take over. It didn't seem right.

They chatted of this and that, though most of it was snippets of gossip Olwen had picked up in the village. Some, Anwen was sure, were exaggerated.

'By the way, I've taken the job of cook at the Big House,' said Olwen.

Violet's eyebrows drew together. She leant forward. 'But who will look after the children while I'm at work?'

Olwen glared at her. 'I'm not that stoopid. I've decided that a young mother's place is in the home with her babbies. I saw Mrs Meredith in the grocer's and she was talking to Mrs Brace about how she wished she could get a cook but realised it was unlikely now before the war ended. Sounded desperate, she did. So I stepped forward. The pay's better than you're getting on the screens. I start Monday. But I'm only doing four days, like you, since Mrs Meredith tolerates Mrs Rhys doing four days too.'

'That's… that's wonderful. Thank you.' Violet looked happier than Anwen had seen her for a long while.

'That is kind of you,' said Anwen, surprised at this development. From hints dropped by Violet, though never directly stated, Olwen was a woman after doing as little as she could get away with.

'No, it's not right,' the older woman went on, 'a young widow being at a male-dominated place of work with all those men sniffing round her.'

Ah, so that was the real reason, thought Anwen. Not so much generous as, once again, controlling. And come to think of it, if she was earning the money, she'd have control of that too.

Anwen felt the shadow go over her before she realised the clouds had once again swallowed up the sun. She pulled down Sara Fach's woolly bonnet, which the baby had partly pulled off.

Violet peered upwards. 'Looks like it's business as usual, as Mr Churchill used to be fond of saying.'

Anwen thought she was referring to Olwen at first, but soon realised she was talking about the weather.

'Talking of Mrs Meredith, I also heard her tell Mrs Brace that her daughter has just been sacked from her job in the overseer's office in Rhymney,' said Olwen.

Anwen leant forward. 'Oh no, I hadn't heard that.' She missed her time with Elizabeth on the allotments, seeing her only on Sundays at church now. Still, she seemed much more content these days. 'Did you hear why?'

'Something about the man whose job it had been coming back from the war with an injury, his knee blown off or something.'

Anwen shuddered. 'Poor man.'

'Mrs Meredith was pleased as Punch about it. Seems to think her daughter might be settling down soon.'

Violet glanced questioningly at Anwen, but she could only shrug back. She felt a disappointment in knowing nothing of this new life of Elizabeth's. She stroked Sara Fach's hair and her mind wandered as Olwen gossiped on.

–

'You ready to go to the allotments, Idris?' said Hywel, eager to get out of the house, with his sister being in another of her bad moods. He wasn't sure what had brought this one on, but there she was, stabbing the needle into the fabric and tugging it through the other end.

'Aye. I'm looking forward to it,' said Idris. 'Fresh air and good tilled soil.'

They were in the middle of calling farewell to Enid when there was a loud banging on the front door.

Idris went ahead. 'I'll get it. Probably Florrie Harris visiting with more gossip.'

Hywel took this opportunity to ask Enid, 'What's wrong with you, *cariad*? Punishing that fabric, you are.'

She stopped briefly. 'Me? Nothing. Nothing at all.'

Which almost certainly meant there was something. He had no opportunity to pursue this further before Idris's voice was heard crying, 'What's all this about now? Didn't you harass me enough last year?'

'It's not you we've come to see, it's Mr Llewellyn.'

Before Hywel could comment to his sister about it, Idris came back into the kitchen with Sergeant Harries and PC Probert.

Enid put the sewing down and jumped up from the chair. 'What's happened?'

Harries didn't reply to her directly, saying instead to Hywel, 'We've had a report that you were spotted going down the path behind James Street, towards the bookshop, the early hours of Friday 11th May, the night Schenck's bookshop was broken into.'

'What? I haven't been out that late at night since the pit disaster last July.'

'Do you know what,' said Idris, towering over Harries. 'This sounds rather like that accusation against me last year, when I was arrested for beating up Cadoc Beadle.'

'Hang on a moment,' said Harries.

'And who on earth was out at that time of night to report on anybody? Who's to say they didn't do it, just like the husband of the person who reported me?'

'That's a fair question,' said Enid.

Hywel was having difficulty saying anything, so shocked was he. Who could think he was capable of such a thing, especially against a kindly gentleman like Mr Schenck?

'Saw you from their bedroom window, they did.'

'That would mean someone on James Street,' said Idris.

'Or Bryn Road,' Enid hissed accusingly.

Hywel realised immediately to whom she was referring. 'Olwen Jones?' Surely even she wouldn't stoop to such lies.

Sergeant Harries' wide-eyed expression and fleeting glance at Probert confirmed Enid's assumption, even before he stuttered, 'We-well, I'm not about to be giving away sources, but if you'd let me finish. I have no reason to believe that she, I mean, they, were correct in their conclusion, as there are no streetlamps down that lane. Not that they'd be on that time of night, even without the restrictions.'

'Then why on earth are you here?' Enid shouted.

'Settle down now, Mrs Rhys,' said Probert. 'You never used to be one for hysterics.'

'It's been reported, so it's our duty to follow it up, see,' said Harries. 'Also, the thief would have had to climb over a high back wall as the gate was bolted, and then had to climb in a small window. So they'd had to have been agile, see, and I don't think you are particularly, since the, um…' He pointed to Hywel's leg.

It was certainly true that he couldn't bend his leg like he used to. For once, it might have done him a favour.

'So you're not arresting me?'

'Goodness, no. This visit's just a formality, that's all, so if the person who reported you asks if we followed it up, we can say we did and that we're confident you weren't involved.'

Hywel took a deep gulp of air and breathed out. He was relieved, yet at the same time furious. It was one thing Olwen stopping Violet from seeing him, but making up stories to get him arrested? He kept his composure, not wanting the sergeant to have any reason to change his mind.

'We'll be going now,' said Harries. 'And you can forget this conversation ever took place.'

Hywel showed them out. When he returned Enid said, 'Of all the nasty, malicious snakes in this village, that Olwen Jones would take some beating. As bad as Esther Williams she is, worse, for at least she did see Idris walking out when she reported him, even if he wasn't guilty. But Olwen must have completely made it up. But why?'

'To keep me right away from Violet.'

Enid sat back down and picked up the sewing. 'Would she go that far?'

'I rather feel she would. I do admire Violet, I can't deny it, but I've only tried to be a friend to her. We met up a couple of times, just for company like, but Olwen found out about one of the times, from Rose Pritchard.'

'There's another snake to add to the list. And her a thief. Wouldn't be surprised if she was the one who broke into poor Mr Schenck's place.'

Hywel picked up his cap. 'Let's just get out of here. I need that fresh air and to do some digging.'

'Aye, mun, get the anger out of your system,' said Idris. 'For Olwen has surely shown her true colours now, even to the police. Let's go via the gardens and tell Anwen, for she did take little Sara there. Come on.'

Halfway down Edward Street the men spotted Elizabeth walking up to the pavement from the allotment.

'Good afternoon!' She waved to them and caught them up. She was wearing her usual gardening garb. 'How are you?'

'We're just heading off to the far allotment,' said Hywel. 'What are you doing here this time of the day? I thought you were working in Rhymney.'

'I was. But the man whose job I was doing has been given a medical discharge, having been shot in the knee. Since it's a sitting job it's perfect for him to return to.'

'I'm sorry to hear that,' said Idris. 'I had the impression you were enjoying it.'

'I was. But at least I won't have my mother complaining about it every day.' She sighed. 'I'm off to the Alexandra Street allotment, since Mary Jones reckons they need some help there.'

'Anwen's in the gardens, so we're just popping along to, um, tell her about... well, Sergeant Harries called by.' He gave her an outline of what had occurred, though didn't let on about Olwen Jones.

'Why, that is frightful. Who would do such a thing? I'll pop into the gardens with you, just to say hello. I haven't seen Anwen in a while.'

They reached the Workmen's Institute and crossed over to enter via the top gate.

'Oh look, Violet's there too,' said Elizabeth. 'And her mother-in-law, by the looks of it.'

Hywel regarded Idris who looked as cross as he felt. He wished Elizabeth had not accompanied them; hopefully she'd move on quickly, for this would not be pleasant.

—

'All I'm saying is, I hope Miss Elizabeth doesn't think she can barge into our lives again, now she'll be free in the day once more.' There, Violet had said it. With any luck, Anwen wouldn't be so keen to invite her to everything from now on.

'I don't know who she thinks she is, Miss High-and-Mighty from the Big House, bossing us about but wanting to be our friend,' said Olwen.

'I think that's unfair,' said Anwen.

'Bringing me her gifts at Christmas as if we were friends.' Violet remembered the jams, which, although delicious, had highlighted her shame that she could not afford to give anything back.

'The classes shouldn't mix,' said Olwen. 'It's a recipe for disaster. Now I'm to do working at the Big House, I don't intend to hobnob with the manager's family.' She looked at Anwen pointedly.

Violet was aware of Anwen turning her head away, maybe dismayed about her friend being criticised. She wondered briefly how Olwen and Enid would get on, working so closely together.

Anwen turned back to say, 'Um, I don't think—'

'I'm afraid I agree with Olwen—' Violet interrupted.

Anwen nudged her and she turned around, still talking.

'Oh.' Violet came to an abrupt halt.

Elizabeth was standing there with Hywel and Idris, looking bewildered and more than a little hurt. 'I need to be going now.' She scooted down the path, breaking into a run until she reached the bottom gate.

Well, Violet thought, it was unfortunate that Elizabeth had heard her opinion, but it would perhaps give her something to think about. And hopefully it would put her off seeking her company again.

'Was that necessary?'

Hywel's eyes were so ablaze with fury that Violet felt afraid. It seemed an overreaction for what she had said.

'I'm sorry that she overheard, but she did rather intrude on our lives before.' She said this with as much confidence as she could muster, hoping they'd see that her opinion was reasonable. After all, she had mentioned this to Hywel. 'I do wonder what she wants with us and whether she's spying for her father.'

Hywel pointed a forefinger at her. 'You are turning out as bad as her.' The finger's position moved towards Olwen.

Violet felt sick. Whatever had brought this on? She looked down to where the children were still playing, glad they were out of earshot.

'Says the man who can't keep his hands to himself,' growled Olwen.

'You're a wicked, vile piece of work—'

'Hywel!' exclaimed Violet. 'That's not necessary. She's only trying to—'

'Yes, Uncle Hywel, I do think you're taking this too far, even though it's unfortunate Elizabeth overheard,' said Anwen.

'Taking it too far?' said Idris. 'I'd say he's only just beginning. And I'm with him on this one.'

Violet had the feeling there was something more here than her harsh words.

Olwen waved them away. 'Men, you're all alike. No doubt sticking up for Miss Meredith because she's young and pretty, even if she does look ridiculous in those clothes.'

Did Hywel perhaps have feelings for the manager's daughter, Violet wondered. She couldn't see anything coming of that, but even the thought that he might admire another woman was like a punch in the gut.

'I had a visit from the police,' Hywel started.

'That doesn't surprise me,' said Olwen, though Violet noticed her face pale a little. 'You're a wrong'un, and no mistake.'

'Why don't you just shut up and listen?'

'Idris, don't be so rude!' Anwen admonished.

Hywel carried on. 'Apparently someone who overlooks Schenck's back yard reported seeing me in the early hours on the night they were broken into.'

He hadn't said Olwen, but that's who he was implying it was. It was like when Esther had reported seeing Idris near Cadoc Beadle's. Violet had only recently told her mother-in-law that story. And yesterday, after the incident in the grocer's, Olwen had gone out for a walk by herself, which she seldom did. Violet stood and walked backwards, away from her.

'Was that you, Olwen?'

'You know it was, for I told you I'd seen him.'

'No you didn't!'

Anwen rose, cuddling the baby to her. 'Either way, you are the one who's been allowing this awful woman to stay,' she confronted her friend.

Olwen pulled a sad face, no doubt meant to provoke sympathy. 'What a thing to say, and my son not ten months dead. I've put myself out, yes, left the comfort of my own home to look after my daughter-in-law and the little ones.'

'I think you're happy for her to stay, Violet,' said Hywel. 'That way, you have an excuse not to try and get over your tragedy and get on with the rest of your life.'

Violet's head was spinning. Was she using Olwen as an excuse? She could have insisted she leave months ago, yet it had never seemed the right time and the woman had always had convincing arguments. Not knowing what else to do, she ran down to the children, taking their hands.

'We've got to go now as it looks like it could rain.'

The cloud was only light, but she needed to be home, away from Hywel's accusing presence. She hurried to the bottom gate, not hearing what was said next. If only she could lock the doors against Olwen, but she knew she couldn't. She felt she was looking after her mother-in-law as much as the other way round. It was her punishment for her wicked thoughts regarding Hywel. It was all her own fault.

–

It wasn't long after Violet got home that she heard the back door bang shut with some force. The children's train set had already been set up in the front room to keep them out of the way. She headed now to the scullery, shaking with anger but also nerves. Confrontation was something she always endeavoured to avoid, but at least putting a room between her and the children should keep them from hearing what was about to ensue.

As soon as she opened the door, Olwen launched in with, 'Well thank you very much for running off like that.'

Violet shut the door before she replied. 'Please keep your voice down, for I would rather the children were not upset.'

'Hm! You didn't worry about me being upset, being set upon like that.'

This woman was infuriating, twisting it round like she was the victim. She would have to go, extra wage or not. Her nerves could stand it no longer.

'How dare you tell the police that you saw Hywel on the night of the burglary! And to sneak off to the police, a week after it happened, behind my back, just because I came across him by accident in the grocer's. Because admit it, that's why you did it.'

Olwen sniffed and stuck her nose in the air. 'I might have been mistaken about the figure I saw.'

'Mistaken? You couldn't see anything down that lane in the early hours from your bedroom.'

'There's no harm in telling the police. Better to report it and it turn out not to be the case than to ignore it and let someone get away with something.'

Violet wagged her forefinger at Olwen, stepping closer. 'You only did it to spite Hywel, and to spite me. I don't remember the last time you were nice about anybody, or smiled, except at the children. Even them you try to boss around. You are an evil witch who sees badness in everything.' The last sentence came out more aggressively than Violet had intended, leaving her quite shocked at her own temper.

Olwen backed away until she was leaning against the sink. 'Evil, am I? More like you're going mad. Look at the face on you.'

Violet stepped forward once more. 'If I'm mad I've been driven there by you, trying to control my life.' She threw her hands up in desperation.

The older woman put up her arms as if to protect her face and started screaming. 'Keep away from me. Don't attack me.'

'What are you going on about now? Keep your voice down.'

Olwen screamed once more, long and noisily. 'Nooo, don't hurt me, aghhhh.'

Violet stepped back, bewildered. The woman had gone crazy, and no mistake.

Despite her best efforts, the children came running in, their faces fearful.

'Why's Mamgu screaming?' said Clarice.

At the same time, there was a rapping on the back door and she heard their neighbour, Mr Prowse, shouting, 'Are you all right?'

The door suddenly opened and he and his wife flew in, in time to hear Olwen scream, 'No, don't hurt me, Violet, I didn't mean no harm.'

The neighbours looked in alarm at Violet, Mrs Prowse clutching her husband's arm. Her stomach churned with fear. Olwen was trying to make out she was going to injure her in some way. She thought quickly.

'I have no intention of doing anything to you, you silly woman. But I've a right to get cross when you tell lies to the police about my friends.'

The Prowses seemed to relax, now regarding Olwen with doubt.

'Yes you were! You had your hand raised to hit me.' She broke down into sobs which in turn started Clarice and Benjy off.

The neighbours now frowned at Violet. She went to the children, placing an arm around each. 'Hush now, *cariadon*, Mamgu's just unwell.' She bent down. 'Clarice, you be a big girl now and take Benjy back to the front room, all right?'

The little girl nodded and scooped an arm round her brother to lead him back out of the scullery.

Violet lifted her hands to demonstrate what she'd actually been doing. 'I put them up like this in frustration, that is all.'

Olwen pulled her mouth into an ugly pout. 'You're mad, you are. This is not the first time you've attacked me. You need help.' Olwen ran past the neighbours and through the door into the garden. Violet went to the opening and watched as her mother-in-law escaped through the gate.

'I'm so sorry about that,' she told the neighbours. 'I'd just found out she'd reported Mr Llewellyn, who you'll remember used to lodge with me, to the police for being in the lane behind here the night the bookshop was broken into. He wasn't, but she's taken against him, see, and is trying to get him into trouble.'

The Prowses didn't look totally convinced by this explanation. Violet realised that it didn't preclude her attacking Olwen for doing it.

'I'm not best pleased,' she went on, 'but certainly didn't attack her.'

Mrs Prowse frowned doubtfully, but said, 'Aye, well, she never does seem a happy soul. Can barely manage a greeting when we sees her in the garden or the street.'

'Well, we'll keep an ear out,' said her husband, 'just in case she starts up again.'

Or if you start up again, is what she suspected he meant. Yet she'd never been any bother in the six years she'd lived here. It was so unfair.

The pair left and Violet headed to the front room to check on the children. She knelt next to them.

'Why Mamgu upset?' said Benjy.

'Why were you going to hurt her?' said Clarice.

'I wasn't. She was confused, and, as I said, not well. Now come on, dry those tears.' She produced a handkerchief from her pocket, noting that the fabric was so thin on the seam of her skirt there that it had shredded. She dabbed their eyes in turn. 'Now, who is riding on the train today, and where are they going?'

The children chatted on about the journey. Violet's head throbbed, the trauma of what had occurred today pressing against her skull. She tried to work out how to make Olwen finally leave, going through several scenarios. Perhaps she should write to Brynmore, tell him to come and collect his wife. She should have done so ages ago. What had she been thinking?

'Hello?'

The faint voice, a man's, came from the kitchen. Her heart jumped. Had Olwen fetched the police?

'I'll just see who that is,' she told the children, rising. 'You stay here and continue your game.'

She was surprised to see the doctor in the scullery, with Olwen cowering behind him.

'Dr Roberts, what are you doing here? Unless it's to treat my mother-in-law's hysteria.'

'See, I told you she swings from violent to normal. Threatening me with a fist, she was, not fifteen minutes since. The Prowses next door saw. She needs a spell in the asylum if you ask me. And those poor babbies being exposed to that temper. Good job their mamgu's here to take care of them.'

'The Prowses saw no such thing and you may ask them yourself, doctor,' said Violet, determined to hold her temper to give no credence to Olwen's false words. 'They came over because she was screaming blue murder when I simply got cross.' She explained what she'd been told by Hywel and how it was false.

'False, is it? It's not false that you've been like a bitch in heat for that Hywel, and that was even before my dear Charlie was gone.'

'How dare you, you lying witch!' Violet had had enough now.

Dr Roberts put a hand up to stop the argument. 'Mrs Jones – senior, that is – would you please leave me with Violet for a while.'

Olwen's frown became a victorious smile. 'I will be with the children in the front room when you need me.'

Dr Roberts waited until she was gone, checking through the kitchen door and then closing it.

'How have you been feeling, Violet?'

'I am stressed, doctor, and certainly I am still mourning Charlie, despite what she says. But I'm not mad. Driven mad, yes, by her constant nagging and spying, but that's quite a different thing to *being* mad.'

'It is, but when I have seen you in chapel, you do not seem your old cheerful self, even given that Charlie has not been gone a year.'

She sighed and leaned against the sink. 'I am grateful to Olwen for bringing more money into the home, but it comes at a price and it's wearing me down. She is not an easy woman.'

'I can imagine. But still, you seem to have grown thinner in the last months, and you've never been well built.'

'Is it any wonder, with the food shortages? The children get the best food first.' Though Olwen wasn't beyond saving some nice portions for herself, and she was eating 'luncheon', as they called it, up at the Big House four days a week.

'I'd be surprised if most people weren't getting skinnier, for it's hard to get fat on veggies alone, and that is certainly our staple diet at the moment. And the veggies on the allotments haven't done so well this year, so we haven't even got as many of those.' Violet became aware she was rambling.

'Food shortages are a worry, but I detect something more with you, Violet. You don't look well.'

'I'm tired and fed up, that's all. Olwen is good with the children but not so good helping around the house, so even when I had the job I was doing a lot of the work here. That's no excuse to send me to no asylum.'

Dr Roberts huffed out a small laugh. 'I'm not keen to send women there unless I absolutely have to. I believe there are other ways to deal with melancholia, for that's what it seems to me you have. But let me ask you a few questions first. Perhaps we could go into the kitchen and sit down.'

'But the children—'

'We'll make sure the door is firmly shut and will speak quietly.'

Violet led the way, pulling out a chair at the table to sit there, rather than the seats by the fireplace. The door to the front room was open, so Dr Roberts stepped over to shut it.

The doctor sat and took a notebook along with a fountain pen from his bag. He put on a pair of round spectacles. 'Do you feel restless, always wanting to be on the move, or tired most of the time?'

Violet considered this. 'A bit of both, I suppose. I do tire easily, but then I feel like… like, oh, I dunno, like I need to get away and *do* something.'

He wrote a few notes, though she didn't know what as one side of the book was flipped up, concealing them.

'Do you have trouble sleeping?'

She thought about this. 'I go to bed exhausted but yes, I do have trouble. Or, I'll go to sleep quickly and wake up halfway through the night.' Often she'd been dreaming, knowing her dreams involved either Hywel, Charlie or Olwen, or sometimes all three, but could never quite pinpoint what had happened.

'Do you ever consider harming yourself?'

'No!' she said. 'Of course not. And before you ask, I don't think of harming anyone else.' That wasn't quite true. She'd have happily slapped Olwen a few times, if she hadn't known it would cause endless trouble. This aggressive tendency in herself was awful and hadn't existed before her mother-in-law had turned up on her doorstep.

He asked a few other questions about her physical symptoms.

'What I suggest, first of all, is to take some exercise, a walk out with the children. I've seen you working on the allotments; that will help too. And to make you feel calmer, I suggest Dr Williams' Pink Pills. They're good for melancholia. You need to send for them here, post free.' He wrote an address on the last page of his notebook and pulled it out for her. 'They're two shillings and ninepence a box.' He wrote that down.

She looked at the paper. 'Two shillings and ninepence? I don't have that to spare.'

'It might be worth trying to save some money for them. They have good minerals in them, ones you should be getting from your food. However, if you really can't afford them, then you could pick some chamomile flowers or lavender, and make an herbal tea. Both are good for calming the nerves.'

'I have lavender in the garden and have seen chamomile on the hillside.'

'Good, you try those then.' He stood to put his book and pen away. 'I must be on my way now. Mrs Jones caught me in between visits, making it sound so urgent I had no option but to come.'

'I'm so embarrassed, doctor, that you've been troubled with this.'

'It's not at all unusual, you know, to feel so down after the death of a loved one, especially considering the circumstances under which he died.'

She nodded. It wasn't the feeling down that got to her as much as the constant battle between sadness at Charlie's death, joy in seeing Hywel and guilt as a result of the two. Was there a cure for guilt, though?

Olwen came out of the front room at this juncture, closing the door behind her. She folded one hand in front of the other across her stomach.

'Well, where are you sending her, Dr Roberts?'

The doctor regarded Olwen over his glasses. 'I'm not sending her anywhere. There is no need. It's not unusual to be suffering from melancholia after the death of one's husband. I've suggested some herbal remedies and hope you'll keep an eye on her.'

Olwen pinched her lips in. 'I'm sure you're wrong, doctor. The girl needs time away, to rest.'

'Rest would certainly do her some good. Perhaps you could help out a little more to allow her to do that?'

'*I* have a job. No, it would be much better to send her away.'

'And who would look after the children while you worked? You really haven't thought this out.' Violet was determined not to be a helpless spectator to this conversation.

'That wouldn't be your concern—' Olwen started.

'That's enough, Mrs Jones, senior. I am not having Violet committed. Now, I must get on with my round.'

When he'd gone, Olwen turned a furious face towards her. 'Told him your lies, I suppose.'

'I leave that to you, Olwen. I think it's about time you went home, don't you?'

'Go home? This is my home now. And the doctor told me to keep an eye on you, and so I shall. And if there's any more talk of me *going home*, I shall get Dr Roberts back. Or better still, I shall go over his head and get someone higher up to come, and make sure you're put away for a very long time. Now, I'm going out to collect some leaves to add to the supper. Don't you be going anywhere.'

She picked up her hat from the chaise longue and pinned it on her head before leaving.

Violet swallowed hard. She was stuck with Olwen, and furthermore, she had no one left to talk to about it. She'd lost Hywel's and Anwen's respect, and no doubt would lose that of others once they got to hear what Olwen had done. There would be some very lonely years ahead.

Chapter Twenty-Two

Standing at the bedroom window to clean it one afternoon, Anwen wasn't surprised to see Idris running up the road, Hywel limping quickly, just behind. Both had their heads down against the rain. She'd been cleaning the glass, taking the opportunity whilst the baby napped, wondering how long it would be before she saw them. She thought about Violet, as she'd done several times that day, trying to work out how to mend that situation. But there seemed no way to do it, not while Violet insisted on letting her mother-in-law stay.

She hung the cloth over the bucket and leaned closer to the window, confused at first as to why the two men were now belting across the allotment there. The reason soon became apparent. Running away from the side of the field were four lads. She threw the window up to get a better look. Idris and Hywel were hollering. It was then she noticed the boys had a box each. They must have been stealing vegetables, and in broad daylight too. They'd maybe thought nobody would notice in the downpour.

The two men soon came to a halt, standing and watching as the lads disappeared down the end house of Lloyd Street. After a few moments they both turned and made their way back towards the house. This was the first bit of trouble they'd had at the allotments since the plot behind McKenzie Cottages had been vandalised last year. They'd eventually discovered this had been down to her own father, along with Edgar Williams, Prosser the Meat and a few of their thuggish friends.

Anwen came down the stairs as Idris and Hywel were removing their coats and moaning about the loss of the precious veg.

'I don't suppose you saw who it was,' Anwen asked. 'I couldn't make them out from the window.'

'Oh yes, we know all right,' said Hywel, his expression dark. 'Two of them, anyway.'

Enid opened the door from the kitchen. 'What's up?'

'Let us get in and we'll tell you,' said Hywel, pushing his wet fringe back.

'You're just in time for a cup of tea,' called Cadi from the stove.

'You haven't got a drop of whisky to go with it, have you?'

'What's wrong, *cariad*?'

'We've just chased Christopher Williams, Cyril Davis and a coupla others off the allotment,' said Idris. 'Had a pile of the veggies, they did.'

'Cyril and *Christopher*?' Anwen said, surprised and disappointed. 'Cyril's a bit of a scamp, but Christopher's always been such a nice boy.' She recalled rescuing him from his bedroom last summer, where he'd been tied up by his father.

Enid tutted several times. 'Like father, like son. What he's been through with Edgar and with him going to gaol, and having to live with Esther, who I swear is quite mad, well, it's enough to turn the nicest boy into a criminal.'

'Let's not get carried away calling them criminals yet,' said Cadi. 'It's bad of them, don't get me wrong, but it might only be youthful high jinks.'

'I'll give them youthful high jinks,' said Hywel. 'That was climbing trees and making bonfires in the woods when I was their age. I'm going to report it to Sergeant Harries. Maybe Christopher and Cyril will give up the other names too. I'm going to nip it in the bud before it gets out of hand. Like last time.'

'There's ironic, you reporting someone to the police,' Idris laughed.

'Aye, that had occurred to me, but at least I'm not lying.'

'It's probably for the best,' said Cadi. 'But after you've had that cup of tea.'

'It's an age since I came in here,' said Gwen, sitting herself down on one of the chairs provided by Mr Schenck in his bookshop. She looked up at the tall shelving and breathed in deeply. 'Mm, smell that. Paper.' She picked up the new Edgar Rice Burroughs, *The Son of Tarzan*, and looked at the front page.

'Are you sure you want to be out and about if you're not well?' Anwen asked, concerned at how she'd been coughing on their way here.

'I'm absolutely certain.' It was said with exasperation.

'I'm only looking out for you.' Anwen stepped back from the travel shelves with Sara Fach, who'd been trying to pull books out.

Gwen's face softened. 'I know you are. I do think my mother was overzealous, going to the motorbus to ask Mabel Coombes to tell my manager I was ill and wouldn't be going back to the munitions until after the Whitsun holiday. Goodness knows what they'll make of that. I'm just a bit tired. My wages will be docked two days. And I was supposed to be going to the pictures this evening to see *The End of the Trail*.' She huffed and slumped once more.

Anwen patted Gwen's shoulders. 'Well *cariad*, I'd say you've earned enough up till now to survive without a coupla days money.'

'You're probably right, though why Mam insists I'm unwell then sends me out for fresh air, I don't know. And I wouldn't want to get on the wrong side of management and lose my job.'

'I'd say that was unlikely,' said Anwen. 'They're always advertising for more munitionettes. A couple of days rest will set you up for when you go back. And this Ralph, who I presume you were going to the pictures with, will surely understand.'

'I'm sure he will.' Gwen raised her eyebrows and gave a cheeky grin.

'When are we going to meet him?'

'Not yet.'

Mr Schenck wandered over, having just bid farewell to another customer. His back hadn't regained its usual posture since the break-in.

'Good afternoon, ladies. Is there anything in particular you are looking for?' Even his voice sounded weary.

'Just looking for something that takes my fancy,' said Gwen.

The tinkling bell made Mr Schenck start. He looked round and seemed relieved to see Violet and the children. She spotted Anwen and Gwen immediately and looked set to flee, except the children had already run into the other room.

So far, Enid was on her third day of working alongside Olwen at the Big House. Luckily, her mother didn't have to spend too much time in the same room as the other woman, who worked in the kitchen while Enid cleaned all over the house. However, this hadn't stopped her having a long moan about Olwen when she'd returned home both afternoons. At least they only had to see each other three days a week, since Enid didn't work Mondays and Olwen had Fridays off.

'Hello Violet,' said Gwen, who, although sympathising with what Anwen's family had told her, had no quarrel with Violet. Anwen supposed that was fair enough.

Violet's reply was muted.

'Mrs Jones, good afternoon,' said Mr Schenck. 'How may I help you today?'

She looked self-conscious as she replied, 'I promised Clarice and Benjy we could come and get a new book after school, just from the second-hand section.' Violet pointed to the other room, where they could just spy the children sitting on two tiny chairs by the window, examining a display of books on a stand.

'Ah, bless them. They do seem to enjoy their trips here.' Mr Schenck gave them an indulgent smile. 'They are always so well behaved too. Not like some I have had in recently who should know better.' He looked glum at the memory.

'Have you had more trouble, Mr Schenck?' asked Violet.

'Indeed I have. The day before they stole the vegetables, Christopher Williams and the other boys were in here, making a hullabaloo. I believe some of it may have been a distraction to steal books. Despite the great number, I am quite well acquainted with my stock and also keep a book with the titles in. I do believe there are a few missing, some Arthur Conan Doyles and an Oscar Wilde or two among them. Nothing obvious, like some of the new editions, but maybe other items. I had to ask them to leave, which, as you can imagine, did not go down well.'

'I'm so sorry you've had to put up with that,' said Violet. 'You provide such a wonderful service and so many lovely books to escape into, it is upsetting to hear of people disrespecting you.'

He gave a wry chuckle. 'It certainly would not be the first time and seems to run in the family.'

'Ah yes,' said Anwen. 'I remember that incident last year with Esther Williams and her band of cronies, coming in here to tell you to shut up shop and do something more useful. The cheek of the woman!'

'You and Mr Hughes defended me admirably,' said Schenck, bowing his head.

'Have you reported it to the police?' said Gwen. 'It could be they're the ones who broke into your shop.'

'I think stealing vegetables and shoplifting a few books is one thing but breaking in quite another. I wouldn't want to get them into trouble for something they probably didn't do.'

'Oh dear,' said Anwen, spotting a figure outside, looking in at her in a most unpleasant manner. 'I fear there could be more trouble.'

They all followed her eyeline.

'It wouldn't be the first time she has caused an argument in here,' said the bookseller. 'From what I hear, she is as proficient as Mrs Williams in looking for trouble.'

'Oh sweet Lord, here she comes,' said Gwen.

The bell above the door clanged, announcing the arrival of the sour-faced ex-cook, Rose. Her blonde curls were dishevelled from the wind.

'I see you're all congregated here, like the three witches in *Macbeth*,' said Rose.

From being bowed, Violet pulled herself up straight. 'Witches, indeed. I leave that kind of performance to you and your mother, always tittle-tattling everyone's business in the butcher's, much of it not true.'

'You want to be careful I don't get my father to ban you from our butcher's altogether,' said Rose.

'I do not believe he would be allowed to do that in the current climate,' said Mr Schenck. 'For it is the only butcher's shop in the village. Apart from which, I do not believe your father would want to lose the business.'

Rose didn't have an answer for this. Instead, her attention went back to Violet. 'But it's not all untrue, is it? For I saw you and that Hywel Llewellyn, sneaking down the end house of Lloyd Street back in February. You're a bad woman, Violet Jones. And now you've got Mrs Meredith telling lies about me. I heard her, two week back, and that Hywel was there, and *him*.' She plunged her finger in Mr Schenck's direction.

'Unless you have come in for a book, Miss Pritchard, could I respectfully suggest you leave?' he said. 'We do not want to be upsetting the children now, do we?' He nodded his head towards the other room. 'If you want to return later, when these young ladies have gone, and have a quiet look round, you are, of course, welcome.'

'As if I'd buy a book when I can get them for nothing at the library at the Workmen's Institute. I've looked in here before. Too expensive, they are. No, I came in to have words with

Violet, who is spreading Mrs Meredith's lies about me being a thief.'

'I have done no such thing!' said Violet. 'I heard about the argument two weeks before, but I don't know why you think I'm responsible. Did Mr Llewellyn make such a claim?'

Oh dear, thought Anwen, this could turn into another argument if Violet believed her uncle had said something out of turn.

Before Rose got to reply, Gwen jumped up off the chair. 'If anyone is lying, it's you, Rose Pritchard. You lied about stealing up at the Big House and now you're lying about Violet and Hywel. We've all known Hywel since he moved here, what, fifteen years ago? He's Anwen's uncle and has been like an uncle to us all, and if we want to walk along the street and chat to him, we will! And one day, if Violet chose to walk out with another man, being a widow like, I'm sure it would be none of your business.'

'You're all bloody bitches and I'll see you all in hell!'

Clarice came running into the room, calling, 'What's wrong, Mam?'

Violet hunkered down. 'Nothing's wrong, *cariad*. Just grownups getting a bit cross. Don't worry. Let's go back to Benjy.'

She took Clarice to the other room and shut the door behind her. Anwen felt a huge relief at her leaving.

'What is this shouting about?' Mirjam Schenck came through a door at the other end of the shop, remaining in the doorway.

'Mind your own bloody business,' screamed Rose.

Sara Fach jumped and burst into tears. Anwen walked up and down, trying to soothe her. 'There there, *cariad*, there there.'

'I would rather you did not address my wife in that way,' said Mr Schenck, looking unusually cross. 'For she has done nothing to you.'

'Of course, Saint Mirjam, isn't she, like Margaret Meredith, on this committee and that, organising good works to raise money for the soldiers. Sick of bloody hearing it from my father. "Why don't you and your mother do some good works for a change," he says. Well it's all right for them what's got time to do it. I've got to work.'

'As has my wife, for she does all the accounts for this business.'

Anwen had often wondered why Mrs Schenck rarely served in the shop. And even though she was active in organising many of the activities in Dorcalon, she seldom made much of an appearance at them. That had been particularly true since the war had begun.

'What, sitting down all day, writing? That's not hard work,' said Rose.

Mirjam's head went down and she shuffled her feet.

'Of course it is!' said Gwen. 'You just wouldn't have the head for it. Perhaps you should try a stint at the munitions, instead of flitting in and out of your father's shop whenever it pleases you.'

'What, and go all yellow like you, you mean?' She laughed far too loudly. 'You used to be pretty at one time. A right show-off. No man would look twice at you now.'

Being a few inches taller than Rose, Gwen was able to look down her nose at her, in the way Mrs Meredith or Esther Williams might do.

'Well that's where you're wrong, for I am walking out with a gentleman. I don't suppose you can say the same. I'm not a nasty little thief who tries to get other people in trouble. I doubt any man would look even once at you, and no wonder. Who'd want a nasty little liar like you as a sweetheart?'

Rose let out an almighty roar and leapt at Gwen, who moved so fast that Rose tripped over the chair next to her. She pulled herself up quickly. Anwen hurried away with the baby to stand next to Mrs Schenck. She thought Rose was going to have another go at Gwen, but instead she bounded to the nearest bookshelf, immediately pulling out books and hurling them to the floor. Mr Schenck and Gwen tried to stop her. Mirjam burst into tears, setting the baby off again. Rose's flailing arms caught the faces of those trying to restrain her.

As Gwen was about to grab one of her arms, the door opened once more and the welcome figure of Sergeant Harries stepped inside. Behind him was PC Probert. They sprang into action and soon had Rose Pritchard restrained. Gwen went to Mrs Schenck, placing a comforting hand round her shoulder.

'I am – all right, thank you,' the older woman said haltingly. Her English had never been as good as her husband's. 'I go now to our rooms.' She made a hasty retreat and shut the door.

Sara Fach had calmed down now and was sucking her thumb. Anwen and Mr Schenck explained to the sergeant what had happened. Rose all the while was shouting that they were liars.

'Do you want to press charges?' the sergeant asked Mr Schenck.

He rubbed his chin, considering. 'I am always one for as peaceful a life as possible, especially now war is raging around us. I will give you one more chance, Miss Pritchard.'

'Are you sure that's the right decision?' said the sergeant. 'Too mouthy by far, this one, and has got away with far too much.'

'I am sure.'

'Still, we'll take her to Rhymney station to caution her. A little time behind bars to cool off wouldn't go amiss.'

'You'll be sorry,' she called, as the policemen led her away.

Chapter Twenty-Three

Violet was roused from her sleep by a vague noise she couldn't quite make out. It sounded like people running down the road, shouting. Maybe a drunk being noisy. She looked out of the window, onto the street, just catching sight of the backs of several people as they disappeared into the mist. It obscured the dim light of pre-dawn that was more obvious high up on the other side of the valley. As she opened the window to lean out, she caught a faint glimpse of another couple of people as they appeared out of Lloyd Street, further down the road and opposite.

Her breath caught. Surely there couldn't have been another mining accident. She switched the light on and looked at the clock on the mantelpiece. Twenty-five past four. She rushed to get dressed, ignoring the corset which took too long to fiddle with. It wasn't like she had much flesh to pull in. At the back of her mind she thanked God that Hywel wasn't on the night shift. Nor Idris or Gwilym, she added to herself.

When she reached the landing, Olwen's door opened.

'What on earth is going on? There's a terrible din coming from the houses over the back, and I thought I saw flames.'

'Flames?' She rushed down the stairs.

Olwen followed, whispering loudly, 'Where do you think you're going?'

'To see if any help is needed,' she said, grabbing her shawl off the hatstand and throwing it round her shoulders.

'And what help would *you* be?'

She ignored the suggestion that she was useless. 'Tell the kiddies when they wake up where I've gone. I'll be back when I can.'

'What a to-do, and on a Whit Sunday as well.'

'I'll be back in a while.'

She rushed out the door before her mother-in-law could find some argument to keep her there. There was some light in the sky to her left, enough for her to see her way down. A few people were ahead of her. They turned onto James Street, so she followed on round the corner.

It gradually became apparent that there was a crowd outside the shops on the next corner, where the confectioner's, the empty baker's and the bookshop stood. As she got closer she realised there were flames licking the air from Mr Schenck's shop. The crackling noise it caused mingled with the shouts of the people. She wrapped her arms tightly around herself, giving in to the immediate urge to cry. What if the family were hurt – or worse?

People were gathered on the road in front of the park. It was a relief to see Anwen and Gwen, until she remembered what had happened. She wiped her tears away. Closer to her, she spotted Maurice Coombes' wife, Mabel, who'd been in Violet's class at school.

'What's happened?'

'Oh Violet! Hywel, Idris and Noah have gone in to find Mr and Mrs Schenck.'

'What, in that?' She pointed to the burning building. 'Where's the fire engine?'

'Someone's alerted Phillips the Fire and he's fetching it down.'

It was at that moment they heard the roar of an engine. Soon, its bright red body and gold engine casing came into view through the gloom. The ladder stretched at an angle from the front to the back, where it sloped down. The bell was being clanged frantically. A cheer went up from the crowd.

Violet looked back towards the shop. 'How long have the men been in there?'

'I dunno. A coupla minutes?' Mabel took hold of Violet's arm and held on. 'I hope they're all right.'

Bethan Schenck, Noah's wife, rushed over to them. 'Mabel, where on earth are they? My mam's taken the children to her house. I don't want them out here, or tucked up in bed next to a burning building. Oh Lord, where is Noah?'

The last few words came out on a sob. Violet took her hand. Bethan's two children were the same age as Clarice and Benjamin. Violet couldn't bear the idea of another pair of babbies without their da.

'Out of the way everyone,' called Sergeant Harries, ahead of the fire engine. 'Let Phillips the Fire do his job.'

The crowd moved to the opposite pavements on the cross-roads. Four other men ran to help with the equipment. Violet caught sight of Cadoc Beadle in the crowd, struck for a second by the oddity of it. He'd not been seen out since his beating.

Bethan moved away from the women and ran over to the policeman. 'Sergeant, some more people should go and look for Noah and the others.'

'We can't be sending more men in, not until we've got a bit of water going. They shouldn't have gone ahead in the first place.'

'But Sergeant Harries—'

'Now step back, Mrs Schenck. We'll send more men in just as soon as we can.'

Bethan burst into tears, a long, moaning wail issuing from her mouth. Violet and Mabel went to her once more, leading her a few yards away. Suddenly she stopped. They all looked towards the shop. Out of the front door stumbled Idris, holding on to a swaying Jozef Schenck who wore a long, striped night-shirt. Both men were coughing. The three women ran to them, not heeding the sergeant's order for them to stay back.

'Uncle Jozef,' cried Bethan, 'where are Noah and Aunty Mirjam?'

'And Hywel,' said Violet, unable to stop herself.

'I don't know,' said Idris, struggling to speak. 'They went to find Mrs Schenck.'

'Mirjam, Mirjam,' Jozef groaned the name with difficulty, followed by something in Dutch. 'She'd been restless. I think – must have gone to, to – other bedroom to sleep, so as not to disturb me. I must go back.'

'No, Mr Schenck, you can't,' said Violet.

'Dr Roberts is here with Sister Grey,' someone called.

'Come on, Mr Schenck.' Mabel took him from Idris. 'You need to see the doctor.'

'And you must see the doctor too, Idris,' said Violet.

She'd barely got the words out when Anwen ran over, giving her a strange look as she pulled Idris away.

Violet and Bethan held onto each other, staring at the shop, as the flames inside licked ever higher.

—

'Noah, where are you?' Hywel spluttered, staggering out of what appeared to be the front room of the flat above the bookshop. The early morning light wasn't helping much.

Mrs Schenck hadn't been in the bedroom with her husband when Noah had burst in, he and Idris following on. Overcome with smoke and confusion, the older man hadn't known where she was. As Idris had led a resisting Mr Schenck away, Hywel and Noah had gone to find his wife. Noah had called that he was going to check the kitchen, which appeared to be on the other side from the room Hywel had just exited. There would be other rooms, but it was hard to see which way to go. His eyes stung from the acrid smoke, making them water, whilst the searing heat was starting to make him feel dizzy.

'Noah? Noah! Are you still in the kitchen, mun?' He'd barely got the last word out when he started coughing. It might be best to check, in case Noah had found his aunt there and needed help. He pulled his scarf away from his neck and wrapped it round his face, covering his nose.

The smoke was less fierce here, at the back of the house, and it was clear there was no one in the kitchen. Back in the hall he heard someone calling. The voice became clearer.

'Hywel, Hywel!' There was a rasping cough. 'Help me.'

It was coming from the area beyond the front room. Struggling down what turned out to be a narrow corridor, he made out a door. He flung it open. 'Noah?'

'Here, I'm here, mun,' Noah's disembodied voice yelled, but it was coming from further up the corridor.

Through the smoke came two figures. Noah was dragging his aunt along. She was gasping for breath.

'Help me – get her – downstairs,' Noah rasped. 'There are – flames – bedroom.'

Hywel plunged forward and tried to help his friend, but it was hard because three people couldn't fit side by side down the narrow passage. He realised his leg, the one that had taken the bullet, was aching, as it still did on the odd occasion. He was limping once more.

At the top of the stairs, Noah said, 'I'll go in front, you go behind, and we'll get her down between us.'

As they were getting into position, Mirjam roused herself. 'Jozef, where is Jozef?' she screamed.

'He's gone—'

Hywel's muffled 'ahead' was barely out, when she tugged herself away from the men. What she'd intended to do he wasn't sure. What happened next occurred so quickly he could do nothing to stop it. In her effort to jerk away from them, she tripped on the top step and fell into the fog of smoke on the landing. He watched as if in slow motion. The last thing he remembered was something hard hitting his leg as her flailing foot swept him off his feet, and then a shriek of panic from Noah.

'We have to send people in to get the others out,' Bethan was howling, tugging the arm of Sergeant Harries' uniform once more.

'No one goes in until we have this fire under control,' shouted Harries. 'Now stand back, all of you.'

By now PC Probert had turned up on the scene, with another, even older, ex-policeman, recently dragged out of retirement. They spread their arms to herd the rest of the crowd away. There were murmurs of protest, but they all did as they were told.

Bethan pulled Violet well out of earshot of the policemen. 'I'm going in, I don't care what he says.' She rushed off immediately.

Violet felt her pulse thud inside her head twice before she followed on. This was idiotic. She had two young children.

'Bethan, wait, think about your kiddies.'

She tried to grab hold of her, but Bethan shook her off. Violet followed on, regardless. She could always change her mind if it proved too hazardous. If no one did anything, they'd surely perish. They might have simply collapsed near the door. It was worth a try, wasn't it?

They felt the heat intensify before they reached the building. Although the flames seemed to be on the left of the shop, who knew what they'd find inside? Sergeant Harries' voice hollered out warnings to them to keep away as they entered the door. Soon the footsteps of someone rushing up behind them were heard. She expected any moment to be grabbed by Harries, but then she heard Idris's voice.

'You two should go back.'

Bethan shouted, 'No,' and ran in.

'Violet, please,' Idris pleaded. 'You have young children.'

Shame at her willingness to run in to rescue Hywel overwhelmed her. She nodded and stepped back as Idris rushed in after Bethan. She was about to turn around when she was almost knocked over by the diminutive Twm Bach, dashing past her.

Hurrying back outside, she saw Anwen at a distance crying and calling Idris's name. What a fool she must have looked, running in after Hywel. Enid was with Anwen now, holding her hands. Gwen seemed to have disappeared. No, there she was, coming towards her.

'Why did you go over?'

'I was trying to persuade Bethan not to go in.' This was at least true, if not the whole story.

'Shame she didn't listen. They're taking Mr Schenck to the hospital. I hope they come out soon. This is terrible.'

They huddled together to watch as the men fought the flames which were now licking out of the top window on the left side of the shop.

'Someone should go and help them,' Anwen shouted. She was shaking and starting to whimper.

From the crowd somebody else ran towards the burning building.

'Oh my goodness,' said Violet. 'He can't be well enough to—'

But she didn't get to finish before Sergeant Harries began to yell at the next disobedient member of the public, but to no avail.

–

'Twm, what are you doing here?' said Idris, as the smaller man caught him up, already coughing.

'You were the main reason – we got out of the mine during the disaster last year, so I'm not – letting you risk your life alone here.'

'Come on then.'

The two of them rushed through a haze of white smoke. To the left of the shop, in the section with the children's and history books, the flames were leaping high. Idris felt a brief sorrow for all the lost books that nobody would ever rifle through with delight again.

Because Idris had not long come out, he knew that the door at the rear was where they should head. They were both coughing almost continuously. Twm was right to compare it to the mine disaster, where the choking gases of the afterdamp could easily have killed them.

They just made out Bethan in the dark space beyond the door. Even during broad daylight there wouldn't have been much light here, with its north-easterly aspect, without the dark grey smoke making it difficult to see.

'The stairs – are here – somewhere,' Bethan huffed. 'Ouch.' She seemed to fall from view.

'Where's – she gone?' Idris coughed.

'I'm here. There's something here. Oh God, bo – bodies.'

'*O duw, o duw*,' wailed Twm, panting heavily.

There was a long groan.

'Someone's alive!' said Bethan. 'Who's there?'

'Hywel,' he said. 'I'm here with, with – Noah, I think.'

Idris tried to sigh with relief but only ended up coughing again.

Hywel appeared as he hauled himself up. 'And Mrs Schenck's – here too. Slid down – we did. Help us.'

'What the – the – hell are you doing – here, Bethan? Aunty Mirjam's still, still,' Noah coughed, 'at – top of stairs. I – think.'

'I'll go,' said Idris.

'No!' came a new voice. 'You've done enough. And it's time I made amends.'

'Mr Beadle?' said Hywel, pulling Noah up. 'Don't be daft, mun. You're not well enough.'

'Out of – the way! It's the – the least – I can do.' The last words were spluttered in his haste to get up the stairs.

'Let's go,' said Twm. 'We, we – can't stay.'

'Where are they?' said Violet, the urge to cry bubbling to the surface again.

'Oh Lord, please let them be all right,' said Gwen.

Mabel returned to Violet's side. 'Haven't they come out yet?'

The two women shook their heads. The water being sprayed at the building from the fire engine did at least seem to be doing some good at last, but it still wasn't enough to make those inside safe.

Sergeant Harries stood watching, lifting his helmet to scratch his head. All of a sudden, he leapt towards the building and entered it.

'About time!' said Mabel. 'Letting ordinary folk risk their lives while he stands there watching.'

The crowd moved closer, despite warnings from the two older constables. Harries soon re-emerged, followed by Idris, Hywel, Bethan, Noah and Twm. A cheer went up. Anwen ran over with Enid. A wave of relief washed over Violet. Hywel was bent over and coughing, but he was alive. How she wished she could run to him.

'Idris, why did you have to go in again?' Anwen admonished him while throwing her arms around him. 'There are plenty of strong young men here could have gone.' She looked round accusingly at the crowd there.

'Where's that idiot Cadoc Beadle?' said the sergeant, glancing around. 'I thought he'd be with you.'

'He went back to get Aunty Mirjam.' Noah tried to catch his breath as he pushed his fair hair back from his face. 'Where's Uncle Jozef?'

'He's been taken to the hospital,' said Harries. 'Which is where you all belong.'

'I'm not going anywhere until Aunty Mirjam's brought out,' said Noah. 'And look, they're getting the better of the fire now.'

'Please, please go.' Bethan put her hands together in the manner of prayer. 'You're not breathing right. I'll stay here for Mirjam.'

But as she said this, Cadoc appeared through the door, half carrying, half dragging Mrs Schenck out. Noah limped towards them with Bethan, followed by Dr Roberts and all three policemen.

Mrs Schenck wasn't looking good, with her face pale and eyes closed. And her clothes were scorched on one side. Violet looked away, afraid of what else she might see.

'You should have left me, left me to die,' she raved.

'Aunty Mirjam, you're safe now,' said Noah.

'No, no, I'll never be safe.' She hollered out a pitiful lament and fainted.

Dr Roberts checked the pulse on Mirjam's neck. 'We must get her to the hospital. You there!' He pointed to four middle-aged men. 'I've a blanket here. Come and carry Mrs Schenck.'

They did as they were told, conveying her gently but quickly ahead of the others. Noah was now willing to be led away.

Anwen held on to Idris. Violet was desperate to do the same with Hywel, but after the rumours that had gone around the village, and now the row with the family, it was impossible.

'Where's Mr Beadle gone?' said the doctor, looking around.

'We were so concerned with Mrs Schenck we didn't notice him leaving,' said Anwen. 'He's been a recluse since his accident and doesn't like attention.'

'You're probably right,' said the doctor. 'But someone ought to go to his home and make sure he's all right, and bring him down to the hospital.'

'We'll do that,' said David Keir, the union representative, beckoning his two mates.

Several other men were chosen to help people down to the hospital. Violet, Gwen and Mabel watched as the casualties variously limped and shuffled down Station Road, past the grocer's store. The sky above the mountain on the other side of the valley was yellow, with swirls of pink and lilac, showing that the day was well and truly on its way. The crowd were moving to watch Phillips the Fire get the upper hand on the flames, when there was an outbreak of shouting from near the park entrance.

'There she is. I bet she started it.' Florrie Harris was pointing a gnarled finger at Esther Williams, who was walking towards them.

Esther came to a standstill. 'I saw the smoke and came to see what was going on.'

'Just saw the smoke! Listen to her. She could see the fire all right from her bedroom, pretending she doesn't know what's going on. Bet she started it. She always did say Mr Schenck should shut down for the duration. Now she's got her way.'

Esther looked genuinely shocked, but also frightened. She backed against the railings of the gardens. Several accusing voices shouted insults at her.

Gwen let go of Violet and came forward. 'And I heard from a reliable source that you were wishing bad things on Mr Schenck not long ago. What were the words? Something about people getting their comeuppances.'

'That's right,' called another voice in the gathering. 'I heard that too.'

'It wasn't aimed at Mr Schenck. It was aimed at Rose Pritchard,' said Esther.

Rose stepped out of the throng. 'I don't recall you saying that to me, you liar.'

'You'd already left. Your father had fetched you back. It was when we were outside the bookshop, about four week back now. With Mrs Meredith.'

'It was aimed at everyone there, I was told,' said Gwen.

Violet nudged her. 'Let's not get involved.' She knew Gwen had got that third-hand from Anwen, via Idris.

'And I heard your lad Christopher tried to steal books from Mr Schenck and got thrown out,' said Florrie. 'Another reason for you to be resentful.'

'Now, now,' said Sergeant Harries, coming between them with his arms out at his sides. 'We shouldn't be jumping to conclusions.'

Esther was already hurrying back in the direction of her house and Rose had disappeared back in the crowd.

'Now all back to your homes,' said Harries. 'Though I'm sure the Schencks would appreciate some help clearing up when the time's right.' He looked back at the shop forlornly. 'Let's make sure first these folks involved in the fire are being treated. Then we'll worry about whether someone started it, or if it was an accident. And believe me, if I find out it were deliberate, it will be a sorry day for the perpetrators.' His bushy eyebrows almost met in the middle as he glared at the crowd.

Violet looked back briefly at where Esther had disappeared round the corner of the park. Whatever verbal poison she'd been spitting at Mr Schenck and the others, she couldn't quite believe she'd have done this.

Chapter Twenty-Four

Violet pushed the back door open, guiding Clarice and Benjamin into the scullery. The walk out this morning hadn't yielded as much information about the fire and those involved as she'd been hoping. There'd been no news while they'd been at chapel yesterday either. Then the persistent rain after dinner had precluded any walk she'd been hoping to have with the children and Olwen that afternoon. But no news was good news, or so people often said. Violet reflected that this had not been the case for many of the families awaiting news of their men on the Front. She pictured Charlie, desperately trying to hold on to his image, but it was soon replaced by Hywel. She was particularly eager for news of him after the fire.

She shook herself. Not today. She had passed the bookshop while she was out, and a sorry state it had looked. Clarice, sensitive soul that she was, had burst into tears and, inevitably, Benjamin had followed suit. Most who'd passed by had shaken their heads and said what a terrible thing to happen. Only a few had said nothing. This had included Polly's awful new family, though Polly herself, dragging behind, carrying baby Herby, had looked back at the scene with uncharacteristic concern.

'Take your coats off,' she called as the children were about to enter the kitchen. 'I'm doing you some dinner now.'

The weather today had also descended into cloud and rain. Clarice removed her coat. It was getting too short for her now. Perhaps she should take some of those baby clothes to Mrs Bowen, like Gwen had suggested a while back, and get some money for a bigger second-hand one for her. Benjy was struggling to get his coat off, so Clarice put hers on the table and helped him.

The children were already sitting down at the kitchen table when Olwen returned from her half-day at the Big House. Mrs Meredith had given her some time off for Whit Monday.

'Having dinner already? An egg each with their bread and dripping? That's a little extravagant.'

'They're from the hens Gwilym is looking after. He gave me one each for the children as we passed by to admire the chickens earlier.'

'Hmph! You could have scrambled them and shared them between the four of us.'

Violet could only think of an impolite reply, so said instead, 'We're having dinner early because it's the Sunday School treat this afternoon. Though I don't see them getting much of a parade in this weather.'

'They shouldn't even be having the tea!' Olwen exclaimed.

Clarice's face fell. 'We're not having the tea?'

'Yes, you are, *cariad*,' said Violet. 'Don't worry.'

Olwen crossed her arms and thumped them against her body. 'The Food Controller advised against such indulgence because of the shortages. I read it in the newspaper.'

Violet looked down at the sad faces of her children. Poor little mites, having even this small treat spoiled, and by their mamgu too. 'Pastor Lewis's wife, Anabel, told me the local grocer's were able to supply the food, so they decided to go ahead. So that's good, isn't it *cariadon*?'

The children cheered, their little mouths turned up in smiles.

'Hmph. I'd like a word in the scullery.' Olwen sniffed and stepped stiffly towards the door.

Oh, what now?

'You eat up,' said Violet, leaving the children to it.

In the scullery, Olwen stood in the middle of the room, head tipped up, as if she owned the place.

'On my way back, I had the misfortune to be waylaid by that Florrie Harris. Told me she was at the fire yesterday morning and saw you.'

'You already know I was there.'

'She said you tried to run into the burning building, and that Idris stopped you. She said that Hywel Llewellyn was already in there.' Giving her head a short, stern nod, she pushed her lips out at the same time, as if she'd made her point.

Violet knew now where this was going. Her face heated up, but she played innocent anyway. 'Yes, I was running after Bethan Schenck to stop her going in. Idris didn't realise that's what I was doing. I'm hardly going to run into a burning building when I've got two babbies to look after. That's why I tried to persuade Bethan not to go. But she was frantic with worry about Noah, poor woman. Luckily everyone came out, though I've not heard how they all are, particularly Mr and Mrs Schenck.' She was prattling on, hoping to distract Olwen from her line of thinking.

'That's not what it looked like to Mrs Harris. She thought you might be running in to save that Hywel Llewellyn, after the rumours she'd heard.'

Violet was starting to lose her temper but knew it would be dangerous to give in to it so said calmly, 'And I wonder where she heard those rumours.'

Olwen took a step back and sniffed once more. 'I presume we'll be having some dinner soon too.'

'I've had some pigeon scraps with bread already. There's some left for you which I'll fetch out. I'll make some tea first. Unless you'd like to do that.'

Olwen scowled. 'I've been at work all morning, not out admiring chickens.' With that, she stomped back to the kitchen.

–

As Violet was finishing the drying up, there was a knock on the scullery door. Gwen entered.

'I've come to see if you'd like a walk to the park before the kiddie's parade,' she said. 'While there's a break from the rain. It's much milder now too. And I've the latest news about the casualties yesterday.'

A rush of warmth coursed through Violet's body. The euphoria was fleeting; it could be bad news. Gwen's expression gave nothing away.

'So, how are they all?'

'Idris, Bethan and Twm Bach came out of hospital yesterday afternoon,' said Gwen. 'Hywel and Noah came out in the evening. Hywel's resting now and still got a bit of a cough, but is otherwise fine. Bethan's parents are looking after her and the family.'

'That's good news at least,' said Violet, though the fact Hywel was still coughing worried her.

'The Schencks are in hospital still, but Mr Schenck is sitting up and talking. They say Mrs Schenck has some minor burns on her arm. She's recovering though she's still sleepy.'

'Poor Mrs Schenck,' said Violet. 'Sleep's probably the best thing for her. What about Cadoc?'

'Well there's a strange thing, nobody's been able to find him. David Keir and some others searched his house. He must have gone off for a walk, which is maybe what he was doing when he saw the shop was on fire. Though it's an odd time to go for a walk and no mistake. Someone knocked again this morning but there was no reply and they left him to it. Perhaps he doesn't want to be bothered with people.'

Olwen tramped in. 'I thought I heard voices.'

'Hello Mrs Jones, I'm just telling Violet the news about those involved in the fire and rescue yesterday.'

'Oh yes, I'm sure you are,' said Olwen sharply, pursing her lips and crossing her arms.

Gwen looked a little baffled. 'Anyway, we're going for a walk. Um, would you like to come too, Mrs Jones?'

'You're not going, are you?' Olwen said to Violet, her tone reproachful. 'The parade doesn't start till three o'clock.'

'We're taking advantage of the dry weather,' said Gwen. 'My goodness, you wouldn't think it was nearly June now, would you? What a terrible spring we've had.'

Violet had the impression her friend was trying to engage Olwen in friendly conversation to get on her good side. She'd seen so many people do this, probably knowing how quickly she got cross. But her mother-in-law's lack of interest in how the casualties were doing was shocking. Violet felt lucky that Gwen at least still called for her, given how rude Olwen could be. She'd learned her own lesson after being so rude about Elizabeth. It was quite unforgiveable of her.

'You have to put up with the weather the good Lord sends,' said Olwen. 'And no, I won't be accompanying you.'

Violet gave a silent sigh of relief.

'I suppose you'll come out later to see your grandchildren at the parade and the tea,' said Gwen.

'No, I will not. The Food Controller said there should be no teas so I will not be attending on principle.' Olwen turned abruptly and went back to the kitchen.

Gwen frowned. 'What was that all about?'

'Take no notice,' said Violet. 'You know what she's like.'

'Is she objecting to me giving you news of Hywel?'

Violet hesitated. 'You know she got the wrong end of the stick.' She waved her hand to dismiss it.

'You and Hywel did seem to be getting on well. There's nothing wrong with that. In fact, it's a shame Olwen's caused such a rumpus that you've fallen out with Anwen's family.'

Violet's stomach knotted. 'We got to know each other a bit when he lodged here, that's all.' She shrugged.

'He's a nice man,' said Gwen. 'Kind. And not too much older than you. If you ask me, it would have been a good thing for you both, to—'

'You shouldn't say such things,' Violet said in a loud whisper. 'Especially not with Olwen' – she gestured towards the kitchen door – 'here. Anyway, the row was my fault too, as I was rude about Elizabeth.'

'Yes, I heard that. I don't think your opinion was quite as unreasonable as they made out. You know she asked me along to the cinema last August, but never asked again, so I guess she wasn't that keen on my company. Felt a little offended, I did.'

'You could have invited her,' said Violet.

'Goodness, no! She's higher class so I wouldn't presume. And it wouldn't have been a good idea, given the circumstances. Never mind that, shall we get going in case it rains again?'

Violet fetched the children and they were soon ready and out of the door. In a way it was lucky that Olwen disapproved and wouldn't come; at least she'd have some peace from her.

'How is your mother-in-law getting on with her job at the Big House?' Gwen asked as they walked along the pavement.

'I've no idea really. I've heard more complaints about Mrs Rhys than anything else.'

'Oh dear, have they fallen out at work?'

'No, but it sounds like the atmosphere is very chilly between them. Olwen objects to Mrs Rhys bringing instructions from Mrs Meredith, though I don't know what else she could do.'

It was a wonder to Violet that Elizabeth hadn't seen to it that Olwen was dismissed before she'd even started, but she kept this to herself.

Reaching Edward Street and turning onto it, they watched the workers on the allotment. Gwen waved to Idris and Gwilym, who were looking at the chickens. Clarice and Benjamin skipped ahead, holding hands.

Gwen sighed. 'It's just as well we decided not to go on that trip to Barry Island today that Anwen suggested a coupla months back, with the fire and the bad weather and all. Besides, what with the railways not running excursion services this year, the trains would have been packed.'

'And the fares have gone up by fifty percent,' Violet pointed out, wondering how a trip to Barry would have worked with Anwen's family now falling out with her.

'I suppose. But when this is all over, one of the first things we should do is take a trip to Barry,' Gwen announced.

'What if it's, say, November?' said Violet.

Gwen tutted. 'Then we'll have to go to Cardiff for afternoon tea instead, and go for a walk around the arcades and Cathays Park.'

Turning onto Jubilee Gardens they both stopped to survey the ruined bookshop. The walls were still mostly standing, but the window frames were burnt and the glass smashed. Beyond the large shop windows there were piles of charred books and scorched bookcases. There was a group of men outside shovelling bits of debris. Twm Bach was wielding a wheelbarrow, taking the rubbish to where several lads were sorting it into neat piles. No doubt the council scavenger would bring his horse and cart to collect that which could be reused.

'Twm seems to have the scouts involved in tidying up the bookshop,' said Gwen. 'Look, there's Jenkin and Evan.'

'Hello there,' Twm called when he spotted them.

Violet noticed Clarice's face fall once more at the sight of the shop. 'Why don't you take Benjy into the park and have a look at the flowers, *cariad*.'

The little girl linked hands with her brother and they crossed the road to the entrance of the park.

'You're all doing a good job here.' Violet was impressed that so many had come out to help the Schencks.

'Aye, well I likes a good book, me, so it's sad to see the place like this. It were lucky that the house and shop either side weren't affected. Fortunately, Mr Schenck has insurance so he'll get the money to fix it up. Quite a few have volunteered to do it in their spare time, given how thin on the ground skilled builders are now.'

'That's wonderful.' Violet felt a drop of hope nudge at the misery. Never mind the Olwens and Esthers of this world, there were generous people too. 'I wonder if the books were insured,' she said. 'I don't suppose he'll be able to replace some of the second-hand ones.'

'Sergeant Harries is here with a detective,' said Twm, 'having a look round. I heard them say the back door had been forced.

They also found a pile of burnt books, as if they'd been put there purposefully to start the fire.'

'My goodness,' said Gwen, shaking her head. 'Whoever it is, I hope they catch them quickly. I thought we'd got rid of people like that when they arrested Iolo Prosser, and the others.'

'Aye. Fingers are pointing at Mrs Williams,' said Twm, 'I don't see how she'd have the strength, really.'

'If she needed strength Christopher might have helped,' said Gwen, 'being led astray by that gang.'

'No, it wasn't Esther,' said Violet. 'She's got a mean tongue, but that's quite different to setting a blaze.'

'Well she's been out around the Gardens several times today,' said Twm, 'telling anyone who'll listen that she's not responsible. Apparently she's lost all her sewing work because people believe it's her, especially since the police have been to her house. And Christopher's gone off to stay with a friend at McKenzie Cottages, through shame, according to her, though he's got nothing to be proud of. Up in court he'll be before long for the veggie thefts, and no doubt fined.'

'Well, that's a point,' said Violet. 'Florrie mentioned yesterday that Christopher's gang tried to steal books and were thrown out by Mr Schenck. I hope Sergeant Harries knows that.'

'Knows what?' said the sergeant, coming out of the charred front door.

With him was a miserable-looking man in his fifties, attired in a grey suit and bowler hat. He had a pencil moustache.

'If you know anything, we'd appreciate you telling us,' said the detective, peering at them with dark, beady eyes.

Violet wished she'd kept her mouth shut. She didn't want to be questioned by this officious-looking man, nor have Christopher's gang hear that she'd told on them.

As she hesitated, Gwen repeated the information.

'We are already aware of that,' he said dismissively.

'And are you aware that Rose Pritchard, the butcher's daughter, was rude to Mr Schenck not long ago?'

'I'll make a note of it, though I doubt it has any relevance—'

'No relevance?' Gwen interrupted. 'But she's a known thief. She stole from the Merediths when she was their cook, didn't she, Violet?'

'Yes. But she's never been known to set a fire.'

'If I need any more information, I'm sure Sergeant Harries here will question you again.' He walked off, clearly dismissing them.

Constable Probert came running out of the building, his eyes bulging. His face had gone pale. 'Inspector Strong, you need to come in here, now.'

The detective and Harries were soon following Probert back in.

The men working on clearing up gathered round the front door, muttering to each other. Soon, others who'd come out for afternoon walks were joining them.

'Come on,' said Gwen, dragging Violet towards the group. 'They might have found some evidence.'

'I'm not sure I want to,' said Violet, anxious about what they might have discovered. But Gwen pulled her along, not to be dissuaded.

Five minutes later the policemen re-emerged, stony-faced.

'What have you found, then?' Twm Bach called. 'Do you know who set the fire?'

The detective crossed the road and walked away down Gabriel Street.

'There's rude. What have they found, sergeant?'

Harries regarded Twm and then the rest of those gathered, his hands behind his back. Slowly he pulled one hand out and held aloft a pair of round spectacles. Violet clasped her mouth, feeling sick.

'I fear we have found Cadoc Beadle.'

Chapter Twenty-Five

It had been six days since Hywel had helped out at the fire, and the first day he'd felt completely well. Being underground in the pit had been a struggle, the walls of the narrow passages seeming to close in on him, like the smoke in the bookshop.

He was in his three-piece suit now, having just returned from Cadoc Beadle's funeral with Idris, Gwilym and their brothers. The scouts had formed a guard of honour in their uniforms, while both Jenkin and Evan had spoken movingly in the chapel about him. Brave, that was. He doubted he'd have done such a thing at sixteen.

The five of them sat in his kitchen now, being served cups of tea by Enid. Anwen sat next to the stove. On a blanket at the side of her chair was Sara Fach, chewing one of the wooden cubes she was playing with.

'He was lucky, was Cadoc,' said Enid, 'that they recorded a verdict of death by misadventure, else he'd not have been allowed a Christian burial.'

Evan and Jenkin glanced at each other and Hywel knew they were thinking what he was, that it was more likely Cadoc had gone back into the fire willingly, that he'd wanted to die. Why else would he have returned? There'd been no one else to save. For what reason had he even been out that early in the morning when he hadn't been out for months? He'd lived right at the end of the village but it was possible he'd heard the fire engine's bell clanging, for it made quite a noise. Whatever the reason, he'd had no cause to go back into the building. How come nobody had noticed? Too busy with the casualties, no doubt. He'd not been happy since he'd woken up after his attack, that's all Hywel knew.

Both boys were now looking down at the table, their faces a picture of misery. Cadoc's death had hit them hard, what with him being their scout master since they'd first enrolled, and lately with their regular visits to him.

'Were there many there?' said Cadi, bringing in some potato bread rolls and some sliced corned mutton.

'Aye, downstairs in the chapel was almost full,' said Idris. 'A lot of the young men have passed through his scout troup, including me and Gwilym here, though we weren't in it for long. Not like these two.' He indicated the boys.

'I'll miss him mun, I'll tell you,' said Jenkin forlornly. 'I was hoping he'd get well and lead us again.'

'The most fitting way to honour him is to do your very best at scouts,' said Enid. 'That's what Mr Beadle would have wanted to see.'

'I wish now we hadn't gone banging on his door when the boys ran away to enlist,' said Idris. 'It can't have helped matters.'

'Mr Beadle never encouraged us to enlist,' said Evan. 'In fact, when we said to him we wished we could go to war he said there was time enough for that when we was eighteen.'

'He did that,' said Jenkin. 'But it weren't you what knocked six bells out of him, so you're not to blame. It's that Edgar Williams what's responsible for his death, as sure as if he'd killed him at the time.'

'Let's not dwell on that,' said Hywel. 'Edgar's locked up, so at least there was some justice.' He took a sip of the tea that Enid handed him. 'I don't know about you lot, but since the sun is shining, and I've been either down the pit or indoors, I could do with a spell on the allotments, blow the cobwebs out.'

'That's a good idea,' said Idris, taking a side plate from the pile and helping himself to some bread and mutton. 'There's lots to do. Are you coming over today, Gwilym?'

'Not to the far allotment, no. I've got a job to do with the chickens here, getting that barbed wire in place round their run. I know they've caught the boys what stole the veg, but I'm not taking any chances. If someone comes in the dead of night, they'll have to negotiate that little lot first. What about you boys? Do you fancy helping Hywel and Idris out?'

'We're helping at the bookshop,' said Evan. 'Once we've got it properly cleared, they can start rebuilding it again. Mr Breckon's got us scouts organised on a rota.'

'Mr Breckon!' said Enid. 'I forget he's actually called Tomos Breckon. Always Twm Bach to everyone, he is.'

'It wouldn't be very respectful for us to call our scout master by his nick name,' said Jenkin.

'No, I suppose not. You're good boys for helping out. I hear Mr Schenck's been staying with Noah and Bethan since he came out of hospital three days back.'

'That's right,' said Evan. 'And Mrs Schenck was due out today, Mr Breckon told us. I think the pair of them will be staying next door for a while yet.'

Sara Fach chose this moment to have a little grizzle. She dropped the block she'd been holding and slumped a little. Anwen picked her up and placed her on her lap, smoothing down the white pinafore over her blue dress.

'I dunno what's wrong with her today. I'm afraid she might be going down with a cold. I was thinking of going over to the allotments myself, just across the road here, but I don't want to leave her with Mamgu too long.' Anwen looked pained as she said this. She joggled the baby on her knee. The little girl didn't giggle like she normally did. Instead she lay against Anwen with her thumb in her mouth, eyes fluttering shut.

Hywel wondered if she was worried it was more than a cold. The baby looked perfectly healthy, but then so had Anwen's brothers, Tomos and Geraint, before the consumption had stolen their lives as youths.

'Don't you worry about me,' said Cadi. 'And I'm sure it's just the sniffles. I can pop over the road to fetch you if need be. She'll probably want a nap soon anyway.'

Enid sat at one end of the table, her face puckered. It was the way she always looked when the conversation turned to Sara Fach. She still had no interaction with her at all, treating her like she wasn't there, unless the baby came near her when she was crawling. Hywel could understand why she was upset, but she was only a baby after all. She'd certainly melted his heart and he was quite happy to refer to himself as 'uncle' when he spoke to her. Enid always humphed when he did this.

'All right,' said Anwen, 'if you're sure.'

'Yes, I'm sure,' said Cadi. 'I love my time with the little sweetheart.' She looked over at Enid with a small shake of her head. 'Now eat up everyone, for I managed to scrape together enough ingredients to make some bakestones. I'm sure you'd all like one before you get on with your work.'

'Thanks Mrs Rhys,' said Evan. 'I haven't had once since, um, oh. Since Miss Meredith brought some to Mr Beadle in the winter.' His head went down once more.

Hywel patted his shoulder. The quicker they ate up and got out to some activity the better.

–

Hywel had slept only fitfully since he'd gone to bed. He slid out now and clicked on the light before looking at the fob watch on the tiny homemade table. Five to three. Maybe he'd read his book, *Frankenstein*, try to free his mind of all that had been swirling around it. By all, he meant Violet.

He plonked himself on the bed. She'd been at chapel that morning, with Olwen the Ogre, who, as usual, was causing trouble, claiming she wanted to sit at the front because she had hearing problems. A likely story, given she seemed to overhear things only too well. Those who'd already secured the seats gave them up reluctantly. Violet's face had flushed pink and she'd looked awkward.

Oh Violet, Violet, Violet. Despite what she'd said about Elizabeth, who'd sat with them this morning, and despite Olwen's cruel act in reporting him to the police, he couldn't stay angry at her. In his heart he knew there was something wrong. It was the look of tragedy deep in her eyes that went beyond losing Charlie.

If she'd had any other feelings for *him* beyond a friend, they'd certainly have flown now, since his harsh words to her. Yet what else could he think, other than that she was complicit in Olwen's malice, if only by not sending her away? And now, even after her mother-in-law had tried to get him locked up, she still hadn't sent her packing.

He placed his fingers lightly round his throat as the lump formed. What was the point of getting upset about it? He could do nothing, and if he attempted to help, it would make the situation with Olwen even worse.

A cup of tea, that's what he needed, for his throat was dry. He'd be dog-tired come his shift, but he would be if he lay awake all night in bed too. After dressing he picked up the book, remembering now that he'd finished it before lying down last night. At least there were another two to be read on the bookcase in the front room, ones he'd borrowed from the Institute library.

While he waited for the kettle to boil, he went to fetch the Conan Doyle. He fancied a Sherlock Holmes mystery to fill his mind.

As he lifted his hand to pull it out, there was an almighty hollering from outside. He dismissed it as a fox initially, but it didn't quite ring true.

The sound had stopped by the time he'd reached the curtain and pulled it back. He peered into the street, towards the allotment, but it was still too dark to see anything, despite a wisp of light appearing above the mountains. Perhaps if he turned the light off in the room he could— there it was again. It was a woman's scream, he was sure of it. He ran to the front door.

He pictured Violet running across the field from Bryn Road, chased by Olwen spouting curses. Reading too much gothic fiction had stoked his already vivid imagination.

Out of the door, he picked his way across the road, his eyes still adjusting to the dark. It was chilly and he was only in his shirtsleeves. The noise of the distress rumbled on, becoming a piercing scream before he reached the other side. There was someone by the chicken run, he was sure.

He heard a door slam and was aware of someone else heading across the road.

'Is that you, Hywel?'

'Yes, Gwilym. What on God's earth is going on?'

'Thief, I reckon.'

That made more sense than his ramblings.

His eyes had now adjusted to what was in fact a dim light. He and Gwilym did a circuit of the chicken run, being careful of the barbed wire placed most of the way round. On the far side they stopped dead, looking down at the cause of the noise.

Someone else had not been so careful.

Rose Pritchard screamed once more on seeing them. 'Bloody get this off me. I can't move.' She was sitting on the ground, her dress and shawl well and truly caught up in the wire, along with her boot which was entangled.

'Shouldn't have been trying to steal chickens then, should you?' said Gwilym.

'I wasn't bloody stealing chickens; I was out for a walk.'

Hywel couldn't help but laugh at the ludicrous claim. 'In the middle of the night? Don't give me that.'

'You've got away with too much recently,' said Gwilym. 'Mrs Meredith and Mr Schenck might not have pressed charges, but I will.'

Two or three other men had come out on the street now, including Hywel's neighbour, old Mr Norris.

'I'll bloody press charges against you,' said Rose, 'putting up dangerous wire for people to have accidents in. Look at my hand bleeding.' She lifted it up to show a nasty scratch.

'Well it do serve you right,' said Mr Norris. 'We're all witnesses to you here.'

'Get me out!' she screeched.

'Not until I've fetched Sergeant Harries,' said Gwilym. 'If these gentlemen would be kind enough to keep an eye on you.'

'Of course,' said Hywel. 'Though I don't think she's going anywhere.'

—

This was just like old times for Anwen on the allotments, her and Elizabeth chatting on a warm afternoon as they worked. Neither of them had spent much time here in recent months, what with Elizabeth's job and Sara Fach. The two of them were hoeing a large patch, ready to sow seeds for early winter veg. Elizabeth stopped, took a deep breath and leant on her hoe.

'Not used to the physical work now then,' Anwen joked, 'after sitting in an office for several months.'

'It's a nice change, being outdoors, especially on a sunny day like today. I can't say I won't miss making my own money, though. My parents' monthly allowance to me always came with such a lot of conditions I felt free of while I was working.'

'Can the man who came back to the job really manage, with a blown-off kneecap?'

'It's the perfect job for him really. I don't resent giving it back to him; I knew it would only ever be until the war ended. I just wish more of this work was open to women in the first place. We could do so many of the jobs that we're denied.'

There she was, in crusading mood again. Anwen had missed that too. 'After the war, the Suffragettes could restart their campaigning.'

'I do hope so, for even with the prospect of votes for women over thirty, there is so much more to fight for. We've merely climbed the first couple of steps of a very long, winding staircase.'

And maybe she'd join in, Anwen mused. She wondered what Idris would have to say about it, though he was all for women having the vote and having better rights.

'I was wondering,' said Elizabeth, 'about Violet. Have you spoken to her recently?'

'I certainly have not,' said Anwen, feeling guilty despite her resolve. 'Quite apart from what she said about you, I'm frankly amazed she still hasn't got rid of Olwen after that nonsense about Hywel.'

'I wouldn't take it out on her for too long. What she said hurt, I won't deny it, but I can understand a little why she might resent me. The three of you have been friends for such a long time. At your wedding, I think she was put out that I helped Gwen get you dressed, and not her. I can understand that too. I hope, in time, she'll come to trust me. I didn't mention anything about it to my mother, as I didn't want her sacking Olwen before she'd even started work and depriving Violet of money. I imagine she's in a difficult position, with Olwen being willing to work and helping her out with finances. She needs friends.'

'Gwen is still popping round and went to the children's parade with her.' Anwen had been a bit miffed about that. 'Though Gwen's not around so much now, with her having a young man.'

Elizabeth leant forward with interest. 'Who would that be then?'

'I don't really know anything about him.'

'How curious. Look, there's Gwilym coming over, all clean and changed. Probably going to check on the chickens.'

'He's become a bit obsessed since Rose was arrested, worried that others will either steal the hens or the eggs.'

'We shouldn't be surprised Rose was caught red-handed, after stealing food from our pantry. Hello Gwilym!' she called.

Anwen and Elizabeth walked over to meet him.

'They seem like happy little ladies.' Elizabeth looked down at the hens. 'That's a nice big run you've built them.'

Gwilym started throwing grain into the run. 'Aye, I wish I could let them out for a bit, but I dare say they'd ruin the veg.'

'Indeed. Now there's Sergeant Harries heading this way. Looks like he's on a mission.'

'Hello there,' he called, as he got nearer. 'I thought I'd find you here after your shift. Thought you'd be interested to hear that your chickens aren't the only thing that Rose Pritchard's been stealing.'

'Did you search her home?' Anwen asked.

'Certainly. I thought there'd likely be evidence of other thefts, and I was right.' His head held high, he bounced on his heels, looking most pleased with himself. 'Never mind them detectives, I've been doing a little detecting myself.'

'What did you find?' Elizabeth asked when he didn't enlighten them.

'Books from the bookshop, no less. I've talked to Mr Schenck and he confirms that Miss Pritchard has never bought a book from there, though she's been in at least three times.'

'That sounds right,' said Anwen. 'She claimed when she came in the shop, only two days before the fire, that she'd never buy a book there when she could get them from the library.'

'Did she now? Mr Schenck didn't mention that, only that she'd caused a row and had flung some books off the shelves.'

'So what are you thinking, Sergeant?' said Elizabeth. 'That Rose was involved in the fire?'

'Seems highly likely. And the break-in a bit before when some money and papers were taken. Didn't find them at her house, but the money's likely spent and the papers thrown away. And there are the half-dozen other minor thefts that have been reported in the village. Anyway, she's been arrested with all those charges. Shouting her 'ead off about it not being her, though she admits to stealing books from the bookshop on two other occasions. Seems pretty conclusive to me. It's up to the courts to decide now.'

'In that case,' said Anwen, 'would you pass the word around the village so that people don't continue blaming Esther Williams? I know she's not a nice woman, but she's lost work because of it. And nobody should be blamed for something they didn't do, should they, Sergeant?'

She could tell by the sheepish look on Harries' face that he knew she was referring to Idris's unsound arrest last year.

'Yes, quite right,' he said, rocking on his heels once again. 'Best be going now.' He touched the rim of his helmet. 'Good day to you all.'

He ambled slowly off, the three of them watching until he was out of earshot.

'Would Rose really have set a fire to the bookshop?' said Anwen.

'I reckon so,' said Gwilym. 'Got a real malicious streak, that one.'

'Who else could it be?' said Elizabeth. 'She's the one who had the argument with Mr Schenck. And there was another argument last month, involving Mrs Schenck too, so my mother told me. She loses control very easily.'

Gwilym replaced the lid on the large tin where he kept the grain. 'Aye, I was there too. It was the day after the theft. Rose was pretty nasty to him and his wife. It is odd that the theft of the money and papers came just before that argument and the fire not long after.'

His eyes widened. Strolling along the side of the allotment was Mrs Meredith in a pristine navy skirt and matching jacket. Her hat was large and decorated with several long feathers. It seemed a little ornate for a Monday afternoon in the village.

'I'll be getting along to the far allotment,' he said, scampering off before Elizabeth's mother caught them up.

'Good afternoon, Anwen,' said Margaret as she approached. 'So you're out helping with the allotments too.'

'Yes. I don't do much now, what with Sara Fach.'

'How is little Sara now? Enid does not speak much about her.'

Anwen experienced that mist of gloom that always shrouded her when she thought of the problem of her mother and baby sister. It was a constant sadness.

'She's growing quickly, and already crawling. When she's a bit bigger and can walk, I'll bring her over to the allotments with me. She'd enjoy playing with the other children.'

'I dare say you'll be giving her a little niece or nephew to play with soon.'

Anwen produced the customary smile in response to this question. 'All in good time. Sara needs my attention for now.'

'Quite so. And who knows, it may not be too long before Elizabeth is in a position to start a family.'

Anwen had never seen such a wide smile on Margaret. She turned to Elizabeth for an explanation. 'What's all this then?'

Elizabeth's face had turned a deep crimson. 'There's really nothing to it.'

'Oh come, come,' said Margaret. 'You haven't told Anwen about Ralph?'

'No, for I feel there's really not a great deal to tell.' She was getting flustered, which was not like her.

Ralph? What a coincidence, what with Gwen's young man... No, it surely was coincidence.

'Well I think he's a very good catch, our Mr Tallis, the councillor. I've met him on several occasions and such a *charming* man he is too. It's high time you brought him home, Elizabeth. Do you remember him, Anwen, from his visit about the allotments? I believe you were there.'

'Yes, I do recall him.'

'And fancy him turning up at the cinema the same time as Elizabeth! It was surely fate. Of course, you'd know about that, for I believe your friend Gwen was there too.'

'When they went to see *The Battle of the Somme*?'

'That's right.'

Elizabeth closed her eyes briefly and looked uncomfortable. Neither she nor Gwen had mentioned Mr Tallis being there, despite both of them, separately, relating the contents of the film to her. Something told her Elizabeth didn't want Gwen to know about her relationship with Tallis, and that in itself was strange. What had she to hide, unless she knew he was also walking out with Gwen?

'Sergeant Harries was here not long ago,' said Elizabeth, 'to say they'd arrested Rose for the fire and theft at the bookshop, as well as the attempted chicken theft.'

'That doesn't surprise me in the least,' said her mother.

'I think Anwen might have doubts about it being her.'

'Really?' Margaret looked askance at her.

'Sergeant Harries doesn't always come to the right conclusion with the evidence available, but simply the easy one. Like with Idris last year,' said Anwen.

'That was certainly a travesty,' said Margaret.

'And if she isn't guilty of those particular crimes, then the real villains will go free,' said Elizabeth.

'Yes. And I was thinking,' Anwen began, wondering if she should be saying this. 'Well, it's just that there have been a few other thefts in the village, as the sergeant said, but all of these started happening after Polly Coombes moved back.'

Margaret visibly trembled. Anwen guessed she didn't want reminding of her son's mistake.

'Polly seems a bit afraid of her husband, Gus, and the family are all troublemakers. Look at the way they behaved at the sports day.'

'It's certainly worth looking into,' said Margaret. 'I'll have a word with Lavinia Perryman, as her husband is Chief Constable. Now, I shall continue with my daily constitutional. Don't be too long, Elizabeth, for Mrs Jones is cooking the dinner earlier this evening. I have a meeting with the Netley Hospital fundraising committee. I think now your work is terminated, you should come and give a hand. Good afternoon, Anwen.'

'Good afternoon, Mrs Meredith.'

Margaret unfurled her parasol and put it up as she walked daintily away. Elizabeth rolled her eyes and tapped her mouth as she gave a fake yawn. They both giggled. Business as usual for poor Elizabeth.

Anwen wished she hadn't mentioned Gus Smith. Being unhappy about Polly's return to the village, Mrs Meredith might use this as an excuse to get rid of them. They could certainly do without such troublemakers, but she was worried about Polly. How strange that that should be the case.

Her mind turned back to Gwen. There were surely two Ralphs. She'd ask Gwen about his surname, just out of interest, but it was unlikely to be the same man.

Cadi was preparing dinner that evening. Anwen had just come down from putting Sara Fach to bed in the cot they'd recently acquired from a neighbour of Idris's parents. Just as well, as she'd grown out of the crib that Bethan Schenck had lent her soon after the baby had arrived.

For the last few hours she'd worried about the Ralph question. The more she thought about it, the more it bothered her. When Gwen had accidently revealed his name, hadn't she followed it up with something about Elizabeth, as if she'd been reminded of her? Did she know they were both walking out with him? It didn't sound like something Gwen would put up with.

'I'm going to pop round to see Gwen before dinner,' Anwen told Idris, who was sitting at the table reading the *Monmouth Guardian*. 'There's something I want to discuss with her.'

'That sounds mysterious,' he said.

'It's probably something and nothing. I'll tell you later. Keep an ear out for Sara Fach.'

He nodded. 'Of course. I'll check on her soon.'

She fetched her shawl and left by the front door. Despite being June, with the sun shining most of the day, it had become a little chilly by the evening. She was soon at the back of James Street, going through the garden gate of number forty. As luck would have it, Gwen was standing in the yard, a cigarette in her hand.

'I didn't know you smoked?'

'Only a little. Ralph started me off. I quite enjoy it, though it makes me cough a bit.'

That was something she could do without, given that she'd been a lot chestier since working at the munitions.

'Gwen, I was wondering about this Ralph.'

'All will be revealed in good time. He needs to sort something out first. There's someone else interested in him, and they're not taking no for an answer. That's all I can tell you. He's afraid I might get the brunt of her anger if she finds out.'

There was unquestionably something wrong here. She was going to come right out and say it. 'Is your Ralph, Councillor Tallis?'

Her friend's mouth opened wide in surprise. 'How do you know that?'

'I'm guessing this person who's interested in him and not leaving him alone is Elizabeth.'

'Goodness, you should be Sherlock Holmes! How did you work that out? Did Elizabeth mention him to you?'

'Oh Gwen. There's no other way to tell you this, but he's walking out with Elizabeth too.'

'Is that what she claimed?'

'No, she didn't, it was Mrs Meredith who mentioned him. She knows all about their relationship.'

Gwen threw the cigarette on the ground and stubbed it out with a rather stylish cream shoe comprising three straps. 'Elizabeth must have told her that, but it's not true. It's all in her imagination.'

'Is that likely?'

'Then she's simply lying.' Gwen folded her arms round her waist, a determined expression on her face.

'No Gwen. That's the kind of thing Rose would do, or Polly before she married Gus Smith. Elizabeth's not like that. And she's not the kind of person to pursue a man if he's not interested. She's a modest sort. She doesn't have Tom's self-confidence, nor his vanity.'

Gwen's head flopped forward, and she stood like that for a while. 'As much as I hate to say it, I believe you could be right. All this cloak and dagger stuff, and we've been walking out for the best part of nine months, but still he's wanting to keep it a secret. And it's not like I see him very regularly. I should have known he was too good for the likes of me.'

'Gwen, he hasn't… you know…'

'What, tried his luck with me? He's hinted at it a couple of times, but I've made it clear I'm not that kind of girl. I did think it strange that Elizabeth should chase him. I'm supposed to be seeing him tomorrow evening. He was going to pick me up in his car at the end house of Mafeking Terrace. I dunno what to do now.'

Gwen slumped down onto the low garden wall, her head in her hands. Anwen wondered if she was going to cry. She sat next to her. 'I'm sorry I had to bring you this news. I didn't want to see you get hurt.'

'I was getting quite fond of him too. Thought I'd fallen on my feet, him being a councillor and estate agent. Not that it was the only reason I walked out with him.'

'No, of course not. I think we should teach Mr Tallis a lesson. What do you think?'

Gwen didn't reply for a while, then said, 'Yes. Ralph Tallis will regret the day he took advantage of my trust.'

Chapter Twenty-Six

Anwen had agonised all the next morning about telling Elizabeth the news of the not-so-charming Mr Tallis. There was one thing for sure: if she found out some other way that Anwen knew he was seeing both her and Gwen, she might not take kindly to it. At the same time, she was loath to upset her friend.

She was cleaning the front room now, with Sara Fach crawling round the old rug. The baby was picking up each of her coloured wooden bricks in turn, examining them with a serious expression, before moving on to the next. The table in there had been folded down and pushed to one side to give her more room. Anwen often brought her in here to play, as there was more room – and it was out of her mother's way.

Going to the window, she pulled the curtains open a little wider and peered out. There were a few women on the allotments, some with children either helping or running around the grassed edges. Elizabeth was there, kneeling down on the soil with a trowel. If she didn't do it now, she never would.

She picked the little girl up. 'Come on, *fach*, you'd like a bit of fresh air, wouldn't you?' In the kitchen she called, 'Just taking the baby for a walk.'

Cadi poked her head through. 'Right you are.'

Outside, the sky was a brilliant blue, not a cloud in sight. It was also warmer than it had been of late, making Anwen wish she could be out working on the land. But she didn't want to take too much advantage of Cadi's good nature. Apart from which, her mamgu had a few sewing jobs to catch up with. She closed her eyes and soaked up the sunlight. It was a way to delay the unwelcome task. But the quicker she did it, the quicker it would be over.

Elizabeth pulled herself up when she spotted her. 'What a glorious day. It makes one glad to be alive. And how lovely to see Sara Fach.'

How Anwen hated spoiling the day for her.

'Could I have a word, Elizabeth? It's a bit delicate.'

'Why, yes, of course.' She put the trowel down. 'Let's have a walk around the perimeter.' As they started on their lap, Sara put her hand out towards her. Elizabeth took it and waggled it, making the baby giggle. 'How sweet. She really does have the loveliest nature.'

'Heaven knows where she gets it from, for it's not from either of her parents.'

'From her grandmother, I should think, like you.'

'Thank you for saying that, though… I'm not so sure you'll still think it when I tell you, well, what I've got to tell you.'

'Oh dear, that sounds serious,' she said on a long breath.

'Gwen has been walking out with someone.'

Elizabeth clasped her hands in front of her chest and beamed. 'But that is *good* news. I know you'll wonder why I should be so enthusiastic about it, but, well, it does make things easier for me. The reason I was so reluctant to—'

'Please, I haven't finished.' Anwen stopped as they reached the part of the field just past Gwilym's house, where it curved to go down towards Lloyd Street. 'I found out last night that Gwen has also been walking out with Mr Tallis.'

'What? No!' she laughed. 'You are mistaken. Gwen has been pestering him ever since we watched *The Battle of the Somme* at the cinema. But he's been politely putting her off. I'm afraid to say she's become a bit of a nuisance, according to Ralph.'

By the way Elizabeth said his name, Anwen could tell she was more than fond of him.

'And that's exactly what he's told Gwen about you.'

The smile melted away. 'I don't understand. Are you saying Ralph has told Gwen about me? He was trying to keep it under wraps for her sake.'

'What I'm saying, Elizabeth, is that Ralph has been walking out with both of you this last nine months, but instructing you both not to tell the other, giving the reason that each of you is pestering him. He's been deceiving you both.'

Elizabeth's expression drooped into wretchedness. 'But why would he do that? Are you sure Gwen isn't just... It sounds terrible to say it. Could she be imagining that her pestering him is a relationship?' Elizabeth looked hopeful.

'Why would Gwen tell the same story you have unless Tallis told her it? And how would Gwen be in a position to chase him unless she was actually meeting him somewhere? She doesn't move in his circles.'

Elizabeth let out a long, distressed sigh. 'I will have to have a word with him.'

'I don't think that's a good idea. If he's willing to deceive you both, no doubt he'd come up with some excuse. He's picking Gwen up this evening, at the end of West Street. She and I have a plan.' Sara Fach started to wriggle, clearly wanting to be down on the ground. 'I'll have to be quick. She's getting restless.'

'It's a shame you don't have a pushchair for her. She'd enjoy that.'

'Elizabeth, are you listening?'

'Yes, yes, you have a plan. All right. What have you got in mind?'

–

Anwen and her friends had passed the chapel on Gabriel Street, and still Gwen and Elizabeth had not given each other more than a cursory greeting. Anwen had done most of the talking on the way, though that had been little enough. Elizabeth walked stiffly, with her parasol up. Gwen strode ahead of them, as if determined to get this over and done with. Anwen was not at all sure this was a good idea now, but it was better than either Gwen or Elizabeth tackling Tallis about this on their own.

Gabriel Street became Mafeking Terrace with its short line of houses, the front gardens bigger than any others in the village. At the end of the terrace was a lane that led to the back gardens.

'Gwen, if you wait on the pavement, Elizabeth and I will hide up the alley here. You know what to do when he stops.'

Gwen nodded. Elizabeth folded down her parasol as Anwen led her to a hedge, where they concealed themselves. They waited around five minutes before at last they heard a motorcar approaching. Elizabeth peeped through a gap.

'That's him now,' she whispered.

The car did a one hundred and eighty degree turn in the road, then reversed into place on their side, facing Rhymney. With the engine still running, Tallis got out of the car and made to open the door for Gwen.

'This is our cue,' said Anwen, noticing Elizabeth had gone pale. Nevertheless, she followed her out.

Tallis didn't notice them at first, so absorbed by Gwen's presence did he seem. It was only when Elizabeth said, 'Hello Ralph,' that he spun around in shock.

'Elizabeth! What on earth——?'

'Am I doing here? I could ask you the same.'

'I should like a few answers too,' said Gwen, whose smile had now become a glower.

He looked from one to the other several times, not even registering Anwen.

'Well, um, you see, I offered Gwen a lift as she was wanting to go into Rhymney, didn't I, Gwen?'

The jolly smile he put on was in the hope Gwen would comply, Anwen was sure, but it didn't work.

'No I didn't, Ralph. You offered to take me to the Theatre Royal and Empire in Merthyr.'

'I, that is—'

'You're clearly fond of going there,' said Elizabeth, 'for you've taken me there a few times.'

'Yes, we've been once before too,' said Gwen. 'I dare say if we compared notes we'd find we'd visited quite a number of the same places.'

'I have no doubt at all.' Elizabeth crossed her arms. Gwen adopted the same posture.

'So, Mr Tallis,' said Anwen, getting more than a little irritated with this man. 'What is your explanation? Do you maybe have an identical twin brother, like in Shakespeare's *Comedy of Errors*?'

Tallis had the good grace at least to look ashamed.

'No, I thought not. You're just a scoundrel who thought he could deceive two decent women. Or perhaps you have more than two sweethearts you're walking out with.'

He looked astounded. 'No, of course not! It was only, well, I liked them both and didn't know who to choose.'

'What?' yelled Gwen. She lifted her handbag and started beating it across Tallis's arm and chest. He lifted his arms to protect himself.

Anwen stepped forward to take hold of her arm. 'That's enough now Gwen.'

'That man is the, the – he's a rascal! As if it's acceptable to be walking out with two ladies just because you can't choose. Oh!'

'My dear Gwen,' said Tallis. 'You can hardly be called a lady now, being the class you are.'

Gwen pulled herself away from Anwen and gave Tallis a sound slap across the face. He reeled sideways a few steps before his hand went to the spot and his face crumpled in pain. As Anwen pulled her away once more, Elizabeth stepped forward.

'You have disappointed me, Ralph. I thought you a decent man. More fool me for being taken in. And more fool you for treating us so shabbily. Now, good day to you, Ralph, and goodbye. Should we have the misfortune to meet anywhere in the future, I will simply act as if you are a stranger.'

With this, Elizabeth turned her back on him.

Tallis composed himself. His left cheek was cerise. He spun round and got back into the car, pulled hastily away and headed back towards Rhymney.

Gwen let out a long breath. 'I'm glad that's over. The nerve of the man.'

'He's a cad,' said Elizabeth. 'I shall not hesitate in telling Mama what he has done and no doubt she will let all and sundry know. He will not play that trick again in a hurry.'

'Oh, but I'd rather people didn't know he'd made a fool of me,' said Gwen, her brow crumpled.

'Do not worry, I will not let on who the other party was.'

They stood awkwardly, not regarding each other.

'Gwen was telling me on the way, Elizabeth,' Anwen started, hoping to shift the subject, 'that her family has received a letter from Henry, and it looks like the men might be moving more into the action again. Have you heard from Tom at all?'

'It's so worrying, after what's been in the newspapers the last few days,' said Gwen, her anger turned to anguish, 'what with the French being attacked. They were mown down by the enemy, it said. And that Kaiser has been telling his troops to be angry and show no mercy and take no prisoners. I was hoping Henry would be in the rear lines till the end of the war.'

Elizabeth's brow puckered. 'Yes, I have read that too. We received a missive from Tom yesterday. He was sent a while back to make up numbers in the depleted 114th Brigade, which also implies they're going to be shifting out of the rear line soon.'

'The 114th is where Henry and the others are!'

Both fell silent again. Anwen now regretted this hastily chosen subject as it had lowered the mood of her companions even further.

Elizabeth pulled herself together first. 'Now, I think I could do with a walk on the hill, especially since it's such a lovely evening.' She put her parasol back up. '*Noswaith dda.*'

Anwen and Gwen replied in kind. Elizabeth walked with some speed up the lane towards Twyn Gobaith, which lay behind the houses. The other two turned to walk back along Mafeking Terrace.

'What on earth is a missive?' Gwen asked.

'She meant a letter.'

'Then why couldn't she have said that?'

'It's not her fault, what Ralph did. You shouldn't get cross with her.'

'Oh, I know. It's just so – I don't know. I'm so glad I hadn't got around to telling my parents about Ralph,' said Gwen.

Anwen linked arms with her friend. 'I'm sorry, Gwen. You've never seemed that interested in anyone before. It must be quite a blow.'

'It is. I think Gwilym was a bit fond of me, back when I was about sixteen, and I did think of encouraging him for a while. He's a nice-looking young man, but I knew he wasn't the one and didn't want him getting too fond. Plenty more flowers on the hillside.'

'You mean plenty more fish in the sea,' said Anwen.

'Never been fond of fish. Flowers, on the other hand…'

Anwen laughed. 'I'm glad you can see the funny side of this.'

'What else can I do? It was good while it lasted, but I guess I never really thought a man like him would stick around for long. I'm not a lady, remember.'

'Nonsense! Any man would be proud to have you on his arm. You wait and see, there'll be someone out there for you. And maybe you'll meet him quite soon.' She crossed her fingers behind her back.

'Maybe. We'll see.'

–

Hywel and his family took the route home through James Street after chapel on Sunday, ambling along with Gwen's family. He was chatting to Mr Austin about a talk they'd both attended at the Workmen's Institute the night before, on the Scottish Highlands.

It was another glorious day, the sky like an azure blanket laid over them, the air warm. The service had not been as awkward as the last three with Violet and Olwen as this time they'd sat at the opposite end of the hall.

Anwen and Gwen were talking in muted tones about something. Cadi was carrying Sara Fach, singing a little song to her. Enid, as always, steered clear of the baby, walking ahead to talk to Gwen's mother and mamgu.

They weren't halfway down the first terrace, when Olwen passed them, holding on to the children's hands, hurrying them along. Violet, following on, looked out towards the pit as she passed.

'Come along, come along,' Olwen nagged, her nose in the air. Poor little Benjy was crying that his legs hurt. 'The quicker we get away from the ne'er-do-wells, the better.'

'Who are you talking about, Olwen Jones?' Enid called. 'If there are any ne'er-do-wells around here, it's you, with your false accusations.'

'Mam,' said Anwen. 'Let's not get her started. Especially as you have to work with her.'

Violet's head dipped down as she hurried to take Benjy's hand from Olwen.

'They've disappeared round the corner now,' said Enid. 'Anyway, Olwen knows better than to start any trouble with us all here. What an awful woman she is. She seems to have a hold over Violet, though I don't understand what. Still, Violet's made her bed and she'll have to lie on it.'

An unbidden image formed in Hywel's mind, of Violet lying on a bed in a nightie, her hair loose and spread out around a pillow. He felt a hot shame, lowering his head in case anyone should guess his thoughts. With all that had happened, his feelings for her were as deep as ever. If only…

'Isn't that a police motorvan?' Gwen's mother pointed ahead.

Sure enough, there was a large, black vehicle with a driver's cab at the front, parked up outside number twenty-one. Detective Inspector Strong, who'd investigated the bookshop fire, was standing outside the house. The two older constables, and another couple of policemen Hywel didn't recognise, were removing Gus, his sister Hilda and her husband Vic from the house. All were in handcuffs.

'Well I never,' said Enid. 'I always knew they were wrong'uns.'

'I wonder what they're being arrested for,' said Gwen.

Sergeant Harries came out of the house and spotted them. He frowned.

Gus twisted around, trying to escape the constable's grip. Seeing them standing on the edge of the pavement, he shouted, 'Yeah, you can all stare if you like, but I found that woman's papers, her from the bookshop.'

'Get him in the back.' Strong pointed towards the two open back doors of the vehicle.

Gus wouldn't be shifted. 'Not before I've had my say, so the people in this village know what they're up against. German she is, not Dutch like everyone kept insisting. Born in Berlin, it says on her papers.'

'You're a damned liar!' Enid cried.

His mother, Frances, who'd now appeared on the doorstep, yelled, 'No he's not, I've got the proof. You'll see.' She disappeared inside but was soon back with the incriminating evidence.

Detective Strong tried to grab it off her, shouting, 'Where were you hiding those?' but she ran across the road, brandishing the papers. She shoved the appropriate one in Enid's face. Hywel looked over her shoulder. Sure enough, Mirjam Schenck had been born in Berlin.

'See, see, she's an enemy she is,' said Frances.

Detective Strong marched up and snatched the papers. 'I'll take those. They're evidence.'

'Makes no difference,' said Hywel. 'She married a Dutchman so that makes her Dutch.'

'Yes,' said Enid. 'She's done a lot of good in this village, always quietly, behind the scenes, never puffs herself up like some. I don't care where she was born. She's a good woman.'

Strong took hold of Frances. 'You're coming with us too as you're clearly involved.'

Polly now appeared on the doorstep, baby Herby in her arms.

'What about Mrs Smith here?' one of the constables called, pointing to Polly.

'What, that imbecile?' Gus shouted. 'As if I'd have told her anything about it when she can't keep her blabbering mouth shut. Always wittering on about stupid things.'

Polly snuggled Herby in closer and lowered her head.

'What on earth is going on here?' Polly's mother, who lived four doors down, came out of her door and walked along the street. 'Don't know why I'm surprised you're being arrested. You were never good enough for my daughter.'

'Shut up, you old cow,' said Gus. 'That foreign sod and his missus deserved what they got.'

Sergeant Harries pushed him towards the motorvan. 'That's enough of that.'

'Wait a minute,' said Hywel, getting closer. 'Are you saying you're responsible for the fire as well as the break-in before-hand?'

'He should have paid up the money I asked for to keep quiet.'

'Shut ya mouth, ya silly sod,' Vic yelled at his brother-in-law before being shoved into the vehicle.

'You were blackmailing him?' said Anwen.

'Enough of this,' said the Inspector. 'Get this lot into Rhymney. We'll question them there.'

Quite a crowd had gathered by this point, other people on their way home from the various chapels and the church. Sergeant Harries came towards them.

'On your way all of you now, that's the end of the show. Apart from you.' He pointed to Anwen.

Despite his words of dismissal, people gathered in once more.

'The next time you have something to say about a crime, come and tell me, see. That's the second time you've got Mrs Meredith to go above my head to the Chief Constable in Rhymney.'

'You should do your job right then,' called someone in the crowd.

'I don't understand,' said Anwen. 'I only pointed out that they were troublemakers and could be suspects. What happened to make the Inspector arrest them?'

The motorvan drove past and the sergeant cleared his throat. 'Well, it seems that the Chief Constable looked into Gus Smith's background by ringing up a colleague in London. Turns out they're wanted felons there and had skipped the area, see. Plus Gus and Vic had already skipped conscription.'

'You knew they were troublemakers,' said Hywel. 'Look at the sports day and the St David's Day concert. You should have thought of them yourself.'

There was a murmur of agreement among the crowd.

'And who are you to tell me my job? We were right to arrest Rose Pritchard, for she is a thief, and although some of the charges will be dropped, there are others she'll be going to court for. Now, if you'll excuse me, I've jobs to get on with, especially as my constables have been commandeered by Inspector Strong. Good day to you.' He touched the brim of his helmet and walked off.

Polly's mother, still standing outside the front door with her daughter, said, 'I told you this marriage would come to no good. You should have left him when I suggested it.'

'But he did threaten me so,' said Polly, eyes wide, 'and didn't think twice about giving me a slap.' She was different to the old, brash Polly, with her cheeky, suggestive smile. 'And I was afraid for poor little Herby's safety.'

'Well you can come 'ome now he's gone. Don't think he'll be gracing the doorstep for a while.'

'I'll need to fetch my things, such as they are.'

Knowing what a low opinion Anwen had of the young woman, Hywel was surprised when she stepped forward to say, 'I'll give you a hand, Polly. This must have been a real ordeal for you.'

'Yes, me too,' said Gwen. 'I'm really sorry he treated you so badly.'

Polly looked close to tears. 'Thank you for your kindness. I'm not sure I deserve it really.'

'Nonsense,' said Enid, joining them. 'Come on, Hywel and Idris will help with anything heavy. Let's get you and the babby settled into your mother's.'

It was a shame Enid wasn't as sympathetic with their own family baby, thought Hywel.

Chapter Twenty-Seven

'There's nothing like a walk on Twyn Gobaith to blow the cobwebs of all these troubles away,' said Anwen as she and Gwen headed back down the hill towards the fire station behind the Workmen's Institute.

'We've certainly had a few of those recently,' said Gwen. 'I do miss Violet's company. And the children, for they are such merry souls and do cheer me up no end.'

'Aye. But what can we do? There's no talking to her while Olwen is there, let alone anything else. Anyway, I'd better get back. It was good of Idris to look after Sara Fach so I could have a walk. Now she's crawling and a bit more interesting, Idris does like to play with her.'

'He's a good husband. You did well there.'

Gwen's faraway look gave Anwen the impression that Gwen was thinking of her own unmarried status, and what might have been with Ralph Tallis. Despite what she'd said about him being a rascal, she wouldn't be at all surprised if her friend's heart was a little bit broken. It prompted Anwen to confide to Gwen something she'd been keeping inside.

'I think Idris is hankering after a baby of his own. Ten months it's been since we married, and not a sign of one.'

'These things can take time,' said Gwen. 'My parents were married two years before Henry was born.'

'I suppose.'

They'd walked a little further before Gwen said, 'I do feel that I'd rather not see Elizabeth for any length of time for a while. I know it wasn't her fault, but she's a reminder. Maybe when I've got over it a bit.'

Anwen said nothing but her heart sank. Her friendships were falling apart around her and she felt helpless to do anything. Coming round the side of the Institute, she spied Mr Schenck in the distance, standing in the road, looking towards his semi-demolished property.

The shopkeeper spotted them, giving them his customary bow, although he was attired in overalls as opposed to his usual neat suit. 'Good afternoon, ladies.'

'Good afternoon, Mr Schenck. I suppose you heard about them arresting Gus Smith and his family,' said Anwen.

'Yes. The sergeant came directly afterwards to inform me. I realised, of course, that those papers were missing, even before Mr Smith came into the bookshop to blackmail me. But I didn't give in to his demands, for who knows how long it would have carried on. I only thought he'd tell people, not that he'd set the building on fire.'

'What a wicked family they are,' said Gwen.

'At least we have been able to source some materials, as difficult as it's been, and will be able to begin work rebuilding the bookshop soon.' He tipped his head to one side and regarded it sadly. 'Whether people will return, knowing now that my good lady wife was born in Germany, I have no idea.'

'The crowd who saw Gus's family arrested were quite supportive of you, I feel,' said Gwen.

'That is heartening, though I dare say not all will feel like that. Dear Mirjam's parents moved to Amsterdam when she was ten. That is where we met. She has no sympathy with the Kaiser and his expansionist plan. But people might only consider that she is German by birth. Still, the men helping here have been kind. And I dare say there are worse things happening in the world. Excuse me, I must go and help. Good day, ladies. I hope you will return to my bookshop when it is open again.'

'Of course we will,' said Anwen. 'Please, do pass on our best wishes to Mrs Schenck.'

'Yes, do,' said Gwen. When he'd crossed the road, she whispered, 'He's always such a patient, forgiving man. I wish I could be like that.'

'You'll get over Ralph Tallis in time.'

'I wasn't thinking of him.'

But Anwen was sure she was.

–

Violet had never felt so lonely as she did at that moment, despite joining a long queue of people outside the butcher's. Several of them jostled to see what was available through the almost empty window that was normally full of hanging hams and other treats. Only two scrawny rabbits hung there today. The jostling resulted in the people at the front being shoved into the doorway and knocking into others.

'Stop that now!' Gertie Pritchard's voice could be heard barking from within. 'There's no point shoving. You won't get served any the quicker. In fact, I'll be throwing out anyone who doesn't behave.'

Violet greeted Rhonwen Evans in front, who she knew only vaguely, then pulled Benjy in closer to her so that someone could pass them on the pavement. Today was her twenty-third birthday. Olwen had clearly not remembered and therefore had not reminded the children, so that they'd failed to produce even a homemade birthday card. Last year, Hywel, who'd still been lodging with her, had organised them, buying some small treats on behalf of the children and taking them to pick wildflowers on the mountain. She felt the hurt swell up in her chest, pushing it back immediately. There'd been a card and a brief letter from her parents, that was all, but nothing from her sister. There'd not even been anything from Gwen, who'd only nodded at her politely in church in the last couple of weeks. She'd looked sad, and Violet had wondered whether she'd done something else wrong.

No point in getting upset here. And who was she, to have her birthday remembered? Oh, but it was nice to be considered just a little bit important by others sometimes.

Mr Schenck came up the road from Noah's house, smarter today than he had been recently in his overalls.

'Good morning, Mrs Jones,' he said, as he joined the queue behind her. 'My good lady wife has sent me out to seek some meat. The queue seems to get longer each day.'

'I'm afraid, despite it being just after nine, that there will be little left by the time we reach the shop.'

'I hungry,' said Benjy, looking up with appeal in his eyes.

'You had breakfast,' she said, in case anyone thought she hadn't fed him today. It had only been bread and some tinned corned beef scraps, but it was more than she'd had. Her stomach grumbled, confirming this fact.

'Ah, the young are always hungry,' said Mr Schenck. 'Noah's children, young Anika and Eduard, are always twittering like baby birds for food.'

Rhonwen Evans turned towards them. 'Well our poor children and grandchildren aren't going to get the food they need all the time the supplies coming in are being bombed by the U-boats. I feel for my poor Mabel and her little Lily. And it's not like the separation allowance is as much as her Maurice was bringing back from the mine. Look sharp, like, we're moving up.'

The queue shuffled along a few feet. The older woman standing in front of Rhonwen, who Violet recognised from her years sorting coal, turned round. Her face was grubby, as if soap never quite got all the coal dust off. 'I don't think this war is going to finish anytime soon, look you. Not from what my Jim read in the newspapers. Over one hundred and fifty killed yesterday in that raid over London, and over four hundred and forty injured. Highest toll ever, they reckon. So it's not just the Zepps what's causing trouble now. And them aeroplanes seem a lot speedier too. Who knows but they might be nipping over our way.'

'I 'ope not,' said Rhonwen, 'for we've enough with pit explosions and scoundrels setting fires, without bombs as well, haven't we Mr Schenck?'

'We have that, Mrs Evans.'

By this time they'd reached the door. Violet could detect the odour of fresh meat and saltiness.

'We go gardens, Mam?' said Benjy.

'Maybe later, *cariad*,' said Violet. 'You'd like some meat for your supper, wouldn't you?'

'I like eggy,' he said with conviction.

'We'll see what's left at the grocer's.'

At last they were in the shop itself. Rhonwen went forward to be served by the assistant. It looked like Violet might get Gertie Pritchard, which she didn't relish. But Rhonwen was finished more quickly than the other woman, so Violet was fortunate to get the cheerful young lad who was not yet old enough to be conscripted.

She looked at what was on offer at the counter. No 'proper meat', as Olwen would have put it. A bit of cow's liver and other offal, some tripe and a couple of pigeons. Then there were the rabbits in the window.

'Not a lot of choice, is there?' said the other customer, regarding Violet while her purchase was wrapped.

'It's not our fault,' said Gertie. 'Lot of meat's being sent to the Front and we're left with the scraps. And there aren't the farm workers there were. Been conscripted, they have. Don't know how we butchers are meant to survive.' She handed the parcel over.

As she left, the customer muttered, 'That's why your daughter goes thieving, is it?'

'What was that you said?' Gertie lifted the meat cleaver.

'Nothing. Nothing at all.'

The customer walked towards the door and Mr Schenck stepped up to the counter.

'I'm not serving you,' said Gertie. 'Your wife's an enemy. I'm not feeding the enemy.'

'His wife is officially Dutch,' said Violet. 'And you can't refuse to serve him.'

'I think you'll find I can do whatever I like in my own shop.'

'I don't think you can,' said Winnie Price, who was now near the front of the queue. 'You're the only butcher in the village. Against the law that'll be, not to serve someone. But here's the person to tell you.' She put her hand to her mouth and called, 'Sergeant Harries! Over here.' She beckoned him.

He was soon in the shop, huffing in exasperation. 'What's the problem *now*?'

'Mrs Pritchard is refusing to serve Mr Schenck because she says his wife's German,' said Violet.

'As I understand it, she has Dutch citizenship,' said Harries.

'I bet this is about Rose being arrested for breaking into the bookshop,' said Winnie. 'But that's the police's fault, not Mr Schenck's.'

'I am *not* serving a German sympathiser, for that's what he'll be, married to a German.' She crossed her arms and stood her ground.

Stanley Pritchard came into the shop with a tray of fresh mutton pieces that made some of the customers who could see it whisper excitedly. 'What's all this, then?' he said to his wife. 'Refusing to serve customers? You can stop that right now, Gertie, for I'm not refusing to serve no one.'

'Very wise,' said the sergeant. 'I'll leave you to it then.'

'Now find out what it is that Mr Schenck wants and get it wrapped up for him. I'm not having any more trouble in this family, you hear?'

Gertie glowered at her husband, then regarded the bookseller with cold eyes. 'What can I get you, Mr *Schenck*?'

Violet was glad to escape the shop with her offal and mutton pieces. The latter had made a dent in her purse, but it was the most meat she'd been able to purchase for a while. She'd make a stew and bulk it out with vegetables from Mr James and as much as she could gather from the hillside and woods.

About to head up to the greengrocer's on the corner of Edward Street, she saw a familiar figure go through the doors.

'There Aunty Anwen,' said Benjy, pointing up. 'We see her?'

'Not now,' said Violet. 'I've got to go to the grocer's first.'

Benjy pushed out his bottom lip in disappointment. 'I wish we could.'

She rubbed his hand affectionately. She wished she could too.

And even more so, Hywel.

—

It had seemed a long service today at the chapel, what with the minister's sermon being full of fancy words and ideas that Violet was hard pushed to keep her mind on. It had consequently wandered, tempting her to look across the aisle to where Hywel was sitting. They were only this close because she and Olwen had been late to chapel and had had to sit where they could find two seats. Benjy was perched on her lap. Clarice was in the Sunday School in a room next to the one they would soon gather in for a cup of tea.

'Hmph!' said Olwen, alerting Violet to an upcoming moan of disapproval. 'I see that Gertie Pritchard's turned up today. Never seen her in here before. Not God-fearing people, them Pritchards.'

Violet wondered what constituted a God-fearing person in Olwen's mind, given the threats she'd made to have her committed. The horror of that menace hung over her. She hugged Benjy closer, trying not to imagine what it would be like to miss your own children growing up.

'Shift along now,' said Olwen. 'I want my cup of tea.'

Violet did as she was told, carrying Benjy through to the other room. Clarice soon spotted them and left the side of her Sunday School teacher, Miss Mabe, to run to them.

'Can I take Benjy to play with my friends in the other room?' she asked. 'Miss Mabe bringed toys for us.'

'Of course you can, *cariad*,' said Violet.

Once they'd fetched their tea, Olwen joined a group of women discussing the abdication of King Constantine of Greece in favour of his son. Violet stood on the perimeter, looking around for Gwen, the only good friend she felt she had now. She spied her in the middle of the room, but she was disappointed to see she was talking to Anwen.

Gertie Pritchard stood nearby, her head tipped to one side as if listening in.

'German sympathiser that King is,' said Winnie Price. 'Maybe now the son's in charge, Greece will come in on the side of the allies.'

'Bit late for my Brenda's Harold,' said Mollie Prior. 'Killed at Mametz, he was.'

'We know, dear,' said Winnie. 'But with more countries getting involved, maybe the rest of our boys can come home the quicker.'

Gertie stepped towards them. 'Everywhere they are, German sympathisers.'

'Oh, now don't you turn this into another outburst about Mr Schenck and his wife,' said Winnie.

Most of the other women nodded in agreement, except for Olwen. 'I agree with Mrs Pritchard. Can't be too careful. We should be ejecting the likes of the Schencks from the village.'

Violet desperately wanted to defend Mr Schenck but was afraid once again of what her mother-in-law would do. Unfortunately, Enid chose that moment to pass by.

'I don't know why I'd expect any other opinion from you, Olwen Jones.'

'I'm allowed an opinion,' she said. 'As is Mrs Pritchard here. There are too many people in this village should be brought to book, including lechers. Some men should keep theirselves to theirselves and leave poor widow women alone.'

Why did her mother-in-law have to twist the subject back to that? Violet wished she could be anywhere else right now. Even the asylum seemed a saner place than this. Her heart thumped in her chest and she found it hard to breathe. She wanted to run away but couldn't move. It didn't help that other groups of people were starting to pay attention and she felt the room moving in on her.

Enid leant her grimacing face forward, getting ready to throw back a comment, but she was stalled by Gertie.

'Talking of lechers and Harold Prothero, what about those soldiers in our village who've brought back more than tales of war?'

'What do you mean?' said Winnie.

Molly Prior stepped towards Gertie. 'That's nobody else's business, look you.'

'Of course it is,' said Gertie. 'Don't want more people getting the pox, do we?'

'The pox?' squealed Olwen.

'Yes, like Mrs Prior's son-in-law, Harold, gave to her daughter, Brenda.'

The young woman in question, who'd been close by talking to the minister's wife, fled the room, barging past people. Violet feared what might be coming, though she knew she was free of syphilis. Anabel Thomas moved swiftly away.

'You stupid woman,' said Molly. 'Where the hell did you hear such a thing?'

'Keeps my ears open I do, in the shop. Amazing it is, what you hear. Reckon the soldiers are having a right old time, getting up to all sorts with the French whores. Wouldn't be at all surprised if all the wives were infected.'

'My Charlie wouldn't have got up to those tricks,' said Olwen.

'Mrs Pritchard, could I ask you to come this way please,' said Pastor Thomas, appearing through the throng. Anabel must have been to fetch him.

'Yes, go away,' said Molly. 'For you're not a regular here. In fact, never shown your face before.'

'Not till I've had my say. The soldiers' wives here need to watch out they don't have the pox, especially your Violet.' She pointed at Olwen. 'For she'll be spreading it round the village, if what you say about the men here chasing after her is true.' She turned towards Enid. 'And, of course, she's been seen with your brother Hywel, so he probably has it now.'

Pastor Thomas tried again. 'That is quite enough, Mrs Pritchard.'

'You can shut up too,' said Gertie.

Where was Elizabeth when she could be really useful, thought Violet, for she had more authority than most. She hadn't seen her in chapel today.

Hywel came charging through the congregation out of nowhere as Enid said, 'Don't you talk about my brother like that.'

'And don't talk about my son like that,' said Olwen, turning against Gertie now.

Her son, not her daughter-in-law, not Violet. No, she had no worth. Who cared about her reputation and feelings? Violet was on the verge of screaming. Maybe she really should be in the asylum.

'I suggest you don't talk about anyone like that,' said Hywel, 'for it's slander you'll be taken to court for.'

'To hell with you, for it's not slander when my Rose saw you, and her,' she jabbed her finger in Violet's direction, 'hiding away on the path at the end of Lloyd Street. God knows what you were getting up to but no doubt you'll get the pox too, and serves you right.'

Violet's head was spinning. How had a conversation about the Greek king become about her and Hywel and... Her thoughts stalled as she dropped her teacup and blackness descended.

–

Anwen panicked when she saw Violet slip to the ground in a faint. About to run to her side, Gwen beat her to it. It was probably better not to go, what with Olwen kneeling next to her, shouting that it was all Gertie's fault. The pastor's wife hastily cleared the broken china.

Hywel leant over her, calling, 'Violet, Violet.'

'Get away from her you, you depraved creature,' Olwen shouted.

He rose immediately, but took only one step back, his face filled with concern.

Anwen wondered what to do for the best. Then she remembered Dr Roberts had been talking to someone by the pulpit as she'd come through for her tea. He didn't seem to be in this room, so maybe he was still there. She ran out, spotting him in the same place.

'Dr Roberts! Come quickly. Violet has passed out.'

The doctor leapt forward, following her into the other room. A path cleared for him.

'What happened?' he asked, hunkering down next to Violet.

Gwen moved out of the way to give the doctor room and stood with Anwen, but Olwen wouldn't budge. The room was now silent, all eyes towards the source of the trouble.

'It were her,' Olwen hollered, pointing to Gertie. 'Her and her filthy talk of the pox and French whores and of soldiers giving it to their wives here.'

'Stop yelling, Mrs Jones,' said Dr Roberts. 'You are not helping.'

'I'm only telling what I've heard,' said Gertie. 'That Brenda Prothero got the pox from her Harold. Makes sense the other soldiers would pass it on too if they've all been to the whore-houses. Now it looks like Violet's got—'

'That's enough,' said the doctor, taking her pulse and examining her. 'Now, what happened?'

'She just fainted,' said Olwen. 'I hope she's not pregnant.' She glared at Hywel.

'Don't you be looking at me like that,' said Hywel, 'for I've done nothing like you're thinking. And Violet is a respectable woman, despite what you say. You're the one with the dirty mind here... And you.' He looked towards Gertie.

There was a groan and Anwen was relieved to see Violet coming round. What could be wrong with her? She'd become even thinner of late. A chill ran through her. What if it was the consumption? Since Sara's death, she'd been obsessed with the disease, seeing it in everyone who was a bit poorly.

'How do you feel?' said the doctor.

'I – I feel lightheaded, and a bit sick.'

'What did you have for breakfast?'

Violet thought for a while. 'Nothing. Saved it for the children.'

'When was the last time you ate something?'

'Had a bit of bread and dripping for supper.'

'That's not enough to keep a body going,' he said. He looked up at Olwen. 'Do you not have food enough in your house?'

'She could have had the leftover mutton and veg, like me. She chose not to.'

'There wasn't enough,' Violet said weakly.

'Nonsense,' said Olwen. 'You're just having one of your funny turns, you know, doctor, like I was telling you about?'

Funny turns? Maybe she *was* ill, thought Anwen. Then another possibility occurred to her: she was giving all the food to the children and to Olwen, and going without.

'I have not been having funny turns,' said Violet.

'What I'd like to know, doctor,' said Molly Prior, 'is why Gertie here thinks my Brenda had the syphilis, for that's what she's meaning by the pox. For she didn't, did she, doctor? You can confirm that.'

The look of appeal in her eyes led Anwen to suspect there was something in the story.

Dr Roberts stood up. 'Mrs Pritchard, you should not be talking about people's illnesses. Now I don't know where on

336

earth you got this piece of tittle-tattle from, but I don't want to hear again that you've been spreading unfounded rumours around about illnesses.'

'And what are you going to do about stopping me, doctor?' said Gertie, taunting him. 'Besides, the pox isn't an illness, it's a curse from the devil.' Her voice got louder as she shouted, 'I don't want no one with the pox in my shop. You might infect me.' She swept her arm round to indicate the group of women, including Winnie and Molly.

'What's all this now,' said Stanley, rushing through the room. 'Just been told that my wife's causing a to-do – again!'

'Aye, and the police'll be here soon too,' said the man who'd evidently alerted him, 'for Harries is being fetched from the Methodist chapel.'

'She says we'll not get served at the butcher's no more,' said Winnie.

He went red in the face as he bawled, 'This is the last time I'm going to tell you, Gertie. No one is banned from our shop! What are you even doing here? You're Catholic. Now get home before you cause more trouble.'

There was the sound of running feet and Sergeant Harries appeared through the crowd. 'Stay where you are, Mrs Pritchard. This is not the first time I've been called to speak to you. One more time, and you'll end up in a cell, like your daughter. You understand?'

'You should be dragging her off now,' said Enid. 'She's had enough warnings.'

'Don't try and do my job for me, Mrs Rhys.'

Gertie made no reply. Instead she jammed her fists into her hips and, sucking in her lips, she stomped off, just ahead of her husband.

'Come on, get up now,' Olwen told Violet. 'Lying around here won't do. Let's fetch the children and get you home to rest.'

She smiled sweetly at everyone, but Anwen wasn't taken in by her apparent benevolence. There was something not right here. Hywel glanced over at her, his slight frown conveying that he was thinking something similar.

'I'll come and visit you later,' Gwen called as Olwen helped Violet towards the room the children were in.

'Don't bother yourself,' said Olwen. 'I'll look after her.'

'I will call in,' said the doctor.

'No, no, she's fine now.'

Hywel shook his head and joined Anwen at the same time as Gwen and Enid. Anwen was glad that Cadi had taken Sara Fach home halfway through the sermon, when she'd got fidgety and noisy. She'd felt fidgety herself. Pastor Thomas's homilies tended to be much more philosophical than those of the last minister.

People dispersed, muttering about the latest rumpus. The four of them were about to walk away when Dr Roberts called her name.

'Anwen, I gather you and Violet have fallen out.'

'Not just me, the whole family,' she said.

'Her mother-in-law has said some wicked things about Hywel,' said Enid.

'I am rather worried about her and the influence of her mother-in-law,' said the doctor.

'She could have sent her packing long since,' said Enid. 'But she's kept her there. If it were that bad, she'd tell her to leave.'

'I'm not sure that is the case,' said the doctor. 'I probably shouldn't be telling you this, but a month ago, Mrs Jones senior fetched me to the house, telling me that Violet had gone mad and needed locking up in an asylum.'

Anwen and Gwen said, 'Oh no,' the same time Hywel said, 'She what?'

The doctor stayed them by lifting his hand. 'I felt, on talking to her, and visiting a couple of times since, that Violet is very down, but there is no indication she needs locking up. Mrs Jones, however, has mentioned it every time I've seen her. What with that, and Violet getting thinner, which I'm sure is due to her not eating properly, I feel there is something awry here and that Violet needs her friends to look out for her, for I can't be there every day.'

'I knew there was something amiss,' said Hywel.

'I don't understand,' said Enid. 'Then why would Violet keep that vicious harpy in the house? She's been controlling her life since she got there.'

Anwen bit the side of her lip. There was only one conclusion she could reach. 'Do you think, doctor, that Olwen is not so much concerned about Violet's mental state, but just trying to get her locked up?'

'Yes, I rather suspect she is. I've seen it before, normally with husbands who want to be rid of their wives. It's too easy, when someone has melancholia, to conclude they're going mad.'

Hywel did up his jacket. 'I've a good mind to go round and sort this out, once and for all.'

'I'm not sure that would be the right approach,' said the doctor.

'No,' said Anwen. 'But it is time we took action. I think there is something Gwen and I can do.'

'Really?' said Gwen.

'Yes. Come for a walk and we'll sort out a plan. I've got an idea.'

'Are you going to tell it to us?' said Hywel.

'Later. All I'll say is that it's about time we involved her family. Now, don't you go doing anything silly while we're gone.'

Enid took his arm. 'I'll make sure he doesn't.'

Chapter Twenty-Eight

'Can we go walk on Twyn Gobaith today, Mam?' said Clarice, as they approached their house after school the next day.

'Not today, *cariad*. We'd better get home, for Mamgu will be home earlier today.'

She guided the children down the alleyway to enter round the back. How she wished she had a house on Edward Street or Alexandra Street, with a back garden that looked onto Twyn Gobaith. That would have been a treat indeed, instead of one that looked out on other houses.

'Mam, can me and Benjy play in the garden?'

Violet came to. 'Yes, of course. You look after Benjy now and don't go outside the gate.'

'No, Mam.'

In the scullery, she filled up the kettle and took it to the kitchen. It was overly warm in here, the stove being lit to boil the water and make the stew she'd have to start on soon.

While she was fetching down the cups from the dresser, she heard the clamour of childish voices. Probably a noisy game, but she'd better check.

She'd only got as far as the scullery when the door opened and there stood her mother. Violet stepped back in shock, which only increased when her father came in behind her.

'Mam, Da?'

Her mother surged forward, enfolding her in her arms. 'How are you, *cariad*?' She stepped away to survey her. 'You are looking terribly thin.'

'I'm fine.'

Her father came forward to kiss her cheek. 'How have you been then?'

'We know how she's been,' said Doris.

Violet was confused. 'You didn't write to say you were visiting.'

Doris undid her jacket and fanned her face. 'If we'd done that, no doubt there'd have been some excuse made for us not to come.'

'Why would I have done that?'

There was more noise outside the door, which was flung open wider to admit the children pulling a third person along.

'Look Mam, it's Tadcu Jones.'

'Brynmore! Why are you here too?' Then it occurred to her. She walked backwards, towards the kitchen door. 'I don't know what you've heard from Olwen, but it's not true. I'm perfectly sane.'

'I think you've got the wrong end of the stick, love,' said her father-in-law.

Ioan gathered the children up from Brynmore. 'I'll take the kiddies out to the garden while you explain.'

'Come on Tadcu Wynne,' said Benjy, pulling on his sleeve.

When they'd gone, Doris said, 'It wasn't Olwen we heard from, it was Anwen and Gwen. In fact, they came to see us yesterday. Took a trip down on the train, they did.'

'But why?' Could this be to do with her fainting in church? She was still confused.

'They're of the opinion that Olwen is trying to get you committed. Apparently she's been trying to persuade Dr Roberts for ages.'

'How would they know that? Anwen isn't even talking to me, nor any of her family, because Olwen, well…'

'We know,' said Doris. 'Olwen has been obsessed with the idea that you and Hywel were up to no good.'

'Mam!' Violet went red. 'It's not true. He was only a friend, trying to be supportive.' She leant her weight against the table.

How many times had she said that? Much of the time it felt like she was trying to persuade herself. 'And I do miss Charlie.' This was true, even if it was the old one she missed, not the domineering one of latter years.

'Violet, love,' said Brynmore. 'We know you miss Charlie, but he's not coming back. Olwen has taken it hard and I think it turned her brain a bit.'

'I don't understand what happened with you and her,' said Violet. 'Did she leave you? She never gave that impression, but she never seemed to want to go home either.'

'I wish I knew. I kept writing, asking her to come back. I had the impression you needed her here. In fact, Olwen hinted that you'd asked her to stay.'

She shook her head. 'I didn't. I thought she'd go home after Christmas, but didn't want to push it as she seemed to like being with the children. Later, I appreciated having someone to look after them when I had to work, and then I was grateful she was bringing in some money. By then I think she had the idea she was staying forever.'

'What about all this nonsense about you going to an asylum?' said Doris. 'Dr Roberts told Anwen and Gwen. I tell you, I was that furious I was all for coming yesterday, but Anwen persuaded us to meet up with Brynmore first, to discuss things. Why on earth didn't you tell us?'

'Dr Roberts shouldn't have been saying anything.'

'He did it for your wellbeing.'

A quite unexpected urge to cry overtook Violet. Tears streamed down her cheeks and she found herself weeping. Despite what had happened, Anwen did still care about her, it seemed.

'Oh lovey,' said her mother, hugging her. 'There, there now.'

'I was afraid if I didn't go along with what she wanted, that she'd get me committed and I wouldn't see the children grow up. It happened to that woman in the village when I was about twelve. Louise someone, do you remember her?'

'I certainly do,' said Doris.

'She was diagnosed with melancholia after she had her second baby and was taken away to the asylum in Abergavenny. I think her children ended up with her mother and the father left the village altogether.'

'Louise Bennett. Yes, I remember her. That was back in Dr Howell's time. I wonder whatever happened to her. Anyway, you're not to worry about that. It's not going to happen to you.'

'I've felt so tired and weak lately, I didn't have the strength to fight Olwen anymore. I thought you'd come to help put me away,' she sobbed.

'No,' said Brynmore. 'But we are going to sort this out once and for all. Olwen did tell me after Charlie died that she wished she could go back to when he and his sister were little. I reckon that's why she wanted to look after Clarice and Benjy.'

'Hello?' came a voice from the hall.

'It's Olwen.' Violet straightened herself, took a handkerchief from her skirt pocket and wiped her eyes. Her pulse was thumping in her head. Despite her mother's words, what if her mother-in-law persuaded them she *did* need locking away?

Olwen marched in with confidence, until she noticed who was there. She came to a sudden halt. 'Brynmore? Doris? What on earth is going on here? I suppose you wrote to them to come, did you?' She frowned at Violet.

'No, she didn't,' said Doris, coming to within three feet of her.

'Well it's just as well you're here, for there's been all sorts going on. She's got the melancholia, has Violet, and now you can help me persuade the doctor to—'

'Don't go any further,' said Doris. 'I know you've been trying to get my daughter locked up, and I'll not stand for it, you hear?'

Olwen pursed her lips and regarded them as if they were silly children. 'You don't know the half of it. I've been duty bound to protect the honour of this family. You should know there's been a man sniffing about—'

'We know all about it,' said Brynmore, 'and it's time you stopped interfering. You've caused a rift between Violet and her friends and it's got to be mended. What you did, trying to persuade the doctor to put Violet away, is terrible. It's time for you to come home, Olwen. And let's hope that all the people you've upset in the village – and I believe it's quite a few – can forgive you. I think it's you what needs the doctor.'

'I'm not going back to Bargoed. I've got a job here and Violet needs the money.'

'If she needs help and some money, that's up to Ioan and me to sort out,' said Doris. 'You can go home or not, that's up to you, but there's no place for you here anymore, do you understand?'

Olwen didn't budge. 'I think that's up to Violet. Not said a word, she hasn't, so I'm guessing she doesn't agree with you.'

Violet lifted her weight from the table and went towards her mother-in-law. She had nothing to lose any more, so she could say what she wanted. 'It's time you went home, Olwen. You should have gone after Christmas. I appreciated your help, but it came at an awful high price and having you here has not been pleasant.'

Olwen didn't budge. 'There's thanks for me putting myself out for you.'

Even now Violet couldn't see her leaving. The possibility of it had been a blessed dream for so long but seemed as far away as ever. No! Something in Violet snapped. Enough was enough. What she said next poured forth in a rapid outburst.

'Putting yourself out for me? When did you do that? When you were saving food for yourself but not for me? When you were telling the children off all the time for no good reason? When you ruined Christmas as Anwen's? When you were spying on me and accusing me of all sorts and embarrassing me in front of people? When you told the police you saw Hywel in the back lane the night of the bookshop break-in, when you couldn't have done? When you pretended that I'd attacked you to the neighbours and Dr Roberts, and that it wasn't the first time? When you expected me to feed you on my widow's pension and contribute nothing when you first arrived? When you insisted I work rather than get a lodger, which would have been handier with the children? When I was working and had to do the cleaning in the evenings because you'd done nothing? When you were working, but insisted on looking after all the money, keeping us short and not lifting a finger at home?' Violet came to a halt, exhausted by the tirade.

'Good Lord, you've a lot to answer for!' said Doris. 'No wonder Violet's so thin. You were starving her!'

Brynmore tutted and shook his head. 'What on earth were you thinking?'

For a long while Olwen eyed each of them, her jaw clenched. At last she spoke. 'Right, if that's how you feel, I know where I'm not welcome. I will pack my things. Brynmore, you will come and help me.'

He followed her out to the kitchen. Violet felt the gloom of the last six months lift from her slim body. She was giddy with relief.

'Good riddance to bad rubbish. I'll put the kettle on, shall I?' said Doris.

'Yes. I could do with a cup of tea. The kettle's already on the stove.'

'Righty ho. Why don't you go and tell your da it's all over.'

'Let me just pull myself together and I will.'

Doris left the room. Violet took several deep breaths, bathing in the knowledge that she had her house back again.

But there was still Hywel there, round the corner, unobtainable.

'One thing at a time,' she told herself, then went to find her father.

'So, are we going to meet Hywel?' asked Doris, as they sat round the kitchen table drinking tea.

'You already know Hywel,' said Violet, hoping the topic would soon be over.

'Yes, but we've not seen him since things changed.'

'I like Nuncle Hywel,' said Benjy.

'It's *Uncle*,' said Clarice. 'Silly!'

His little face fell. 'I not silly.'

'Why don't you get your train set,' said Ioan. 'We'll have a chuff around the track.'

'It's in the front room,' said Clarice, jumping off the chair and making for the room in question.

Ioan helped Benjy down and they followed her.

'I'd still like to meet up with Hywel,' said Doris, 'find out what his intentions are.'

'Oh Mam, if he ever had any intentions, he hasn't now. He must hate me after what Olwen did, and I did little to help the matter.'

'It wasn't your fault though.'

'But I was also rude about Miss Elizabeth and she overheard me and they got cross with me about that too.' The guilt of that still laid heavily on her.

'Well, either way, I'm going to pop round to see Enid. Marvellous it was, to see her walking at Easter. Good friends, we used to be.'

'Don't say anything to Hywel.'

'As if I would.'

While her mother was gone, and her father was occupied with the children, she took the opportunity to do the washing up and clear up the kitchen. She'd have to think about dinner soon. It was odd, doing normal things, not worrying about Olwen. Would her parents be stopping for supper? She'd managed to get some more mutton today. It might stretch if she used all the vegetables she'd bought. What was she going to do without Olwen's money?

'By the way,' said her father, in the doorway. She jumped and laughed.

'Oh Da, don't creep up on a body like that.'

'When I helped Brynmore bring the bags down, he told me he'd found some money in a drawer. Olwen admitted she'd been keeping back half her wages.'

'I did wonder about that. I knew she wouldn't be earning eighteen shillings a week like Anwen as she was doing fewer hours, but I did think five shillings a week was a bit low.'

'Brynmore thought you should have it.' He handed over some coins. 'She'd been saving four shillings a week, so there's sixteen bob there. He said he earns a good enough wage at the pit and they don't need it. It was bad she held it back when you were struggling on the widow's pension.'

Violet considered the coins. They'd certainly help fill the gap for a few weeks. Then she'd have to consider what to do next. She placed them into the pocket of the apron she was wearing.

'Only me, come with a guest,' Doris called, as she opened the back door.

Violet took a hasty breath when she saw it was Hywel, who looked rather awkward.

'I hope you don't mind me calling around,' he said. 'I'd like to apologise for the way we treated you after Olwen spoke to the police because I know now it wasn't your fault and that you were in a difficult position what with her threatening you with the asylum and being such a bully and—'

'Slow down,' said Doris, 'for we can hardly make out what you're saying.'

'It's all right,' said Violet. 'I understood it well enough. I'm sorry Hywel, for the way Olwen treated you. And sorry for ignoring you and putting an end to our friendship, because I did enjoy your company. But Olwen, well, she made it too difficult.'

'I know she did. I'm sorry to the heart of me I didn't see the full extent of what she was doing to you. I should have realised you weren't a willing participant.'

347

'And what are your intentions towards my daughter?' said Doris, crossing her arms and lifting her not insubstantial bust.

'Mam, he has no intentions!' said Violet. Really, if it wasn't one embarrassing situation, it was another.

'Actually, I do,' he said. 'I know the year isn't up since Charlie's passing just yet, but I've been wanting to tell you for months exactly how I feel. From our few meetings, I thought you might feel the same. I suppose now is the time to say it. I love you, Violet.'

He pressed his lips together and he looked in some kind of pain, maybe worried at what her reaction would be. She knew what she wanted to say, but she'd never been good at saying these kinds of things, not even to Charlie in the early days. What she felt for him was like a huge bag of emotions caught in her chest that threatened to suffocate her if she didn't let them out.

'Come on *cariad*, what have you got to say for yourself?' said Ioan.

'I love you too, Hywel, I really do.'

'I think this is our cue to leave, Doris.'

The soppy look on her mother's face became surprise. 'What? Oh, yes, of course. Let's see how the children are doing.'

After they'd gone, Hywel and Violet walked into each other's arms and held on tight. When he bent to kiss her, she was ready for his warm lips. He sighed and she giggled, stalling the moment.

'Why are you laughing?' he said.

'I thought women were meant to be the soppy, sighing ones. According to the novels I've read.'

'Men can be soppy too. And what else could I do but sigh with pleasure now we're together at last? And I hope for a very long time.'

'Me too,' she said, and leant towards him to be kissed once more.

Chapter Twenty-Nine

'I can hardly believe it's your wedding day tomorrow, Uncle Hywel,' said Anwen, pouring some more water into the teapot for their post-dinner drink.

'You can't believe it?' he said. 'I never thought I'd get married, not since, well, Catrin.'

'Catrin?' said Anwen.

'Oh, *her*,' said Enid, sitting at one end of the table sewing a button onto Hywel's good shirt.

'My first love. Or so I thought,' he explained.

Anwen listened as he told her about this young woman he'd never mentioned before. 'Well, you are full of surprises, Uncle Hywel. How are you feeling, about tomorrow?'

'Nervous.'

Enid looked up. 'At least it will be a better August Bank Holiday Monday than last year, which was the day after the memorial for our dead soldiers. Nobody felt much like celebrating then.'

'No, least of all Violet, of course. But it's a new start for her.' Anwen hoped her mother wasn't going to be in this mood all day. 'I'm so glad she's made it up with Elizabeth, and invited her to the wedding.'

'She was touched when she heard that Elizabeth hadn't made a fuss to her mother about employing Olwen because of their money situation,' said Hywel.

'It's hard to believe that Violet will be Mrs Llewellyn from tomorrow,' said Enid. 'A bit like the royal family changing their surname.'

'Not quite the same as changing your name from Saxe-Coburg-Gotha to Windsor,' Hywel laughed. 'She won't have to change it by royal proclamation.'

'Talking of the Germans, did you read this in yesterday's newspaper?' Idris lifted it up.

'About the Welsh Division fighting?' said Hywel. 'Yes. Looks like they're in the thick of it again after being in the back lines nearly a year.'

Anwen relieved her husband of the paper. 'Gwen and Elizabeth were afraid this might happen.'

'They're fighting at a place called Pilckem,' said Idris. 'They reckon it's the battle which the world has been waiting for, as they put it.'

Anwen put the lid on the pot and left it to brew. 'I don't like the sound of that. Didn't we lose enough men at Mametz Wood? Though I suppose it might mean it will be over soon. It's been three years now. That's surely long enough.'

'Who knows,' said Idris. 'According to the report, the Welsh troops have more or less defeated the Kaiser's top soldiers, the German Guards Fusilier Regiment.'

Enid stopped sewing and looked at him. 'I hope our boys are all right. My goodness, so much has happened since the war began. Things will never be the same again.'

The others all nodded but didn't comment. Anwen found it hard to imagine now how she'd survived the last few years; her father's violence, her sister's death, Idris breaking off with her. She should think herself lucky, but there were a couple of things she still prayed for.

She popped the cosy on the teapot. 'It's coming up to two o'clock and I said I'd meet Gwen at the back. We're going to decide what flowers to pick for Violet's bouquet tomorrow.'

'And we're going to have a look at the lavvy,' said Hywel. 'It's not flushing proper, like.'

Anwen laughed. 'Uncle Hywel, that's a very unromantic thing to respond with when we're talking about flowers for your loved one.'

Half smiling, half grimacing, he replied. 'It is, sorry, but it needs doing see.'

She looked up at the ceiling, thinking about her sister sound asleep in the cot upstairs. 'I don't think Sara Fach's going to wake up in the next five minutes.' She regarded her mother, hoping, as she did every other time, that she'd say something like, *I'll listen out for her.* It was never to be.

'We'll be near the house, so we'll hear her if she hollers,' said Idris.

'All right, thanks.'

When Anwen reached the bottom of the garden, her friend was just approaching the gate.

'A bit cloudy today,' Gwen called, pulling her shawl more tightly round her shoulders. 'And not very warm for August. Hope it's better tomorrow.'

'Me too. Now, what flowers shall we pick? Twyn Gobaith is filled with wildflowers, too, which we could use.'

'That sounds lovely. What are those pink flowers near the house? They're pretty.'

'Zinnias. Let's have a look.'

They sauntered down the centre path, chatting about the following day. As they neared the house, they heard the holler of a baby in distress.

'Oh no, Sara Fach,' said Anwen.

In her hurry to get to the tot, she tripped over the watering can, which had been left on the side of the flower bed, taking Gwen down with her, amid clattering and hollering.

'What on earth?' said Idris, rushing from the outside toilet. 'Here, take my hands.' He held them out to help the women up.

'Didn't you hear the baby crying?' said Anwen as she straightened herself.

'What crying?' he said.

Sure enough, it had stopped. That wasn't like Sara Fach at all. There must be something wrong. She ran through the scullery and into the kitchen, only to come to a standstill by the door. Gwen caught her up, almost knocking into her. Anwen thought she must be seeing things at first, for there, in between the two armchairs by the stove, was her mother, cradling the baby and singing the Welsh lullaby 'Suo Gân'. *Slumber child, upon my breast, it is snug and warm...*

Anwen recalled her father singing it at Sara's funeral, that grim, January day, twenty months ago. Tears coursed down her face, of sadness for Sara, of joy for Sara Fach. One of her prayers had been answered.

The men came up behind, leaning over the women to see.

'What's happened then?' said Hywel. 'Oh.'

'I'm back,' called Cadi, coming through the scullery. 'What's the hold-up here?'

Gwen and the men moved to let her in. Anwen turned to her and smiled.

'Oh my.'

Enid came to the end of the song. 'I know you're all surprised, but I've been doing a lot of thinking. After all the nastiness with the Pritchards, and with Olwen trying to get Violet committed, I realised I was becoming as bad as them with all my resentments. I'd had enough of being imprisoned in the bedroom, unable, or unwilling, to walk, and then, when I was mobile again, the anger and hatred became a new type of gaol. I don't want that anymore.'

Anwen went to her mother and cuddled both her and Sara Fach. 'I'm so glad you've changed your mind, Mam.'

'Come on now, none of this sentimentality. I suspect this little one needs her napkin changing. I'll just take her upstairs.'

Enid walked towards the hall and Idris took her place next to Anwen, placing his arm around her.

'There's marvellous, isn't it?'

'Oh yes, it's a prayer come true.'

Chapter Thirty

'Those whom God has joined together, let no man put asunder. In so much as Hywel and Violet have consented together in holy wedlock, and have witnessed the same before God and this company, having given and pledged their faith, each to the other, and having declared the same by the giving and receiving of a ring, I pronounce that you are husband and wife. I ask you now to seal the promises you have made with each other this day with a kiss.'

Violet looked up into Hywel's eyes. They were brim-full of love and she knew she'd made the right decision. She hoped Charlie was somewhere in the great beyond, looking down at her and wishing her well. Hywel bent forward to kiss her. She closed her eyes, tipping her face up in eager anticipation of his warm lips.

When they turned, ready to walk back down the aisle, little Clarice, adorable in her yellow dress and posy of wildflowers, gazed up at her. 'I got a new da now?' she said.

'Yes, *cariad*, you've got a new da,' Violet laughed, the tingle swelling out from her heart and infusing her body with joy.

'You hear that, Benjy, we got a new da,' she told her brother in the front row, standing with his grandparents.

'New da for Benjy and Clarry,' he said, his chubby face beaming.

The tears welled up and spilled over Violet's bottom lashes. Hywel kissed her cheek and took her hand, leading her down the axisle of the chapel to the strains of Mendelssohn's 'Wedding March'.

Gwilym and Idris were already opening the main doors as the couple approached. Warm air rushed in. Anwen followed on behind with Gwen who was holding Clarice's hand.

The couple stepped onto the threshold and looked out onto the village of Dorcalon as Mr and Mrs Llewellyn. Violet gasped with delight. The sun was shining across the valley, lending a golden glow.

'Look at that,' Hywel said, hugging her to him. 'Raining this morning, and now a lovely summer day. The children will be happy that they can play in the garden.'

As if to confirm this, Clarice and Benjamin ran to the couple, giggling with delight when they saw how sunny it was. Violet took her daughter's hand while Hywel took his new son's. Together they looked out on the lush landscape beyond the pit, and a fresh future of hope.

A letter from Francesca

First of all, a very big thank you to everyone who read the first in the *Valleys* series, *Heartbreak in the Valleys*. I was bowled over by the wonderful response it received, along with the many positive reviews.

I was particularly touched by people's reaction to the hardship endured by my characters at this period of history. Some have said that they didn't realise just how difficult it was for the inhabitants of working-class areas like the Welsh Valleys at this time. That I've been able to convey even a small sense of their struggle and fighting spirit, as well as tell a story people have enjoyed, has been very encouraging. Over time, the sheer hard slog and sacrifices of those whose work formed the backbone of the nation, not only in Wales of course, but in other industrial areas too, have faded from people's memories. It's fascinating to get a glimpse into the past.

When I started writing the sequel to *Heartbreak in the Valleys*, I knew immediately that I wanted Violet to be the star. I was keen to explore her story, the mousy housewife married young and stuck in her shabby house with her two little kiddies, struggling to keep it brushed, scrubbed and polished clean, always playing catchup. But of course, I discovered there was much more to her than that. She is symbolic of many women from that time, who battled daily to keep a spotless home and to get a meal on the table, many left without a husband. I hope you've enjoyed reading her story.

If you'd like to discuss the novel with me, or discover more about it, I'd love to chat with you on social media here:

Facebook: www.facebook.com/FrancescaCapaldiAuthor/
Twitter: @FCapaldiBurgess
Or you can visit my blog here:
www.writemindswriteplace.word-press.com

Best wishes,
Francesca xx

Acknowledgments

Once again, I'd like to thank Keshini Naidoo and Lindsey Mooney at Hera Books for giving me the opportunity to tell a second *Valleys* story, and for all their hard work in bringing it to fruition. They've been brilliant to work with. Thanks also to Jenny, whose editing skills have been invaluable.

I'm grateful to my friends and fellow writers, Angela Johnson, Elaine Roberts and Karen Aldous, whose friendship and encouragement, and willingness to natter endlessly about writing, has kept me going through my writing journey.

I'd like to acknowledge the value of the many writers' and readers' groups on Facebook, especially during lockdown when it's been impossible to meet up for talks and socials. A special hello to the authors of the Strictly Saga group, whose video and messaging chats have been supportive and fun.

Last but not least, a big thank you to my children, Carmela, Peter, Giovanna and Jack, for all their encouragement.